TH OPPOSITE OF MURDER

SOPHIE HANNAH

HODDER &
STOUGHTON

First published in Great Britain in 2026 by Hodder & Stoughton Limited
An Hachette UK company

The authorised representative in the EEA is Hachette Ireland, 8 Castlecourt
Centre, Dublin 15, D15 XTP3, Ireland (email: info@hbgi.ie)

1

A CIP catalogue record for this title is available from the British Library

Hardback ISBN 978 1 529 35295 5
Trade Paperback ISBN 978 1 529 35296 2
ebook ISBN 978 1 529 35296 2

Typeset in Sabon LT Std by
Palimpsest Book Production Limited, Falkirk, Stirlingshire

Printed and bound in Great Britain by Clays Ltd, Elcograf S.p.A.

Hodder & Stoughton policy is to use papers that are natural,
renewable and recyclable products and made from wood grown in
sustainable forests. The logging and manufacturing processes are expected
to conform to the environmental regulations of the country of origin.

Hodder & Stoughton Limited
Carmelite House
50 Victoria Embankment
London EC4Y 0DZ

www.hodder.co.uk

THE
OPPOSITE
OF
MURDER

Sophie Hannah is a *Sunday Times*, *New York Times* and Amazon Kindle No. 1 bestselling author whose books have sold millions of copies and are published in 51 countries. She was the first person to write and publish new Hercule Poirot mysteries, at the request of Agatha Christie's family and estate. In 2023 she won the Dagger in the Library Award for her body of work, and in 2013 she won the UK National Book Awards Crime Novel of the Year prize for her novel *The Carrier*. Sophie is also an award-winning poet whose work is studied at GCSE level across the UK, and has been shortlisted for the TS Eliot Award. Her murder mystery musical, *The Mystery of Mr E*, was released as a feature film in 2023. Sophie is the founder and coach at *Dream Author Coaching*, and her recent self-help book about how to make brilliant decisions, *The Double Best Method*, was an Amazon top ten bestseller.

Sophie lives with her husband, grown-up children and dog in Cambridge, where she is an honorary fellow of Lucy Cavendish College.

Also by Sophie Hannah

For JS Mayville and Gemi Danes – gone but never forgotten.
And maybe not even gone forever, who knows?

1

JEMMA

This is my story and no one else's.

In it, I am a killer.

That has nothing to do with what I did or didn't do. I'm talking about who I am, not who I want to be or have the potential to become.

I felt myself switch over in an instant; something broke inside me and something new and powerful sprouted up in its place. If I didn't know better, I could almost believe that a button had been pressed, so startling and sudden was the change. And it wasn't brought about by me murdering anyone. That's something I've never done, and hopefully never will. It's the other way round: because I now know myself to be a killer on the inside, I have to stop myself from killing. You don't need to strangle someone with your bare hands, poison them, stab them or shoot them in order to be a murderer.

The being is the chicken and the doing is the egg.

Marianne would say, 'Ah, but which comes first, the chicken or the egg? If it's the egg – and it might be, or else that question wouldn't be asked as often as it is – then you've got it the wrong way round.'

She is never not speaking in my head.

When I tell it in my favourite way, what I'm about to tell the police, that's how it always starts: *This is my story and no one else's. In it, I am a killer.* And I might never have become one if someone else hadn't given me the idea – someone who was a killer before me, who tried but didn't succeed. That's neither an excuse nor a distraction.

If stories were buildings, that detail would be a load-bearing wall. It's funny the way just hearing about someone who tried to do something, even if they failed, plants it in your mind as a possibility.

My favourite way to tell the story is silently, only to myself and far from this cold, humming, brightly lit building, so that no one can sully or distort what I know to be true. But somebody has to be the first to risk the huge leap from concealment to honesty, and I don't think anyone ever will apart from me. And I crave clarity, more than happiness or freedom or safety. Sometimes I think it's all I need and want: all of the truth, plainly laid out. Nothing else matters.

I'm here to tell my part of it. To give a statement, and I'm pretty sure those are always the unaltered words of the statement-giver, even if it's a police officer who notes it down or types it up. It's a comforting idea: my statement. My words, which no one will subsequently be allowed to change.

Meanwhile, the sergeant on the desk with the bleached blonde hair and red lipstick has already misunderstood me, so the distortion of my story has started. She's apologised three times for how long it's taking the promised detective to come and deal with me, convinced I must be finding the delay distressing.

Nothing could be further from the truth. I'm making the most of this waiting time. I feel calmer than I have in weeks. The ordeal of deciding is over – *Was I really going to do it?*

Yes, I was – and the next ordeal, the telling part, hasn't started yet.

The sergeant has no idea that I want this small pocket of waiting time to stretch as far as it can. She assumes that, since I've said I'm here to confess to a murder, I must want to rush into the confession room and get it over with.

Interview room, I correct myself. This is a police station, not a church: the perfect secular space for giving up your secrets.

Ollie thinks most people don't understand what's behind the need for secrecy, and he's right. It's one of the things he said when I saw him in July, and I knew immediately, as soon as I heard it, that it was a truth I wanted to memorise and think about later. 'Our secrets are our property – no one else's,' he said. 'So is what we've made them mean. Once other people get their hands on them, the meaning's up for grabs. Then it feels as if our property is being stolen, and then those others tell more people still, and soon our version's in danger of becoming the minority report. Like in . . . *Minority Report.*' He grinned. I nearly smiled back but stopped myself. We'd loved that movie and watched it together more than once. Ollie was trying to leverage my emotional attachment to the memory, hoping I'd stop demanding that he tell me the truth.

He miscalculated. Our happy memories have lost their power to make me happy, and I knew he'd only said it to distract me from the answers he knew I wanted.

Why wouldn't you tell me, Ollie? I might not be here now – in danger, being a living, breathing danger to others – if you had. Don't you realise? Don't you care?

I wipe my eyes. A new person, a man, has taken over behind the reception desk, and the bleached-blonde sergeant is heading towards me, probably thinking I'm crying about being kept waiting. This reception area is strange. The deep windowsills are all wood that's been stained almost orange and, behind its protective wall of glass, the reception desk is the same. I can't tell if it's fake wood or just badly and excessively varnished. The floor is yellow square tiles that I'd expect to find in a conservatory, not a workplace. They look too domestic, somehow. So does the desk, which has a curved end that makes me think of a kitchen island.

The blonde sergeant sits down next to me. 'I'm really sorry about this. I've no idea where DC Waterhouse has got to, but it's getting ridiculous. Let's find a free room and you can talk to me instead.'

'I don't mind waiting,' I say. 'I need to talk to a detective.'

'I used to be a detective, if that makes you feel any better. Might be one again soon too, if I'm crazy enough to agree.' She raises her eyebrows slightly. 'Long story.' She's twitchy. Can't sit still in her chair.

'I don't mind waiting for DC Waterhouse.'

'Well, I do,' she says. 'I think we're done waiting. Come on. Follow me.'

I don't want to move. What if DC Waterhouse appears as soon as we've gone?

'Look, I'm not convinced Simon's on his way,' she says. 'DC Waterhouse, sorry. I think he might have fibbed and said he was, while actually intending to disappear and let everyone down. Because he's a *dick*.' She sighs, pushing her hair back from her forehead with one hand. 'Sorry. Shouldn't have said that, but on the other hand, I'm his wife, so maybe it's fine.'

'You're his wife?'

'Yup. You married?'

I nod.

'Also to a dick?'

I'm startled by this and don't know what to say.

4

'Is it your husband you've killed? What's his name?'

Why the hell would she think I've killed Paddy? 'He's called Paddy Stelling, but . . . I haven't done anything to him. He's alive. Why would you think . . .?'

'Women who look like you don't kill people, unless it's their violent boyfriends or husbands, in self-defence,' she says.

'Paddy's never been violent.'

'Can you tell me the name of the victim? Speaking of names, I'm Sergeant Charlotte Zailer, but you can call me Charlie.'

'The victim?'

'The murder victim. You're here to talk about a murder, right? Though I'm fairly sure you haven't killed anyone. Am I right? If I believed for one second that you'd actually killed someone, you wouldn't still be sitting in reception.'

'Marianne Upton is her name.' I hear the words first, like something I've hurled at myself, then feel them inside me, tumbling down and down. I scrunch my hands into fists to stop them from reaching for something that isn't there.

I can't undo this now. Everyone will find out. There will be a knock on the door of Marianne and Dad's house. That's how it will start . . . because Marianne will need to be warned . . .

'I'd . . . Please, can we just wait for DC Waterhouse?' I say, because I'm really not sure about this woman at all.

She looks as if she's about to argue with me, but thankfully decides against it. With a disapproving twist of her red-lipsticked mouth, she turns and heads back to the other side of the reception area.

Once she's left me alone and it's safe, I pull my laptop out of my bag and open it. I try to put on the face I'd be wearing if I were about to open something work related – next term's budget spreadsheet or something like that. I like my job because it's completely stress-free and no one ever complains about me doing things the way I want, but I can't pretend that being the bursar for a tiny independent school is the most thrilling career in the world. Still, I have a boss who's happy to be in charge only in theory while leaving me to my own devices, so I regard myself as lucky. I'm not good with authority figures, thanks to Marianne. It's ridiculous, but when anyone suggests I might like to consider doing something that wasn't my idea in the first place, my immediate thought is always: 'Here comes tyranny'.

I open the diary folder on my laptop, knowing exactly which entry I need to read before I speak to any detective. I'm so nervous, it's hard to think straight, and I could do with reminding myself of why I'm here – of what I both desperately want to do, and can't allow myself to do.

Here it is: July 7, the entry that feels like the most important of all the ones I've written since I started writing this . . . journal or book, or whatever it is, on my laptop. The first word is '*Marianne*' . . . It makes me feel sick, the way everything has to be about her.

If she didn't exist, I wouldn't be a killer right now. I wouldn't need to tell the police a story about murder.

As I read, I start to have the feeling that something's not right – something about my own words. It's almost as if . . .

No, that's ridiculous. These are my words. No one else wrote them. I remember writing them. Starting with the word '*Marianne*' . . .

Marianne pushes open the door of her study with a 'Ta-daaa!'. She's put on a special dress for the occasion, a long black kaftan I've never seen before with a silver brocade pattern around its square neck and lines of sequins down its sides: glistening slug-trails on dark ground. On her feet are shiny black sandals with matt black soles as thick as bricks and elaborately bumpy arrangements near the toes: white lace bows and pale pink pearls. She has painted her toenails the same pink; same shade of lipstick too.

Marianne hardly ever bothers with dresses or make-up. I've known her for nearly thirty years and I've seen her done up like this no more than five times. Normally she wears a floppy white or pale blue shirt, dark blue jeans and the plainest, flattest flip-flops on her always-bare feet. She boasts about her good circulation – how she never feels the cold – and about how she doesn't need to look smart because she knows she is smart intellectually. Only last week she boasted, 'I'm the scruffiest nearly-seventy-year-old I know, and I'll still be dressing the way I did in my early twenties when I'm a hundred and ten.'

Arm still outstretched, she stands back to give me an unbroken view. I look, but there's nothing.

7

Her study – or rather, the room that used to be her study – has been stripped of all its contents. She has dressed up like this – her 'glad rags', she calls them – to show me emptiness. A destroyed room.

The three windows have marks around them, suggesting the presence of curtains and blinds at some point, but they're all gone. The walls are patchy pink-beige plaster, like skin that has suffered one trauma after another. Shelves have been torn down, light fittings pulled out. None of it has been done with care. Covering the floor is a fuzzy grey substance, unevenly distributed; there are thicker clumps and sparse patches.

I haven't seen the inside of this room for seventeen years, but the three windows are just as they have been all this time in my memory. One, large and rectangular, overlooks the black wooden barn and the thin gravel path that separates it from the house. The second is tiny and square and offers a glimpse of what Marianne calls her 'show-piece', the formal, walled section of the front garden. The third is the size and shape of a large car wheel and faces the wildflower meadow at the back and the lodes and fens beyond.

Dad took an instant dislike to this room when we came to look round the house in 1998. He said it jutted out from the side of the house in a way that was jarring, and thought the odd assortment of clashing window styles made it look untidy.

'Oh, Gareth, don't be so unimaginative.' Marianne laughed at him, delighting in his wrongness as she always did. In her eyes, Dad has never been someone whose thoughts needed to be taken seriously. 'Things don't have to be identical to belong together,' she said, providing him with his new opinion, to be learned by heart. 'These windows are the perfect trio. Think of an orchestral trio. You'd want violin, cello and double bass, wouldn't you? Not three boring old identical violins.' This winning argument was perfectly calibrated to silence all opposition. She's a master at those.

All three windows look mistakenly designed and clumsily placed, but for some reason Marianne enjoys pretending things work that don't.

Like me and Paddy.

When Dad and Marianne bought the house in late 1998, Marianne immediately claimed the room Dad had 'pooh-poohed' as her own. Throughout all the years that she kept its door locked and the key hidden, she never stopped trying to provoke him by singing the praises of its ill-matched windows. 'It's so clever,' she told every visitor loudly, with one eye on Dad, who never seemed to notice or react. 'It's not only that they're different shapes and sizes, it's also that the views are all wrong, but deliberately so – at least, I'm sure it must be deliberate, since the house was built when architects still cared about beauty and attention to detail. I refuse to believe it's by chance that the biggest of the three windows reveals far too much of what no one really wants to see: the side of an old, weather-worn barn. And the smallest one reveals just enough beauty to tempt you over to it in order to see the most stunning garden, but if you step even a foot back then you can hardly see it any more. Somehow, that makes the best view feel even more special than if you could see it easily from anywhere in the room.'

Over and over, she would recite the same lines to different guests, who would then be told they weren't allowed to see any of it for themselves because the study was sacrosanct. 'Just for me, and no one else,' Marianne would say with a shrug, as if nothing could be done about it. She only started to give her 'room I can't show you because it's my private sanctuary' speech in 2006, the year I chose Paddy and ended my relationship with Olly. Before that, her study was a perfectly ordinary and accessible part of our house.

For many years, I believed it was a coincidence that both these things happened at roughly the same time.

I never heard any guest question why Marianne's study couldn't be glimpsed by anybody, or the door opened even for a brief glance. She made sure always to offer a generously thorough tour of the rest of the house: 'It's quite something: the most romantic old rectory – well, it was a rectory at one time – that's *so* like something out of a Jane Austen novel, but not in a civilised village in Hampshire or anywhere like that. No, just plonked down in this flat Fenland village full of squat, beige brick bungalows where nothing ever happens – a place that, frankly, is fit for nothing but sugar beet and barley farming – and *I love it*. I adore the contrast, the . . . *unexpectedness* of it.'

I wonder if dolling herself up as if for a fancy cocktail party in order to show me this ravaged room had the same appeal for her: the clash factor. The unexpected.

She has won again and she knows it. I'm shocked, though not surprised to be, so that isn't her victory. I was expecting to be blindsided by whatever I saw inside this room – as shocked as I felt when she offered to show it to me as if it were no big deal, after keeping it hidden from the whole family for seventeen years. The unexpected part is how gutted I feel, as gutted as Marianne's study has been; I'd hoped to be surprised by a presence, not an absence – by the answer, whatever it might be. Instead, new questions seethe and swarm in my mind.

Marianne turns to face me, grinning. There's pink lipstick on the side of one of her front teeth.

She can smell my desperation to know, as strongly as I can taste it: a thick sourness in my mouth.

'What was in here, before you got rid of it?' I ask.

'How do you know it hasn't always been like this?'

'It wasn't like this when we moved in.'

'True,' she says. Marianne can sound like the fairest person in the world when she wants to. 'Do you remember the wallpaper, when we first came here? This was the only papered room – all the others were painted plain colours, but this one had grass-green wallpaper with a pattern of small pink tulips. Should have been gorgeous but wasn't. Brought to mind a sickly person with a painful rash.'

'What was in here before today that's now gone?' I ask, choosing my words carefully. 'No one locks their family out of a room for so many years if there's nothing in there.'

'Well, someone might,' says Marianne. 'People will do all sorts of irrational things if you leave them to their own devices.' She laughs, then points. 'There was a lovely leather chair there, under the round window. And I had my battered old velvet chaise longue by the tiny window, so that I could read with my feet up and see the best part of the garden at the same time. I had a matching desk and captain's chair set, too – medium oak, green leather.' She sighed. 'And framed photographs everywhere – so many of those. All of family. Always and only family. You were in nearly all of them. Whereas your house contains no photographs of me. It's all right, I don't mind any more. But I had at least twenty of you, on shelves, up on the wall—'

'So, where's it all gone?' I snap. She's won again: made me lose my cool. She feigns a look of surprise at my outburst, which she knew would come. It's what she's been waiting and hoping for. 'You haven't just moved a few pictures. You've reduced the room to a shell.'

'A more useful question than "Where?" would be "Why?" '

'If I ask why, will you tell me?' I stop myself from adding, *I know that, somehow, the reason is linked to Olly.*

'I can't believe you haven't worked it out already,' Marianne says.

I pull in a long, deep breath. 'Why have you got rid of the contents of this room? I'll never work it out. If you want me to know, tell me.'

'You don't know I've got rid of anything. I might have moved it all.'

'Why?'

'Because of you.' Her feigned meekness makes me want to scream. *Just a brief, simple answer*, her tone proclaims. *Just the truth, unadorned.* 'Because you made a phone call, didn't you? To Norman. N.P. Pelphrey, as you would think of him.'

The name is instantly familiar. *N.P. Pelphrey, N.P. Pelphrey* . . . Where have I heard it? It was recently, I know that much. An image of me sitting on Dad and Marianne's bed appears in my mind. That's right, they were out and I was in their room because . . .

Oh, no.

N.P. Pelphrey. In the search results on my phone.

There is nothing this can mean apart from the worst thing.

I try to breathe, but the air in my mouth and throat feels like a solid chunk of something too hard to inhale.

'Norman Pelphrey told me what you asked him to do,'

Marianne says. 'Did you think you *just happened* to fail?' Her emphasis advertises her contempt for all things that occur by chance, that are not orchestrated by her.

Yes, that's exactly what I thought. I made a request and a man – N.P. Pelphrey – told me to forget it, in a tone that was blunt-verging-on-rude. I decided his response was typical of the rudeness of a lot of people these days – not noteworthy at all.

And then, all the others . . .

I wonder how much danger I'm in, and what kind of danger, now that Marianne knows what I did. Tried to do.

She smiles. This is the bit she's been looking forward to most: forcing me to watch her savouring the full extent of my failure.

'That's why everything had to go.' She nods in the direction of the empty room, then moves towards me and pulls me into a hug that stinks of the only perfume she ever wears, a peppery, leathery vanilla smell that I've come to loathe. My body is rigid, fossilised in her arms. 'Don't worry,' she says. 'I'm not angry. In your shoes, I'd have done the same.'

Except you'd have found a way to succeed.

'Like mother, like daughter, eh?' she whispers next to my ear, and it occurs to me that what I need is for her to die. I want to make that happen.

I want it more than I've ever wanted anything.

2

Monday 30 October 2023, 5.20 p.m.

JEMMA

Like mother, like daughter, eh?

I didn't include the words that fought to get out of my mouth in response, because I was too scared to say them: 'You're not my mother. You never have been and you never will be. You're my enemy.' I remember thinking to myself as I typed, my tears hitting the keyboard harder than my fingers: *Sorry, but no. If you were too much of a coward to say it, then it doesn't get to be part of the story.*

I slam my laptop shut, my heart hammering as if it's still happening now: the shock of that moment, that conversation, being alone with Marianne on the top floor of the house. I knew she wouldn't do anything to me then and there, but the look in her eyes and her 'You've done it now' smile were unambiguous: she wanted me scared.

I guess I've just proved to myself that my writing has the power to deliver an emotional gut-punch, so if I ever decide I want to go public with this diary, or book, or whatever it is, maybe it will be of interest to somebody: the story of how I, a murderer in my heart, stopped myself from committing a murder – that's how I'd describe it.

I feel a strong urge to open the file I've only just closed and look again. Was there something wrong in there? Did my eye skate over a line or phrase that needed fixing? I could swear my mind snagged on something, but it was subliminal and didn't fully register. And maybe I'm being paranoid. If I am, I blame my present location a little bit – an eerily impersonal police station reception area – and Marianne a lot. If she hadn't stolen and read all the other diaries I've ever kept, I'd probably still be handwriting in notebooks with turquoise and purple ink pens like I always used to until 2006, when my diary of the moment went missing and never reappeared. Before then, Marianne had always returned them to wherever she'd found them in my bedroom, once she'd had a good nosey. Not the 2006 diary, though. Clearly, she wanted to read and reread my thoughts from that crucial year: the one that contained the end of my relationship with Ollie and the beginning of me and Paddy trying to make a proper go of it together.

Nice way of putting it, Jemma. It would have been quicker and easier to say 'the year I chose Paddy and dumped Ollie', but let's not make things any more painful by assigning responsibility, shall we?

My words on the subject of Ollie getting dumped and Paddy being declared the winner of the 'Who-Gets-To-Be-Jemma's-Boyfriend' competition were evidently so important to my stepmother ('Wicked enough to convince anyone that Cinderella really didn't know how lucky she was', as my best friend Suzanne once said) that she decided to deprive me of them forever. I'm sure my 2006 diary was one of the things she kept locked inside her study, before she gutted it.

Where is it now?

'Oh, she's got it stashed away somewhere, for sure,' Suzanne said, after I told her about Marianne showing me the empty, stripped room. 'She was way too invested in your love life and which boyfriend you chose.'

I thought but didn't say, *I don't care where it is, as long as I don't have to read it again. Too painful.*

'Jemma? Is it okay if I call you Jemma? Are you all right?' The dyed-blonde sergeant is hovering over me again. What's her name again? That's right: Zailer. Charlotte Zailer. I didn't notice her coming over. 'Will you come with me to an interview room so that we can talk about this properly?' she says. 'And I'll need an address immediately, assuming there's a body to be found.'

'A body?'

She leans in closer. 'You said you wanted to tell us about a murder, remember? When you first came in? Then just a minute ago, I asked you for the name of the victim. You said "Marianne Upton".'

'There's no body,' I manage to say, praying she'll decide to leave me alone. 'I'll explain the situation to DC Waterhouse when he gets here.' I'll make his arrival my fresh start. As soon as I see him – a detective who deals with murders – I'll pull myself together. Somehow.

'Would you like a glass of water? Jemma, I do need Marianne Upton's address.'

Not yet. I need to explain first.

'Oh, no,' Sergeant Zailer mutters. I look up. She's staring over my shoulder, looking angry. 'Here he comes, breaking new records for whatever's the opposite of "in mint condition". I thought he'd gone home, but no such luck. Too late: you wanted him? You're about to get him.'

I'm not sure she's thinking straight. I never said I wanted DC Waterhouse specifically. I've got no idea who he is and didn't know his name until I walked in here today. All I said

– with no idea if I was using the correct terminology – was 'a major crimes detective who's experienced at dealing with murders.'

I turn and see a tall, broad-shouldered man walking towards me. He stops when he reaches my side, and blinks at me. There are patches of stubble on his face. He looks stunned – as if he's just come round from a general anaesthetic and found himself standing, fully dressed, in a police station's reception area. His probably-once-white shirt is creased and sweat-stained, his greying dark hair just long enough to look untidy.

'Simon Waterhouse,' he says abruptly; it's almost a grunt. 'You Jemma Stelling?'

I don't know what I was expecting, but it wasn't this.

'She's here to confess to the murder of a Marianne Upton,' and says there's no body,' Sergeant Zailer tells him, pronouncing each word distinctly, as if this is his first encounter with the English language. *His wife. Who thinks he's a dick.*

I wonder if there's a different police station I could go to. Silsford, maybe – that's not too far. These two are making me want to run away, but they probably won't let me leave given what I've already told them. Then again, maybe they'd shrug and say, 'See you.' There's something not quite right about either of them, and both of them together.

It's as if they're impersonating police officers. Badly.

'Why's there no body?' Waterhouse asks me.

'Can we go somewhere more—'

'Why no body?'

Feeling his words like something tightening around me, I take a deep breath. 'I haven't killed her yet.'

'For God's sake.' Sergeant Zailer lets out an expansive sigh. 'Then . . . how about you carry on not killing her, or anyone else? Then there'll be no problem, will there? I think you're a fantasist time-waster who probably has no clue that planning a murder is also a serious crime.'

'If I hadn't come here, she'd have been killed today,' I say. I want to explain everything properly, from the beginning, alone in a room with a serious, attentive detective. At the same time, now that I've started, I can't stop talking. 'Her murder would be happening now, but it isn't. Instead, I'm here talking to you. But . . . I've got a fully worked-out plan, one I've been working on for months. And I'd have got away with it. No one would have been able to prove it was me. If it weren't for the fact that I've got a thirteen-year-old daughter, I'd have allowed the inevitable to happen, but I don't want to risk—'

'What "inevitable"?' asks Sergeant Zailer.

Hasn't she been listening to me?

'I think I know what you mean, but I don't want to assume,' she says.

I spell it out. 'Marianne's murder. That's the inevitable. Or it was, before I came here. Which I did because I can't take even the tiniest risk of going to prison and leaving my daughter alone, so—'

'Alone? What about your husband, Paddy Stelling?' Sergeant Zailer emphasises his name, as if she suspects me of inventing him.

DC Waterhouse isn't looking at either of us. He's staring straight ahead, unblinking, like a dubious piece of public art that no sensible organisation would want in its foyer.

'Anyone who's only got Paddy is effectively alone.' The words are out before I can stop them. 'Even if he were different, which he never can be . . . I don't want Lottie to have a convicted murderer as a mother. I'm already a murderer inside – that won't change – but I'm not yet a murderer who's committed a crime, and it was getting more and more obvious every day that I would soon become one if I didn't do the unthinkable: come here and confess, like I am now. I tried a hundred times to tell myself, "Don't do it, don't think about the plan, don't take the next step", but it wouldn't go away. I started to do things to—'

DC Waterhouse yawns in my face.

'What the hell is wrong with you?' I ask him.

'He's having a bad day,' says Sergeant Zailer. 'Carry on, since we've got this far. You'd started to – what?'

'Lay the groundwork. Despite all my fears and attempts to rein it in, I was acting like someone who was going to do it. It took up every inch of space in my mind: that I could make Marianne not exist any more, and so easily. Without any negative consequence, apart from the big one: living with the risk of getting caught, maybe one day actually getting caught. However much you imagine you've thought of everything, that can always happen, can't it? That's why I had to come here. This is the only way for it to be over. If I tell you what I'd planned, then I'll never do it. My life will go back to normal, which isn't wonderful, but it's so much better than *this*. And there'll be no risk of Lottie losing her mum to a long prison sentence.'

'Telling us will be enough to stop you from doing it?' Sergeant Zailer asks. 'Is that the idea?'

I nod. I knew it would work, and I can feel a subtle difference already. The evil that's been burrowing into me for so long is still there, but it's loosened its hold and is now standing off to the side. There's distance between us. 'Telling the police kills my plan stone dead,' I say. 'Now, if anything were to happen to Marianne, you'd know I was behind it. The chance of me getting away with it would be zero. So please, can one of you take my statement?'

I'm no longer sure that my first choice is DC Waterhouse.

Charlotte Zailer might only be a sergeant and not a detective, but she seems far more skilled when it comes to interacting with other humans. 'And . . . I think you probably have to tell Marianne, don't you?' I direct this at Waterhouse. Let Marianne get a visit from him; I'd enjoy imagining that, if I knew it was happening. 'You'll need to warn her, presumably, that I've come in and said all this? I mean, there's been a threat to her life. I assume you have a duty to inform her.'

'According to you, the threat is now non-existent,' Sergeant Zailer points out.

'You're not going to warn her? What, you're just going to take my word for it that I won't do it now?' These two don't give a toss, clearly. Maybe their top priority is keeping their to-do list as light as possible. 'I don't care, as long as you take my statement. It has to be on record: how I was going to do it and get away with it.' The police deciding I'm no danger to anyone and sending me home is not good enough. Nowhere near.

DC Waterhouse has started to walk away. 'Follow me,' he calls over his shoulder, and then: 'Which room?'

How am I supposed to know? You're the one who works here.

'Four.' Sergeant Zailer calls out, her voice echoing along the tiled corridor. 'Go on.' She nods at me for emphasis and I realise I need to move. Follow. Even though no one who wanted to improve any aspect of their life or anyone else's would allow the weird, dead-eyed detective-husband to lead them anywhere.

I've nearly caught up with Waterhouse when Sergeant Zailer calls after me. 'Jemma?'

I turn.

'If he breaks during the interview, come and find me,' she says.

31st May 2006

That bitch. Cruel dictator bitch. She's basically told me I have to love Paddy and I'm not allowed to love Ollie, as if it's up to her how I feel about anything or anyone!!

It's the most unfair thing in the world. It feels like a tragedy. My love for Ollie has not one single tiny grain of badness or wrong-ness in it. I love him for the extraordinary person he is. There is no purer, more altruistic feeling that could exist. It's unbearable to know that I have to spend the rest of my life deprived of him and, even worse, to think of him forever going without the endless, amazing love I know I'd give him, which he deserves more than anyone I've ever met. When I think about his sheer goodness, with no trace, spot or stain of anything bad in it, I want to cry.

Ollie isn't like most of us. He's different. There's nothing tainted or compromised about him. When I was with him and thought I might actually get to keep him, I felt my own inner taint start to dissolve. Not that I'm a bad person, but most of us, me included, are sometimes driven not by the highest moral principles but by slightly more squalid motivations: making sure we're okay at other people's expense. Ollie would never behave like that and he's proved it. You don't become a firefighter if you're as self-serving and venal as most of us are. You have to be willing, day after day, to walk into burning buildings and risk your life in order to save others.

Ollie's strength of character, his exceptional bravery, his kindness — most people don't have those qualities. And he's so modest too, and so, so beautiful. I'll admit it: his beauty is part of the tragedy — that snatched-away, once-in-a-lifetime chance to have something perfect. How gorgeous would any babies be who had him as a father?! It makes no sense to torture myself by thinking about it, but I can't stop.

The hardest part of this ordeal is not that he's being forcibly removed from my life by a tyrant. That sort of cruelty, or something equally evil, happens to so many people in this pain-filled world — they lose homes, jobs, loved ones, often not as a result of unavoidable natural disasters but because of the wickedness of a human monster or monsters. And everyone, quite understandably, feels desperately sorry for them — but there would be no sympathy for me, even if I were honest about how I feel. No one would understand. I could well be the first person this particular awfulness has ever happened to. No one on this planet has felt what I'm feeling now — at least nowhere near as strongly — for someone who is forbidden to them for the particular cruel, senseless reason that Ollie is to me.

If they knew about it, people would say there's something unnatural about the strength of my love for Ollie, and how much I want him back. The only person who might understand my predicament is Ollie himself, because it's his predicament too. From him to me, from me to him, it's the same: a palindrome of loss. Oh, I'm sure he doesn't feel as strongly about me as I do about him. Not yet, anyway. But I know he would, and soon, if only we hadn't been forcibly separated. Ollie is a strong-feeler — unlike Paddy, whose reaction to most of life is a shrug and a 'Who cares?' He's so inert so much of the time. I've met stuffed toys who have more agency, ambition and vision. Yet Paddy — the one who smokes joints all day long and keeps getting fired from one crappy bar job after another — is the one I must now somehow brainwash myself into preferring. How the hell am I going to manage it?

It's true that I did once think he was lovely. That was before I met Ollie, obviously, but still. Maybe I can feel that way about Paddy again, if I try? There was a time when I'd have said, 'Anyone who fires him, it's their loss,' and 'Who cares about a bit of weed? We've all done it.' But that was before he behaved so despicably, before his endless, callous demonstration (it felt endless at the time, though it did eventually end) of his complete and utter unwillingness to commit. Can I revive the way I felt about him before that unforgivable display of ingratitude? It was really the worst . . . let's call it 'Romantic Relationship Vandalism' I've ever seen done by anyone ever to someone they know adores them.

Stopping describing his behaviour as 'unforgivable' would be a start, I suppose. The trouble is, I don't want to forgive him. The real question, and a far more interesting one than 'Do I want to?', is 'Do I want to want to?'

Every time I try to untangle the mess of all of it, a panicked scream rises up inside me: No, no, no! Don't just accept this! Do something, anything.

What can I do, though? The Tyrant has made it very clear that I'm never going to see my beloved Ollie again.

3

Monday 30 October 2023, 5.40 p.m.

CHARLIE

Charlie Zailer resisted the urge to follow and take charge of matters herself as she watched Jemma Stelling turn the corner and disappear after Simon. He couldn't do her any serious psychological harm, could he? How resilient was Jemma? It was a question Charlie doubted Simon would be asking himself. His mind was occupied by one thing and one thing only, and had been for the last week: the wreckage that his working life had become, in such a shockingly short space of time.

The new superintendent, Fran Whittingham, had started at the beginning of the month. Exactly seven days ago, she'd announced that Simon's team was to lose two members. The jobs of DI Giles Proust and DS Sam Kombothekra were being relocated to Lincolnshire Police as part of a regional collaboration on serious and organised crime, and if Proust and Sam didn't want to follow them to a new building and county, then Superintendent Whittingham was afraid there was nothing she could do about that; their presence at Spilling Police Station would no longer be required.

Simon had been wandering around like an upright corpse

ever since he'd been told the news last Monday. Though he kept denying it to Charlie, she was convinced he was now actively doing everything in his power to get himself fired. 'Why not resign, if you want out?' she'd asked him. 'We could get by on my salary, just about.' He wouldn't answer, would barely speak about it.

In his present, messed-up frame of mind, would he think to check whether Marianne Upton – Jemma's prospective murder victim – was alive and well? Charlie had an uncomfortable feeling about Jemma Stelling, who might well be in denial about already having committed this murder she seemed so preoccupied by. The eyes gave it away: the 'How did I end up here?' shock, the dark glow of something once tidy and self-contained, now spiralling . . .

But who was this Marianne Upton woman? If Jemma had killed someone, why wasn't it her husband? That's what Charlie would have expected. Evidently something was seriously wrong on the marriage front. What was it Jemma had said? Her daughter would be better off parentless than relying only on Paddy? A criticism as specific as it was devastating.

Someone needed to establish, and quickly, who was alive and who was dead. A detective – which meant not Charlie herself. Not any more, or not yet, or both. She started to move, feeling as if she was chasing her own thoughts, which were galloping twice as fast as her legs could go.

Did she want to go back to CID? To Simon's team in particular? Trying to manage him at home was enough of a struggle. Would Simon mind? If she told him – asked him – and he responded with anything but uncomplicated delight . . .

Right. Great. Have you ever met your husband?

'Who better than you to rein him in without making him feel persecuted?' the new super had said with a warm smile.

'He knows you're not against him. Anyone else comes in as his new skipper, he might view them with . . . well, a certain amount of hostility.'

Only if, by 'a certain amount', you mean the biggest possible amount in the whole history of amounts, Charlie thought.

Shit, had she just blurted out something about maybe being a detective again to Jemma Stelling? Yes, she had. And now Jemma was with Simon, and it wasn't impossible that she'd . . .

No, Jemma would be too busy talking about her own problems. A random police sergeant's career plans would be the last thing on her mind. Still, this was a 'note to self' moment: the outbursts and oversharing had to stop. The more unstable Simon became – and so far today he'd been acting as if he hoped to set a new record – the more together Charlie would need to be. They couldn't both lose their jobs.

Charlie stopped at the open door of the canteen, out of breath. A quick look around the hall revealed no Colin Sellers, no Chris Gibbs, no Sam Kombothekra.

They're probably at The Brown bloody Cow.

There was no point trying the CID room. Simon and his team were never in it any more, which the new super would have noticed. The unofficial boycott had started with Simon, of course. The others, incapable these days of raising the mildest objection to anything he suggested, went along with it as if it was all perfectly fine and there would be no consequences. *Dicks.* Yes, Simon was a talented detective who deserved admiration, but since he'd solved the murder at Tevendon a few years ago – or perhaps since COVID, which had been the year after – there had been a subtle shift of attitudes and power; they'd all started to treat Simon like some sort of murder-solving guru and had started to quote his wise words at Charlie whenever they got the chance, on subjects that ranged from the proposed Culver Valley congestion charge to the canteen's new serving hatch.

This never used to happen. And Charlie had heard all of them at one time or another – Gibbs, Sam, Sellers, even DI Proust – parroting Simon's objections to CID having been moved to a different floor of the building. The Snowman, as DI Proust was known by all who were well acquainted with his iciest, most chilling moods, had lost the glass cubicle that had once separated him from his team, and protected them from him.

A few days ago he'd grumbled to Charlie that 'Waterhouse is quite right: even prisoners get their own little cell, which they are compelled to share with only one other person.' Those first four words had nearly knocked her off her feet – the Snowman had been in the habit of praising no one but himself, for as long as Charlie had known him. That, however, was before Waterhouse worship broke out in the building and took hold of everyone like a mania. Charlie knew for a fact that if Simon suddenly decided he loved the new CID room, the rest of them would too.

Fat chance of that. Hardly anything ever climbed any higher than its starting point in Simon's estimation, which meant that their designated space in the building was being shunned by all of them. No wonder the new super had decided a restructuring of the team was necessary; had they really, none of them, seen it coming?

Charlie had her phone in her hand and was about to ring Sam when she heard the sound of a male voice drifting towards her along the corridor: 'And I think it's gonna be a long, long time . . .' She smiled and looked up, knowing before she saw him that Gibbs was nearby. Several years after Sellers had turned vegan in order to impress his girlfriend, Gibbs still found it entertaining to sing Elton John's 'Rocket Man' at him, his theory being that rocket leaves must be all his friend was eating these days.

Sellers, by Gibbs's side, told him to fuck off and waved at Charlie at the same time. 'All right, Sarge.'

'Got a task for one of you,' Charlie said.

'You're a bit late for Daily Tasking,' said Gibbs. 'And you don't get to assign us jobs – you're not our skipper. Rumour is you might be soon, though.'

'What?' How the hell did they know? Heat rushed to the surface of Charlie's skin.

'It's true, then.' Gibbs grinned. He never missed an opportunity to enjoy someone else's discomfort.

'No, actually. Currently untrue.'

'You'll get a shock if you come back,' Gibbs said. 'Things aren't how they used to be.'

'I'm well aware,' said Charlie, remembering what the two detectives standing in front of her now had looked like when she'd left CID all those years ago. Sellers had been at least four stone heavier, with sideburns. Now he was a gangly string bean with a buzz cut. Gibbs, meanwhile, had discovered cycling and the gym and had bulked out. He had muscles that bulged even when he wasn't exerting himself. 'God, I still can't believe it,' she said. 'Both Sam and the Snowman. Leaving.'

'It's no big deal.' Gibbs shrugged. 'People leave jobs all the time, don't they?'

'You're gutted about it,' Sellers told him. 'It's okay, you can admit it. We're all gutted. Waterhouse has taken it hardest, obviously.'

'He'll get better under you,' Gibbs told Charlie, prompting a smirk and a chuckle from Sellers. 'I didn't mean it like that.' He sounded indignant: how could anyone think that he, Chris

Gibbs, prolific creator of obscene innuendo since the early noughties, would ever make a lewd remark? 'I meant, she's the only solution. She's got to come back.' He turned to Charlie. 'You know it too. Why are you holding out?'

Because it's not my fucking job to save you lot from a mess of your own deluded making.

'Seriously, it'd be good for all of us to work with you again,' Gibbs snapped as if it were a reprimand. 'Not just Waterhouse. Anyway, where is the Wandering Twat-strel? Something big's come in. We've tried The Brown Cow. He's not there. Not in the canteen either.'

'Interview Room Four with a woman who came in to confess to a murder she hasn't committed yet,' Charlie said.

'You what?' Gibbs looked unimpressed.

'I know. She's hoping her confession'll act as a deterrent. I think she's a bit doolally.'

'I pity her if she's chosen today to waste Waterhouse's time,' said Sellers. 'To be honest, I'd rather leave him where he is, mood he's in, but we need him. Murder case came in ten minutes ago. Sounds like an odd one too: massive house with the kind of garden a scrote could hide in for hours, if not days, without anyone spotting him. We're talking, like, acres. Woodland,' he added, pronouncing the word suspiciously, as if he wasn't necessarily prepared to believe in such a thing, even if other people did. 'This one needs all of us. If we shoot off there now, can you send Waterhouse over, soon as you see him?'

'Where?' Charlie asked. Simon's team's last four cases had been drug dealers shooting each other in the Culver Valley's murder capital, the Winstanley Estate, where there were no massive houses.

'Sleatham St Andrew,' said Sellers.

'God, that's miles away. Up near Lincolnshire.'

'Never been a murder there before,' said Sellers. 'Not that I can find, anyway.'

'That's because there's only about ten people living there,' said Gibbs.

'3,751, actually. I looked it up.' Sellers smiled proudly.

Charlie had started to walk away. 'If I see Simon I'll tell him, but I can't make him drive to Sleatham St Andrew if he'd rather mope around here ignoring all his work and freaking everyone out.'

'Can't you try to—' Sellers began hopefully.

'Nope,' she said. 'I've got a huge heap of my own admin that I've been neglecting, and I need to follow up on this weird non-confession, in case Simon doesn't. Looks like I'll be the one tracking down Marianne Upton, making sure she hasn't been killed recently. Lucky me.'

'Are you winding us up?' Sellers looked ready to laugh if it turned out to be a joke. 'Marianne Upton?'

'Don't tell me you know her?' said Charlie.

'That's our vic's name,' Gibbs said. 'The woman who's just been murdered in Sleatham St Andrew – she's called Marianne Upton.'

2nd June 2006

I hate her. I HATE HER.

I've got a new nickname for her, which is how I'm going to think of her from now on: 'Mai Tai'. It's her favourite cocktail. (She ordered one when we were out for dinner last night, which is what made me think of it.) In my version, though, it's spelled differently: MyTy, short for 'My Tyrant'. She won't be able to hear the spelling in my head when I jokingly call her it. All it will mean to her is the drink.

Anyway, that's what she is: a fucking tyrant, however much our mutual nearest and dearest would passionately defend her and deny it. I know exactly what his reaction would be:

'Oh, come on, that's not true.'

Yes, it is.

'She's just trying to make sure . . .'

I don't give a shit.

Here's how I know she's a tyrant: I allowed her to have a complete and total victory over me and it still wasn't good enough for her. When she told me that was it, no more Ollie, I didn't argue. I nodded meekly and said all the right things — everything she wanted to hear. Since there was no way for me to change anything — nothing I could think of immediately, at any rate — I accepted it all without question and did my absolute best to act as if I was happy with her decision. And guess what? My total compliance wasn't enough for her. Ever since I said, 'Of course, whatever you want,' as deferentially as I could, she has secretly suspected me of Having My Own Thoughts About Ollie That Aren't The Same As Hers – a heinous crime in the eyes of a dictator. Still, what could she do? She had no proof. I've deliberately kept all my thoughts and my sadness to myself. Actually, let's call it heartbreak, because it goes way beyond sadness – I don't think I've felt as desolate ever before in my life as I do about this. And she knows I'll only deny it if she attacks me for thoughts she can't prove I'm having, so instead she's waging a pro-Paddy, anti-Ollie propaganda campaign.

I didn't notice until she made her second not-so-subtle attempt to brainwash me. The first was so pathetic, I didn't register it as anything more than a pinprick of pain: she told a story about the one time Paddy and Ollie met. According to her, Ollie criticised Paddy 'unfairly' afterwards, in a way that demonstrated that 'there was something not right about him, because who would say that?'. All Ollie had done was ask if Paddy was maybe a bit selfish, after seeing him stretch his legs out and take up nearly all of a sofa, apparently not noticing that I was squished into a corner at the end of it. Ollie didn't think it was right that Paddy let me perch uncomfortably like that for twenty minutes, on my own sofa in my own house, while he extended his legs and hogged most of the space, and God bless him for that. I fully agreed. I've often wondered what went wrong with Paddy's upbringing that he actually thought behaviour like that was acceptable. I should never have let Ollie and Paddy be in the house at the same time – that was wrong, and I shouldn't have let my curiosity get the better of me. I'd wondered for some time if seeing the two of them together might clarify the pecking order even further in my mind, and boy did it do that.

As for the idea that there's something seriously wrong with Ollie because he dared to criticise Paddy . . . I resisted the temptation to say, 'Anyone who meets Paddy Stelling and instantly thinks, "Hm, he seems a bit shit in some quite important ways", and then points out some of those ways, is a perceptive and helpful person, if you ask me — the kind of person who ought to be listened to.'

I didn't realise that the Tyrant's apparently offhand observation was part one in a carefully planned programme of character assassination, so I didn't think much more about it. It was only when part two of the anti-Ollie brainwashing initiative was delivered over the breakfast table this morning that I twigged what was going on. 'I've been thinking,' she said. 'There was always just something off about Ollie. I should have seen it sooner. That whole palaver on the way to the Cotswolds should have woken me up.'

I gritted my teeth as she explained why something so minor — a well-intentioned and harmless request Ollie had made months ago that was completely understandable if you were anything but a monster — proved that he was somehow terrible and dangerous. Small explosions of hurt ripped through me as she spoke and I realised that, if she chose to, she could subject me to this unobtrusive form of torture whenever she felt like it, forever: endless negative jibes at Ollie, all delivered in an 'Isn't this a fascinating observation?' tone.

I know what she's trying to do: goad me into defending Ollie. She reckons if she keeps the accusations coming, I'll eventually go wild and scream, 'How fucking dare you? I love Ollie! He's amazing! You're so wrong about him!' That's why 'tyrant' is an accurate description. Stalin and other political dictators tried to find out who secretly disagreed with them so that they could have them killed. Luckily, the Tyrant doesn't have a secret police service working for her. Anyway, she's wasting her time. I'll never give in, never give up my love for Ollie. And I won't be provoked into declaring it, either. I'm no masochist, but I think I might be the world's biggest . . . something. I'm not sure what yet. Darer — maybe that's the right word. Plotter.

Interestingly, the more I nod my acceptance and allow her victory to stand, the more anxious and jumpy she seems. I've definitely unsettled her by seeming so compliant. She's wondering more and more every day: am I trying to lull her into a false sense of security so that she'll be caught off guard when I finally . . . what? She must be racking her brains for the answer.

I'd better start doing the same because, whatever she might suspect, the truth is that I don't have anything brilliant planned.

Yet.

That's something that needs to change.

4

JEMMA

'Killing Marianne was an obsession from the second it occurred to me,' I tell DC Waterhouse. 'But it had nothing attached to it at first, nothing practical that linked it to the real world. It was like this . . . sinister backing track to my life that I couldn't switch off, always playing beneath the surface. I could handle it, though. Hoped it'd go away. It didn't. And then I thought of how exactly I'd do it. And one word kept popping up in my mind: "foolproof". I know nothing ever is, really, but . . . even if I'd been suspected, there would have been no evidence, given the solid-seeming alibis involved.'

Waterhouse says nothing. I get it: why add to the barrage of words, when it's all pouring out anyway? I haven't stopped talking since we sat down, and he's barely looked in my direction. It's lucky I came here ready to tell the whole story. These conditions would discourage all but the most determined from saying anything at all.

I wonder if Interview Rooms One, Two or Three are any more plush or welcoming. Probably not. Or maybe they ran out of comfortable furniture and paint that wasn't a hideous bright blue before they got round to doing up number Four. I

39

thought I liked the colour blue until I walked in here. There are no armchairs, rugs or pictures, nothing to soften the hard edges – only shouty signs about various things we all need to beware of or report, as if reminders of all the bad things that aren't in the room might distract from what is: this dead-eyed detective, the horrid, pock-marked table between us, the long, high window that must have been positioned to make it as hard as possible for anyone to see anything. My only view is of a slice of beige brick wall.

'It's not matricide,' I say. That's got to be the worst of all crimes: killing your own mother. 'I mean, it wouldn't be, if I did it. Marianne and I aren't blood relations. Though any mention of that was banned from the word go. I was instructed to call her "Mum". First time Dad introduced her to me, she told me she was my mother from now on. I was seven years old. My mum had died less than three months earlier. Dad knew how devastated I was by her death, yet he nodded along enthusiastically as if Marianne was saying something welcoming and lovely. I remember thinking, "No, you're not my mum. I don't have a mum any more. You're a stranger, telling me lies." It all just felt so wrong, especially because Dad didn't seem remotely bothered by any of what she was saying.

'He smiled and beamed and did everything short of jumping up and down with joy, as if Marianne's arrival in our lives was a wonderful treat for both of us. Just . . . so, so oblivious and deluded!'

I knew I'd be whacked by guilt for saying that, and that's how it feels – like a deserved blow – but I'm still glad I said it out loud. Why didn't Dad flinch at the wrongness of what Marianne was asking me to do? And there was more wrongness to come, none of which he raised so much as the slightest objection to: the ragged gasps Marianne made sure to produce whenever I mentioned Mum – and each time the air would stiffen around me, so that I soon learned not to do it; the three photos I had of me and Mum together that disappeared from my bedroom. I'd pushed them into three of the four corners of my mirror frame. Later that same day, I came back from school and they weren't there. Dad shushed me when I told him, and jerked his head towards the door as if to say, *Not now. Too risky.* Except later never came. He didn't return to the subject and neither did I. I understood, somehow, that something frightening might happen if I did, something that could cause a lot of problems for Dad.

Then a week before the second anniversary of Mum's death, he asked me if I'd mind if we didn't make what he called 'a big song and dance' about it. According to Marianne, that was what we'd done for the first anniversary, and it had made her feel unappreciated, insulted, unloved and a range of other painful emotions she had no wish to experience again. It was clear Dad needed me to cooperate, so I did, because I was eight years old, he was the only parent I had left, and I could feel his desperation for a happy ending pressing down on me like one of those machines they use to crush old cars.

The most painful thought in the world, the one I'm so used to pushing away, fills my mind before I can stop it: *Once a child has lost her mother, happy endings aren't possible.* That's why Lottie can't lose me, ever. I need to get this over with, quickly, so that I can get back to her. What will Paddy have told her? All I said in the text I sent him was that I was going to the police station and I'd be back as soon as I could. Nothing else, no explanation. Should I have added, 'Don't tell Lottie where I am'? It didn't feel necessary at the time; I assumed it would be obvious to Paddy that he shouldn't tell our thirteen-year-old I'd gone to the police without knowing the full story.

I have to stop doing this: taking for granted that he'll behave like a responsible adult.

'Shouldn't you be taking notes?' I ask Waterhouse.

'I'm not.'

Right. I could have told him that. I did, except in the form of a question.

I'd expected him to start with the formalities – taking down my full name and address – but he didn't produce a pen and paper or any sort of recording device when we came in here. That part must come later. Maybe he's going to listen first, then make me go over it all again while he writes it down. That's how the police know you're telling the truth, if none of the details of your story change when you repeat it.

'Foolproof,' he murmurs.

'That's how it felt at first, yes. It landed kind of fully formed in my mind a few hours after I'd been to see my ex-boyfriend Ollie in July. It felt like a gift from something outside of me. Like it was meant to be, you know? Decreed by fate – and yes, I know how crazy that sounds. I think that's partly why I've got this deep-down dread that there's nothing I can do to stop it happening. But that's not true,' I add quickly. 'What I'm doing now – telling you – will stop me.'

Waterhouse looks no more curious than he did a minute ago. There's something oddly soothing about his unresponsiveness.

'Ollie and Marianne had been – have been – keeping something from me, ever since he and I broke up in 2006. In July when I went to see him, I asked him to tell me what that thing was. He wouldn't. Though he did admit eventually that he was withholding something, which at least proved to me that I wasn't going mad.'

A different kind of confession is pushing to come out, one that has nothing to do with murder. 'For a long time, I thought

Ollie was the one,' I tell Waterhouse. 'You know, the one I'm meant to be with, if you believe in that kind of thing. In a way, I still think that, even though he won't tell me the truth. He's also not the one I have a child with, which matters. Paddy – that's my husband – might not be perfect, but he loves Lottie, and she adores him. I'm not going to deprive her of her dad if I don't have to. And I don't, which suits Marianne down to the ground. She's determined to keep me and Paddy together. God knows why.'

'That why you want to kill her?'

Finally, a question. 'I don't. I want the opposite,' I say. He can't be listening properly. 'To stop myself from doing a terrible thing that can never be undone. She's my daughter's grand-mother. I think Lottie probably loves her.'

All the things that have made me loathe and fear Marianne are things she's said and done to me. As far as I'm aware, she's only ever been kind and generous to Lottie.

Waterhouse amends his question: 'Why did you want to kill her enough to make a plan to do it? Can't just be because there's something she and your ex aren't telling you.'

I see the stripped-bare study as clearly as if I were still inside it: walls like wrecked human skin, the top layer peeled off; grey fuzz underfoot.

'She orchestrated a nice little torture scene, with me as the victim. It wasn't physical, the torture. She put on a sequinned evening dress to do it, not plastic overalls, Dexter-style – but that's still what it was. That's what pushed me to the point where I just . . . snapped.'

Stepping things up a level. Letting me know I was in danger. Which meant Lottie was in danger of losing her mother. I say none of this, because I can't prove it. I'm here because I want to make it impossible for me to kill Marianne – that's the official line, and it's part of the truth, for sure. A big part. No one needs to know that I'm equally afraid she might kill me, or arrange for someone else to do it, or that I'm certain the little scene she orchestrated on 7 July – her sequinned dress, the stripped study, the mention of N.P. Pelphrey – was a death threat.

How can Waterhouse want to ask nothing at this point? He's not even looking at me.

'You know who Dexter is, right?' I say, mainly in the hope of keeping the conversation going. 'Fictional serial killer on telly?'

'You're talking as if you've killed Marianne Upton already.' Waterhouse sounds bored. 'You say you snapped, but you haven't. If you had, she'd be dead.'

'Maybe that's the wrong metaphor, then,' I say. 'But something changed in me after her little psychological torture experiment. I wasn't an ordinary person any more. I was a murderer. On the inside, I mean. I was just . . . completely different from how I'd been before. From that point on, I knew I was going to do it. I could feel it bulging in my brain, the reality of it, as if it had happened already. It was like . . .' It's almost impossible to explain to a person who has never experienced it. 'Like it already existed in the future, as a . . . a done thing. It was never going to leave me alone unless . . . The *only* thing that was going to stop me was this: coming here, telling you my carefully worked out, foolproof plan, so that I could never get away with it. Even then, I thought, "Don't be ridiculous, there's no need to do something so extreme. Just don't kill her. Decide you're not going to do it and then don't do it." But telling myself that didn't work, didn't make it go away, and I started to panic, especially when I noticed I'd attached a time and a date to the plan in my mind. I knew when exactly it was going to happen. Can you guess?'

'Guess what?' Waterhouse asks.

'It was going to be today. This afternoon.' I glance down at my watch and feel a tiny detonation of relief in my chest. The moment I chose for Marianne's murder is now well and truly in the past; safely gone, never to return. 'I put it in my diary weeks ago: 30 October, 5.15 p.m.' A harsh laugh escapes from me. 'How self-sabotaging can you get? But it's the diary-writer mentality: once you're hooked, you need to get it all down, all the important things. It's Marianne's fault I became a diary addict. She started laying into me one day when I was about Lottie's age, as if I was a moron who'd really screwed up: how could I be a teenage girl, with all the complicated emotions that entailed, and not keep a diary? She was going to buy me one, and I was going to *love* it, and write in it every day, and one day I'd thank her for it . . . blah blah blah, on and on she went. Did I have no life of the mind that I felt was worth recording? What was I, a human being with a soul, or was I soulless? She actually asked me that.'

Happily, I've forgotten most of the specifics of Marianne's viciousness from my childhood, but a few incidents have embedded themselves like thorns – mostly the ones witnessed by Dad, who never questioned or objected. The funny thing was, I didn't expect him to. I knew he had no more power in our home than I did, and of course he wouldn't want to risk his 'Special Subordinate' status.

'It took me ages to realise all Marianne wanted was to be able to spy on me,' I say. 'The diary thing wasn't about soulfulness, it was about surveillance. She was right, though: I quickly got hooked. Wrote down nearly every thought I had between the ages of thirteen and eighteen. The state I must have been in, emotionally? Suzanne says it's hardly surprising my diary was my best friend until she came along.'

'Thirtieth of October, 5.15 p.m.,' Waterhouse repeats in a dull voice.

'Right.' I feel dizzy suddenly, and squeeze the back of my neck with my left hand, hoping it might send more blood to my brain. 'There was something about seeing my murder plan in black-and-white on my laptop screen, the date and time all neatly laid out in 12-point Times New Roman—'

'You type your diary?' Waterhouse cuts me off. 'Onto your computer?'

I nod. 'Haven't always, but I do now. Perhaps if it had been handwritten, it wouldn't have felt so much like I was typing up an official execution order.' I shudder. 'When I read it back . . . It sounds like a cliché, but every part of me turned cold. I knew I had to try and stop it, but at the same time I . . .'

There's no reason to hold back. He knows why I'm here.
Say it.

'At the same time, I wanted to kill her so much. I still do. And I'm also glad I didn't, glad I thought of this as the only way out: coming here, telling you everything. It was the only way to make sure I didn't ruin my daughter's life by ending up in prison.'

'The plan can't have been foolproof, then,' says Waterhouse. 'Not if you were worried about prison. Make up your mind.'

'Nothing like that's ever foolproof.' I shouldn't have to tell him this. 'When you start to feel sure you'll get away with it, that's when you're really in danger.'

'Is that a fact?'

He seems to hate me. I'm not sure why. I'm trying to do the responsible thing and prevent a crime from happening. 'I think so, yes,' I say. 'Anyway, this is going to work, this . . . deterrent I'm creating for myself now, by telling you. 5.15 on 30 October has come and gone, and if anything ever happens to Marianne in the future, I know I'm the first person you'll suspect, which is enough to make me drop the whole idea. And . . . I mean, I'm assuming you'll be making contact with her at some point and telling her there's been a threat against her. Isn't it normal to . . . I don't know, warn people in situations like this? Not that you need to, because, like I said, there's no way I'll do anything now.'

I have to hope Marianne won't risk harming me either, if she finds out about this. Surely knowing that she and I are now on the radar of a murder detective will be enough of a deterrent.

'I just need to tell you how I planned to do it, and then I can go,' I tell Waterhouse.

He yawns. Makes no attempt to rein it in, either.

Time to ramp things up. I hadn't been planning to bring up what happened eleven years ago, but desperate measures and all that . . . 'In case you're wondering, it wasn't me last time,' I say matter-of-factly. 'It was someone else who tried to kill Marianne in 2012. I've no idea who.'

Ha. That got him. His eyebrows just shot up, like they were trying to slap his hairline. I guessed right: he had no idea. Neither he nor Sergeant Zailer reacted with particular interest when I first mentioned Marianne's name.

'There was an attempt on Marianne Upton's life in 2012?' he asks.

I nod. I've become expert, by now, at detaching my concept of what happened from the scene itself. I can talk about it easily these days, without seeing what I found when Paddy and I got back that night: the blood on the kitchen floor, the shrunken, grey skin around Marianne's bulging eyes, the red and white inside of her neck . . . I translated it into image-and-emotion-free words soon after that night, and now I can think and say all the colours and the adjectives, and use them as a distraction from what they mean and a barrier to stop me going back there in my mind.

'She survived, and the person was never caught,' I say. 'If that hadn't happened, I'm not sure killing her would have occurred to me as a possibility earlier this year. I'd probably have carried on thinking murder was something that only affected other people, never me or anyone close to me.'

'This is starting to make more sense.' Waterhouse inspects his hands. 'It was you in 2012. You got away with it, and it's been eating away at you. The guilt, the regret. You want to see if confessing makes you feel better, but can't risk admitting to an attempted murder because that's an actual crime. Obviously it hasn't occurred to you that conspiracy to commit murder is just as much of a crime, but leaving that aside for now . . . How am I doing so far, guess-wise?'

I feel as if I've just been addressed in a language I don't speak. 'What?'

His head dips forward, though he keeps his eyes on me. Can't be bothered repeating himself.

Standing up, I say, 'Is that the best you can do? No wonder you and your cronies screwed it up in 2012. They must all be as shit as you.'

'I didn't get anything wrong in 2012,' he fires back and, at last, there's some energy in his voice. 'Hadn't heard of Marianne Upton until you mentioned her today.'

'Really? Well, it was detectives from Culver Valley CID, your colleagues, who made no progress whatsoever and let an almost-killer go free. Tell you what . . .' I move towards the closed door. 'I'm going to find another police station, one with proper professionals in it who—'

'Leave whenever you like. I'm not stopping you. None of this is going on the record, by the way.'

'What do you mean?'

'What I said. There'll be nothing in our files or on our system to say you ever made a threat against Marianne Upton. And no one's going to be warning her about anything.'

I don't understand. If he isn't planning to put any of our conversation on the record . . .

Does he . . . Is it possible that he wants me to kill Marianne?

As if on cue, he says, 'She must be a pretty unpleasant character if all these people keep wanting to murder her. So go on.' He gestures in the direction of the door, a sweeping motion. 'Do it if you want to. Get away with it if you can.'

5

Monday 30 October 2023, 6.15 p.m.

CHARLIE

'All right, so what the fuck do I do?' Charlie cupped her hand around her phone and her mouth. She was in the corridor outside the canteen, having called DS Sam Kombothekra. Finding somewhere more private to speak would have taken too long.

'Go in and . . . Wait, let me think,' said Sam. 'Yeah. Interrupt them, pull Simon out. Tell him about Marianne Upton's murder and let him go back into the room with it in his arsenal, ready to produce it in whatever way he thinks'll get the most out of Jemma Stelling. Or not produce it, if he thinks . . .' Whatever he said next was inaudible. 'I don't know. My brain hasn't caught up yet. Give me a second. The main thing is, don't just steam in and tell them both that Marianne Upton has been killed.'

'Obviously. Why do you think I rang you?'

'I think I might want to be there when Jemma hears the news, actually. Assuming she doesn't already know Marianne's dead. I want to see the look on her face when she's told.'

'Great minds suspect alike,' Charlie said. 'She's killed her, hasn't she? And we're her alibi. Nice, neat, middle-class Jemma

Stelling. You should see her, Sam: beautiful, glossy hair. Slightly horsey face, attractive in a sturdy way – capable-looking. Like, she'd have the best-stocked first-aid kit. She's every inch the lovely, middle-class mum – and like all scumbags who think they're untouchable, she came here to boast. She thinks she's in the clear because she had police eyes on her at the exact time Marianne was killed. She wants to taunt us, rub it in our faces – "I am a murderer, no, really, I am." Coming as close to confessing as she can, feeling safe enough to get off on the thrill of the risk she's taking.' Charlie sighed. 'You're absolutely sure Marianne Upton was murdered between 5.10 and 5.30?'

'I am,' said Sam. 'Or rather, I will be once I've checked. But, yeah, basically I am. Her husband Gareth – Jemma's dad – was on a Zoom that started at five and was supposed to finish at six. Important work meeting, loads of people from all over the world involved. Marianne showed up in the background and spoke to Gareth. Ten past five, he says that was, and luckily the Zoom was recorded, so we'll be able to watch it and see for ourselves. Then at 5.20, she rang Gareth on his mobile. She had time to say only a few words: "I'm just by the car. I don't suppose you could bring me out my—" And that was it. He heard her make a funny sound, then the phone went dead. He decided it was probably nothing, told himself she'd just lost reception – where they park their cars, you often can't get a signal. He tried to convince himself all was well, thinking Marianne would either ring back, or decide she didn't need whatever it was she'd forgotten after all, or come back to house and get it. Then at 5.25, worried about the strange noise she'd made and having failed to convince himself all was well, Gareth abandoned the Zoom meeting and went out to the garden. He found Marianne lying dead next to her car, face down. Stabbed in the back multiple times.'

'Perfect timing on Jemma Stelling's part,' said Charlie. 'What if her helper and doer-of-dirty-work for her murder plan was her dad? Could Gareth Upton have killed Marianne himself at 5.25, immediately before he saw her dead next to her car? Perhaps he omitted that crucial detail from his story.'

'He was wearing the same clothes when uniforms arrived as he'd been wearing all day and in his Zoom meeting,' Sam told her. 'Not a trace of blood on them.'

'Couldn't he have got changed twice? In and out of his murder outfit?'

'No time. Uniforms were at the scene at 5.30, less than four minutes after he rang for help at 5.27. Even if he could have quickly got changed, there wouldn't have been time for him to wash. There'd have been blood on him, and there was none. He also didn't have time to hide his murder outfit, as you call it, or dispose of the murder weapon, any of that.'

'Right,' said Charlie. Then someone else must have played the role of helper. 'Jemma Stelling got here just before five,' she told Sam. 'She was with me in reception from then until 5.25, when I handed her over to Simon.'

'She's out of the running, then.' Sam sounded disappointed. 'Spilling to Sleatham St Andrew is half an hour minimum. Late afternoon, it's closer to an hour. She can't have done it.'

'Sam, she got someone to do it for her. Obviously. That's what all this confession bullshit has been about. She's counting on us not being able to prove who her helper was, or that she had one, or prove anything against her at all.'

'I'm hopeful we'll solve this one,' said Sam. As well as being his team's only true gentleman, he was also its chief optimist. 'If anyone can get the truth out of her, Simon will.'

'You're kidding, aren't you? In the good old days, absolutely, but he's currently a wreck who can barely put one foot in front of the other.' Tears prickled Charlie's eyes. 'It doesn't help that you're pretending you're totally fine with the Lincolnshire move, Sam. He knows that's crap, and he hates being lied to, even if you're only doing it to make him feel better.'

'Charlie, I can't discuss that now. Listen, don't pull Simon out of the interview. Let him finish it. I'm going to leave Sellers and Gibbs holding the fort here with Gareth Upton and the uniforms, and I'll come back. Don't let Jemma Stelling leave the building. I want to talk to her myself.'

'I'll tell her the skipper of Simon's team wants to hear her story first hand,' said Charlie. 'She'll love the idea of getting proper attention from the head-est of honchos. I'm telling you, she's giving the performance of her life here today.'

'Barbarism,' came a voice from behind.

Charlie turned and found DI Giles Proust standing nearly close enough for her to inhale his breath – something she had no wish to do. She stepped back.

'"Head-est of honchos",' he intoned. 'Lax, Sergeant. Lax.'

'You're having a go at me for my choice of expression? I'm talking to Sam, not the Queen. I mean, the King,' Charlie corrected herself, preparing to be savaged for monarch amnesia.

'Laxness leads to barbarism.' Proust stood straight as a pencil, legs together, arms by his sides. 'Has led to it, I should say. And now we're unprepared.'

Charlie nearly asked, 'For what?', but caught herself in time. There was no need to encourage him to stick around and take up more of her time and attention.

'How long can we expect to carry on doing it and getting away with it?' he asked, glancing up at the ceiling. 'Defiling the English language, defiling our institutions, defiling the values and concepts we've relied on for centuries?'

'Sir, I really need to—'

'Don't worry, Sergeant. You'll soon be rid of me.'

Promise? How soon?

'There's a war being waged against me and my kind. You, Sergeant, have been recruited, without your knowledge or permission, by the other side.'

'I'm not sure what you mean, but I'm sorry about what's happened,' Charlie told him. 'With your's and Sam's jobs.'

'Something is happening to many more people than me and Sergeant Kombothekra,' said the Snowman. 'By the time you've worked it out, it'll be too late.'

He started to walk away, then thought better of it. 'Waterhouse won't be able to blind himself in the way you can,' he said. 'He's already having trouble pretending. And you have to live with him, don't you? So don't expect an easy ride.'

With that, the Snowman stalked off at a pace so regular that it seemed almost automated. No one could have called it fast or slow.

Charlie shuddered, cleared her throat and put her phone to her ear. 'Sam? You still there?'

'I am. Charlie, I'm really worried about him.'

'You heard it, then? You're going to need to back me up, that he really said all that.'

'I think he might be having a full-scale breakdown,' said Sam. 'Trouble is, I'm not sure anyone's noticed, given . . . well, what he's like normally.'

'I'm actually shivering from that crap he just spouted. If you tested my blood now, it'd be ten degrees down from where it was before he opened his gruesome gob. What's wrong with him?'

'You haven't heard the half of it.' Sam sighed. 'It's all mad, but . . . it's also intricate and well thought out. He's invented a whole made-up world in which everyone's out to get him and—'

'Sergeant Zailer?'

Charlie jumped at the sound of a shaky female voice she knew she'd heard before.

Jemma Stelling. *Thank God. Anyone but Proust.*

'I need you to listen to me, before I do something I'll regret forever.' Her face was pink and she was shaking. Fleetingly, Charlie wondered if she too had been accosted by the Snowman.

'What's happened, Jemma?' Charlie held her phone at an angle so that Sam could hear. Plainly, something was wrong. This wasn't a woman on her way out of the building after an interview that had gone smoothly. How the hell had she ended up all the way over here, anyway? The canteen was nowhere near either the interview rooms or the entrance to the building. 'Is DC Waterhouse okay?' Charlie knew she should have asked if Jemma was all right, not Simon, but at this precise moment she couldn't bring herself to care about this woman she was pretty sure had colluded in a murder.

'I don't think he is, no,' said Jemma. 'He's either evil or he's lost it. He's just told me I should murder Marianne if I want to. Do you have any idea how easy I'd find it to . . . to just go and do that, right now? To kill her?' She'd started to cry.

'He said what?' *Please let this be a joke.*

'I'm glad you're shocked.' Jemma looked relieved. 'I half thought you'd say the same thing: "Kill her if you want to." Thought I might be trapped in a mad world where all the cops encourage you to murder people. Because that's what's just happened. I didn't imagine it. He really said it, all of it.'

'Where is he now?' Charlie asked her. Her suspicions in relation to Jemma Stelling had shrivelled to nothing. This was too good an act to be an act.

No. Your resistance is lower now that it was before; that's the only change. Your trust in Simon's taken a dive and you're desperate to plug the gap by trusting someone else.

'He said he was going home. Seemed to think his work for the day was done. He even . . . He praised me.' Jemma shook her head. 'I told him how I'd planned to kill Marianne and he . . . made a suggestion. Look, can you please take down my statement, since your husband obviously doesn't care?'

'What suggestion did he make?' Charlie asked.

'He advised using a gun instead of a knife,' said Jemma. 'To avoid the risk of getting too close and leaving physical evidence. Said I'd be less likely to end up in prison for murder if I changed that one bit of my plan.'

4th June 2006

Heard from my friend Rosie today for the first time in years. She rang out of the blue this morning and asked how I was. Obviously I couldn't tell her I feel as if my heart's been ripped out and stamped on. She wouldn't have listened even if I'd told her — she's still as obsessed with the Royal Family as she's always been, and I could barely fit in the words 'I'm fine' before she started ranting on about poor Prince Charles and poor Camilla and all the horrid people who don't understand their great love, as if she knows them personally and can speak authoritatively on their behalf.

Ridiculous. But it reminded me of a conversation she and I had years ago, about love and the restrictions that are imposed on it sometimes. Again, the bloody Royal Family was the topic of conversation, as it pretty much always is when you're talking to Rosie. I've no idea why or when she decided that Charles and Camilla being kept apart by family expectations is the world's biggest ever tragedy, but that's definitely what she thinks. 'We're so lucky, aren't we?' she said wistfully. 'I mean, we can choose for ourselves, marry whoever we want.'

I probably agreed at the time. Because yes, if you're not the heir to the throne, you probably do assume you'll have complete freedom of choice when it comes to love. And yet my love for Ollie must remain mute, gagged and silenced. And do you know what? I don't feel in the slightest bit sorry for the Royals, with their immense wealth and many beautiful homes and castles. They know from birth that they're part of a structure in which duty and family are valued more than individual freedom. If you'd grown up as a Royal, you'd surely mind less when you couldn't have what your heart wanted; it would be the norm. Everyone around you, all your relatives, would be thinking not only of themselves but of the greater good. Sacrifices, when they were made, would be recognised and valued — whereas I can't even talk about mine. As a non-Royal, I'm supposed to be 'so lucky' because there's nothing stopping me loving whoever I want, with no family restrictions whatsoever.

What an infuriating lie. The truth is that only some of us have the benefit of that supposed freedom of choice. Others, like me, have hearts that we're expected to switch on and off depending on a tyrant's whim.

6

Monday 30 October 2023, 6.20 p.m.

GIBBS / SELLERS

Detective Constable Chris Gibbs stood on the gravelled driveway on the house side of the turning circle and watched as his skipper, Sam Kombothekra, drove away from Devey House, home of Gareth Upton and, until earlier today, of his wife Marianne too. Gibbs marvelled at how far Sam's ride could get and still be on the Uptons' property, inside the grounds of this Grade II listed former rectory; the car was a tiny spot in the distance now, yet still hadn't got as far as the tall stone gateposts. If Gibbs were to drive the exact same distance from his own home, he'd be closer to work than to where he lived.

He wished he knew what had come up that meant Sam needed to go back to work in such a hurry. All he'd said was, 'It's Gareth Upton's daughter, Marianne's stepdaughter,' without adding whether this person was dead, alive, at the nick, or somewhere else. A few more words would have helped, but Sam had allowed no time for Gibbs to press him for further information.

Jemma Stelling was the person he assumed Sam had been referring to. That was the name he'd been given: Gareth Upton's only child. Thirty-eight years old, and worked from home three days a week as a part-time bursar for a small private day school. The rest of the family were all here: Gareth himself, seventy years old though he had a full head of hair and looked younger; Gareth's son-in-law, Patrick Stelling, known as Paddy, also thirty-eight; and Paddy and Jemma's thirteen-year-old daughter, Lottie.

Not for the first time, Gibbs marvelled at how much you could learn about people from taking their basic details. Paddy Stelling had been either unwilling or unable to define himself without reference to other family members when Gibbs had spoken to him earlier. 'I'm Jemma's husband,' he'd said, before Gibbs had been told who Jemma was. 'Marianne's son-in-law, and Gareth's—' He'd tried again, looking somewhat numb and stunned in the face of all that was unfolding around him. Then a third attempt: 'Lottie's dad.'

He sounded confused as he said all this, as if he were trying to guess at his own identity, rather than clarifying it for Gibbs's benefit. Gibbs had often thought that being at a victim's home surrounded by their relatives in the immediate aftermath of a murder was a bit like being one of the few humans left in *The Walking Dead*. He and his colleagues were the living, and the surviving family members were the zombies – ghastly grey faces contorted by pain and incomprehension – and you felt sorry for them, of course you did, but you also weren't allowed to show how much you really didn't want them anywhere near you. In theory their affliction wasn't contagious, but you never quite believed that. He'd never voiced these thoughts to anyone, suspecting it was just him and not a general thing.

To be fair, Paddy Stelling didn't seem distraught in the way that Gareth Upton did. Nor did he appear to be in shock like his daughter Lottie, whose stunned, staring eyes Gibbs was starting to find unsettling. Stelling seemed more . . . provisional, somehow, as if he wasn't sure who or where he wanted to be. Asked what he did for a living, he'd said, 'Oh, I'm not really anything,' and then, seeing that more was expected of him, he added, 'I'm working at a branch of Café Nero at the moment. Not sure how long I'll be there.'

Gareth Upton had done his best, through his tears, to recite what Gibbs guessed was his usual word-for-word description of himself: 'A software writer, supposedly retired, in fact busier than I've ever been. I'm what's commonly known as a boffin.' He'd then wiped his eyes and named several companies he'd worked for and advised in the past. Gibbs hadn't heard of most of them, but understood both that he was supposed to be impressed and that Upton found it comforting to recite the details of his CV; his wife might have bled out in the grounds of their house after being stabbed multiple times, but no one could take away his illustrious career history.

Imagine work being the thing that makes you feel safest. Gibbs swore under his breath as he realised that would have been true for him before the new superintendent turned up and started messing with something that had been working fine without her.

Speaking of which . . . where was Waterhouse? Was he ever going to get here?

Gibbs turned to go back inside, then changed his mind. There was something uninviting about Devey House, even aside from the shellshocked atmosphere. Despite its many large windows, it felt shadowy and oppressive. There was too much dark wood, and densely patterned wallpaper everywhere that gave Gibbs an ache behind his eyes: a different pattern in each room.

It wasn't an attractive building on the outside, either. There were lumpy bits sticking out of its sides, rooms sprouting out in unexpected places. Sellers had said the house was named after the architect, Somebody Devey. Gibbs wondered if he'd been drunk for part of the design and building process, unable to restrain himself.

Instead of going back in, he started to walk across the lawn to where SOCOs in protective suits were clustered around Marianne Upton's body. The police doctor was still there, a new guy, young enough to be Gibbs's son. So far, the only thing he'd been able to tell them was that Marianne had been killed with a large knife and probably not one of any particular distinction. It hadn't been left at the scene.

She wasn't the first wife Gareth Upton had lost in tragic circumstances. Jemma's mother, Nancy, had died of ovarian cancer in 1992, when Jemma was seven. Upton had done the most crying Gibbs had seen from him so far as he'd tried to convey these facts, though he'd attempted, unconvincingly, to offer a consolatory voice-over: 'Thankfully, Marianne came along soon afterwards. She was a wonderful wife to me and mother to Jemma. I felt very lucky.' Gibbs had wondered if Upton's second marriage had been one of those in which any and all fond mentions of the first were strictly forbidden.

Lottie Stelling, silent until that point, had quietly corrected her grandfather: 'Marianne was Mum's stepmother, not her mother.'

'Yes, of course, sweetheart.' Upton had put his arm round her and given her a squeeze, apparently unaware that he'd just been issued with a warning.

As he got closer to the cordoned-off area that contained Marianne's body, Gibbs spotted something in his peripheral vision and turned to his left. Paddy Stelling was about a hundred yards away, leaning up against the side of the house, eyes closed, head back against the wall. Was he meditating? Thinking hard about something? Maybe he just wanted to get away from everyone else.

He was shivering from the cold, wearing a stripy shirt, nothing warmer over it. Gibbs felt himself shiver too, and pulled the zip of his coat higher so that its padded collar stood up, covering his neck.

Why wasn't Stelling with Lottie, looking after her, reassuring her that, however frightening and weird life felt now, everything would be okay? Poor kid was only thirteen. You wouldn't leave your daughter alone in the house with police when something like this had just happened.

Come to think of it, why hadn't Paddy Stelling and his daughter arrived together? He'd driven here alone, and then Lottie had turned up later, driven to Devey House by—

As he was thinking about her, Gibbs saw her striding across the vast lawn towards him: Suzanne Lacy, Jemma's best friend since school – which was all very well, but didn't explain why she'd been the one to bring Lottie here when the girl's own father had done the exact same drive earlier. And Suzanne had been the one making drinks for Lottie, feeding her from Gareth and Marianne Upton's fridge, explaining to her that it was fine to forget about homework today, promising to ring school and explain in the morning. Paddy Stelling, meanwhile, had been wandering around acting more like a lost child than a parent: staring into the distance, shaking his head, rubbing his face with his hands as if he had no idea what he was even doing here.

Suzanne jogged the last part of the way, and was out of breath by the time she reached Gibbs. She was short, athletic-looking, with large grey eyes, strawberry blonde hair pulled back into a ponytail and black-framed glasses. Dressed in black Nike leggings, blue and white trainers and a sky-blue hoody, she reminded Gibbs of his secondary school PE teacher, though Suzanne had told him earlier that she worked for an exam board ('tighter security than Guantanamo, but you could try bribing me if you've got school-age children').

'Where's Paddy?' she said now. 'Did he ask you?'

Gibbs gestured to his left, where Stelling was now sitting, knees pulled up to his chest, still by the side of the house. 'Ask me what?'

Suzanne gave a dismissive snort. 'Taking some him-time. I see. Some more, I should say. You'd have thought thirty-eight years might be enough, but obviously not.' She sighed. 'If you talk to him and can be arsed, tell him I'm cooking a proper meal – lasagne with a rocket and mango salad – and it'll be ready in about an hour. Will Jemma be back by then? Is that why Sam's gone back to Spilling, to bring her here from the police station? That's what I sent Paddy to ask you. Clearly he didn't bother.'

Sam? DS Kombothekra to you, mate.

So Marianne Upton's stepdaughter was at the nick. *Interesting.* Gibbs tried not to be annoyed that Suzanne had known before he did.

'I asked Colin but he didn't know,' said Suzanne.

'If you mean DC Sellers . . .'

'Yeah, I do. Isn't his name Colin?' she demanded impatiently.

'I don't know any more than he does,' Gibbs told her.

'Jemma was with you lot when Marianne was killed, though, yes? At the station? Sam said she sent Paddy a text saying she was heading there at around 4.45.'

'You seem to know as much as I do,' said Gibbs. 'Maybe more. Do you know why Jemma went to the police?'

Suzanne made a brisk, dismissive noise. 'Never mind that,' she said. 'Someone around here needs to start thinking about Oliver Mayo in relation to what's just happened.'

Gibbs knew who Mayo was: he'd briefly been suspected of the attempted murder of Marianne Upton in November 2012. *Bonus: two unsolved crimes for the price of one.* 'We've hit the jackpot today,' Sam had said sarcastically, but Gibbs had heard a determination in his voice that wasn't normally there. He knew how much Sam wanted to be able to present the super with two solves – one current, one cold – before he left for Lincolnshire.

'I heard Sam and Colin talking about Ollie before Sam left,' Suzanne said. Gibbs wished she'd stop with the Christian names, like she was a primary school teacher and they were kids in her class. 'They seem to think he's in the clear again – lucky old him. Same exact line as 2012: psychotherapy session with a client at his practice in Cambridge. All sounds very provable, doesn't it?'

'Meaning?' asked Gibbs.

'Genuine question,' said Suzanne. 'How many psychotherapists or people who've had therapy do you know personally?'

Gibbs thought about it, then answered truthfully: 'One.'

'I know quite a few,' said Suzanne. 'Clients who think the therapy's really helped them tend to be excessively worshipful of their shrinks. We're talking levels of gratitude that might well extend to fake alibi provision. So . . . if you want my honest opinion? I've never been convinced by the "Ollibi", as I call it – Ollie Mayo's alibi from 2012. Marianne said, "Oliver" when Jemma asked her who'd tried to kill her, when she could hardly speak. Jemma was the one who found her, after the attack.'

'Why would Oliver Mayo want to kill Marianne?' asked Gibbs.

'In 2012? Don't know. This time?' Suzanne smiled. 'Maybe he'd finally got sick of whatever twisted game it was that the two of them were playing.'

Even from the top floor of Devey House, the smell of lasagne was strong. Sellers knew it was pointless trying to resist; Suzanne Lacy had told him, with no equivocation, that she was a brilliant cook, and he'd never been the best at exercising willpower. He was supposed to be vegan these days, but he hadn't eaten since lunchtime and was hungry enough be having doom-laden thoughts about how awful it must feel to be actually, truly starving if it felt this bad to be as hungry as he was, after having had only a sandwich and a small cake for his lunch.

He'd be fine. There was no way Sondra, his girlfriend, could find out he'd eaten meat if he didn't tell her, and he was more likely to chop off his own head than ever do that.

Paddy Stelling appeared behind him. 'I heard footsteps and I thought it might be Lottie,' he said, looking past Sellers and through the open door to what had once been Marianne Upton's study. 'She really stripped it back, didn't she?' he said.

'First time you've seen it like this?' Sellers asked him.

Paddy nodded. 'Jemma described it to me. She saw it in July and it was empty then. She wanted to show me – brought me up here once when we came round to see Gareth, and Marianne was out, but the door was locked.'

'Why lock up an empty room?' Sellers wondered aloud. He was grimly fascinated by the gutted study with the non-matching windows. He'd come up here as much to get another look at it as to avoid the smell of lasagne in the hope of preserving his veganism. The whole house seemed filled with a haunted, hollow atmosphere, as if nothing inside it was quite real, but this room was the only one that looked exactly like the feeling Sellers had had ever since arriving here.

'Don't know.' Paddy shrugged, shifting from one foot to the other. He had a typically square-jawed 'handsome man' face, fair hair, golden stubble. Sellers didn't doubt that most women would find him attractive, if a little on the short side – that was assuming there was still anything most women agreed about these days, which, from what Sondra had told Sellers, there wasn't.

Having taken a few steps in the direction of downstairs, Paddy changed his mind and turned back. 'Jemma texted me earlier, saying she was going to speak to the police.'

'Right.' Sellers waited.

'Marianne hadn't been killed, though, when she sent the text. I heard Gareth say she was killed between 5.20 and 5.30, so why would Jemma think to go and speak to the police before that? I mean . . . did she? Do you know where she was when Marianne was stabbed?'

This was unexpected. 'Are you saying you suspect your wife of murder?' Sellers asked him.

'No.' Paddy looked confused. 'Just that . . . I'm not exactly sure where she was when Marianne was killed, and . . . well, I know where everyone else was. Gareth was here, in a Zoom meeting. Me and Lotts were at home – and Gareth can tell you that, too. He saw us in our kitchen when he FaceTimed to tell us the news. It'd be nice to know for sure where Jemma was, that's all.'

He couldn't have done a better job of implicating her if he'd tried, though Sellers was certain that wasn't his intention. A shrewder man than Paddy Stelling might have worked out that seeking reassurance that his wife isn't a killer from a detective involved in a murder investigation is a dangerous route to take.

'Did Jemma have a reason to want to kill Marianne?' Sellers asked.

Paddy's face tweaked in apparent irritation, as if an annoying fly had buzzed past his nose – something distracting and not worth bothering with. Without answering, he turned and headed downstairs.

Sellers was about to follow him when he heard a noise. It might have been someone whispering, and had come from behind the half-closed door of Gareth Upton's home office, the only other room on the house's top floor, across the landing from Marianne's empty study. Sellers walked in and found Lottie Stelling sitting cross-legged on the floor, next to a gigantic computer, as big as Sondra's orange Smeg fridge at home.

'What are you doing up here?' he asked her.

She stood up immediately, as if he'd said it was illegal to sit on the floor. 'Nothing. What were you doing in Granny's room?'

'I wasn't. I . . . Didn't you hear your dad just now? He said he'd been looking for you.'

Lottie stared at him. 'There's nothing in Granny's study any more,' she said. She was tall for a thirteen-year-old, with dark brown hair, parted in the centre. Her school uniform – maroon jumper, pale grey trousers – looked too big and baggy on her, and her heavy black eye make-up and pale pink lipstick both looked as if they'd been plastered on in a hurry. Around her neck was a small silver pendant on a chain: a rectangle with four thin bars going across, each one with a tiny coloured gemstone set into it.

'Is there something that makes you want to go in there?' she asked Sellers.

He was about to say, again, that Paddy was looking for her, but changed his mind. 'Yeah,' he admitted. 'I couldn't tell you what it is, though. You?'

'I didn't go in, and I don't want to. I've only been in here,' she said in a tight voice. 'Granny never let anyone in. The door was always kept locked.'

'It was locked when we got here,' said Sellers.

'Did you find the key on her? On her dead body?' Lottie asked, her eyes widening. 'She always kept it with her, wherever she went. One time it fell out of her sleeve. I was the only one who noticed. She tucked it back in before anyone else saw.' In a quick, jerky movement, Lottie darted past Sellers on her way out of Gareth's office. The rest of what she said was muffled by the creaks her feet made on the stairs: 'I'm going down to wait for Mum. Don't stay in Marianne's room too long. You might have dreams about it. I used to.'

Why 'Marianne' suddenly, and not 'Granny'? Sellers thought.

She'd dreamed about it? Her grandmother's study, that she'd never been allowed inside? Perhaps it wasn't that surprising: the idea of a locked room was a powerful . . . thingamajig; Sellers couldn't think of the word he wanted.

Was he going to cross the threshold and inspect the noth-ingness of the empty room for a third time?

He walked in, looked at his polished shoes on the decaying carpet underlay, turned round and walked straight out again.

There. Done. Not that he needed to prove anything to himself.

He'd started to make his way downstairs when Gareth Upton appeared in front of him, travelling in the opposite direction, with two meshes of red lines where the whites of his eyes used to be. Sellers hoped Upton wouldn't be one of those elderly people who were dead from grief within a fortnight of their spouse dying.

71

'I was looking for you. Could we . . .?' Upton gestured towards the top floor of the house. 'I need to talk.'

'About?' It sounded serious. Sellers hoped this wouldn't mean a delay to his encounter with Suzanne's lasagne.

'It's about Marianne's will,' said her husband.

7

Monday 30 October 2023, 6.30 p.m.

JEMMA

The door closes and Sergeant Zailer's gone. I'm alone. I didn't hear a key turn, but I get up anyway and walk over to the door to check. Not locked. The door opens easily.

That's good. I'm free to go if I want to.

I close the door, go back to my chair and reach into my bag for my phone, sure that by now Lotts will have decided Paddy's explanation of where I am and what I'm doing is insufficient and sent me a 'Where the hell are you, Mum?' message.

Damn. My phone's out of battery. A flash of panic passes through me. I should have texted Lottie directly in the first place. Instead, I sent the explanation for my absence to Paddy, knowing he's a much less efficient communicator than our daughter; knowing he wouldn't immediately hit reply and demand more information. For today only, until this task is done, I need things to be a little vague and blurry – and for that, Paddy Stelling is always your man.

I'll think of a convincing story to tell Lottie later. And Paddy. I can hardly say I came here to stop myself committing the murder I've been planning for months. Suzanne heard the unedited version, late last night – I always tell her everything

– but no one else. Nobody wants to hear something so disturbing about their mother or their wife, however true it might be.

It's fine. I force myself to breathe fully and deeply for a few seconds. Lottie will be fine. Hopefully it won't be too much longer before the most senior detective gets here. Sergeant Zailer said he was on his way. "The head honcho", she called him.

There's a small table in front of me, and I've got my laptop with me, so . . . I pull it out of my bag, open it and go straight to the file called 'Diary'. Until DS Head Honcho turns up, I can write about what's happened so far with Sergeant Zailer and DC Waterhouse.

I'd be embarrassed if anyone knew how hard I try when I write my diary. The effort to turn it into something that might one day have readers who aren't me – that might even be publishable . . . Though of course I could never publish it while Dad and Marianne are alive.

Listen to Lady Muck, still waiting for her adoring fans to turn up.

Most lonely, confused children invent imaginary friends to keep them company. After Mum died and Dad became preoccupied with keeping Marianne happy to the exclusion of all else, I invented an imaginary cheering audience that followed me wherever I went and whooped ecstatically at everything I accomplished: good exam results, victories in school netball matches, getting asked out by a fanciable boy. Except the person these non-existent fans couldn't get enough of wasn't me, Jemma Upton. In my fantasy life, which for many years felt more real to me than my real one, she was called Lady Muck. That was her stage name – or, I should say, mine. Mum used to call me it as a joke when I asked for breakfast in bed or for more marshmallows to be added to my cup of hot chocolate. 'All right, Lady Muck,' she'd say affectionately as she got up to get me whatever it was I'd asked for.

The nameless hordes of devotees I'd invented hung on my alter ego's every word. Most of what she had to say was about Marianne Upton, naturally – formerly Marianne Taggart, a woman who had gone with alarming speed from being Lady Muck's mother's good friend, whom she'd met on a garden design course, to being the fiancée and then the wife of Lady Muck's poor deluded father. Wasn't it the day before Nancy Upton's funeral that Marianne had first been spotted at the Upton family home, tiptoeing out of a bedroom that was definitely not yet hers? Why, yes, it was. And hadn't her hand lingered a suspiciously long time on Gareth Upton's arm at the wake, after the funeral?

Why, yes, it had.

Lady Muck's audience applauded fanatically whenever she produced her punchline: Marianne must have set her sights on this father and soon-to-be-spare husband long before Lady Muck's mum had died.

I open my diary file and start to scroll down, looking for where the last section finished so that I can start writing a new one about the events of today. I'm nearly there when something stops me in my tracks. At first I think it's just a typo, but there it is again. I was right: something wrong *had* snagged in my mind when I'd looked at it before.

I scroll up a bit, then down. It's everywhere: the same mistake over and over. I feel light-headed and force myself to take three deep breaths. It can't have been the computer that did this. And I know it wasn't me . . .

Ollie's name is spelled wrong. I've now seen four of them: 'Olly' instead of 'Ollie', in three separate diary entries.

No one would spell his name like that except for . . .

A memory comes back to me: 2006, Ollie sitting in the kitchen at Devey House, fending off the attack on his name more charmingly than I'd have thought possible if I hadn't witnessed it with my own eyes: *You're right,* he told Marianne. *It probably does work better spelled with a 'y'. Certainly looks better written down, and I can see the argument for fewer letters. Haha! Why add unnecessary clutter? If I were starting from scratch, I think I'd opt to be Olly-with-a-y for sure, but the trouble is, I'm just so used to the way I've spelled it all my life.*

I had cut in at that point. Told him there was absolutely no need or reason for him to justify the spelling of his name, which was his business, and none of my stepmother's.

I grip the edges of the table in front of me. How many 'Olly-with-a-y's am I going to find? Is it just these four, or . . .

In my panic, unable to focus on how to get back up to the top of the document, I decide the fastest way is to close it, then open it again.

There it is in the very first entry: 'Olly'. Spelled the wrong way.

This is my diary, mine and mine alone, that no one else even knows exists.

Or do they?

I didn't do this. It wasn't me. I spelled it right every single time. I'd never get Ollie's name wrong.

Someone's done it, though. Someone has broken into my diary file and left their snide, taunting calling card.

There's only one person I know who'd do that.

8

'Wordle,' said Suzanne Lacy. She and Gibbs hadn't moved from their spot just past the turning circle in front of Devey House. Gibbs fought back the urge to say the rudest thing he could think of: something to make her shrivel up and feel shame forever. She'd led him on, if only very briefly – allowed him to believe he was on the verge of an important discovery in the case. Her mention of a twisted game that Oliver Mayo and Marianne Upton had been playing together had raised his hopes, which plunged right back down, like a lift that reaches the top floor and then has its cables cut, at the mention of something as anodyne as the world's favourite online word game.

'Ask Jemma when she gets here,' said Suzanne. 'It was the first thing Marianne did when she woke up every morning: solved that day's Wordle puzzle. She kept trying to get Jemma to play it, but Jemma wasn't interested. And . . . I think Ollie must have been, though I can't prove it.'

'So, you're saying Marianne and Oliver Mayo . . . what, had some kind of Wordle thing going on? Is that what you meant by a twisted game they were playing?'

'I think that was an element of it, yeah,' Suzanne said. 'A harmless game within the twisted game.' She looked at her right wrist, which had a pale watch-shaped mark on the skin, but no watch. 'I'd better go and check the lasagne isn't burning.'

'I don't get it.' Gibbs stood in front of her, stopping her leaving. 'You need to explain.'

'I need to get back to the kitchen.'

'I'll come with you, then,' he said. Together, they started to walk towards the house. There was no sign of Paddy Stelling when Gibbs turned to look. He must have gone back in.

'All I've got is a theory, and absolutely no evidence that it's the truth,' Suzanne warned him.

'Go on.'

'One night last year, I stayed over at Jemma's after we'd had a bit of a boozy night,' Suzanne said. 'Next morning we're having breakfast and Jemma's phone buzzes. Marianne. And she's sent her Wordle result for that day, the grid. I don't suppose you know . . .?'

'Know it well, unfortunately,' said Gibbs. 'My wife does it religiously every night before bed, then sends that stupid box thing to everyone she's ever met since the day she was born.'

'Oh God, one of those,' said Suzanne.

'I wouldn't care, but it's like she expects me to get excited. She'll go, "It's *bread*. Today's word is *bread*!" Like, so what? I don't play it, and I don't give a shit.'

'Here's the strange thing,' said Suzanne. 'Marianne's been doing Wordle since it started, but she'd never sent her result to Jemma before. Not once. But this particular morning she did, and she sent a message with it too: "Send to Jemma. No words, only the grid." Jemma said, "Why's she telling me to send this to myself?" I said, "She obviously meant to send it to someone else. She must have got mixed up and pressed the wrong contact on her phone because you were in her mind. Freudian slip of the finger." Jemma replied to her, saying, "I'm Jemma. Have you sent this to the wrong person?", to which Marianne sent back a stupid-yellow-face-crying-tears-of-laughter emoji and a "Yes, sorry! Meant to send it to Paddy!" Which was a fucking lie.'

Suzanne's expression hardened. 'She's never texted Paddy in her life, according to Jemma. The whole thing was just . . . odd. I figured it must have been a pretty important word, if Marianne thought it worth sending to anybody with that instruction: "Send to Jemma". What could it possibly be? I wondered. So, later, when I wasn't with Jemma any more, I found Wordle and had a go. Guess what the word turned out to be?'

'No idea.'

' "Howdy".' Suzanne stopped walking. They'd reached the front door. 'We probably shouldn't discuss this inside,' she said. 'Can you think of any reason why Marianne would encourage her son-in-law to send the word "howdy" to his wife? Because I can't. I think – no, I'm sure – that message was meant for Ollie Mayo, not Paddy. I just can't prove it. I think it was Marianne telling Ollie, "Here's a clever, cryptic, flirty way to get in touch with Jemma after all the years the two of you haven't spoken." Why she wanted him to do that, I've no idea. She'd been dead against him and Jemma getting together – like, basically gave the impression she'd die if it happened, and almost insisted Jemma and Paddy stay together – so I've no idea why she'd suddenly encourage Ollie to get in touch with Jemma.'

'What did Jemma think?' Gibbs asked.

'That Marianne was trying to mess with her head for some reason. It was one of her favourite hobbies – but she didn't agree with me that Ollie had to be the person that message was meant for. Said there was no proof, and she's right – there isn't. Look, even if it's true, and I *know in my bones* that it is, that doesn't mean Ollie killed Marianne. All I know is, Marianne said on the night of the attack in 2012 that he was the one who'd done it, before she started insisting it wasn't him.'

'Why would she lie to protect the person who'd cut her throat and left her bleeding to death on the floor?' Gibbs asked.

'Your guess is as good as mine,' said Suzanne. 'Jemma agrees with me, for what it's worth. She'll tell you herself when she gets here: she's thought for a long time that Marianne and Ollie are keeping some kind of secret from her – that there's something dodgy going on between them.'

'Her stepmother and her ex-boyfriend?' Gibbs frowned.

'I know. Gross, right? But Jemma's convinced, and I'll admit, after everything she's told me, I am too.'

'Can I ask you something else?' said Gibbs. 'How come it was you who brought Lottie here, not her dad?'

Suzanne's mouth flattened to a disapproving line. 'For some reason, Paddy decided he couldn't bring Lottie with him. Probably thought he could protect her, I don't know. Instead of ringing me and asking me to sit with her – I mean, I was at work, but I'd have dropped everything – Paddy rang an old acquaintance of dubious character. A bloke.' She shook her head. 'Effectively a stranger, too – Lottie's barely spoken to him. The only thought in Paddy's head was who could get there soonest. Fine, he wasn't thinking straight after hearing about Marianne's murder, but I mean, when is he? Look, did you take in what I said about Ollie before? Whichever client gave him his alibi in 2012 needs putting on the spot, big time, to see if they're telling the truth or not. Are you going to do that?'

'You still haven't told me how you ended up bringing Lottie here.'

'Why does it matter?' said Suzanne impatiently. 'She was freaked out by being dumped in the care of this dude immediately after hearing her gran had been killed, so she texted first Jemma, who didn't respond, and then me. I rescued her and brought her here, where she obviously needs to be, with her family. Not with a not-even-close-any-more male friend of Paddy's, the very last person Jemma would ever trust with . . .' She seemed to change her mind mid-sentence. 'Well, she'd never entrust Lottie to him. That I'm sure about.'

She started to move towards the house, saying, 'I'll have to apologise to everyone for a charred lasagne if I don't get in that kitchen right now. Please follow up on the Ollibi, okay?'

'What? Oh – right. Mayo's alibi.'

'Since she went to see him in July, Jemma's been insisting he didn't do it in 2012,' said Suzanne, 'but that's not what she thought at the time. Very much not.'

Gibbs followed her in the direction of Devey House, falling gradually further behind as she sped up. He wondered if he'd read too much into her words or if she had meant to imply that Jemma had trusted the not-even-close-any-more friend with *something*, if not her daughter. Or that Suzanne thought she might.

Gibbs shook his head, deciding he'd probably read too much into what she'd said, and put it out of his mind.

'Will you take all of them away?' Gareth Upton asked Sellers in a deadened voice, looking around his home office. By 'all', he meant the various . . . Sellers didn't even know what to call them. Technological devices, maybe – though that description brought to mind smaller things like phones and the Nintendos his kids had played with when they were little. Upton's home office was full of enormous monitors and large grey and black hard drives the size of filing cabinets. 'I built most of them myself. I don't suppose . . .'

'What?' asked Sellers.

'Nothing. I was just going to say, I don't suppose it matters. I don't feel up to doing much. Can't see myself . . . You know.' Speaking seemed to be an effort for him. He wasn't crying at the moment, but there were still wet patches on his face.

'Would you maybe like to go and lie down for a while, Mr Upton?'

'No. I'd have to wake up again, wouldn't I? Don't want to do that.' He looked around, as if to remind himself where he was. This room had been designed to look as masculine as possible, thought Sellers, with none of the colourful, elaborately patterned wallpaper that filled most of the house. Even the study that Marianne had stripped bare, which Sellers could see across the landing, was somehow more feminine.

He wondered if it had been furnished and full or empty in Lottie's dreams. She'd said she 'used to' dream about it, which implied long ago, when presumably the room had some stuff in it – but if Lottie had never been in there . . .

Sellers dragged his eyes and attention away. Who'd have thought that a shell of a room could be so much more interesting than one that contained lots of things to look at and a speaking human? Gareth Upton was clearly in so much pain, it was hard to be in his company. Sellers rose from his chair and started to say, 'Mind if I close the door?' at the same time that Upton said, 'I don't know what I'm supposed to do without her. I'm sorry. I'm just not . . .'

'Not a problem. Take your time.' Sellers sat back down again, waiting for this new round of crying to stop. He forced himself to look at the room he was in, and not the one that seemed to be calling out to him. The walls of Gareth Upton's home office were grey, like most of the computers standing against them, and the wooden floorboards had been painted an even darker grey. There was nothing on the walls apart from two enormous canvases, both portraits of Marianne Upton. In one, she was a full-bodied orange outline on a white background, but somehow still recognisable as herself. The other was a more realistic, traditional portrait of her sitting in a high-backed armchair, smiling. Her bobbed silver hair shone; Sellers thought it was clever how the artist had done that. The second was by far the superior painting, he thought.

Aside from the pictures, there were no decorative or softening items in the room: no lamps, no ornaments on shelves; no shelves, in fact, for ornaments to go on – not a single one. No rug, coasters, cushions, throws. Sellers thought of himself as a fairly blokey bloke, but even he would have had a cushion or two. He could have done with one now, in fact. The room's only chair apart from the one behind Gareth Upton's desk was minimal and Scandinavian-looking – less like a chair and more like a slender metal ruler folded in half.

'We'll get all the computers and stuff back to you soon as we can,' Sellers said, once Upton had composed himself.

'Please do. If it becomes possible to distract myself with work in the coming days, then I'd like to.'

Sellers inclined his head in the direction of Marianne's empty study. 'Do you know why your wife stripped her study bare?' he asked.

Upton looked disorientated. 'I . . . no,' he said eventually.

Was he lying? Hard to tell. All Sellers could see was a mess of a man. Upton had a soft, round fleshy face, straw-like hair that stuck out in every direction, and a small, piggy squiggle of a nose. Together, these features might have given him a rather comical aspect if he hadn't been so obviously distraught.

Interestingly, Marianne had been attractive for a woman her age. Getting on for beautiful, even. Sellers looked again at her portrait: bow-shaped mouth, long slender neck, dark blue eyes. Why had she married a man who looked like the cuddly-toy version of a scarecrow? For his unquestioning obedience and devotion, perhaps.

'I do know,' Upton said.

'Sorry?' said Sellers.

'Why Marianne destroyed her study. I do know why. I'm sorry, I wasn't trying to mislead you. I thought you'd asked a different question. She was convinced that Jemma was trying to break into her room, invade her privacy. Please don't think badly of Jemma. She wouldn't normally think to snoop like that. She found Marianne . . . difficult.'

'What was in there before?' Sellers asked.

'Nothing untoward,' said Upton. 'A little writing table, like the sort a Victorian lady might have had. Marianne called it her desk but that was my little joke: "Desk? Call that a desk? *This* is a desk."' He patted its glass surface. 'I could never understand how she got by with something so dainty.'

'You must have seen her study, then, and been inside it, if you saw her desk?' said Sellers.

'A couple of times, yes. If Marianne and I were the only ones home, she would sometimes leave her study door open, if she knew she'd be going in and out. And I mean, I wouldn't have dreamed of setting foot over the threshold without an invitation. She knew that.'

'What was in there, apart from the dainty desk?' Sellers asked.

'Other furniture. A chaise longue, chairs, a rug. Lamp, cushions. The shelves were stuffed with books, notebooks, photographs.'

Everything that's missing from this room, then.

'Where's it all now?'

'Clearabee took it all,' Upton said. 'They're a company that comes and takes away anything you don't want any more. She didn't give them any of the personal stuff – the books or the photos. We squirrelled those away for safekeeping. Everything else went, though.'

'Including the shelves,' said Sellers. 'And the carpet.'

Upton nodded.

'Why? Marianne not wanting Jemma to see her personal possessions, books, photos – that makes sense, I guess, but removing shelves and the carpet seems a bit extreme.'

Upton sighed. 'If you'd known Marianne, you'd understand. She saw every part of that room as hers, and for her only. Yes, even the carpet. On one level it was really only the photos she couldn't risk Jemma seeing, but . . . all of it was her kingdom and she was determined to . . . protect it.'

By destroying it? Sellers was hardly about to argue that Marianne Upton couldn't have been as crazy as that when her husband was calmly advising him to the contrary. Most people were bonkers in at least a few little ways, Sellers knew.

'What did you want to tell me about her will?' he asked Upton.

'My wife has – had – a lot of wealth. You're going to find out about her will, I expect, so I wanted to tell you before you do, and to urge you to . . . well, to disregard it. Nobody would kill a person for taking them out of their will, especially not when it happened so long ago, but even if they would, Jemma and Paddy have no idea. I'm the only one who knows, and I'm very much hoping that nothing about what's happened here today means they need to find out it was ever any different from how it is now.'

Interesting. Sellers didn't plan to disregard any of this.

'Are you saying Marianne used to have a will in which Jemma and Paddy Stelling were beneficiaries, and then she changed it and cut them out?' he asked.

Upton began to cry again, but there was a nod in there too. Confirmation.

Sellers waited.

'Shortly after their marriage, she made a will. We both did. Mine's the same now as it was then: Jemma and Lottie. Everything goes to them. But Marianne, who was worth significantly more than I am—'

'What did she do again?' Sellers asked.

'Before she retired, she worked part-time at the museum in Silsford,' said Upton. 'Very part-time. That wasn't where her money came from, though. That was from her father. An American.' This was stated in a tone that suggested it explained everything. 'Victor Taggart, his name was. He invested in a friend's company in the 1940s – a company that turned diamond particles into the sharp edges of oil-drilling devices, I think. I'm not sure I ever quite followed the details. Thanks to him, Marianne inherited millions. She very much wanted to leave some of her wealth to Jemma and Paddy when they first got married, and she suggested £500,000 for Paddy and a million for Jemma.'

Sellers tried not to look as startled as he felt.

'I thought it was extremely generous of her,' said Upton. 'The rest would be divided between me and a number of charities she supported. She's always given a lot to charity.'

'When and why did she decide to cut out Jemma and Paddy?' asked Sellers.

'She made her new will in December 2012. As for why . . . I'm afraid I can't tell you.'

December 2012. That wasn't even two months after someone

86

had tried to kill her by cutting her throat. There had to be a connection, surely. 'Mr Upton, anything you know, I'm going to have to ask you to—'

'I don't know. Hence why I can't tell you. I meant what I said: it's *can't*, not won't. Marianne let me in on exactly as much as she wanted to and no more.'

'You mentioned before that Marianne couldn't risk Jemma seeing the photos in her study,' Sellers said. 'Why? Could I see those photos? You kept them, right?'

'You'd be none the wiser.' Upton smiled sadly. 'They're family photos, that's all. But Marianne didn't want Jemma to know that she . . . well, she played Happy Families in that room. She picked out photos that had us all smiling or laughing – Jemma especially. As if there was no resentment from Jemma towards Marianne and never had been.'

'But . . . everyone picks the best, smiliest family photos to display,' said Sellers. 'Would Jemma have thought anything of it?'

After a few seconds, during which Sellers guessed he was wrestling with difficult thoughts, Upton said, 'It would have been humiliating for Marianne. The photos were evidence that she cared, and wanted something that she saw Jemma as depriving her of. She never . . .' He cleared his throat. 'She didn't ever like to give any power away. She always had to have all the power.'

Sellers eyed her portrait again. Yes, he could imagine it. 'You're sure Jemma and Paddy don't know about the changed will?' he asked.

Upton nodded. 'As I said: they didn't know about the first will, either. I don't think inheriting money from Marianne has ever crossed either of their minds.'

Having not met Jemma and barely having spoken to Paddy,

Sellers disagreed. How could you have an elderly relative worth millions and not be constantly wondering if you'd be quids in one day?

'Please tell your colleagues: there's nothing associated with the will that provides a motive,' said Upton. 'And . . . I *really* don't want Jemma and Paddy to find out they've been done out of something they never even knew they had, if you know what I mean. They'll both have assumed everything of Marianne's is coming to me, I'm sure.'

'I don't suppose you know who's getting their million and a half instead?' Sellers asked.

'I don't know for sure, but my guess would be a trust fund for Lottie. Or else the charities and I will each get a little more. Which they don't know and I couldn't care less about – and whatever the arrangement is, it's been in place since December 2012. There's no reason why someone upset by it or hoping to gain should have waited eleven years. The will is completely irrelevant, all right? It has nothing to do with any of this.'

And that's why you've invited me in here for a special discussion about it, thought Sellers. *Because it's so completely irrelevant to everything.*

6th June 2006

    This morning, the Tyrant (MyTy — though that nickname is too contrived and I don't think it's going to stick) brought up 'that ridiculous palaver on the way to the Cotswolds' again. She ambushed me as I was walking up the stairs, and found a stupidly contrived way to drag it into the conversation. She'd obviously been fretting about my lack of response the first time she mentioned it: I didn't roll my eyes or accept her invitation to criticise Ollie, and she wanted to give me another opportunity to do either or, ideally, both.

    I had no intention of saying anything disloyal about lovely Ollie, so I tuned her out as she went on and on about why his behaviour had been 'creepy' and how we'd all had a narrow escape. Predictably, her version of the story was full of exaggerations and outright lies — that he'd gritted his teeth at one point, that his tone had been 'frosty and weirdly detached'. What crap!

    Here's what really happened: we were driving to the Cotswolds, to a house with a heated indoor swimming pool that we'd rented for the Christmas holidays last year. Ollie had spent the last three Christmases with his dad but this year his dad was in Australia, staying with his sister and her family.

    As a thank you for inviting him to join in with our Christmas holiday, Ollie had insisted on driving us to the rental house in his car. It was a black seven-seater — a hand-me-down from Ollie's dad, Mark — that had 140,000 miles on the clock but was nevertheless smooth and comfortable and in far better condition than either of our rickety old bangers.

A couple of hours into the journey, we met some heavy-ish traffic on the M25 and had to slow down to around twenty miles an hour. Quite cheerfully (with absolutely no 'weird detachedness' or 'gritted teeth', and I should know because I was sitting next to him), Ollie said, 'We should probably ring and let them know that we might not be there by four.'

'What are you talking about?' I laughed. 'We don't need to do that. Are you joking? Please tell me you're joking.'

'No.' Ollie looked confused. He frowned as if to say, Why would I be?

'We're picking up the keys from a pub, Ollie — a very busy and popular one. They'll be open until at least eleven o'clock, and we'll be there by half past five at the latest.'

'Oh.' He sounded surprised and looked so reasonable, as if he wanted to do everything he could to persuade himself that I was right. 'But . . . I thought you'd told them we'd pick up the keys for the rental house at four? Or did you say "around four"?'

'I said four, but—'

'Then shouldn't we let them know it might not be four on the nose?'

I took a deep breath and tried again. 'Ollie, they'll still be open whether it's four, five or six, and the keys will still be there too.'

'I'd rather ring, if that's okay?' he said tentatively, and as he said it we came to a slip road next to some services and he took the exit, as if we'd all agreed he should do what he'd suggested and call the pub. 'I'll do it myself, if you give me the number,' he said. 'Sorry, but . . . I don't like leaving people hanging or wondering. I don't want them to worry we're never going to turn up.' He laughed nervously, and was clearly doing everything he could to make his unpopular opinion more palatable to the rest of us. 'What if they rent the house to someone else?' he said. 'They might have a waiting list. I want to ring, even though I know it means you're all going to mock me for years.'

Since he'd already taken us off the motorway and was insisting he'd do it himself if I didn't want to, I rang. I teased him about it afterwards, but I didn't really mind. 'Just for the record,' I said, 'four o'clock, in this context, means "Not before four" – so that the cleaners can get the place ready. It doesn't mean, "Turn up at four on the dot or it's all over." ' We were all laughing at him now, egged on by my sarcastic tone, which I hope was also affectionate. 'We've paid for the cottage in full, plus a security deposit. They can't give it to someone else. It would have been fine. God, I bet they wish all their rental guests were as considerate as you!'

I remember thinking that excessive precision about timings and arrangements might be a fireman thing. Sorry – firefighter. If your job was saving people's lives by hauling them out of burning flames, then presumably if you said you'd be at work at four and turned up at six, some people might end up burned to blistering crisps amid the ashes that were once their homes. Or at the very least, you'd inconvenience your equally life-saving colleagues who had been relying on you to turn up on time so that they could get some rest before their next night-shift.

Speaking of heat, this little episode en route to the Cotswolds made my Christmas so much better. I had a new, warm glow inside me, because Ollie had said we'd all be mocking him 'for years'. He expected to be around, in my life, for a long time!! This was proof that he assumed he'd soon be a firmly installed part of my family. (I can hardly bear to think of that now, given what's happened.)

I think it's because of this – the family thing, how much I wanted him to become part of mine and what I knew about his own awful, neglectful family – that I hated the Tyrant more than I've ever loathed anyone before for using this particular story against him.

He'd been so thrilled — and by that I mean visibly ecstatic — to be invited to join the Uptons' Christmas holiday, and would have been horrified if he'd known anything he'd done during that week had been viewed as wrong or creepy by anyone. All he was doing was trying to make everything run as smoothly as it possibly could. And yes, maybe he was a bit ridiculous in his paranoia that our rental house might be given to someone else if we didn't show up on time. There was probably part of him that could barely believe he was about to have a nice week away with a family he was hoping to become part of soon, and that nothing would go wrong. That'd be totally understandable given that his mum, while she was alive, always palmed him off on her sister and went on holiday without him, and his dad was AWOL from his third birthday until he was seventeen. And when we're afraid something will go wrong, our fear can make us act like a bit of a fool or a control freak. Poor Ollie!

I can't work out why the Tyrant thinks that reminding me of how considerate Ollie was that day helps her pro-Paddy campaign in any way. Paddy would never anticipate the hypothetical worries of a pub landlady he'd never met, or think ahead and question whether our amazing Christmas might be ruined by lateness or a failure of a communication. He'd assume it was someone else's job to take care of all the practicalities.

'The whole thing was so sinister,' said the Tyrant, lying through her teeth. I was in that car with her when it happened and she showed no sign of thinking it was anything but sweet and amusing, like we all did. She's trying to rewrite history. 'It's all about control with Ollie,' she said. 'You can see that, right?'

I managed not to say, Oh, my God! Never ever in the history of the world has a blacker pot ever slagged off a more innocent kettle.

'Here's what I think,' I said instead. 'I think Ollie was the one who was starting to worry, and didn't want to admit it. He knew he'd be anxious all the way there if he didn't ring, and he wanted to put his mind at rest. The best bit was that we ended up getting there at five to four anyway.' I smiled.

The Tyrant glared at me. Once again, I had failed to provide evidence that I had laid down my own thoughts and feelings about Ollie and adopted hers instead.

It simply wouldn't do. She had no intention of letting me get away with that.

9

SIMON

Simon Waterhouse was curious about this Marianne Upton woman, who more than one person seemed to want to kill. He suspected she was as upper-middle class and well turned out as Jemma Stelling, and it was highly unusual to find ladies of nearly seventy of that sort in the role of murder victim.

He decided he was probably curious enough to drive back to the nick, though he'd only recently left there and was now at home. He stood motionless in the hall of his and Charlie's house, his coat still on. Did he want to take it off? He didn't think so. What he wanted was to know more about the attempt on Marianne Upton's life in 2012.

Maybe he could stay put and make a call . . . No, he couldn't. *Damn.* He'd left his phone and his police radio at the nick, deliberately, so that no one would be able to contact him. It had seemed like a good idea at the time. And he and Charlie hadn't had a landline phone for years.

He'd told Jemma Stelling he was going home. He'd meant it, too. And he'd done it. So what if he'd spent half an hour sitting alone at a table in The Brown Cow first, with a pint glass full of tap water from which he hadn't taken a single sip?

He'd gone home eventually. Anyway, it was up to him what he did.

You're cracking up. Get a grip.

Seconds later, he was slamming the front door and jogging back to his car, keys in hand.

By the time he'd got as far as Spilling High Street, he felt calmer. Everything was under control. Indulging his curiosity wasn't disallowed by the new rules he'd made for himself, though obviously it would depend on what he did with whatever he found out. That was where the breaking of resolutions might creep in, but only if he let it. And he wouldn't.

Get it together.

Had he really told Jemma Stelling to murder her stepmother if she wanted to? Yes. He had. *Good.* If he got fired before Sam and Proust left, at least he wouldn't have to watch them go.

Ten minutes later, pulling up in the nick's car park, he briefly considered trying to identify the car of the new superintendent, Fran Whittingham, so that he could piss on or otherwise vandalise it. The idea didn't appeal to him enough to bother. Not his style.

The uniforms' nickname for the new super – Dooper – had stuck. 'Dooper, Dooper, why'd they have to hire you?' Sellers had taken to singing whenever he and Simon walked past her office, to the tune of ABBA's 'Super Trouper'. Sometimes, if Sellers had overdone it at The Brown Cow over lunch, he'd throw in another line too: 'Pooper Scooper, when's she gonna fire you?'

It was a good question. Soon, probably, now that Simon was encouraging murders. Knowing he'd never be able to prove her wrong in her assessment of his professional shortcomings, he'd found himself fantasising about defeating Dooper some other way. Fat chance. She'd soon have him living on benefits and wishing he'd obeyed more than a handful of orders since the start of his police career.

Luckily, Jemma Stelling was about as capable of committing murder as Simon's socks were. Dreaming up an oh-so-clever plan was one thing, but she'd never have put it into action. She was a trapped-in-endless-emotional-bullshit person, not an action person. Whatever her manipulation was about, murder wasn't the aim. Simon's best guess was that she wanted two things: to make her fantasy feel more real by getting it immortalised in an official police statement, and – most importantly – she wanted to scare Marianne Upton out of her mind.

I'm assuming you'll be making contact with her and telling her there's been a threat against her. Isn't it normal to warn people?

That's what Jemma had said. She'd made the point twice. She was Simon's least favourite kind of person: shamelessly telling a tiny fraction of a story and pretending it's the whole thing, expecting you to hang on their every word and not notice you're being manipulated.

He locked his car and walked through the slicing wind up the steps and into the nick. Once inside, he headed for the new CID room – the first time he'd done so by choice. He focused on nothing but the danger of running into Dooper, how extremely likely it was, how much he'd hate to lay eyes on her even from a distance.

God turned out to be on his side for the first time in what felt like a long while: he made it to the CID room without so much as a glimpse of Dooper's shiny mushroom hair.

The first person to notice he'd walked in was DS Doug Brodigan, nearest to the door. He still had his coat on and was mopping up some coffee he'd spilled on the top of a filing cabinet. Brodigan was as good a place to start as any, Simon thought. He'd been with Spilling CID as long as Simon had; they'd trained together. Simon had an impression of Brodigan as someone who would prefer to say 'Yeah, course', rather than 'No chance', which made him a promising prospect.

'Waterhouse.' Brodigan looked slightly wary as Simon approached. 'I was sorry to hear about Sam and—'

'No one's dead,' Simon spoke over him. He couldn't stand sympathy. Charlie had said the other day that most of their colleagues, close and distant, were more concerned for him than they were for Proust and Sam. Simon wished she'd kept that observation to herself, though he knew she'd meant well in telling him.

'Sure,' said Brodigan. 'But to lose two members of your team . . . That's rough. Has Superintendent Whittingham—'

Simon cut him off with a terse, 'How likely are you to remember a case from 2012?'

Brodigan looked surprised to be interrupted. Then he nodded. 'Marianne Upton?'

Simon was about to ask how he knew, then realised word must have got round about Jemma's supposedly preventative murder confession.

'Worked that one myself and won't forget it in a hurry,' said Brodigan. 'Bloody odd one, it was.'

'Tell me,' Simon said.

'Formidable lady, was Mrs Upton. Minted, too – massive house in Sleatham St Andrew. Wife, mother, grandmother. She was attacked in her mansion while babysitting her grand-daughter. Had her throat slashed. Nasty. She was lucky to survive – only did because the scrote got her trachea, not her arteries. Could still have died, though, if she'd been found thirty seconds later. Ambulance got there just in time. She nearly drowned in her own blood.'

Simon said, 'Stepmother and step-grandmother, I heard.'

Brodigan shook his head. 'We were given strict instructions by Marianne herself: she was as much the little girl's grandmother, and Jemma's mother, as if they were her flesh and blood. No "step nonsense" would be tolerated – that's what she called it. I remember her saying, "It makes a huge difference, what we decide to call things." I've never forgotten it. She'd always yearned for children and grandchildren of her own, she told me, so why would she let any step nonsense put an unnecessary distance between herself, Jemma and . . . no, can't remember the kid's name.'

'Lottie,' said Simon.

'Right.' Brodigan chuckled. 'I tell you, she was a right old handful, was Marianne Upton, even half dead.' Lowering his eyes and his voice, he said, 'Snowman alert.'

Simon turned. Proust was standing in the doorway of the CID room, holding a file under his left arm and a banana in his right hand. Without being summoned, but feeling a kind of internal pull, Simon told Brodigan he wouldn't be long and moved towards his DI.

'Would you like a banana, Waterhouse?' said Proust. 'This banana?'

'No sir.'

'You've *gone* bananas, though. I brought you this to celebrate. From the canteen.' The inspector held it out and Simon took it. 'Did you encourage a woman to murder one of her relatives this evening?'

'She isn't going to do it. She never was.'

'Maybe was. Definitely isn't going to in the future,' said Proust. 'I see. You haven't heard, have you?'

'Heard what?' said Simon.

Proust nodded, as if in response to an answer rather than a

question. 'We're the sane ones, Waterhouse. Me and you. It's the rest of the world that's abandoned sanity, and we're the ones who have to suffer for it.' He plucked the banana out of Simon's hand and marched out of the room.

'What was that about?' Brodigan asked a few seconds later.

'Not a clue. Could have been his idea of a joke.' Unlikely, though. Normally anyone in the vicinity suffered the scalding agony of an ice-burn whenever Proust deployed what passed for his sense of humour. 'Tell me about Marianne Upton in 2012,' he said to Brodigan. 'Everything you can remember. How was it an odd case?'

'Well, we thought we had it in the bag, but then we had the rug pulled from under us – by none other than the victim herself.'

Simon knew he ought to wait and let Brodigan tell the story in his own way, but he was too impatient. 'Could Jemma Stelling have done it?' he asked.

'Nope. Jemma was in a taxi with her husband when it happened, on their way home after trying and failing to go to London. Loads of witnesses saw them in the taxi queue and the driver confirmed it. No question about it – they were both ruled out very quickly. Normally they stayed in London over-night every Thursday, at the same hotel, while Marianne Upton babysat for little Lottie, but on this occasion their train stopped between Rawndesley and Stevenage and decided it wasn't going any further. You know what trains are like. Eventually the driver headed back to Rawndesley, all the passengers got off, including Jemma and her husband, who got a taxi from there to Sleatham St Andrew. They got back to Marianne's to find that—'

'Wait, she was babysitting at her house, not theirs?' asked Simon.

'In 2012 Jemma and her husband and daughter were living

at Devey House with Jemma's dad and Marianne. On the night of 8 November, Jemma and hubby get back to find an ambulance and a police car pulling up at the same time. Marianne had managed to reach her phone and call – well, whisper – for help. And here was the funny thing: she named who'd done it to her within seconds of them all arriving: "Oliver", she whispered, in response to Jemma asking who'd done it. And Jemma knew who she meant, or thought she did. Her ex-boyfriend was called Oliver. He was a psychotherapist, having previously been a fireman and given that up. Mayo – that's it. Oliver Mayo. And according to Jemma and also Marianne, she didn't know any other Olivers. But Oliver Mayo, it turned out, couldn't have been the one. He was in Cambridge, where he lives, doing therapy with a patient, or whatever they call it.' Brodigan's delivery made it clear that he had no time for such things.

As Brodigan had been speaking, Simon had felt something was out of kilter somehow, and now he realised what it was: this bloody room. It was worryingly quiet – no human voices apart from his and Brodigan's, only the hum of dozens of machines. It was a hellscape: rows of desks and screens; automatons, supposedly human, tapping away at keyboards, no one looking at each other, no chat, no one throwing balls of paper or swearing loudly.

Was this really how Dooper wanted it to be?

'Like I said, no one could think of any other Olivers that Marianne might have been referring to,' said Brodigan. 'Jemma asked her. "My Oliver?" she said. And then, according to Jemma and hubby and everyone else who heard it, the paramedics and everyone, Marianne frowned, as if Jemma had got it all wrong. She had almost no strength left in her by then, but she started trying to shake her head. She whispered, "No, *my . . . my . . .*"

I mean, I wasn't there, but I've heard the same story from five people at least. Jemma says she's sure Marianne was trying to say, "No, *my* Oliver." '

'Why would Jemma's ex want to murder Marianne?' Simon asked.

'Jemma said he definitely wouldn't – wouldn't harm anyone, she was adamant.'

'What about Marianne's husband? Where was he?' It was supposed to be always the husband, though Simon's own experience of murder cases didn't bear this out.

'Gareth Upton was in London,' said Brodigan. 'Like Jemma and Paddy Stelling, Mr Upton stayed overnight in London every Thursday. For work, in his case. Thursday and Friday were his two days in the office. He'd made it in to London where Jemma and Paddy hadn't – he'd gone in on an earlier train that miraculously reached its destination. Lots of witnesses corroborated his whereabouts too.'

'The baby, Lottie Stelling – where was she when the attack happened?' Simon asked.

'Asleep upstairs,' said Brodigan. 'Which means much further from the violence than it would be in a normal house. The staircases at Devey House are long and steep and go round several corners. Little Lottie slept through the whole thing, thank goodness. There were no loud noises to wake her. Oh, and that was the other interesting thing: no one broke in. There were no windows smashed, no broken panes of glass in the door, no busted locks. Whoever did it, Marianne Upton let them in and drank wine with them. Nearly a whole bottle had gone. Jemma swore that same bottle had been in the fridge, unopened, when she and her husband had set off for London. There were two washed-up wine glasses standing neatly by the sink, alongside the attempted murder weapon, which had been cleaned equally thoroughly: a sharp knife from a block in the kitchen.' Brodigan took a sip of his coffee. 'Killer was careful to leave no trace of himself. Locked the front door on his way out and posted the Chubb key back through the letterbox.'

'So Marianne's lying on the floor spouting blood from her neck while he's washing up?' said Simon, trying to picture it.

'Must have been, yeah. Thankfully she had her phone on her, in a pocket. Wouldn't have been able to call for help otherwise. We assumed she waited to ring till he'd left the kitchen, no doubt thinking and hoping he'd left her for dead.'

'Even if they drank wine together, that doesn't mean she knew her attacker,' said Simon. 'Someone interesting could have knocked on the door and been invited in. Any security cameras?'

Brodigan shook his head. 'Marianne was against them in principle – both before the attack and, crazy as it sounds, even more so after it. I did everything I could to persuade her to change her mind, but she stood her ground. "I refuse to act like a victim", she said. "Do you really think those things make anyone safer, or feel safer? They do the opposite." There was no arguing with her. I did wonder at the time . . .'

'What?' said Simon.

'If she had some secret . . . you know . . . dalliance, or something, going on,' said Brodigan. 'I couldn't think of any other reason why an intelligent person, obviously wealthy and with a house that size, would refuse such a basic security precaution. You know, unless there was someone coming and going from the house, shall we say, whose visits needed not to be caught on camera.' Brodigan shrugged. 'For what it's worth, I was convinced she knew him, whoever he was. Knew him well. And yeah, I was always sure it was a bloke, despite the thorough washing-up job that had been done in the kitchen, because Marianne always said "he" when she talked about the person who'd attacked her. When I pointed it out to her, she said, "It's a generational thing. I am officially old. When we old people mean 'any old bod', we say 'he'." She said it like it was true. The rest of the time, she spoke like she was obviously lying and wanted me to know it. Gloating, almost.'

'How d'you mean?' Simon asked.

'She trotted out the same lies multiple times,' said Brodigan. 'Always with a confident smile on her face: she couldn't remember saying Oliver had done it; if she'd said that, she must have been delirious; no, she'd let no one in that night; she hadn't seen the face of the person who'd come up behind her; she hadn't been aware of anyone lurking in the house; she'd drunk some wine alone, but had no visitors. Just lies on top of lies, in that goading tone that says, "You can't prove I'm lying and we both know it." According to her, one minute she was watching television in the lounge, and the next she was coming round on the kitchen floor, covered in blood. No memory of anything that happened in between.'

'What about the physical evidence?' asked Simon.

'Oh, we found fingerprints and DNA from all the people who couldn't have done it.' Brodigan sounded irritated. 'Gareth Upton, all the Stellings. Oh, and Oliver Mayo too. He and Jemma had broken up years earlier but apparently he was still a regular visitor to the house. Not quite sure how that worked, but then again, they're different from us, aren't they?'

'Who?' said Simon.

'Posh people.' Brodigan sighed. 'Though I'm sure most of them aren't quite as determined to protect their would-be killers as Marianne Upton was. She didn't like me defining it that way – as attempted murder. One time she snapped at me, "This has nothing to do with murder. What happened was the opposite of murder!" And if you're about to ask what she meant by that, I'm afraid I can't help you. Made no sense then, and makes no sense now, eleven years later. If only she'd listened to me and installed those bloody security cameras.' Brodigan sounded angry, suddenly. 'It's not the opposite of murder this time, is it?'

'What do you mean? Are you saying . . .' Full of disbelief that he was even asking the question, Simon said, 'Has . . . something happened to her?' at the exact moment that he saw Brodigan's eyes widen. No, he'd had no idea. Yes, Brodigan had only just realised Simon hadn't known and that something else, not the murder of Marianne Upton, must have brought him here.

10

'Can this be quick?' I ask DS Sam Kombothekra. I've been moved to a different interview room. This one has more natural light and smells fresher, thank God. Unfortunately, the improved aesthetic can't make up for the fact that I've been here too long already, and now all I want is to get back to Lottie, check she's okay. Has she had dinner? What will Paddy have given her? Something easy and unhealthy, no doubt.

'It's up to you whether it's long or short.' DS Kombothekra smiles at me. 'You're here voluntarily and you're in charge. So . . .'

'It's just that . . . my daughter, Lottie—' I break off, frustrated by the part I can't say: that I need him to leave me alone so that I can carry on trying to work out what it means that Marianne has been in my laptop diary file and changed the spelling of Ollie's name throughout. Did she read it all, including the part where I outlined my plan to have her killed? Did she get as far as my much better plan: to come here, to the police, in order to make sure I didn't go through with it?

Of course she did. She's read it all, every last word.

Marianne's nothing if not thorough. She'll never forgive me for any of it. If I thought I was in danger from her before . . .

'Lottie's fine,' DS Kombothekra says. 'Safe and well.'

'What?' A knot tightens in my stomach. 'How do you know? Why would you . . . how . . .?'

'When people come in to confess to murders, even ones they haven't committed yet and hope never to commit, we check on their loved ones as a matter of course,' he says.

That makes sense.

Of course she's all right. She's safe and healthy and perfectly okay. Why wouldn't she be?

Why do I have the irrational fear that she's with Marianne at this very moment, having been swept up, in my absence, under that malignant wing?

'Did you see and talk to her yourself?' I ask. 'Did . . . did you tell her about my . . . about why I came here?'

'Yes to the first, no to the second.' DS Kombothekra smiles again. He's tall and handsome with olive skin and green eyes, immaculately dressed in a grey suit and tie. His voice sounds like velvet, and it makes no sense that I feel so much worse than I did an hour ago, but I do. I almost wish I was back in the ugly room with the offensively disengaged DC Waterhouse. I felt more in control then.

I just need to get home. Soon as I can.

Is it strange that a detective sergeant handled a routine safety-check trip himself?

Wouldn't he send a uniformed PC to check on Lottie? Unless . . .

He said Lottie was safe, though. He wouldn't lie about that.

'You seem jumpy, Jemma. We don't have to talk now if you'd rather not.'

'No, I . . . I need to tell you.'

'About your plan to murder Marianne Upton?'

I nod. 'You'll turn the recording into a statement, right? For me to sign?'

Kombothekra nods. He pressed record a few minutes ago, and then the first thing he asked me was if I was sure I didn't want a lawyer to be present. That freaked me out. I'm not trying to get away with any dishonesty here. All I want is to tell the truth and be heard, properly.

'Marianne's my stepmother,' I say. 'I've never loved or even liked her, and I thought I hated her, but I didn't. Not really. Not until 7 July this year, when she . . . she did something that turned my dislike to hatred, and . . . fear. The kind I couldn't ignore.'

Predictably, DS Kombothekra asks what she did.

'Can we come back to that later?' I say. 'I'll tell you the whole story, but the plan to kill Marianne is more important. I need to say all the details and you need to record them.'

'Why is it so urgent that you tell me your murder plan?' asks DS Kombothekra.

'Because . . . every second that I'm not telling you is a second I'm actively considering *never* telling you,' I blurt out. 'Even now, I could decide to lie. I could feed you some rubbish, then kill Marianne in the exact way I've planned, imagining I might get away with it.'

I've never been more tempted, knowing she's read every word of my diary file. To think of her even opening it is like spiders crawling all over me, underneath my skin. Since I found out, I've been fighting with the same thought that won't leave me alone: *You stupid idiot, Jemma. If only you hadn't come here and opened your big mouth. If only you could still do it . . .*

DS Kombothekra looks unperturbed by what I've told him so far, but he's much more put together and harder to read than Waterhouse. Who knows what he's thinking? Will he understand if I tell him that the murderer part of me is now, once again, in the ascendant?

I decide an analogy might work better. 'Do you know any alcoholics?'

He starts to shake his head, then converts it into a nod. Evidently an alcoholic acquaintance came suddenly to mind.

'That's what it's like. My murder plan is like an unbearably tempting, full, sealed bottle of—' I stop, wondering what an alcoholic's drink of choice would be. Nothing as girly and frivolous as any of my favourite drinks, probably. 'The strongest vodka in the world. Telling you every detail of my plan is the equivalent of opening that bottle and pouring the vodka down the sink. Gone forever, no longer available to me. By telling you, I remove the chance that I'll ever try it. If anything happened to Marianne, you'd know it was me. You'd know I'd paid Tom, how I'd hidden the payments—'

'Tom?' DS Kombothekra cuts me off.

I'm going to have to give his surname too. There's no way of keeping him out of this.

'Tom Tulloch,' I say. 'Middle name Ellis. Address: 9 Fore Street, Little Holling. Look, let me tell you everything, okay? And then I'll answer all your questions.'

He nods.

'Paddy and I – that's my husband – we were at school with Tom. The three of us were really close, for years, until Tom treated us pretty shoddily, which ended the friendship. Then he got in touch again about three years ago, wanting to get together, being all cheerful and "Hey, guys, let's hang out", as if nothing had ever happened. He and his girlfriend had split up, and . . . well, the reason we'd lost touch was because of her, indirectly. But now they weren't together any more and Tom wanted to pick up where we'd left off. Paddy seemed to want that too, but I didn't. I didn't think I could. Tom had behaved badly, and I didn't think I'd ever be able to think well of him again, so I said so in the most tactful and least hurtful way possible. I didn't expect we'd ever hear from him after that, but he messaged last year, out of the blue, to ask for . . .' I stop suddenly. 'You probably don't need all this background.'

'Please, go on,' says DS Kombothekra. 'I'm curious to know why you'd hire someone you think so poorly of to carry out a task that involves extreme violence and high risk.'

'You'd understand if you knew the full story. It's really not that relevant or interesting. The important part is what happened when Tom reappeared in my life. He messaged me last year, asking for help. His life had fallen apart, he said. He'd been made redundant and been booted out of a flat by whichever woman had got sick of him most recently.'

In response to DS Kombothekra's raised eyebrows, I say, 'I've never known Tom's love life to be anything but a disaster. He had nowhere to live and no money, and wanted to know if I could lend him some cash, put him up, do anything to help. Oh, and also forgive him for being the shittest friend ever. I told him that of course I forgave him, but sorry, there was no way he could live with us. I didn't want him in my space every day. That would have been awful. Paddy, Lottie and I had only just moved out of Marianne and Dad's house and into our own place. But . . . I did genuinely want to help Tom – mainly just to ease my conscience, knowing I didn't really want him as a friend any more – so I said I'd pay him to house-sit for us while we went on holiday for a fortnight.

It was August 2022 when he got in touch, and we were just about to set off to the Italian lakes, in, like, three days' time. I offered to pay him to live at ours while we were away and just keep an eye on the place. I pretended our burglar alarm wasn't working and that I was worried about leaving the house empty for so long. Easiest job in the world for him, and normally I'd have offered maybe five hundred quid. I mean, he hardly had to do anything – just live in our house for two weeks, that was literally it. But I offered him two grand.'

'That's . . . generous,' says DS Kombothekra.

'Deliberately so. I felt guilty for the extent to which I just . . . didn't want to be around him any more. I suppose, also, I've got quite a bit more spare money than a lot of people.' I shrug. 'Anyway, Tom said yes, and our house was still standing and immaculately clean and tidy when we got back, so . . . no problems there. And then this year, beginning of August, he texted again, asking if I want the same again this summer: two weeks house-sitting for two grand. I didn't, but I did want something else by that point.'

'Someone to kill Marianne for you?' Kombothekra says.

I nod. 'I knew I'd never be able to do it myself. All the ways of killing people I could think of, I just . . . I knew I couldn't. And they all seemed so risky. If I bought a gun illegally, the police might find evidence of me doing that. Plus I'd have to learn how to use it. If I stabbed Marianne myself, I'd probably leave DNA traces, and I'd need to be right next to her to do it – frighteningly close.'

It feels strange to be saying out loud to a stranger all the things that for so long have been no more than an anguished refrain going round and round in my head. 'If I poisoned her, I'd need to buy poison, and, like the gun, that might be a traceable transaction. Eventually I realised: the only way to leave no trace of myself was to get someone else to do it for me – someone whose DNA had never been . . . taken and stored anywhere official. Someone who had no connection at all to Marianne. No one investigating her murder would be likely to suspect Tom any more than they'd suspect any of Paddy's or my other acquaintances who had never met her.'

I sit forward in my seat, nervous tension bouncing inside me exactly as it had before I told DC Waterhouse. 'The official story would have been that Paddy and I had hired Tom to house-sit for us again. We'd paid him two grand, again. Nothing about that would have looked suspicious – we'd done it before, after all. And I've got a history of overpaying for stuff. I'm not short of money,' I explain, in case Kombothekra is wondering. 'When Mum died, she left a trust fund for me that cashed out a couple of years ago. That's when I was finally able to move out of Dad and Marianne's house and buy me, Paddy and Lottie a place of our own.'

'So you could afford expensive house-sitters – and the services of a killer.' The way DS Kombothekra says it, it sounds like the most reasonable thing in the world, though I know that's not what he's thinking.

'I could afford it, yes. I was going to pay Tom five grand to kill Marianne, and the payments would be hidden inside the house-sitting fees. He'd house-sit for us once this year and once next year, each time for a fortnight, and then the year after he'd house-sit for a week. At the same rate as the last year house-sitting, that makes five grand. See what I mean?'

Kombothekra gives me an encouraging smile that makes me want to cry. I know I don't deserve the approval of anyone in the business of crime prevention. He must be hating me, whatever his face looks like.

'All Tom had to do was agree to receive most of the money after he'd done the . . . task. He had to be happy to wait and get the money in stages. I told him almost before I said anything else: if he didn't want to do it, that was absolutely fine, but in which case there'd be no more house-sitting and no more money from me. I knew he'd say yes. He'd have done almost anything to get his hands on that five grand – he'd always been terrible with money and obsessed with it at the same time – and I knew how desperately he wanted to be my friend again. He'd have done anything. I'm not proud of it, but I hinted that it might be possible for things to go back to the way they'd been between us before if he'd help me out with this one thing.'

'I take it he agreed to your . . . proposal?' Kombothekra asks.

'Like a shot. Didn't even have to think about it.'

'And what about the murder itself? Was that up to Tom to improvise?'

'Absolutely not,' I say. 'I worked out every detail. On Mondays at six, Marianne has a yoga class in Silsford. She always sets off in her car at 5.15. It's really secluded where Dad and Marianne park their cars in the grounds – a bit of a walk from the house. Dad grumbles about it all the time when Marianne's not there to tell him off. She doesn't want to be able to see cars from any of the windows. She's obsessed with windows and what you can see out of them.' I'd lost count of how often I'd stood in her garden and stared up at the round window of her study, craning my neck until I couldn't bear the ache any more, wondering what was inside that room that Marianne was so determined to conceal from everyone.

'The murder would have happened on a Monday,' I say. 'Today. I decided a few weeks ago that today was going to be the day: 30 October. Both Tom and I would arrange rock-solid alibis for ourselves. Mine would be genuine, his would be a lie: his brother, Lucas, who would agree to cover for him no matter what, Tom assured me. Tom would wait in the wooded part of Dad and Marianne's garden, having climbed in over the high wall, from Sleatham Forest – the part so dense with trees that no one's ever there. I mean, it's *so* convenient. Would have been so convenient, if it had happened. Tom would have been in position from quarter to five or so, hidden in the trees. When Marianne came along at quarter past and was standing with her back to him, facing her car, about to get in and drive to yoga, he'd run forward and stab her from behind. He'd have worn some kind of protective suit to avoid leaving his DNA at the scene. Said he'd order one online, and a big hunting knife for the violent part. Then once it was done, he'd have disappeared, via Sleatham Forest again, and driven miles away to dispose of everything: the suit, the knife, anything else of his that had Marianne's blood on it.'

I let out a long, slow breath. *There. It's done. Finally. All safely recorded on a police device.*

DS Kombothekra taps his thumbs together. 'Is that everything?'

I can't think of anything I've left out.

'So, are we your rock-solid alibi, then?' DS Kombothekra asks. 'Me, Sergeant Zailer, DC Waterhouse? You being here at exactly the moment that Marianne gets stabbed to death?'

'What?' The size and importance of his obvious misunderstanding makes me weary. How soon will I be on my squashy sofa at home, taking the mickey out of a stupid TV programme with Lotts? *Please let it be soon.* 'No,' I say. 'By the time I

decided I had to come here, I'd changed my mind about . . .'
I break off. 'What? What is it?' Something's not right. I can see
it on his face.

'Jemma, Marianne Upton was murdered today.'

Smooth, calm and clear. No mistaking what he said.

Jemma, Marianne Upton . . .

Murdered. Today.

His words howl in my head, a roar as loud as the sea.

'She was killed next to her car, in the grounds of her house,
just like in your plan,' says DS Kombothekra. 'Between 5.20
and 5.30 p.m. Stabbed several times from behind.'

I can't breathe. Oh my God. *Lottie* . . . What have the police
told her? What does she think I . . .

'And your whereabouts at the relevant time aren't in doubt,
are they, Jemma? You were here. So, I have a few questions for
you, as I'm sure you can imagine. Did you arrange for Tom
Tulloch to kill Marianne Upton today? Did you plan to use us,
the police, as the most unshakeable of all possible alibis? And
– maybe I'm being overly imaginative, but . . . was there another,
even cleverer part of your scheme that you haven't told me
about: confessing to your plan and pretending you wanted to
prevent yourself from going through with it, at the same time
as establishing your alibi?'

Oh, God, oh, God, oh, God. What does this mean? Could
he be making it up? I can't begin to make sense of it, if it's
true. I feel cold all over.

'If I'm right, then you're not the only one who needs an alibi,
correct?'

Dread clutches at my stomach and my throat. It can't be
true. Marianne can't have been murdered while I've been here.
Of course she hasn't. It must be a trick. The police don't trust
me, so they're testing me.

'Tom Tulloch also needs one,' DS Kombothekra goes on. 'His brother, as you said? Or anyone but his brother? Yes, I think anyone but.' His calm demeanour seems chillingly smooth and mechanical now that I'm falling apart inside. 'That's what I'd go for, if I wanted it to seem as if I'd decided not to put the plan into action after all.'

11

SELLERS / GIBBS

O kay, so he wasn't imagining it. Sellers had been right: Lottie Stelling had him under surveillance. Each time he came up to the top floor, she was there too, only a few seconds behind him. Wasn't trying to hide it, either. She was in white pyjamas now, with a large white towelling robe over them that obviously belonged to someone larger. Alarmingly, her face seemed to be smeared in what looked like goose fat. Unlikely, thought Sellers, who had encountered no geese in the grounds of Devey House so far.

'Don't worry,' she said. 'I know it looks gross. I'm slugging.'

Suzanne's voice travelled up from the landing below, 'Lotts! Come and do your teeth!'

Lottie gave Sellers a 'she's so clueless' look. She said, 'I love Suzanne to bits, don't get me wrong, she's my godmother and everything, but . . .' She shrugged. 'I don't know how she thinks I'm going to be able to sleep tonight.'

'I'm really sorry for your loss,' said Sellers.

'Oh.' Lottie looked surprised. 'Thanks. I just meant . . . I'm not going to be able to stop thinking about it all. I mainly still don't believe it's happened.'

119

'Did you love Marianne to bits?' Sellers asked her, interested to see where her 'yes' would fall on the scale of heartfelt to perfunctory to downright unconvincing. If he'd understood correctly, she'd just tried to tell him that she was more shocked than sad.

'She loved me.' Lottie looked away.

Interesting.

'So, tell me,' Sellers changed the subject. 'Is it me, or is it this room?' He pointed at the open door to Marianne's empty former study. 'It's got to be one or the other. Every time I come up here, you're tailing me.'

'Just want to see what you're doing up here.' Lottie chewed the inside of her lip. 'There's nothing in here, but you keep coming up.'

'This time it's because it's the quietest floor of the house, and I had to take a call.'

'If you say so.'

'What do you mean by that?' asked Sellers.

'Nothing.'

'Tell me, Lottie. I won't mind, whatever it is.'

Her expression was severe. 'You didn't need to come up here just because your sergeant rang you. There are loads of quiet rooms on the ground floor, rooms no one ever uses.'

She knew Sam had rung him. Had she eavesdropped, heard the whole conversation? Probably. Sellers' half, at least.

'Lottie Nancy Stelling!' Suzanne yelled again from downstairs. 'Get yourself down here before I have to come up and drag you down by force!'

Lottie half smiled and rolled her eyes at the same time. 'Talk about *loco* parentis,' she muttered, twirling her finger next to her head to signify insanity.

'Hadn't you better go?' said Sellers.

She ignored his question. 'I think you're wanting to find something in Marianne's study, even though it's empty,' she said. 'Same with me.'

'What are you hoping to find?' Sellers wished Simon Waterhouse was here. He'd have known the right questions to ask. Not that he was particularly good at communicating with teenage girls – Sellers nearly laughed at the idea – but he was the best at getting to the bottom of anything that made no sense, the best Sellers had ever known.

Where was he? He'd asked Sam, who had dodged the question.

'Your sergeant told you it couldn't have been any of us, didn't he?' said Lottie. 'We were all somewhere else when Granny was killed.' Again, Sellers noticed the switch between 'Marianne' and 'Granny'.

So she had been eavesdropping. 'You ought to think about a career as a detective,' he told her. Yes, that was what Sam had said: everyone's whereabouts were accounted for, even this Oliver Mayo person who had briefly fallen under suspicion when Marianne was attacked in November 2012. Although . . .

Could the thirteen-year-old kid in front of him have done it? If she hadn't been ruled out, would he suspect her? The police doctor had said it could have been a female killer; no particular strength or brute force is required if you're not squeamish and willing to keep stabbing until you're sure your victim's dead. But a thirteen-year-old?

Pointless to speculate, since according to the update Sellers had just had from Sam, Lottie had been seen standing outside her house near Little Holling with Paddy Stelling at 5.45 p.m., just before he'd set off to drive to Devey House, which meant neither of them could have been stabbing Marianne between 5.15 and 5.30. Equally solid, unfortunately, were the alibis of Jemma Stelling, Suzanne Lacy and Oliver Mayo, who had been, respectively, at Spilling Station, at work in the headquarters of the DWC exam board and at his therapy practice in Cambridge at the relevant time. Gareth Upton, meanwhile, had been Zoom-meeting with work colleagues. All of this had checked out, Sam said: several of his fellow IT boffins had confirmed Upton's presence on the Zoom, and one had already sent the official video recording of the meeting.

'There's a problem that your sergeant probably didn't tell you about, because he hasn't found it out yet,' said Lottie.

'What's that?'

'There's nobody else.'

Sellers waited for her to say more.

'Marianne didn't really have friends, just people she knew slightly from around the village. That's it. No one else would have wanted to kill her, apart from the people the sergeant said can't have done it.'

'Well, someone must have,' said Sellers, thinking about Tom Tulloch, whose name Sellers had heard for the first time on the phone with Sam just now. Uniforms hadn't managed to track Tulloch down yet, but it sounded like a promising lead. Only one thing made no sense to Sellers: why would Jemma Stelling confess to it all, pretending she'd decided not to do it, if she'd decided the opposite? Surely she'd know any sentient detective would think what Sellers was thinking now: that she and Tulloch had to be the killers, with him doing her bidding. And the longer he remained unreachable, the stronger those suspicions would get. Instead, Jemma could have set herself up with a nice alibi that wasn't based at Spilling nick, and said nothing to anyone about Tulloch. He had no connection to Marianne and could have stayed out of the picture altogether.

Lottie made a small, impatient gesture: a quick shake of the head. She'd found Sellers' pat response irritating, and he didn't blame her.

'It's possible your gran knew someone in the village more than slightly,' he tried again. 'It's also possible she didn't know whoever did it. That happens sometimes.'

'What, a complete stranger?' Lottie said scornfully. 'That's not a thing.'

Sellers seemed to be disgusting her more with every word he said, but he wasn't about to give up. 'I'll tell you why I'm up here,' he said. 'I've got a colleague, DC Simon Waterhouse. He's not here, though he should be. If he was, he'd be all over this empty room.'

'Why?' asked Lottie.

The answer felt so obvious, it took Sellers a few seconds to convert it into words.

Marianne's study, locked and secret for many years, then destroyed, then revealed to Jemma in a way intended to taunt her, according to Sam. 'Waterhouse would think it was a puzzle,' he told Lottie. 'A puzzle at the heart of a murder victim's home – he'd think that was worth paying attention to.'

'It's just an empty room, isn't it?' She was sounding sneery again. 'I don't get why you're deeping it.'

Yeah, well, maybe there's quite a lot you don't understand, despite the endless amounts of worldly wisdom you've managed to accumulate over the last thirteen years.

'You mentioned dreams,' he said. 'You used to dream about this room?'

Lottie nodded.

'What happened in the dreams?'

'Nothing much. Just boring stuff, like being by the sea and in this room at the same time. With Granny and Grandad and Mum and . . .' Lottie stopped. She looked caught out. As if she'd done something wrong and then realised she'd been about to give herself away.

'And your dad?' Sellers guessed.

'I mean . . . maybe.' There was no mistaking the tone: she'd said it resentfully.

Sellers was about to ask what she'd meant, when Paddy called upstairs: 'Lottie? Suzanne's looking for you. Can you come down? Now?' He didn't sound to Sellers like a man who expected to be obeyed or was even convinced that he wanted to be.

'Saved,' Lottie said under her breath as she left the room.

Sellers knew he hadn't caught her parting remark by accident. She'd wanted him to hear it.

Gibbs had eaten too much of Suzanne Lacy's lasagne, and had already loosened his belt once. He might have to do it again in a second; his stomach seemed to be still expanding, though they'd finished eating an hour ago. He consoled himself with the thought that his waistline wasn't the only casualty. Sellers's veganism had also gone for a Burton. 'You're a dead man if you breathe a word to Sondra,' Sellers had threatened him, and Gibbs had felt a pang of nostalgia for the old days, when protecting his friend from consequences had involved lying about more exciting things than eating prohibited pasta dishes.

'You wanted to ask me something?' Suzanne appeared in the doorway just as Gibbs was wondering if he ought to start clearing the kitchen table while he waited for her. She was still wearing the blue and white striped apron of Marianne's that Lottie had found for her in the pantry. 'Christ, look at the mess,' she muttered. The debris of the meal was evenly distributed around the room: countertops, table, kitchen island.

'I'm not wasting any more time trying to make Lottie go to sleep. Losing battle! So.' Suzanne pulled a chair back from the table and sat down opposite Gibbs. 'I'm all yours if you want me. Sorry, I didn't mean that to sound . . . I'm not after your body. I'm not after anyone's body, actually, though I am recruiting for a new husband – but I'm prioritising the intellectual connection over the physical this time round.'

Gibbs had no interest in her love life, and feared she was the sort who'd provide endless, tedious detail if given the chance. 'I want to know more about Jemma and this Oliver Mayo,' he said. 'Some background. They stopped seeing each other in 2006, you said?'

'Yes.' Suzanne was focused and serious again. 'They were briefly in touch again in 2010, then didn't see each other again until July this year, when Jemma went to see him in Cambridge.'

'But from what you said before about the Wordle thing, it sounds like you think he and Marianne might have been in touch earlier this year.'

Suzanne nodded.

'Tell me about 2010,' said Gibbs. 'The "briefly in touch" you mentioned.'

'One-night stand.' She stood up. 'Fancy a cup of tea? I'm dying for one.'

'If you're making, yeah. Thanks.'

She made her way over to the kettle, pulling the apron off over her head as she went. 'How about this: I'll give you the lowdown on the never-ending love triangle, and in return, you keep digging for the truth about Ollie. When your colleagues tell you he's got alibis coming out of his ears, don't believe them. I just . . . think he did it, and I don't want my best friend, my goddaughter's mother, to end up married to a murderer if there's anything I can do to—'

125

'Hang on a second,' Gibbs cut her off. Had he missed something? 'Jemma's married to Paddy.'

'Yeah. For the time being.' Suzanne sighed. 'I need to give you the background. Let's start with Jemma and Paddy, because they met first. We were at primary school together, all three of us. Paddy's parents and Jemma's became close friends. Nancy, Jemma's mum, was a piano teacher. At some point Paddy went to her for lessons, though I think he gave them up pretty swiftly. No surprise there! I've never met a bigger giver-up-on-things than Paddy. Thank God he passed his driving test first time, I always think. He'd never have tried again, and with Jemma never learning and them insisting on living in the middle of rural nowhere instead of in a proper place . . . How would Lottie have got to school? And since Paddy has no career, no hobby he's passionate about, no entrepreneurial drive whatsoever, I'm bloody glad he at least does the driving – that's pretty much the only contribution he makes. You know that thing about whether it's better to be Socrates dissatisfied or a pig satisfied? Paddy's a pig who's not really sure if he's satisfied or not – won't commit either way. Ugh.'

It occurred to Gibbs that either he or Suzanne should probably walk over to the door and close it before anyone overheard anything sensitive. He couldn't be arsed; it was too far away. The kitchen at Devey House was the approximate size of a small train station, with a high ceiling and windows taller than Gibbs's whole body. Suzanne didn't seem worried about Paddy walking in or overhearing, so maybe this was nothing she hadn't said before to his face.

'When Jemma's mum died, Paddy's parents were the main ones who looked after Gareth,' Suzanne said. 'They're very looky-after people, a bit too much so. Explains a lot, if you ask me. And Gareth's one of those men who couldn't function on his own – you must know the type. Marianne soon sorted that out. Jemma reckons she was counting down Nancy's last days, waiting to slot into the new wife role soon as she could. Anyway, Paddy's parents started socialising with Gareth and Marianne, which meant Paddy and Jemma saw each other out of school quite a lot. Fast-forward seven or eight years, they decided they fancied each other, and then every time the Stellings and the Uptons got together, Jemma and Paddy snuck off somewhere for a snogging sesh.'

Suzanne put Gibbs's cup of tea down in front of him on the table. 'By the time they're eighteen, the snogging has escalated to where these things usually escalate to, and they've also started arranging to meet up on their own. They're seeing each other, basically – though Paddy won't call it that. He won't call it anything.' Suzanne's mouth twitched as if she'd noticed she'd just swallowed something unpleasant. 'Jemma's madly in love with Paddy by this point. I mean, there's no denying he's an extremely good-looking guy, so we can only assume she didn't notice . . . you know, his entire personality. But there's a problem: he's about to head off to uni and wants to be single while he's there. Still wants to hook up with Jemma whenever he can while they're at their separate universities, he tells her, but definitely not with any kind of commitment or expectation of fidelity involved. University will be full of other girls, and how could he be expected, at his tender age, to confine himself to one?'

Despite Suzanne's outraged tone, it sounded reasonable to Gibbs. Eighteen was way too young to pick one person and stay with them and only them forever. *Bit like fifty-two, then, eh?* Determinedly, Gibbs steered his attention away from his own mess of a love life. It wasn't really a mess, anyway. It worked for him, even if it had involved, for the last twelve years, a girlfriend about whom his wife knew nothing.

'For the next two years, Jemma and Paddy had what the Gen Z-ers would call "a situationship",' said Suzanne. 'Every few months Paddy would summon Jemma for a sesh, and she'd go running. And, no, by "sesh", I don't mean just sex – not any more. By this point, it was a lot more than that. Paddy was dropping hints all the time about how much Jemma meant to him, how she was his favourite, the fittest, all of that. If and when he ever *did* feel ready for a committed relationship, she'd be his first choice. Oh, and he thought he definitely would at some point, so there was hope on the horizon!' Suzanne's voice dripped with sarcasm. 'Maybe when he was, like, thirty, if Jemma was lucky. All of this kept her nicely reeled in.' She paused her narration to take a sip of her tea. 'But, listen, we can't just blame Paddy – not exclusively.'

Gibbs wasn't blaming him at all. He was Team Paddy all the way. Thirty was a good age to settle down. Anything before that . . .

'Jemma spent most of their shit-show, situationship, whatever, pretending to be cool with it all, though it was hellish for her. It was only once it had been going on for about two years that she admitted to me how miserable and lonely it was making her feel. She was seeing other people too, because she knew Paddy was, but she didn't really want to be. She was in love with him. He was all she wanted. So I said, "Then tell him that, you idiot!" I probably said it more sensitively than that, though maybe not.' Suzanne smiled. 'Jemma agreed she couldn't bear to let the on-again-off-again horror show drag on any longer. If Paddy wasn't ready to choose her and only her, then she wanted to call it quits, get him out of her system once and for all and move on.'

Gibbs could remember, at least once, wishing a woman he was involved with would say that to him, give him a chance to opt out.

'She gave him an all-or-nothing ultimatum. They were both, like, twenty, twenty-one by this point. Guess what? He chose nothing.' Suzanne laughed, shaking her head. 'Still wasn't ready, he said. Bear in mind, no one was talking about marriage or living together or anything. All Jemma wanted was a normal boyfriend-girlfriend relationship and not to have to keep hearing about all the other women he was screwing. But Paddy felt way too young, free and single to become a boring old boyfriend, he told her. At least he was honest. I'll give him that: he never lied. And *then* . . .' Suzanne slapped the table with the palms of her hands. 'Along came Ollie Mayo: every bit as gorgeous as Paddy, except tall and dark instead of short and blonde. And . . . well, basically perfect. A firefighter. Like, he saved people's lives for a living: dragged them out of burning buildings. Hero, right?' Suzanne sounded anything but convinced. 'Fell for Jemma straight away, told her he'd marry her and have babies with her tomorrow if she'd let him—'

'That sounds weird. Depending on how soon he said it after they met,' Gibbs qualified, as his suspicions in relation to Mayo shot up a level. Murderers that weren't of the standard scrote variety were often obsessive.

'I generally admire people who know what they want and just go for it,' said Suzanne. 'But I mean, Ollie was *keen*, and I slightly worried that . . . I mean, I'm sure I'm being unfair . . .' She seemed to make up her mind. 'Put it this way: if he didn't kill Marianne, or try to in 2012, then I've got nothing against the man. But as I've said, I think he did. I've had *such* a bad feeling about him ever since the Wordle thing.'

'That happened recently, though,' said Gibbs. 'And you're saying you weren't sure about him from the start. Was that just because of how desperate he was to be with Jemma?'

'Oh, it never came across as desperation. I think he honestly did fall in love with her and knew, or decided, that she was the one for him. I just worried that maybe it wasn't *only* her he wanted. I think the whole package was appealing to him: this house; rich, loving parents who always pick up the bill wherever you go; the whole family-and-home structure. I mean, Jemma didn't think of Marianne either as loving or as her parent, but that's how Ollie would have seen it. He'd have noticed how much she wanted and tried to be a mum to Jemma, in stark contrast to his own mother, and he wouldn't have picked up on the undercurrent of coercive emotional blackmail that went with it. And who wouldn't want to be swept up into all this?' Suzanne gestured around the room. 'I mean, it's grim to be here now, today, but it would have felt very different to Ollie in 2005, 2006. Let's face it, it would have felt a bit like hitting the jackpot. Especially to him, given his family history.'

'Which was?' asked Gibbs.

'Oh, God, the worst excesses of hippy bullshit. Mother was a drug addict who eventually died of an overdose, and his dad ran a martial arts school as well as a small publishing company – really tiny, books held together with staples in the middle kind of thing. I can't remember its name. It was something really bonkers like, I don't know, Lamp-post Pistachio Press. Not that, but not far off. They mainly published weird, political screeds, Jemma said. Ollie spent most of his childhood in a kind of commune-type house in Manchester where everyone slept with everyone else's husband or wife and told themselves it would help to smash the bourgeoisie or some such crap.'

Gibbs felt grateful for his own dull childhood in Swindon: just him, his parents and his brother, doing nothing especially interesting or controversial.

'Ollie's dad had lots of interests, but being a dad wasn't one of them,' said Suzanne. 'He buggered off when Ollie was three, then reappeared fourteen years later, saying, basically, "Soz I abandoned you, do you want to hang out now and then?" To which Ollie replied with an enthusiastic "Yes!", but I mean, it really was just now and then, Jemma said. Christmases, Ollie's birthday, that was it, pretty much. Ollie was always talking about how much he wanted Jemma to meet his dad, but the useless git kept cancelling on them. Look, I'm not saying Ollie didn't want Jemma for her own sake, because he was clearly besotted from the get-go, but getting to be part of the Upton family would have been irresistible to him too, I reckon.'

'So Paddy and Jemma were done,' said Gibbs. 'Ollie and Jemma started dating when?'

'2005,' said Suzanne. 'And for a while – nearly six months – she seemed really happy with him. She and I had hundreds of discussions where we listed the trillions of ways in which Ollie was so much better than Paddy, but unfortunately Paddy hadn't disappeared altogether. He was still popping up, getting in touch with Jemma every few months and when he did, of course, the inevitable always happened. Sex,' Suzanne clarified. 'God, I still get angry when I think about how that poor, beautiful ultimatum got trashed.' She pressed the flat palm of her hand against the bottom of her neck. 'Once or twice Paddy was even here, at the house, at the same time as Ollie. Jemma spun it as "It'll do him good to be introduced to my actual boyfriend as nothing more than a friend of the family", but Paddy didn't care how he was introduced as long as he got his shag later. I just kept thinking "Surely it'll click into place for Jemma one day. Surely she'll wake up one morning and think, 'Of course, I cannot sleep with Paddy Stelling or think about him for one more second of my life, and look, here's this lovely boyfriend who really appreciates me and treats me well . . .' " Ugh.' Suzanne covered her face with her hands for a moment.

'Did you tell her what you thought?' Gibbs asked. He knew women cared more about their mates' love lives than men did. Even so, it struck him as strange for Suzanne to be as obsessed with Jemma's romantic machinations as she evidently was: Paddy was wrong for Jemma, Ollie was right for her – though not any more, because now he was a killer, if Suzanne was to be believed.

Gibbs tried to turn his misgivings about Suzanne into a suspicion that she might have killed Marianne Upton, but couldn't. She, like everyone else, was provably somewhere else at the time: at work, and it was looking likely that this Tom Tulloch person Sam was liking for it was the one they were after – him and Jemma Stelling.

It was a bizarre story – just strange enough to be true, Gibbs thought. He didn't believe in normal anything or anyone any more.

'I told Jemma what I thought, yeah, for as long as she kept asking me,' Suzanne said. 'Then one day she said, "Guess what?", and I knew immediately what it was from the excited, confused look on her face: Paddy had asked her to be his official girl-friend, at last. Thing is, she really did love Ollie by then, but . . . something weird must have happened in her love-addled brain, because, next thing I knew, she'd ended it with Ollie and she was Paddy's girlfriend. She'd been so sure she'd never be able to have Paddy all to herself, and then suddenly she saw she could.' Suzanne made a face that suggested unfortunate inevitability. 'Never underestimate the allure of the unavailable.'

Or the anti-allure of a person you take for granted, who's been a given in your life for as long as you can remember, Gibbs thought.

'Fast-forward a bit more: Jemma and Paddy get married. Ollie makes no secret of the fact that he still loves Jemma and always will – though to give him his due, he didn't crowd her. Even said he hoped she and Paddy would be really happy together, but . . . yeah, he also said he loved her and if she ever wanted him, he'd be there. Here's the thing . . .' Suzanne leaned forward, nearly knocking over her mug of tea. 'I don't think Jemma's love for Ollie ever really went away. It was like . . . for a while it got forced into hiding, but it never died. And soon she was living with Paddy day in, day out – which can't have been anything but a very undramatic, uneventful nightmare – and Ollie was suddenly the one she wanted but couldn't have. Ollie also had a career: brave fireman! He was dynamic, witty, and charming . . .'

And, according to you, a killer.

'Anyway, long story short, Jemma got in touch with him in 2010, asked if he wanted to meet for a drink. Just as friends. Yeah, right! They ended up spending the night together, after which she rang me in tears, wailing about how Ollie was the one, and she had to be with him, right now. "Perfect!" I said. "Divorce Paddy, marry Ollie – all sorted." And it would have been, if it weren't for Marianne and the fact that Jemma was pregnant at the time, though she didn't know she was when she slept with Ollie.'

'Baby was definitely Paddy's, then?'

Suzanne nodded. 'Jemma and Paddy were living here at the time, with Marianne and Gareth. Paddy didn't notice anything was amiss, but Marianne saw that something was very wrong with Jemma. Christ, that woman was like a KGB interrogator when she realised something was afoot that she didn't know about. She bullied Jemma into confiding in her, then started weeping like *her* heart had been broken – like, for hours, Jemma said. She *insisted* Jemma stayed with Paddy and made it work, and how could she even consider ending the marriage when a baby was on the way, and only a terrible mother . . . etc., etc.'

'So Jemma stayed with Paddy,' said Gibbs.

Suzanne nodded. 'Yup. Struggled on miserably until Lottie was born, and it wasn't any less of a struggle after, to be honest. Marianne bloody-mindedly refused to consider that the marriage might end, so, get this: she designed and *funded* a rescue plan. She'd look after Lottie overnight every Thursday, and pay for Jemma and Paddy to spend those nights in a posh London hotel. The Great Date-Night Marriage Repair Initiative, I called it.'

'Did it work?'

'Not really,' said Suzanne. 'If you've realised you don't want to be with someone, it's not going to help to be holed up with them once a week even in the most luxurious hotel, where you can't get away from each other. I'll tell you what did work, though – can you guess?'

Gibbs couldn't.

'Marianne nearly getting murdered in November that same year. After that, Jemma clamped down on what she called her "silly daydreaming". The Ollie dream was over and she was going to make it work with Paddy, whatever that took. "I'm not going to launch a destructive attack on our family when someone else has just done that in the most horrific way", she said.' Suzanne was shaking her head. 'It was an excuse. Do you want to know why she really changed tack?'

'She suspected Ollie was the one who'd tried to kill Marianne?' Gibbs guessed.

'Hundred per cent,' said Suzanne. 'Not unreasonably, since Marianne had said, "Oliver", when Jemma had asked her who. You know it happened in here, right?' Suzanne pointed. 'Just behind where you're sitting now.'

Gibbs turned and looked. Unsurprisingly, he saw hardly any trace of the incident, eleven years later, only a patch that was lighter and shinier than the surrounding area, as if it had been damaged, then sanded down and re-varnished.

Turning back to Suzanne, he said, 'Does the name Tom Tulloch mean anything to you?' He was expecting to hear from Sam any time now that Tulloch had been found and was being taken in for questioning. He wondered if Jemma Stelling was under arrest yet.

Suzanne nodded. 'Tom was at school with us too: with me, Paddy and Jemma. He was the one I was telling you about.'

'When? What do you mean?'

'Remember I said Paddy left Lottie with someone she'd barely met, when he came here? And Lotts texted me, and I went and rescued her? That was Tom I was talking about.'

12

'I don't understand why you won't drive me to my dad's first,' I say. I should never have accepted her offer of a lift home, should have insisted she call a taxi to collect me. '*Please.* I need to get back to my daughter. I don't want her to have to deal with this without me there.'

'I keep explaining, Jemma,' Sergeant Zailer says. 'The officer who's going to drive you home is—'

'It's not home. I don't live there.' Why the hell didn't I learn to drive when all my friends did? If I had, if I owned a car and had come here in it, I could get up and leave whenever I wanted to. No one's arrested me.

Yet.

While I'm auditing past mistakes, not fully charging my phone before coming here is right up there with the best of them. If I could talk to Lotts for even ten seconds, I'd feel so much better.

'Right. Well, your driver's on her way,' says Sergeant Zailer. 'And we might as well talk while we wait for her rather than sit here in silence. Are you sure you don't want a lawyer?'

'Are you sure you can't remember what I said the last two times you asked me?'

'You're not a criminal. So you seem to believe, at any rate.'

'Look, you *know* I didn't do it. When was Marianne killed? Around 5.30, right?'

'Maybe,' says Sergeant Zailer. 'Though if you were to ask the police doctor . . . Apparently it could have been earlier from a medical point of view. Quite a bit earlier.'

She wants to make her meaning clear, though she doesn't state it directly: by 'earlier', she's suggesting I might have killed Marianne before coming here.

'DS Kombothekra told me the murder happened between 5.20 and 5.30. And I was here then, talking to you and your weird husband.'

'Right. But . . . that isn't the "get out of jail free" card you seem to think it is.'

The word *jail* is one I definitely didn't want to hear. My brain feels slow and heavy, clogged with clumps of solid terror.

I can't go to prison. What if Lottie doesn't believe me when I tell her I didn't do it?

I have to make sure she does, that she's in no doubt.

What I really need is to be able to think, uninterrupted, for at least an hour. Not much chance of that.

Marianne is dead. She's dead.

I can't seem to convince myself it's true. In 2012, when Paddy and I found her lying white-faced on her kitchen floor, blood leaking from the wound in her throat, I had to work to convince myself in the opposite direction. I found a pulse, but she was lying so still, and I was more convinced by the appearance of death than by the slow beat beneath the skin of her wrist.

This time she's really dead. Unkillable Marianne. And I have no idea if my life has been saved or ruined.

'If you really didn't kill her, or get Tom Tulloch to kill her, then someone else did it and we'll find out who,' Sergeant Zailer says. 'Try not to worry too much, but . . . you need to be real-istic. Do you know how rare it is for someone to be murdered at the very moment that someone else, someone who wants to murder them, is confessing to nearly having done it at the exact time that it was getting done? Blimey.' She smiles. 'I don't want to have to repeat that sentence, so I hope you got the gist. Point is: even if it wasn't Tulloch, you're going to fall under heavy suspicion. How does anyone know you didn't hire someone else to do it instead?'

'But . . . that would make no sense. If I'd decided to go through with it, why the hell would I come here and tell you all about it?'

'Great question,' Sergeant Zailer says in a flippant tone. 'Anyway, last I heard, no one's been able to get hold of Tom Tulloch. I wonder why that might be.'

DS Kombothekra must have told her about Tom, because I certainly haven't. 'If you're suggesting Tom did it—'

'The thought did cross my mind, yeah.'

'There's no way,' I tell her. 'Not without me giving the go-ahead, and I didn't. Also, I never told him today was the day.'

Someone knew, though. Dad? Paddy? Not Ollie, surely.

Yes, Ollie's possible too, if Marianne told him all about my laptop diary, and she might have. His name's all over that file, on nearly every page, and she loves nothing more than creating drama.

Loved. Past tense.

I suppose it's possible that someone else altered the spelling of Ollie's name, to implicate Marianne. They'd have known I'd think it had to be her.

She always made sure to spell Ollie's name the way he did, even though it wasn't her favourite spelling. She said to me once: 'If he's determined to get it wrong, we'll all have to do the same, I suppose. It's his name, after all – his choice.'

That was for his benefit, though, and it was seventeen years ago. It doesn't mean Marianne wasn't the one who got into my diary and made those changes. She knew I'd be the only one to see them, and Marianne had no qualms about horrifying me – far from it. After the N.P. Pelphrey incident, shocking and upsetting me became her favourite hobby.

But why would she look there? Why would she think a laptop is where a diary might be found? She was always strictly a pen and paper woman. She refused even to keep appointments and calendar items on her phone or computer – everything had to be on paper, in beautiful notebooks. The first diary I ever had was a present from her and it was more a work of art than an item of stationery.

The old rage burns inside me again as I remember how upset I was when it first went missing – when Marianne 'borrowed' it and read everything I'd written, including some very unflattering things about her. It's embarrassing, how many years it took me to start suspecting her; I totally fell for the 'Jemma's so absent-minded, she loses everything' narrative, even though I should have known I was anything but.

'Tell me about her,' Sergeant Zailer says. 'Marianne.'

'What do you want to know?'

'Why did you hate her so much?'

'Mainly because I was scared of her. It's impossible to love someone you're terrified of. You'd always rather they weren't there. And . . . she had to be in charge of everything and everyone. All she cared about was what she wanted and needed – nothing and no one mattered apart from that. She persuaded me to stay with Paddy, my husband, when she knew I loved someone else more. That's on me, too – I let her persuade me.

I was pregnant with Paddy's baby, so it was my decision. I made my choice for Lottie's sake, my daughter, but Marianne wasn't thinking about me or Lottie at all. She wanted me with Paddy and not Ollie for reasons of her own.'

'What reasons?' Sergeant Zailer asks.

'I don't know.'

'Now that she's dead, you never will.' This is delivered with a twist of, *Didn't think of that, did you?*

'I didn't plan . . . what I planned because of any of that,' I explain. 'Believe it or not, I'm not such a monster that I'd kill someone just because I hated them and they'd lied to me or . . . used me, or whatever.'

'Then why?'

I have no proof of what I'm about to say, but I'm talking to the police, and this really matters, and it's the truth, so here goes. 'I knew Marianne was going to do something terrible to me. I didn't know what, but it didn't seem impossible that she might kill me. I was scared that if I did nothing, I'd . . . The danger felt so real. I started to have nightmares about it. Sometimes I'd catch her looking at me and it was as if she was warning me with her eyes: "You just wait. You'll get what's coming to you." But what could I do? I couldn't come here and report a look I found threatening, could I? She'd have denied any intention to harm me, and everyone would have believed her because of course devoted stepmums don't kill their stepdaughters.'

And even if she never touched me, never hurt me, I knew I would never be free of the terror that she would . . .

'The idea wouldn't leave me alone,' I tell Sergeant Zailer. 'Someone had tried to kill her before. Trying to kill her was a thing that already existed in the world. Don't get me wrong, I thought the attack on her was terrible when it happened, even given the way I felt about her, but everything changed in July. It was the room, the way she'd destroyed her study . . .'

Sergeant Zailer waits for me to say more.

Once the wave of revulsion has passed, I tell her about Marianne inviting me up to the top floor, promising to unlock the door and show me her study's secrets, me and only me. I describe what she was wearing, the contrast between her elegance and the scarred wreck of a room she seemed so proud to have created. As I'm speaking, I have to keep reminding myself that, no, this was not some lurid tale invented by my melodramatic imagination. It really happened, all of it.

'I didn't understand at first why she'd be so eager to show me a room full of nothing,' I say. 'And then, when I understood, I wished I didn't. She'd done it to spite me, because she knew about Norman Pelphrey.'

'Who?' Sergeant Zailer asks.

'A locksmith. Lives in the next village. Marianne found out I'd contacted him. I wanted to know what was in her study that no one was allowed to see. Didn't want to wait much longer to get the answer. I'd spent years rummaging through her bags and pockets, any chance I got. Marianne being Marianne, she never once left the key in a findable place. I still don't know where she keeps . . . kept it,' I correct myself. 'So one day, I decided to contact a locksmith.'

'Norman Pelphrey,' says Sergeant Zailer.

'He was the nearest one I could find. About five minutes' drive away. I rang him and he was sort of . . . weirdly curt with me. I didn't give it a second thought, just assumed he was a rude git.'

'Perhaps he didn't approve of breaking into other people's locked private spaces?' Sergeant Zailer suggests.

'I'm not that stupid,' I tell her. 'I've got a key to Dad and

Marianne's house. I'm officially allowed in every other part of it. Paddy, Lottie and I used to live there. When I rang Pelphrey, I pretended it was my house, my locked room – except I'd lost the key and couldn't get in. Dad and Marianne were out all day. It was the perfect opportunity. No one would have suspected anything was amiss, since I was inside the house already. But Pelphrey couldn't come and help me. Didn't say why. Just dismissed me, rudely. I didn't think anything of it until I tried the two next nearest locksmiths, both in the Heckencotes area. They were both equally rude and abrupt, told me to forget it, basically.'

'So . . . is there a link between rudeness and locksmith work?' says Sergeant Zailer.

'Marianne had paid them off.' I suppose I shouldn't be surprised that she didn't guess. It's too insane to be guessable. 'Those three and more. Anyone in the Sleathams who might conceivably have come out to Devey House. Marianne had pre-bribed them all.'

The look of astonishment on Sergeant Zailer's face is gratifying.

'And they'd all been expecting my call for some time, as Marianne delighted in telling me, immediately after she'd shocked me by revealing the room she'd destroyed. She'd known I'd been trying to get in and failing to find the key, and she'd anticipated my exact thought process. Knew what I'd do next. She was way ahead of me, explaining to any locksmith she could find that her boundary-violating daughter was intent on invading her personal space and—'

'Wow,' Sergeant Zailer says quietly.

'Yeah. They'd all promised to report back to her, once I got in touch, which Pelphrey and probably others dutifully did.'

'Jemma, did you try to kill Marianne in 2012?'

143

'What?' Where the hell did that come from? 'No. Of course not.'

'Who do you think did? And who do you think did it this time, if it really wasn't orchestrated by you?'

'I've no idea.'

'I find that quite hard to believe,' says Sergeant Zailer.

Me too.

'Until July, when I went to see him in Cambridge – two days after Marianne's big empty study reveal – I thought it had to be Ollie,' I say. 'Despite his alibi, which the police told us at the time was watertight. "The Ollibi" – that's what Suzanne called it. But . . . now I don't think it was him.'

'How come?' asks Sergeant Zailer. 'Did he tell you something that changed your mind?'

I nod. 'He told me a lot. Trouble was, every single thing he said was cancelled out by something more important that he didn't say.'

JULY 9, 2023

Well, I've spent the two days wondering if I'm brave enough, and it turns out I am. I've just given my fake name to Olly's receptionist, and now I'm sitting in his waiting room in Cambridge, impersonating his newest patient, Jenny Judge. I liked the alliteration when I thought of the alias, and liked even more that the surname doubled as a declaration of intent. I'm here to judge Olly. That's stage two, though. Stage one is persuading him to tell me the truth.

He works from a tall, rectangular house (I assume it was once a family home) called the Cedarwood Centre – yellow bricks, glossy black-painted door and windows – which sits set back from a busy A-road south of Cambridge city centre, behind a wall that looks much too small for the building that's behind it.

Olly shares the centre with several other therapists, three of whose doors are visible from where I'm sitting, names and specialisms proudly displayed on brass plaques. There's an acupuncturist, a homeopath and a cranial osteopath. Olly's room must be on one of the higher floors. Three little trees in pots stand beside the staircase's glass banister, as if guarding it. The whole reception area is full of greenery – large ferns, grey-green rubbery stalks, flat leaves like

145

oversized hands with holes in them – and there's a sharp gingery-orange smell coming from a reed diffuser on the reception desk.

I wonder if Olly comes down here to greet his clients or if I'll be sent up to knock on his door when the time comes. If I were a psychotherapist, I'd make the effort for a brand-new patient and come and collect them, escort them upstairs. My guess is that's what Olly will do too – he was always charming and polite – which means we'll end up having the 'Yes, it's me, I lied about my name' conversation in front of the receptionist. Shortly after that, I imagine I'll be asked to leave. There's a chance I won't get to see Olly's therapy room at all.

No. He'd never throw you out, whatever you'd done. He loves you.

I've no idea why I'm so sure Olly's feelings for me haven't changed after more than a decade of no contact, but I am – and nearly as strong as my certainty is the fear that I'm about to find out I'm wrong.

I'll love you for as long as I'm alive, Jemm. You know that, don't you? I'll never settle for anyone else. I'd rather be alone forever. That's what he said the last time I saw him, immediately after I made him promise never to contact me again.

I used a fake name today not because I had to but because I wanted to, and my dishonesty doesn't even begin to settle the score. For more than ten years, Olly has known how completely in the dark I am, and he's left me there.

I hear footsteps on the stairs and a man appears: jowly, gangly and round-shouldered, eyes red and puffy. There's a good chance that Olly has spent the last hour making him cry.

Eventually, I'm told to go up. 'Mr Mayo's name is on the door – he's on the second landing.'

I expect my legs to feel wobbly and hollow once I'm on my feet, but instead a surge of energy launches me forward, and I have to stop myself from running, leaping up the steps two at a time.

What if . . .?

It won't happen. For a second, I had a vision of Olly and me falling into each other's arms.

Like I said: won't happen. I hereby forbid myself to fall into his arms, even if they happen to be outstretched in my direction.

His door is open a little. I knock twice, then push it and walk in. He's writing something, leaning forward over his desk. Everything feels suddenly magnified, louder, brighter. Oh, my God, he's still gorgeous: flawless skin, big brown eyes, beautiful glossy dark hair, cheekbones sharp as knife blades. My stomach somersaults. He could easily pass for five years younger than he is, which I'm not sure is true of me and certainly isn't true of Paddy.

Olly is dressed immaculately too: smart shirt, brilliant best-possible-summer blue, and grey trousers. I want to scream and run at him and hit him and . . . and . . .

I'm not going to do any of those things. I might still be in love with him, but I'm also angry and I want answers. And it's probably not technically possible to be still in love with someone you haven't seen or spoken to for so long. It's not that far removed from being in love with someone who doesn't exist.

Without lifting his eyes from his paperwork, Olly welcomes me and tells me to take a seat.

'Jenny Judge, isn't it?' he says.

I hope he doesn't want a response. The sound of his voice has robbed me of mine, temporarily.

Finally, he looks up, and the change in his demeanour makes me want to cry. I have to dig my nails into my palms to make sure I don't. It's as if he's just opened his eyes and realised he's in heaven.

I am his heaven.

'Jemma!' he stammers. 'I . . . I can't . . . Can we . . . Jemma, I've got a client—'

'No, you haven't.'

'I have.' He frowns.

'There's no Jenny Judge. It's me. I used a made-up name.'

'Oh.' I can't blame him for needing to take a few moments to consider this. 'Why?'

'I wanted to talk to you. And I wanted to lie to you. So I did.' Lowering myself into the armchair opposite his desk, I drop my bag on the floor and look around the room. I don't want to miss a single detail. The ceiling is high with lots of tiny lights embedded in it; there's a brass dimmer switch near the door. Tall lamps stand in two corners: one wooden, straight and tall with a square, grey shade; the other shiny metal with a forward-bending head, like a gold robot praying. A large rectangular sash window takes up most of one wall. The view is of a wide, white building across the road with excessive stucco curls protruding from its exterior, partly covered in builders' scaffolding.

Behind Olly's brown leather wing-back chair there's a glass-fronted bookcase full of books about psychology and therapy. He was always an obsessive reader. I still remember the titles of the four books he brought with him when he came with us to the Cotswolds for Christmas in 2005: *Mr Wakefield's Crusade, The Sacred and Profane Love Machine, An Instance of the Fingerpost,* and the weirdest one of all: *Compositional Bonbons Placate.*

At the centre of Olly's therapy room is a large wooden desk with nothing on it but a small laptop and a boastful mug that reads: 'As I Suspected, I Was Right About Everything'. A small coffee table with a white marble-effect top and dark orange painted legs stands on a white rug that's bunched up on one side. No photos, I notice, thinking of Marianne's eviscerated study and her claim that it had once contained lots of photographs of me. I have no way of knowing if that's true or not.

'Jemma, I can't be your psychotherapist.' Olly's voice cuts into my thoughts. 'There are ethical—'

'I'm not here for therapy.'

'Oh. Then . . . I mean, you know what I'll start to imagine if you sit there saying nothing for too long.'

'I don't know what you mean,' I tell him.

'I'll imagine that you've finally decided to leave Paddy. That you want to be with me. You've chosen me.' His voice grows louder and more intent as he goes on. I'm relieved when he says more quietly, 'But . . . I can see from your face that I'm wrong. That's not why you're here.'

That's right. Not why I'm here. Good. Nothing scary is going to happen today, nothing irreversible, today or ever. It's too late for me and Olly. It has to be.

'So what do you want?' he says.

'You'd take me back, then?' I ask, nervous even though I think . . . no, I'm *sure* I know what he's going to say. 'Even now?'

'You know I would. I've never stopped loving you, Jemm.'

My heart wants to leap out of my body and dance around the room, bounce off the ceiling, in between the tiny star-stud lights.

'Why haven't you?' I ask, determined that he shouldn't have an easy time of it. 'I chose Paddy over you, more than once.'

'You were twenty-one,' says Olly. 'And you weren't thinking straight.'

'I was twenty-one the first time. Twenty-five the second time, twenty-seven the third.' Only now does it occur to me that Olly might not think of it as three separate rejections. Perhaps he sees my picking Paddy over him as a single event that went on and on. There was the initial choice in 2006, then my unwillingness to end my marriage after my one-night stand with Olly in 2010. Then in 2012, once Olly had been declared no longer 'of interest' in Marianne's attempted murder case, he got in touch to tell me his feelings for me hadn't changed, and to ask if I'd leave Paddy now. If I would, he promised to love Lottie and take care of her as if she were his own daughter. At that point, if I hadn't been convinced he was withholding something about the night Marianne was attacked, I think I'd have said yes, but I wasn't going to break up my daughter's home for the sake of someone I believed was lying to me.

'I'm thinking straight now,' I say, not at all sure that's true. 'I need you to tell me the truth, Olly. About 2012. Was it you who tried to kill Marianne?'

His eyes dart to the left, then back to me. He's clever enough to know that avoiding eye contact isn't the way to quell my suspicions.

'I know you've got no reason to believe me,' I say, 'but

I swear I won't tell anyone. I won't go to the police. And I'd forgive you – you know I would.'

His eyes widen.

'I *hate* her, Olly. If it weren't for her, I'd have left Paddy *years* ago, when I decided I couldn't bear not being with you for a single day longer. It all kind of . . . erupted one day, all my unhappiness, and I ended up telling Marianne everything. She kind of forced it out of me. And then . . . I was so confused and felt so helpless for so long – as if I didn't have the power to make anything happen at all, even in my own life. And then before I knew it, I'd agreed to let Marianne send me and Paddy to a stupid posh hotel in London every Thursday for nearly a year. God!'

Olly shakes his head. 'Thursday. My least favourite day of the week.'

'Why?'

He seems reluctant to answer. Averting his eyes, he mutters, 'There was a client I used to see every Thursday. Bit of a nightmare.'

Why did that sound so made-up? Is he lying? 'Well, whoever he was, I'd rather spend my Thursday evenings with him than in that hideous hotel with Paddy,' I say. 'Marianne paid a fortune for it, and I hated it. Everything was maroon or purple or red. It was like spending the night inside an aneurysm. Dinner booked for us by Marianne at 7.30 in the blood clot restaurant – it wasn't called that, but it was decorated like one. She never asked us what time we wanted to eat, or if we might prefer to go to a different restaurant occasionally. And we just . . . we accepted it.' I look up at Olly. 'I've never really understood why she was so relentlessly determined that our marriage had to work. I've been thinking that you might understand it better than I do?'

'What do you mean? I've no idea.' He's clearly flustered by the question, wasn't expecting it.

What magic combination of words might make a dent in his determination to keep whatever he knows to himself? 'Olly, she told me you were the one who'd attacked her. "Oliver" – it was a whisper, but she managed to say your name very clearly.'

Olly shifts in his chair. Stares down at his feet. 'It wasn't me.'

'Then, if that's not the secret you're keeping, what is?'

White patches have appeared on his cheeks. His Adam's apple leaps up and down in his throat.

'Now's your chance,' I tell him. 'If you want me to leave Paddy, and for you and me to be together—'

'Do you really mean it? Don't . . .' He stops and exhales slowly. 'Please don't say it unless you mean it.'

'I have no fucking idea whether I mean it or not!' I start to cry. 'Just, please, tell me what you've been keeping from me all these years, you and your partner in deception. And yes, I mean Marianne. I've worked it all out, Olly. Well, not all, but enough. I know you and Marianne are in it together, whatever it is. And . . . the next words out of your mouth had better be a full explanation of what you've been hiding, and why. Start whenever you're ready. I'm listening.'

13

Monday 30 October 2023, 9.45 p.m.

SAM

'I probably wasn't going to do it,' Tom Tulloch told Detective Sergeant Sam Kombothekra, as if murdering someone in exchange for five thousand pounds was something he'd been intending to mull over at his leisure. The two of them were sitting in front of a gas fire that looked like a relic from the 1970s, in the small, overcrowded lounge of Tulloch's brother's semi-detached cottage in Little Holling. There were twice as many chairs in here as the room could comfortably accommodate, giving the impression of a furniture shop that had seen better days.

Like Jemma Stelling, Tulloch seemed entirely unaware that he was likely to be facing a conspiracy to murder charge. Some people were unbelievably out of touch, Sam thought. He'd naively assumed the average man and woman on the street knew basic facts like these. Evidently not: this stupid man in front of him seemed to believe he was in the clear as long as he hadn't physically plunged a knife into anyone. Jemma too. *Fools.*

'I told Jemma I'd do it if she wanted me to, but . . . I don't think she really did.' Tulloch shrugged. He reminded Sam of a

153

gnome: short, pot belly, brown hair and a long fuzzy beard that jutted out into mid-air beneath his chin. 'All she kept telling me was not to do anything yet, make sure not to go anywhere near Marianne unless she gave me the go-ahead. She seemed quite happy to start paying me while telling me to do nothing. Fine by me.'

'What do you mean?' Sam asked him. 'Jemma paid you? Already?' *Please let this turn out to be something useful.* Sam had been feeling utterly wretched since Gibbs had rung and told him to add Tulloch to the 'Indestructible Alibi Gang'. Apparently at 5.45 p.m. he'd been at Jemma and Paddy Stelling's house, a fifty-minute drive from Sleatham St Andrew at that time of day. Suzanne Lacy had met him there, to take Lottie off his hands and bring her to Devey House. Sam didn't hold out much hope that both Suzanne and Lottie were lying, which meant he had precisely no viable suspects for the murder of Marianne Upton.

'She'd already paid me some of the fee, yeah,' said Tulloch. 'Plan was to disguise it as payments for house-sitting. She and Paddy went away in August, I "house-sat" ' – he made air quotes with his fingers – 'so she gave me the first instalment.'

'This August just gone?' said Sam.

Tulloch nodded.

'I see. Do you mind if I ask why you were so willing to accept this particular commission?'

'Do you mean the . . . Not the house-sitting? The murder. Right. Look, I told you: I didn't want to do it.' Tulloch picked up his bottle of beer from the floor and took a swig. 'But I messed things up with Jemma and Paddy years ago, and I wanted to get back in their good books. I've been living here now nearly eighteen months – in this shithole. Don't tell Lucas I said that.'

Lucas, the older of the two Tulloch brothers, both looked and smelled as if he needed a bath. His hair was the stiff kind of unwashed, and gave the impression of having been carved from a solid block of some dark, unsavoury substance. Sam had met him when he'd first arrived, before Lucas had tactfully removed himself to the kitchen. Tom was definitely the cleaner of the siblings, so that was one thing in his favour.

'I was hoping I could stay with Jemma and Paddy for a while,' Tom said. 'Their place is a lot nicer than this – I knew it would be before I'd even seen it. I'd been feeling bad about the way things had gone between us, so I got in touch. And Jemma was all right about it – paid me to house-sit for them last year, to help me out. This was long before any murders got mentioned. I'd told her I was up against it financially, so she sorted me out, and then we kind of stayed in touch – just the odd text here and there. Things weren't back to how they were before or anything, but we were on speaking terms again. And then . . .' He took another sip of his beer. 'Sure you don't want one?' he said, lifting his bottle in the air.

'No, thanks,' said Sam, who feared he might catch a stomach bug if he ingested anything in this house.

'Give me a shout if you change your mind,' said Tulloch. 'So, yeah, then this summer, Jemma decided . . . well, she had a massive problem with Marianne, didn't she? And she knew I was still in dire need of money, so. You know the rest. It sounds daft, but I felt like I owed her one. Well, her and Paddy, but mainly Jemma. I knew she was the one who'd have minded most when I buggered off, all those years ago. Paddy wouldn't have taken it as hard as she did. I don't think he's got strong views about how friends should and shouldn't behave the way Jemma has. She'd have had that ball-crusher Suzanne Lacy in her ear too, telling her I was scum and not to bother with me any more.'

155

'Why did the friendship end?' Sam asked, curious to see if Tulloch's account would be different from Jemma's.

It wasn't, though Tulloch offered a fuller version: his ex-girlfriend had been jealous of his close friendship with Jemma and Paddy, but particularly Jemma. She kept accusing him of preferring Jemma to her, and secretly wishing he was with Jemma – even though Jemma was married, had a baby by this point and had no romantic interest in Tulloch whatsoever. Eventually the girlfriend had made him choose: either the friendship with Jemma and Paddy had to end or she was off. Tulloch had submitted to her pressure and cut off contact with Jemma, Paddy and Lottie.

'It was a shitty thing to do,' he told Sam. 'Especially since I was Lottie's godfather. Well, still am, I suppose, though I haven't acted like it. I was scared, I suppose. Scared of ending up on my own. Stupid, really – I was, what, twenty-five years old? I mean, I'm scared of ending up on my own *now*, when I really am past it, at thirty-eight, but then? I didn't realise how much life I still had ahead of me. Anyway, last year she ditched me – my ex. Since then, I've had no girlfriend, no friends . . . just Lucas, my no-mark brother, for company, and this shithole for a home.' Tulloch twisted the end of his wiry beard around his fingers. 'Probably no more than I deserve, you must be thinking.'

Sam was. He smiled politely. Past it at thirty-eight? What a ridiculous thing to say. Since Dooper had turned everything upside down at work, Sam had been busy trying to persuade himself that he was about to start a whole new exciting chapter of his life in Lincolnshire, aged fifty. The last thing he needed was some no-mark whinger suggesting it was too late for him.

'I suppose I was gambling on Jemma never making me do the actual kill,' Tulloch said. 'I was hoping that, by declaring myself willing, I'd be able to prove to her I was capable of loyalty. To be honest, I kind of thought that might be the only reason she'd asked me – like, maybe it was more about testing me than wanting Marianne dead.'

'You wouldn't have minded having to give back the first instalment of the murder fee?' Sam asked him.

'Wouldn't necessarily have had to,' said Tulloch. 'The house-sitting happened. I definitely did that.' He seemed to be considering the question seriously. 'I don't think Jemma would have asked for the money back,' he said eventually. 'She'd have known I didn't have it to give her. I've got debt coming out of my eyeballs.'

'Do you have a job?'

Tulloch shook his head. 'I've not been doing so well since Janice kicked me out,' he said. 'Can't really . . . settle to anything, you know?'

'Where were you between 5.20 and 5.30 today?' said Sam.

'I was here with Lucas till Paddy texted me. That was about 5.30. Then I went over to his, to mind Lottie. He'd offered me £100 to do it.'

'So you have an alibi for when Marianne Upton was murdered and that alibi is your brother,' said Sam. 'Just like in your and Jemma's plan.'

'Hey.' Tulloch looked offended. 'It was her plan, not mine. And if you're thinking Lucas'd lie for me, you can ask the Domino's driver who dropped off a pizza here just as I was walking out the door. Cold by the time I got back – Sod's law.'

'From which Domino's?' Sam asked.

'The one on Kessin Road in Rawndesley.'

Sam made a note of it. 'If you've got nothing to hide, why weren't you answering your phone?' he asked Tulloch. 'When people act like they don't want to be contacted or found, that tends to arouse suspicion.'

'Right, but I wasn't trying to avoid suspicion, was I? 'Cause I had no idea Marianne had been murdered or that anyone might be thinking I did it. And if it's a phone number I don't know, I never answer. I've had trouble in the past with girls I've met on Tinder. They've rung from different numbers to try and track me down – ones they know I won't link to them.' Tulloch's sheepish smile was one of kinship and commiseration, as if he assumed Sam must be familiar with the problem. 'There are some disturbed people out there,' he said.

14

Monday 30 October 2023, 10 p.m.

SELLERS

Sellers couldn't work out if he was finding Paddy Stelling's company soothing or alarming. The man seemed to have no . . . What was it? Sellers had been racking his brains and failing to come up with a word that described the main thing that seemed to be lacking. If Paddy had been a streaming platform, Sellers would have said content was what was missing. *A contentless man.*

Oomph – that was it. Paddy Stelling had no oomph about him, and spending time alone with him was draining Sellers of what little of the stuff he had left, which wasn't much at this time of night.

The two of them were sitting on tartan-upholstered sofas in a long, thin lounge, half of which had been turned into a library. Gareth Upton had referred to the room twice as 'Mulberry' when suggesting where Sellers might speak privately to Paddy, perhaps because of its wine-coloured curtains and carpet. Sellers knew mulberry was a colour as well as a fruit, and he suspected it was this colour, though he personally would have called it claret.

God, he could have murdered a bottle of red right now. He

wondered if Gareth Upton had any spare. It wasn't the kind of question you could ask of a grieving widower, unfortunately.

'Tell me about your relationship with Marianne,' he said to Paddy. 'Was it good? Did the two of you get on well?'

'All right, I s'pose.'

For fuck's sake, make an effort, man. Sellers was tired, and didn't want to expend unnecessary energy any more than Paddy did. 'Can you elaborate?'

'Marianne was always a bit . . . hot and cold, you know?'

'No, I don't,' said Sellers. 'You're going to have to explain. Please.'

'She used to want us to have a good relationship,' Paddy said. 'She invited me out for lunch once – just me, not Jemma. I thought that was odd, but it would have been rude to say no, I thought, so I went. Free lunch? I'm not going to turn it down.'

'When was this?' Sellers asked.

'Just before Jemm and I got married. Before the starters had even arrived, she locked eyes with me and told me she had a confession to make, that it was serious and I'd better prepare myself.'

Sellers waited – too long for his liking. Was that it – the end of the story, as far as Paddy was concerned? Mentally, Sellers rolled up his sleeves yet again. 'And? Did she confess to something?'

Paddy nodded. 'Told me she really wanted us to be close. To have a proper mother-son relationship, she said, and for that to work, she had to tell me the truth, or else she'd be the world's biggest hypocrite, and she hated hypocrisy more than any other . . . whatever, failings – and then she basically told me that for years she'd feared I was a total shit. Words to that effect, anyway. I told her not to worry about it.'

'Was it something you'd done, or said?' Surely being a total shit required more gumption than this man possessed. Maybe not. It might just be possible to do it in a passive, inert way.

'I'd been a bit of a user in the past,' said Paddy. 'Given Jemma the runaround. In it for myself, not giving much back. I wouldn't have expected Marianne to approve of me then, and she didn't. But now I'd turned it around and she loved me, apparently. Made me out to be some kind of hero for realising I'd been a knob for ages and then being less of one. Most people never change, she said, never improve, but I had. She respected me now. That's why she couldn't let me believe she was just this nice, friendly mum-type under false pretences, without knowing all the hostile things she'd said about me in the past. And then she came out with them all – a big long list, pretty brutal. It was important for me to hear every single one, she said.' Paddy grimaced.

Sellers felt a pang of guilt, thinking of how his girlfriend, Sondra, liked to say that he'd improved beyond all recognition since she'd first met him. She could never, ever find out that he'd eaten beef lasagne tonight.

'Then she got all emotional,' Paddy went on. 'Started crying, saying she should have known all along that I'd come good, that I was a nice guy underneath. Not *demonic*.' Paddy stressed the last word. 'Not *a boil on the arse of humanity*.'

Sellers assumed these were things Marianne Upton had told her son-in-law that she'd said about him previously.

'I never told Jemma, not about the lunch or any of it,' Paddy said.

'Why not?'

'Dunno.' He seemed quite content not to understand his own motivation. 'It was all just weird. I suppose I didn't want to freak her out. Marianne didn't tell her either, I don't think.'

'Did she say anything else, apart from confessing to bad-mouthing you?'

'Yeah, she told me she was going to leave me five hundred grand in her will,' Paddy said matter-of-factly, as if this kind of thing happened to him every day. 'And before you say that gives me a reason to kill her – no, it doesn't. She changed her will again later.'

So he knew about that part.

'Yeah, she told me that too,' Paddy said, seeing the question on Sellers' face. 'Didn't explain why. I didn't ask, to be honest. Her business. But my share went from £500,000 to nothing. Some you win, some you lose, I guess. Not that I wanted her money, particularly. I mean, I didn't *not* want it, but . . . I was kind of neutral on it, you know?'

'You didn't want five hundred grand?' What was wrong with this plank?

'Not especially,' said Paddy. 'Jemma's trust fund and her job, and the bits and bobs I earn, all of that's enough for me, her and Lottie. We're well off compared to most people.' He scratched the side of his nose.

'Do you know when Marianne changed her will, or why?' Sellers asked.

'Must have been about a month after what happened to her in 2012,' said Paddy. 'That's right: the attack was November, and she told me around Christmas. Must have been, 'cause the two of us were in the lounge when she said it and the Christmas tree was up. I don't know why, no. It was like she blamed me for someone trying to kill her, which made no sense. I wasn't in the house when it happened – I was out with Jemma, on our way back from a broken-down train. I had nothing to do with it. But it was like Marianne didn't seem to realise that. She's never forgiven me.'

'For what?' Sellers asked.

'Well, nothing.' Paddy said this as if it ought to be obvious.

'Nothing I know of, anyway. She's been against me since then, that's all I know. Listen, would it be okay if you didn't mention any of this to Jemma?'

'She doesn't know about the will either? The five hundred grand, first given, then taken away?'

'Nothing. I never said anything. Look, you don't know Jemma,' said her husband. 'Give her anything to latch onto and she'll go on about it for months. I did tell her one thing Marianne said to me around the same time, Christmas 2012, and she wouldn't let it go.'

'What was that?' Sellers asked.

'Marianne asked me what I thought was the opposite of murder. I said, "Suicide". She laughed and said, "Wrong", but she didn't tell me what she meant or why she'd asked. I mentioned it to Jemma and she wouldn't stop bringing it up, for weeks, trying to get me to help her work out what it meant.'

'Don't you think Jemma would want to know what you've just told me? It sounds like quite a lot to keep secret from your wife.'

'You don't know the half—' Paddy changed his mind, evidently, and started again. 'It's not a secret. That makes it sound . . . I don't know. It's more just . . . there's no point muddying the waters, is there? Chatting shit about people when it wouldn't do any good. Especially now, when there's enough drama, and Jemma and Gareth don't need anything else on their plates. You know?'

What Sellers knew was that nothing could convince him Paddy Stelling hadn't just stopped himself from blurting out, *You don't know the half of it.*

What else was he keeping to himself because he'd decided it would make everyone's lives easier?

15

JEMMA

It's nearly half past ten by the time I arrive at Devey House. Dad must have heard the wheels on the gravel; he's waiting for me outside and pulls me into a hug as I step out of the police car. 'My darling girl,' he says. 'Are you all right?' What starts as an embrace turns into me holding him up. I stagger under his weight, as the strangest thought occurs to me: he wouldn't have come out to meet me if Marianne were still alive. She'd be in the house too, and he'd know that she would say: 'Why does waiting for Jemma require going outside? She has a key. I'm sure she'll manage to find her way in.'

If I were Dad, and Lottie were me, I'd be outside too. I'd be running through the streets until I found her and brought her home.

I wonder if Dad will start to feel more like a dad to me now that Marianne's gone? Will he look at me and see me, instead of someone who might please or displease Marianne? 'I'm so sorry, Dad,' I say, hugging him. 'You must be in shock.'

'Better now you're home safe.'

This isn't my home, Dad. 'Are the police still here?' I ask him.

'Most of them have left for the night but one's just come back. A lovely chap, actually: DS Kombothekra.'

The unrufflable smiler with the velvet voice. I find it hard to think of him as lovely. 'Do they have any idea who . . .?'

'No. They don't seem to,' Dad says.

'Where's Lottie?' I ask. 'Not asleep, I bet.'

'Suzanne's been valiantly trying to get her to bed, but no luck yet.'

I disentangle myself from Dad and move towards the house. 'I need to see her.'

'She's doing okay.' Dad's following me, out of breath already. He starts to say something else – it sounds like the beginning of a question – but I can't talk any more until I've seen Lotts. The front door has been left slightly ajar and I pick up pace as I get closer.

Suzanne, at the far end of the entrance hall, sees me and starts running towards me. 'Jemm! God, am I pleased to see you!' She rushes over and grabs me, squeezes me tightly. 'Lotts is fine, but – no, don't panic, it's not that sort of "but". She's upstairs brushing her teeth. I was just going to say: she knows about what happened to Marianne in 2012.'

'Shit. I was going to tell her.'

'I know,' Suzanne says.

'Does she know she was in the house when it happened?'

'Everything, yeah. I told her what we know about that night, helped her to try and make sense of it. She didn't seem overly . . . scared or freaked out or anything. Children, teenagers . . . they can't avoid experiencing life, you know? The difficult bits too. Jemm, she'll be fine.'

It's all fine. Lottie's fine.

'Sorry. I just—'

From behind me, Dad says, 'Would you like a cup of tea, sweetheart? Something to eat? I can heat you up some of—'

'Just a cup of tea would be great,' I tell him. 'Thanks.' God, he looks appalling under the bright lights of the hall: grey-faced and precarious, like he could fall to the ground at any moment.

Once he's gone, I whisper to Suzanne, 'Tell me one thing: Lotts can't have done this, right? Charlie Zailer told me they know she was nowhere near Dad's when it happened.'

Suzanne recoils. 'Jemm, what the . . . Of *course* Lottie didn't do it. Who's Charlie Zailer? And yes, it's beyond doubt. The police have spoken to your neighbours, who saw Lotts with Paddy at yours just after 5.30.'

'Jemma?' Paddy's voice comes from behind me, and I realise he hasn't crossed my mind since I got out of the police car. I haven't hoped, or expected, to see him.

He's halfway down the stairs, stops walking when I turn to face him.

'Paddy.'

'Where have you been?'

'You know where I've been,' I say. 'I texted you, remember?'

He looks at me warily, eyes moving up and down as if he can't stand to look straight at me for too long.

How long is it going to take him to ask me why, why for so long, why on the same night that someone murdered Marianne?

Come on, Paddy. It's just words, arranged in an order that makes sense. You can do it.

Perhaps I'm the one who should start asking questions: all the unanswered ones that have been circling my brain all the way from Spilling to here.

Who killed Marianne?

Was it someone who's here now, at Devey House? *Dad . . . Paddy . . . Suzanne?* Because it has to have been one of them, surely.

Only if the killer is the same person who read and altered the diary file.

They must be. Who else could have known the date and time I'd chosen for Marianne's murder? I didn't even tell Suzanne that detail. I told her about my plan and that I was going to the police to make sure I never did it, but I never said how I'd chosen when to go, or that Monday 30 October at 5.15 p.m. had originally been reserved for a quite different event. And I'm sorry, but I just don't believe in coincidences that big and unlikely.

Which means . . . maybe it wasn't Marianne who altered the diary file, changing 'Ollie' to 'Olly' throughout. What if someone else did that, wanting me to think it was her handiwork?

Why? Why would anyone want that?

Who else could have got into my laptop last week, the week before? Dad, Paddy or Lottie, easily. Suzanne, too. All four of them would have tried 'Lottie' as their first guess at my password, and struck lucky. I've never thought to hide my computer or even put it away. And sometimes, both at Dad's and at home, I leave the room for longish periods of time, if I have to take a work call. I fall asleep on the sofa for half an hour, my laptop on the table next to me . . .

I can rule out Tom Tulloch and Ollie, neither of whom had the opportunity.

Unless . . .

I think about the time last year when Marianne sent me her Wordle result, then claimed she'd done it by mistake, that she'd meant to send it to Paddy. Suzanne was sure that was a lie and that Ollie was the intended recipient. And if Ollie and Marianne were still in touch, then she could have been the one who tampered with the diary, and then told him all about it: *Guess what? Jemma's hired someone to kill me. She's even picked the date and time of my execution.* Which means Ollie can't be ruled out as the person who decided to kill her at that precise time, on that date.

My daughter's voice drags me out of my spiralling thoughts. 'Hey, Mum. S'cuse, Dad.' She's hurrying towards me, down the stairs, past Paddy. I run to her, cling to her, burst into tears, which makes it hard to ask if she's okay as many times as I'd like to.

'Calm down,' she says. 'Mum, I'm okay. You're the one who isn't.'

Understatement of the century.

Suzanne says something about helping Dad make hot drinks, and I know she's trying to get herself and Paddy out of the way so that Lotts and I can have a few minutes together alone.

Thank God for brilliant Suzanne.

'Mum?'

'Yes, darling.'

Lottie looks over her shoulder to check everyone's gone. Then she says, 'Was Granny an evil person?'

Something twists inside me. 'I . . .'

'Don't say no one's either completely good or completely evil. That's what Suzanne said before, when I asked her.'

I can't help smiling at this, imagining the restraint Suzanne must have employed for Lottie's sake when talking about Marianne. 'That woman is the devil on steroids,' she was fond of telling me.

'Even if it's true, some people are much more good and some are much more bad,' says Lottie. 'Which was Granny?'

'Why are you asking?'

'Because she's been killed.' Her voice cracks on the last word. 'And eleven years ago, someone tried to murder her then too. So, like . . . maybe there was something quite bad about her if people kept wanting to kill her. That's all I meant. Do you think it's true?'

169

15th June 2006

Suzanne said something earlier that I can't get out of my head. I was talking about how much things can change in a very short time, and I used Paddy's attitude to being in a relationship as an example. I pointed out that he's switched in the space of a few weeks from 'Yeah, I'm sleeping with a few other women, sure, but none of them are as good in bed as you are' to 'You're enough for me now, I don't want or need anyone else'. I said I couldn't help wondering if meeting Ollie at my house — a firefighter, there in his official boyfriend capacity — had anything to do with this sudden transformation. Maybe it brought it home to Paddy that other blokes his age aren't as chicken-shit as he is. He might have reflected on the fact that Ollie isn't afraid to run into burning buildings and risk his life in order to save strangers, and certainly doesn't balk at the even more supposedly terrifying ordeal of Being A Boyfriend, which for years seems to have been Paddy's main phobia.

But . . . and . . . New Paddy has now declared himself happy to be a boyfriend, which should make me feel less bitter, and maybe it will one day if I give it a chance, and no doubt it was disloyal of me to say what I said to Suzanne this morning, but I couldn't resist. Rant bitterly first, forgive later — that's my motto. Or, sometimes, don't forgive ever.

I was thrilled when Suzanne said she one hundred per cent

agreed with me. 'I just can't believe he said it.' She winced. 'He's a douchebag of epic proportions.'

'Obviously he was Old Paddy when he said it. Commitment-phobic Paddy. But, yes, there's no denying that those words did come out of his mouth: "No one else I'm fucking at the moment is anywhere near as good as you", and he definitely would have meant it as a compliment.'

'Oh, for sure,' Suzanne agreed. 'Which makes it so much worse.'

'Right. A clever man would have realised it was an insult, and not said it.'

That's when Suzanne made her interesting, and really quite brilliant, observation: 'It's two insults for the price of one,' she said. 'There's the obvious one — "Hey, just be happy you're easily winning the competition I'm torturing you by forcing you to enter" - but there's a deeper, more subtle insult too.'

I was on the edge of my kitchen chair, waiting to hear more. Surely, I thought, there can't be anything Paddy's done wrong that I've failed to think of and add to my list.

'It's actually so subtle, it's hard to put into words,' Suzanne said.

'Try,' I ordered.

'It's like . . . not being chosen is painful enough, when you're madly in love, but normally when that happens you can at least think, "I'm losing out because he prefers someone else." It makes sense, however much it hurts. But Paddy was saying, effectively, "You're losing out to something I don't value at all and think is crap." The cheek of it! It's like, "I can't have dinner with you tonight because I'm staying in to eat a dog turd I've fished out of a bin." The message is basically, "I don't care enough about you to choose you, even in preference to something I think is worthless." To me, that's the ultimate insult.'

Undeniably true. Every word. And I'm supposed to think that's all in the past now, because along came New Paddy! New Paddy emerged from the ashes of Old Paddy, the one who'd done and said all the despicable things, and arrived on the scene glittering with all the allure of the previously unavailable. I said something like this to Suzanne, who said, 'Yeah, it's a well-known marketing trick: create a sense of massive scarcity, then tell your audience this so-hard-to-get thing is now, amazingly, available. They'll all want it.'

Apart from those of them who would still so much rather have Ollie, I thought, but didn't say.

16

Monday 30 October 2023, 10.30 p.m.

SIMON

'Have you been outside all this time?' Charlie was sitting at Simon's table in The Brown Cow when he walked back in from the garden, blowing on his hands to warm them up. 'For God's sake, Simon. It's pitch black and freezing. What were you doing out there, communing with the stars?'

In his absence, his tabletop arrangement had changed. His empty glass had gone, replaced by a new, full pint of Coke, and there was a sandwich wrapped in clingfilm balanced on top of the Marianne Upton case files from 2012. There ended the list of changes Simon approved of. He tried not to notice the gin and tonic Charlie had ordered for herself.

Simon didn't understand why almost all the adults he knew treated alcohol as if it were nectar from heaven. He'd never been a drinker himself, but recently it had started to annoy him when other people did it. He'd heard on the radio that it was hard for cancer to kill you if your liver was functioning at its highest level. He'd tried telling Charlie that alcohol was poison, but she either laughed at him or said, 'So are killjoys.' Simon wasn't sure he was capable of feeling joy, but this was where he tended to feel least discontent: at his regular table at The

Brown Cow, next to the fireplace, opposite a framed oil painting of a black and white cow (yeah, it made no sense to Simon either) standing side-on between a thick, gnarly-trunked oak tree and a red wheelbarrow. Inexplicably, a large green apple was balanced on top of the cow's head.

This wasn't the original brown cow painting; that one, in which the cow had been an appropriate shade of caramel, had gone last year and taken the smell of old wood with it. Now, under new management, the place reeked of roses and leather, which Charlie liked and Simon hated. So far he'd had no luck tracking down the source of the smell. There had to be a vent somewhere pumping it out, one he planned to bury under dozens of layers of masking tape if he ever found it.

It was half past ten. The pub was empty apart from the bar staff, Simon and Charlie.

'Anyway, well done,' she said. 'You successfully manifested a sandwich.' He'd texted her an hour ago: *'brown cow bring cheese sandwich'*. 'Less successfully,' she continued, 'you left confidential paperwork lying around on a pub table while you went out and . . . did what, exactly, for twenty minutes? 'Cause that's how long I've been here, waiting with your stupid sandwich.'

'I asked for cheese, not stupid. Are we out of cheese?'

'I can't believe you left all this lot just lying here for anyone to rummage through.'

'I don't care about keeping Spilling Police's secrets any more.' Simon was annoyed that he had to spell it out. Didn't Charlie know nothing was the same now that his team was going to be torn apart? That it never would be again? 'I went out to ring Doug Brodigan. Couldn't get a signal in here.'

'You still haven't enabled Wi-Fi calls on your phone, have you?' Charlie sighed.

'Don't know what it means,' Simon said proudly.

'Can I do it for you now? It'll take four seconds.'

'No need. I've already spoken to Brodigan, who confirmed I was right. Made a nice change.'

'What?' Charlie looked confused. 'Simon, you're always right. When aren't you? Oh, for God's sake!' It was convenient for Simon that she could read his thoughts most of the time. Saved him having to string sentences together. 'The super's not doing what she's doing because she doesn't think you're a brilliant detective. You know that. Everyone knows how good you are.'

'It's my fault, what's happening to Sam and Proust. The team. There'd be no exiling of anyone if it weren't for me,' Simon said. 'If I was as good at the job as you say I am, Dooper'd be scared of losing me and she can't be, or she wouldn't be trying to push me out the door by firing the only people I want to work with. If I'd been less disruptive, more conventional—'

'An entirely different person, yeah?'

'—I'd have been a detective no one would have risked losing.'

'Well . . .' Charlie shrugged. 'No one can be a perfect, flaw-less human all the time and in every way. Especially – and I cannot stress this enough – especially not you.' She laughed at her own quip.

'Tell me the truth,' Simon said. 'Anything and everything I've achieved over the past God knows how many years . . . Could I have done it if I hadn't obeyed my gut instincts and nothing else? I don't think so.'

'It might be an interesting experiment,' said Charlie. 'If you're willing to give being obedient a go, you could always ask for a meeting with the super and—'

'Fuck that!'

Two young men behind the bar looked up to see where the outburst had come from.

'She's an over-promoted mediocrity with a puffy squirrel face,' Simon muttered.

'Valid.' Charlie waved the wrapped sandwich under his nose. 'Here, have something to eat.'

He pushed it away. 'I'm not hungry any more.'

'Can I have it, then? I need extra calories to cope with your moodiness.'

'No. I'll probably want it in a bit.' Simon pulled a sheet of A4 paper out of a file and passed it to Charlie. 'See this? It lists all the places Oliver Mayo's DNA was found at Marianne Upton's house after she was nearly killed there in November 2012. None in any of the bedrooms. The most by a significant margin was found in a room described there as Marianne Upton's study – that's the same room Marianne showed Jemma once it was empty, the one she'd kept locked for years and that Jemma had been curious enough to think about trying to break into. Did Jemma tell you about that?'

Charlie nodded.

'It was very much for Marianne's use only and kept locked in 2012, according to Brodigan. She called it her "private sanctuary", he said. Except . . . Oliver Mayo was allowed in, apparently. Marianne told Brodigan herself: Mayo was a regular visitor – had been since he and Jemma had split up in 2006 – and the study was where he and Marianne sat and talked when he went round.' Simon took a gulp of his Coke.

'Right. So she didn't want anyone else to see what was in there, but she didn't mind Oliver Mayo seeing it,' Charlie said.

'Brodigan and his team were obviously given access at the time, and he says there was nothing out of the ordinary in the room. Just what you'd expect in a study: furniture, cushions, pictures on the walls, books and photos on shelves, stationery, pens, the odd ornament. Nothing anyone'd want or need to keep secret.'

'Weird,' said Charlie. 'I can see why Jemma wanted to break in. Must have driven her mad that her ex-boyfriend got to go in there years after they'd broken up. Assuming she knew about it. Maybe she didn't, I don't know. I mean . . .' She frowned. 'Could Marianne and Oliver Mayo have been having an affair?'

'Maybe,' said Simon, 'but like I said, there was none of his DNA in any of the bedrooms. But whatever they were doing, it was secret all right. If you read the interviews with Gareth Upton and Jemma Stelling, they both say Marianne last saw Mayo in 2006, the year he and Jemma split up. Both claimed to have no clue why Marianne said "Oliver" when asked who'd slashed her throat open. But then in the transcript of Marianne talking to Brodigan, it's right there: she tells him Mayo was a regular visitor, *her* regular visitor, between 2010 and November 2012. Nothing on the record suggests anyone spotted this discrepancy or asked anyone about it. There's no interview with Gareth Upton where a detective says, "Your wife says Oliver Mayo's still a regular guest and friend of the family." The discrepancy's just sitting there in the file, easy to miss. So I rang Brodigan, thinking he'd say how stressed they'd all been at the time and they must have missed it, but no. He admitted it: he'd felt sorry for Marianne, so he'd covered for her.'

'What?' Charlie sounded as surprised and disapproving as Simon had hoped she would.

'He felt sorry for this old lady who'd just been nearly killed, so he covered for her. She told him in confidence about the secret meetings between her and Mayo which always happened when no one else was at home, and he agreed not to mention it to anyone, especially not her family. He assumed an affair, he told me.'

'Brodigan admitted all this?' Charlie frowned.

'Only because I led with an admission of my own: that I'd encouraged Jemma to kill Marianne and given her advice on how to do it.'

'I guess it really is true, what I keep hearing,' Charlie said. 'The police don't care about preventing or solving crimes any more. They only care about rude internet posts.'

'Brodigan's always thought it was Mayo, though he was with a therapy client at the time,' said Simon. 'He said it was clear Marianne was lying and proud of it, and there were no other suspects. He wanted to take it further, but his DI said it was uncloseable and a waste of time.'

'I reckon it was an affair,' said Charlie. 'They shagged in the study instead of a bedroom because . . . maybe that was the only room with a lock on the door. I've got an idea: why don't you join your team at Marianne Upton's place – you know, where you're supposed to be – and have a look?'

'They won't be there now, Char. It's late. Don't worry – I'll be getting the answers I want soon enough.'

'Good. Sam and the gang could use your help,' said Charlie.

Simon opened his mouth, then closed it. Nothing good would happen if he explained that wanting to know and wanting to help were two very different things. As for wanting to win, not for Spilling Police's sake but in order to deprive them of that same win, in the spirit of crushing your enemies . . . that was something different altogether.

17

JEMMA

One of the spare rooms at Devey House has a small balcony: black-painted wrought iron, grey metal floor. It's where Suzanne and I used to stand and smoke illicit cigarettes and gossip about boyfriends past, present and future, and it's where we're standing now, at nearly midnight, even though it's freezing and we both gave up smoking long ago. As soon as Lottie fell asleep in the super-king bed in the room behind us, I had a sudden, urgent need for those two absolute essentials, fresh air and nicotine. You can forget about both and imagine you're managing fine without them for a long time, and then the need suddenly hits you.

'Thank you for everything you've done today,' I say. 'You're the best husband-and-father substitute a girl could wish for.'

'What are you going to tell them all about why you went to the police?' Suzanne asks.

'The truth. Eventually. I just didn't want to do it tonight, when everyone's had their fill. It can wait.'

She nods. 'Do you mind if I ask you a sickening, horrible question that I wish I didn't want to ask? But then we all know I'm a terrible person.'

'It wasn't me,' I tell her. 'I mean . . . obviously it wasn't me. It was never going to be me. But it wasn't Tom either. I've no idea who could have done it. Believe me, I'm as shocked and confused as you are.'

'That wasn't what I was going to ask you,' Suzanne says.

'What, then?' I take a long, deep drag on my cigarette.

'Are you happy? Glad? Does it feel . . . good?'

'That she's dead?'

We both turn, hearing a rustling sound behind us. It's Dad. He's ready for bed: blue and white checked pyjamas with a navy trim, beige towelling dressing gown.

There's a smear of toothpaste on his chin and something crusty and darker on one side of his mouth. I can't bring myself to remind him to wash his face. What does it matter what he looks like? This must be the worst night of his life. Mum's death was . . . different. My heart clenches, as it always does when I think back to that day at the hospice. I was seven, so my version of it, at this point, is probably more invention than remembered reality, but in my memory Mum was comforting Dad and me, strengthening our resolve until the very end. And . . . Dad was heartbroken but not desolate, as he looks now; not full of nothing but despair.

I wish Mum were here now, to tell him again that everything will be okay soon, whether that's true or not. And I wish Dad hadn't just heard Suzanne ask me if I was pleased Marianne had been murdered.

How long was he there, in the room behind us? Did he hear me saying it wasn't Tom? Is he about to ask me—

'I should add my voice to the thanks, Suzanne,' he says. 'Jemma shouldn't have needed a father substitute, but she has since her mother died. That's my fault.'

'I was slagging off Paddy, Dad. Not you.'

'You're too hard on him.'

'I disagree,' I say.

'He loves you, and is afraid to show it.'

Suzanne tries to pass me her nearly finished cigarette. 'I should leave you two alone,' she says.

'No, stay,' I tell her.

'Yes, stay,' says Dad. 'I didn't mean to intrude. I need to get to bed, try and sleep. Tomorrow's unlikely to be easier than today. You should both sleep too.' He touches my arm. 'Night night, sweetheart. Love you. I'm sorry I haven't been . . .' He leaves without specifying what he hasn't been.

'Am I?' I ask Suzanne, once he's gone.

'Too hard on Paddy?' She makes a pained, crushed-in-a-mousetrap kind of noise. 'I really want to say "No", because . . . I'll be honest, Jemm, I've never thought he was good enough for you, but . . . Well, more and more, it seems like you've started to think that too. To be as fair as possible to Paddy . . . I suppose it's hard to be your best self when you're married to someone who's thinking the worst of you all the time. You know – living with the constant expectation you're going to get it wrong yet again. Ugh, I don't know what's wrong with me. I'm going soft as a result of sleep-deprivation. I'm normally asleep by nine these days.'

'If I didn't have this terror that, somehow, I'm going to end up in prison for the next twenty years of my life—'

'Hm?' Suzanne looks confused.

'I'm answering your question. Am I glad Marianne's dead? If I wasn't so scared, and if I knew I wasn't going to be blamed, me or . . . or anyone I love . . .'

The thought of Ollie being sent to prison makes me want to howl. I don't believe he could exist or survive there. It's strange: there's always been something about him that makes me want to rescue him as well as be rescued by him. I felt it strongly in July, when I went to see him in Cambridge and knew I needed to protect him from my own justified anger.

'Jemm?' says Suzanne. 'If you weren't scared, then what?'

'Then yes, I'd be glad she's dead. More than glad.' I hold my half-finished cigarette with one hand and flick it with the other, so that it shoots out into the night. 'I think it would probably feel like the best treat I could ever be given.'

Olly doesn't reply immediately. He's not turning away, though, or shifting awkwardly in his chair. Nothing about his body language signals surprise.

He's prepared. He knew he would have to face this unwelcome question one day. 'What makes you think Marianne and I are keeping something from you?' he says eventually in a voice that signals kindness – pity, perhaps – as well as curiosity. I wonder if this is how he speaks to delusional clients: *What makes you think you're the re-incarnation of Queen Victoria?*

'Two days ago, she showed me her study, at Dad's,' I tell him. ' "Today's your lucky day", she said. "I'll unlock the door and show you right now, give you a proper tour." She led me up there, seeming all happy and relaxed, knowing I'd believe I was about to be let in on the secret.'

'And?'

'Empty. She'd stripped it bare, right down to stripping the walls and pulling up the carpet. As a psychotherapist, do you have any theories as to why she'd do that?'

Olly says nothing.

'Lust for complete and total victory – that's my best guess,' I say. 'She knew I was desperate to see anything and everything that was behind that locked door, so she had to remove *every single thing* that had once been in there, every last square centimetre of wallpaper. That's what she did – and then she took me up there to taunt me.'

It'll be easier to say what I need to say next if I'm not looking at him, so I stand and walk over to the open window. On the street outside, two young Chinese women are jogging along the pavement in white vest tops, black Lycra leggings and white trainers. A cyclist nearly knocks one of them over, but manages to slip in between them instead. Once past them, he waves apologetically over his shoulder.

'Do you know what I was thinking about when Marianne took me up to the top floor?' I say. 'When I believed I was about to get the answers I'd been craving for years, before I found out it was all a trick? I was remembering the tongue-lashing she gave you when she caught you trying to open the door to her study, about a month before Lotts was born. Don't pretend you don't remember.'

'Of course I do,' Olly says quietly.

I turn to face him. 'Why the fuck were you at Devey House that day, Olly? Nothing was going on between us at that point. Marianne said afterwards she'd had no idea why you were there or how you got inside. She certainly didn't let you in, oh, no. She just went up to her study and found you on the top landing, trying the door handle, trying to break into her private sanctuary. That's where I come into the story – because I heard her scream at you, didn't I? She made sure I heard – that's why it had to be such an over-the-top bollocking, so there was no way I'd miss it. She shrieked at the top of her lungs that you had no business being there. "How dare you? Get out of my house! You're not Jemma's boyfriend any more, you've no reason to be here." It was all a show for my benefit, wasn't it? Why don't you tell me what really happened that day?'

Olly says nothing but keeps his eyes fixed on me, staring my rage in the face as if it's a punishment he's imposed on himself.

'How about if I start?' I say. 'You couldn't have got into the house unless someone had let you in, and Marianne and I were the only ones there. I didn't let you in, so she must have. The whole big mystery she pretended we were both trying to solve had an obvious answer from the start. I was just too stupid and trusting to think of it for *more than fifteen years.* I believed Marianne's theory: you were so obsessed with me, you'd climbed in through an open window. I'm such a gullible moron, I didn't even think to question it, though God knows why you'd have tried to force open the door to *her* study if it was me you were obsessed with.'

'I've been obsessed with you since we first met, Jemm,' says Olly. 'In a good way, I like to think.' He almost smiles. 'And . . . any truths I haven't told you, I've hated keeping them from you. *Hated* it.'

'Then be honest with me now.'

'I can't.'

Unbelievable. Presented like it's an unchangeable law of nature.

'But I won't lie to you again,' Olly says. 'That I can promise.'

'Yay, lucky me.' I can't keep still. Nowhere I can stand or walk to in this room feels comfortable. 'Do you know when it clicked for me, that Marianne must have let you in that day? It was a few months ago. Paddy and I were having supper with her and Dad, and Dad mentioned a new director of music at church who'd invited him to join the choir. I don't know why it took that for me to make the connection, but it hit me suddenly: Dad had been out at a musical thing the day Marianne screamed at you and chucked you out of the house. They'd both known for ages he'd be out all day. Paddy was out at work. And I wasn't supposed to be there either.'

Olly nods. 'You were supposed to be at Suzanne's.'

'Right. I'd been on my way there when she'd phoned to cancel – her mum had broken her arm and Suzanne had to drive her to hospital, so I told my cab driver to turn round, and headed back home. Marianne didn't hear me come in because she was up at the top of the house in her study. With you, right? You were in there with her, at her invitation. She'd arranged for you to go round that day, thinking the two of you would have the house to yourselves.'

'Yes,' Olly says. It's almost a whisper. 'That's what happened. Except . . . she did hear you come in. You slammed the front door quite hard. We both heard it.'

He meant it, then. He's not going to lie any more. Or is this another clever trick?

'Right,' I say. 'So she had to improvise, quickly. Sneaking you out secretly would have been too risky – I could easily have appeared in the hall and seen you – so she pushed you out of the study, locked the door, and started screaming at you for being an intruder who'd climbed in through a window.'

Olly nods.

'Here's another thing that didn't occur to me for ages,'

I say. 'Her study never used to be locked. There were a few years, after we moved to Devey House, when I could walk in there whenever I wanted. It was full of normal stuff in those days – all the things you'd expect to see in a study. Her sudden need for secrecy started very soon after you and I met. After you and *she* met. I tried to work out exactly when that lock got put on the door – it was early 2006, I think. I went back over it all and worked it out. And . . . you saying you're not going to lie to me any more just isn't enough, Olly. It's nowhere near enough!' The words spill out of me. 'You need to tell me everything and it needs to happen now.'

'Jemma, it changed, it wasn't—' He lifts his hands as if to cover his face, then lowers them again. 'I never wanted to lie to you. I was there, remember, when Marianne told us all? We were having dinner, and she explained that from now on her study would be a no-go area for everyone but her, with a lock on the door. She said it was so she could keep the room tidy and I thought . . .' Olly looks lost for a second, as if he's forgotten what he was trying to say. 'Well, I knew that couldn't be the real reason. You won't remember but you said to me that night: you never went in there anyway, and neither did your dad. No one had ever been in and left it untidy. I was as clueless as you were, until . . . well, until that day. The one we're talking about, when Marianne screamed and threw me out. Before that, I had no idea what was going on. Please believe me about that.'

When I don't respond, he says, 'You believe me, right?'

'I do, but it doesn't matter. What matters is the part I still don't know. What did you find out that day? What's going on between you and Marianne, Olly?'

'I haven't seen or spoken to her for years. The only contact I've had with her since late 2012 is . . . this is going to sound ridiculous—'

'Wordle?' I say.

He closes his eyes. 'I've no idea how you can possibly know that. Yes. I can't remember when it was – last year some time – but one day she sent me her Wordle score. After ten years of no contact. The little grid with the squares, you know? I think she must have thought I was bound to have discovered Wordle and got hooked on it. She was right.'

'It must have been a shock to hear from her after so long. What did you do?'

Olly's face contorts. 'Nothing at first. But then . . . I sent her my Wordle grid the next day.'

I bet you did. Couldn't risk pissing her off, could you, given what she could do to you, given what she knew?

'I only sent my grid, no words. Before you ask: yes, we've been exchanging our Wordle scores most days since then. Not every day. We've each missed a few. But Jemma, I swear to you, from whenever it started until now, that's the only contact I've had with her for the last nearly eleven—'

'You were having an affair with her, weren't you?' I can't believe I've said it. I've made it exist more than it did before; here it is, in the room with us, the reality of it. 'Maybe not since 2012, but at some point, you and Marianne were lovers.'

What else could it be? What other explanation is possible? *If it's true, then please let him lie to me.*

'Having . . . an affair? With Marianne?' His face twists. Then he laughs.

'At some point you wanted it to stop, but that was tricky, wasn't it? Marianne could have told me what had been going on, and you couldn't take that risk. Was that why?'

'Why what?' Olly asks, looking as if he might laugh again.

'Why you tried to murder her in November 2012,' I say.

18

SIMON

Simon had been to Cambridge before, and found he liked it more each time he was here. At first, he'd thought that feeling of being able to breathe more easily was down to being nowhere near home. No one was going to recognise him or approach him. It was true, he'd always felt more relaxed – though also lonelier, that was the disadvantage – in places where he had no ties, but the more often he came to Cambridge, the clearer it became that he liked it for other reasons too. It was colourful and felt alive in a way that Spilling didn't, and the snatches of overheard conversation were eye-opening. Two men walking in front of Simon were having a vigorous argument about whether a treasurer's wife had any right to insist that the organist write an essay justifying his refusal to take communion from a female priest. The focus of the discussion wasn't changing church traditions but rather whether one person could reasonably impose essay-writing duties on another when they had no structural authority over them. Simon knew where he stood on the matter: unequivocally, no.

If his map wasn't lying to him, the Cedarwood Centre, where

Oliver Mayo worked, was going to be coming up any second now on the left. Yep, here it was. As he approached the front door, it opened and two women came out, one addressing the other over her shoulder: ' . . . and I told her, I can't believe any woman likes it. It's like being dipped in the tepid remains of a bowl of cereal.'

Simon hoped Oliver Mayo would prove to be as loud and forthright as the rest of Cambridge, because he had a lot of questions he wanted to ask Jemma Stelling's ex-boyfriend. Was it a good sign that Mayo had willingly agreed to the appointment?

He found himself feeling disappointed as he shook the hand of the man he'd driven for two hours to meet. His first impression was of a cautious, reserved person – shy, even – who had no intention of shouting his mouth off about anything. There was something uncomfortable, also, about his intense focus on Simon. Normally, in the presence of a police detective, particularly after a serious crime had been committed, people experienced a lot of internal drama, whether they were guilty or innocent; their attention would switch back and forth between their interior world and the external one. Sometimes it made them difficult to talk to; they would lose concentration and keep having to reorient themselves.

Not Mayo. His large, brown eyes were two still pools, and Simon sensed nothing behind them apart from a sort of . . . *force of observation* was the only way he could describe it. This felt like a deeper and, frankly, more threatening level of attention than he'd ever had focused on him before. He wanted to shake its weight off him.

'This won't take long,' he said, then silently berated himself for his defeatist attitude. He'd been here less than five minutes, and he was already convinced Mayo would, as politely as possible, give him nothing. 'Thanks for agreeing to see me at such short notice.'

'Happy to help,' said Mayo. 'Is there a new lead? I'm assuming you're here about Marianne's murder, if you're from Culver Valley CID.'

'You've spoken to my colleagues, then? DS Kombothekra?' Simon still hadn't made contact with his team, still hadn't responded to any of the dozens of messages they kept leaving for him.

'Name doesn't ring a bell, and I think it probably would.' Mayo smiled. 'Someone phoned me yesterday evening – sounded young enough to be my daughter. And a lad with a big, round baby face was here this morning from Cambridge Police, spoke to me and the reception staff. Both experiences made me feel very old, and I didn't appreciate the déjà vu. Because of 2012,' he added, in case Simon didn't get it. 'It was uncanny, talking to them. Felt as if I was pulling out an old play script and reciting the same lines as eleven years ago: I was with a client, here, nowhere near Sleatham St Andrew.'

Which is why you got delegated to Cambridge Police. Simon could see the logic: Sam, Sellers and Gibbs would all be thinking of Mayo as having been conclusively eliminated. Still, one of them would probably come and talk to him tomorrow, given that Marianne had briefly accused him eleven years ago before taking it back, and Simon was glad to be getting in first. Beating them to the solve would be . . .

He found he couldn't feel the uncomplicated relish he was aiming for. Dooper was the one he wanted to crush with a resounding victory, not his team. He hated knowing he couldn't help them without adding another solve to the list of cases she was so proud of, those successfully closed since she took over; none of which she'd had any direct hand in, of course.

'Have a seat,' said Mayo. 'Can I make you tea, or coffee?' He gestured towards the small navy-blue kettle on his desk.

Simon wasn't thrilled by the prospect of holding either of the two mugs sitting beside it. One had a slogan – 'As I Suspected, I Was Right About Everything' – and the other, a soppy picture of two green elephants linking trunks and stretching out their front legs towards each other. 'Ordinary tea, milk, no sugar,' he said. 'Thanks. How are you bearing up?'

'Marianne?' said Mayo. 'Shocked but also okay. She meant a lot to me once, but . . . not any more. Not for a long time. My only concern is for Jemma, Marianne's stepdaughter. That's why I was keen to see you today. Neither of the other two, the young ones, could tell me anything about how she is and she's not answering my calls or texts.'

'I doubt she'll have her phone on her today – we'll have taken it.'

'That's a good point.'

'I can't tell you how Jemma's doing, I'm afraid,' Simon said. 'Haven't spoken to her since before she knew about the murder.'

Stupid. Now Mayo was bound to ask him why he'd had cause to speak to her before that.

Thankfully, he didn't. He said, 'Jemma and I used to be . . .'

Did he want Simon to finish the sentence for him? Or to say or do something else? His eyes were searching, questioning, even though he hadn't asked anything. 'She means a lot to me,' he said eventually, and though the words meant something different, what Simon heard was a plea for him to do something, anything, to put Mayo out of his misery. This was not a happy man, he thought.

'Tell me about Marianne Upton meaning a lot to you,' Simon said as Mayo started to make their cups of tea.

'When I first met her, I thought – incorrectly – that I'd give anything to have a mum like her. Mine had no interest in children or family life. And she'd died by the time Jemma and I met. My dad tolerates me at Christmas and buys me the odd lunch, and that's about it. He only really seeks me out when he wants to criticise me. He didn't want me to join the fire service – very opposed to that, he was. Then, not too long afterwards, he didn't want me to *leave* the fire service and pursue psychotherapy.' Mayo shrugs, as if still puzzled by the contradiction. 'But the main thing he didn't want me to do was expect him to be a proper father. And Marianne was the opposite of all that. In every way. *All* she wanted was a happy family. I don't think I realised how much I wanted that too until I met her. I'd never known anyone before who . . . had it as an ambition in that way.'

'She didn't think she already had a happy family?' Simon asked. 'Husband and stepdaughter?'

Mayo's expression darkened. 'Gareth was as devoted as she wanted him, but she couldn't accept Jemma as she was. Jemma's always had a mind of her own. Look, I need to make it clear: Marianne was a dangerous person. Definitely borderline. Some kind of Axis II personality disorder. I'm trying to explain why I didn't see it straight away, that's all. She had something I wanted: a . . . a shared priority. A yearning in common, I suppose you'd call it. So . . . I didn't spot the danger she presented for a very long time.'

Presumably because he wasn't a therapist when he was initially impressed by her, Simon thought. He suspected not many firemen went round diagnosing people with Axis II personality disorders, whatever they were.

'I've looked at the files from 2012,' he said. 'You and Jemma Stelling split up in 2006, yet you were in touch with Marianne after that, visiting her regularly immediately before the attempt on her life in November 2012.'

'That's right.' Mayo handed Simon the slogan mug. It was better than the amorous elephants, Simon supposed, though not by much.

'That's unusual, isn't it? Keeping in touch with your ex's mother?'

'Very,' Mayo agreed. 'Unusual, inadvisable . . . Perhaps just plain wrong.' He sighed. 'I couldn't see it at the time. I thought Marianne and I were . . . friends. Confidantes, really, more than friends. Before you ask, there was nothing romantic or sexual between us, ever, though we both understood without having to say so that nobody could know about our . . . meetings. No one at Devey House,' he clarified. 'Jemma didn't know. Marianne didn't tell anyone, I don't think. Not even Gareth, who would never have gone against her on anything, or expressed disapproval. Oh!'

Mayo winced, then tried to hide it by raising his mug to his face. 'I told my dad, in a futile attempt to bond with him. Desperate stuff! Didn't work. He just sneered and lectured: business as usual for him, showering me with his disapproval. There was nothing to disapprove of at that point, though, apart from the secrecy. Marianne and I just met and talked. That was it, all we ever did: long conversations about things that mattered deeply to both of us. It's thanks to those chats we had that I decided to train as a therapist, so I have Marianne to thank for that at least. It sounds pathetic, but she was the closest thing I could get to being close to Jemma, which is all I really wanted. I've never stopped wanting it.' He made this last part sound like a challenge, as if he was daring Simon to object to it.

'Even though you broke up in 2006,' said Simon, matter-of-factly.

'Correct.' Mayo looked as if he was struggling to maintain his composure. His Adam's apple moved up and down. *Come on, mate, how bad can it still hurt, seventeen years later?* Would Simon still be ranting about Dooper destroying everything that mattered to him seventeen years from now? Christ, he hoped not.

'You said there was nothing to disapprove of "at that point". When was there something to disapprove of?' he asked. 'Later?'

Bullseye. Mayo looked scared. He'd revealed more than he'd intended to.

'What did you and Marianne get up to later that you don't want to tell me about?'

'Nothing,' said Mayo. 'I didn't mean to imply what that sounded like.'

'These deep chats you and Marianne had: they all happened in her study, didn't they?'

A nod of confirmation from Mayo. He was holding his mug in front of his face, perhaps trying to hide behind it.

'Her locked room,' said Simon.

'Yes.'

'How come you were allowed in and her family weren't?'

'She trusted me,' said Mayo. 'There was . . . some personal stuff in there.'

'Such as?'

'Family photos, that kind of thing.'

Simon's impatience must have been visible, because Mayo started to apologise and say how difficult this all was.

'Why would anyone want to keep family photographs secret from their family?' Simon spoke over him. 'Presumably

Jemma Stelling and Gareth Upton were both in some of these photos.'

Mayo nodded. 'They were in nearly all of them. And Lottie. Look, I'm sorry I'm not able to help you—'

'I think you're very able, and I know you're lying,' Simon told him. 'The good news is, you don't need to. I'm not here officially, as a DC working the case. Either case: Marianne's murder yesterday, or the attempt on her life in 2012. There's a strong chance I won't share what you tell me today with anyone, no matter how incriminating it is – especially if you stop bullshitting me and tell me what you know.'

This produced a suitably puzzled expression from Mayo. *Good. Give the shrink something to shrink about.* 'You have a once-in-a-lifetime chance, Dr Mayo, to—'

'It's Mister. Therapists aren't generally Doctor.'

'. . . tell me the truth and get it off your chest, consequence free. Did you kill Marianne Upton? Did you try to in 2012?'

'No. I was with a client, as I've already—'

'Why didn't you and Marianne continue your secret trysts after she survived the attack in November 2012?' Simon asked.

'They weren't trysts.' Mayo's voice had a tremor in it. 'Look, if you must know, we'd been in touch again more recently. No contact at all from around . . . December 2012 until last year and then when we resumed, it was only by text. Exchanging Wordle scores, mainly. Not much else. She didn't invite me to the house again, thank God.'

'Who initiated the texting last year, you or her?' said Simon.

'She did. I didn't want to, but—'

'Then why did you?'

Mayo pressed his eyes shut, then opened them again. 'I swore to myself, if she started angling in for any kind of in-person meeting . . . But she didn't.'

'So you carried on sending her your Wordle score?'

Mayo nodded.

'Mr Mayo, your story makes as little sense as any story would if half of it was left out. By last year, you'd decided Marianne Upton was dangerous, yes?'

After a fleeting look of panic, Mayo gave a small nod of confirmation.

'You must have been afraid of her,' said Simon. 'Or of what she could do to you, maybe. She wanted to swap Wordle scores . . . Was it every day?'

'Most days, yes.'

'And you didn't want to, clearly, but you did,' said Simon. 'What were you frightened she'd do to you, if you didn't go along with it?'

No response.

'Do you know who tried to kill Marianne in 2012, or who stabbed her to death yesterday, if it really wasn't you?'

'No.'

'Could Jemma have done it, do you think?'

'Absolutely not.'

Was he really as convinced as he sounded? 'Can I have the names of the two therapy patients?' Simon asked him. 'The ones who can vouch for where you were – November 2012 and yesterday?'

'I've already told—'

'You haven't told me. And I'm the one asking, aren't I?'

'But . . . you said you weren't here in your professional capacity. In which case, I don't understand why you're here at all.'

'Well, I'm happy to tell you the whole sorry tale if you're

willing to reciprocate,' said Simon. 'The full truth. Everything you know.'

Mayo glared at him, his eyes still full of questions, but now there were accusations there too. How unreasonable, for a detective to come and mess with the head of the good, kind therapist when all he was doing was obstructing the solving of two unsolved murder cases.

'Farida Suleyman,' said Mayo. 'She's the client I was with last night from five o'clock until nearly six. And the night Marianne was attacked in 2012, I was with Belynda Simmonds. That's Simmonds with a D, Belynda with a Y. She's not my client any more – lives in Pembrokeshire now. I was with Belynda here, in this room, when Marianne was nearly killed eleven years ago. Nowhere near Sleatham St Andrew. I'd been Belynda's therapist for fourteen months by then, too.'

'How's that relevant?' Simon asked him.

'It meant the police couldn't suspect me of conveniently producing a new client who'd act as my alibi.'

'How about Farida Suleyman? How long has she been a client?'

'Six weeks, give or take.'

'I see,' Simon said as portentously as he could, but Mayo didn't look fazed. Was he keener to prove he couldn't have done it in 2012 than yesterday? 'What about the story swap idea, then?' he asked Mayo. 'Are you ready to tell me the truth?'

He wasn't expecting an answer and was surprised when one came back instantly. 'No,' Mayo said. 'I'm sorry. Everything I can tell you, I've told you already – though I'm willing to admit, only because you're saying it's off the record, and for some reason I believe you . . .'

That wasn't quite what Simon had said. Still, it looked as if the misunderstanding was about to work in his favour.

'There's more that I haven't told you.' Mayo sighed. 'A lot more – and it in no way incriminates Jemma. In spite of that, I'm afraid you're never going to hear it from me. I'm sorry.'

'How could you believe even for a second that I was sleeping with Marianne?' Olly is crying now, and it feels so wrong. Surely other people should cry in his therapy room, not him. 'How could you think of that possibility and not know straight away that it couldn't be true?'

He seems genuine, but then talented liars always do. I want to believe him more than I've ever wanted anything.

'Jemma, I swear on your life and mine, on the lives of everyone I care about: there has never been anything of that kind between Marianne and me. She was in her fifties when I first met her. I was twenty-two.'

As if that means anything, or rules anything out. 'She's Marianne Upton. She always gets what she wants,' I say.

'Maybe she does and maybe she doesn't,' Olly says pointedly.

'What's that supposed to mean?' Tired of standing up, I walk back to the chair opposite his desk and sit down. 'Are you saying she tried to get you into bed, and you rejected her advances?'

'God, no.' He winces. 'Jemm, you don't know her at all if you think she'd do that.'

'Oh, don't I? I don't know the woman who sent me to bed without any dinner one night when Dad was away for work because she'd found me crying on Mother's Day because my mother was dead? And then the next day, when Dad got back, she told him all about *her* sadness, *her* "ache of betrayal", she called it – how awful it had been for *her*? And *I* was the one encouraged by Dad to be more sensitive and considerate in future?'

'God, she treated you appallingly.' Olly looks aghast.

If you know that, and you love me, then why all the secret meetings with her? 'Treats,' I mutter. 'Present tense.'

'I just meant . . . Marianne has never shown any romantic or physical interest in me and nor would she.'

'Then what?' I snap at him. 'What was it, if not an affair?'

He looks away.

'Okay, let's try a new one: you say you haven't seen her since late 2012. That was when someone tried to kill her. November 2012. Was that someone you? Was that why the two of you didn't keep in touch? Fair enough: seems like the kind of thing that'd put an abrupt end to a relationship, but—'

'Jemma, there are things I can't—'

'But wait, you had an alibi, didn't you? The police were satisfied, so you were in the clear. Who, though, if not you? Paddy and I were together, so I know he didn't do it. Dad was away in London for work. Marianne doesn't have any friends, doesn't really deign to speak to anyone in the village. So . . . I wondered if maybe there was another Oliver, one Marianne might describe as "hers"? Oh – you probably don't know about that, the way she tried to say "*My* Oliver".'

'The police told me at the time,' he says.

'Oh, my God. You know what she meant, don't you?

Or *who* she meant. I can see it on your face. Don't you?'
I yell at him.

'I . . . I think so, yes.' His eyes dart around the room.
Scanning for possible escape routes, maybe.

I want to run at him, grab him, shake the truth out of
his mouth. 'Olly, did Marianne have a different bit on the
side, also called Oliver?'

'No. She'd never have been unfaithful to your dad.'

I laugh. 'And you know this how?'

'She cares about family more than anything else. You
must know that. That's why she hated the words "stepmother" and "stepdaughter". She wanted it all to be . . .
you know.'

'No, I don't. Tell me.'

'Proper,' says Olly. 'Perfect. She loves you, Jemma, believe
it or not.' He holds up a hand, seeing my mouth open in
protest. '*And* she's wrong to think that accurately describing
the relationship – step-parent and stepchild – would make
anything less proper or perfect, and she was breathtakingly
stupid to have tried to grab the "mother" label from the
second she met you, when your mum had just died. *And*
her love for you in no way excuses her appalling treatment
of people.'

'Did she treat you appallingly too?' I ask him. That was
how it had sounded, as if that's what he meant.

'There are things I'm never going to be able to talk
about,' he says in a tight voice. 'I have to be upfront about
that. I'm very sorry I can't tell you everything, Jemma, but
I can't.'

Impossible. He's seriously sitting there saying that he
plans to leave me in the dark.

'Could the other Oliver tell me?' I'm desperate enough

to throw out a wild guess. 'The one with the curly grey hair and the beard that's sort of half-blond and half-ginger? Sturdy build, late fifties? Well, he'd be older now. That was how he looked more than a decade ago.'

The flinch is unmistakable. 'Wh-what?' Olly manages to say.

'You know who I mean, then. Good.' *Please let this work. Let it lead somewhere.* 'Thanks for making it so obvious. Why don't you tell me who he is, the man I've just described?'

19

CHARLIE

'I could be deferential and beat around the bush, or I could just come out and ask for what I want,' Charlie told Superintendent Fran Whittingham.

'So which is it going to be?' Whittingham asked. There was little expression in the voice or on the face. She might have been curious to know what was coming next, or she might have been containing a yawn in her pouchy gerbil cheeks, entirely uninterested in Charlie's thoughts. Her delivery was as grey as the decor in her newly refurbished office, every inch of which screamed, 'I am the work of an interior designer whose idea of taste comes from a magazine in a dentist's waiting room'.

To be fair, there were some touches of other colours in the room too: black and white, if they counted, and a lot of silver that was no doubt meant to add luxury and sparkle – the frame of the large mirror on one wall, the shiny candle holder on the edge of the desk, labelled 'Jasmine', from which a pristine, fat, cream-coloured candle protruded.

Sadly, no sort of shine stood a chance in here; the lustre-extinguishing atmosphere was all-pervasive. The monotonous sound of the super's voice was enough to hurry anyone to the depressing conclusion that silver was no more than grey with fraudulent inclinations. The row of three windows, overlooking leafy Blantyre Park and the lido, only made you feel worse about being in here instead of out there.

As if the presence of a smelly candle on the desk wasn't bad enough (no police superintendent's office should be artificially scented, and anyone who would respond to that statement with a 'Why not?' didn't deserve an answer), there was a framed wedding photograph by its side that Charlie couldn't help viewing as unbearable provocation. *Pretend it's not there*, she told herself, resolving not to look at it again, but the temptation was too strong. The bride in the picture was Fran Whittingham as a much younger gerbil, and the groom was a fair-haired man in a pale grey suit who had a slightly unnatural, bolted-together look about him. Both he and the super appeared to be not just laughing but cackling like nutters, and were bent towards each other at awkward angles, clutching their stomachs, as if they'd recently been poisoned in a way they found especially hilarious.

The picture was bad enough, but far worse was the implausible caption attached to the photo's mount at the bottom, inside the frame. Printed in cursive letters were the words:

Hands down the most magical day of my life. Fran looked like a princess from a dream — Lloyd Whittingham

Charlie was fighting an almost overpowering urge to ask questions about the framed abomination. Was it some kind of test? Did you never get promoted if you failed to spot that it was a joke? Or did the super really decide the photo would be improved by a quote from her husband, about her and their special day?

'Well?' said the super, expressionlessly.

Charlie dragged her eyes away from the picture. Might as

well be direct, she decided. 'I'm not trying to mess you around, but I can't say yes or no to the CID job offer until I know what's happening with Simon,' she said. 'Are you planning to fire him?'

'Sergeant Zailer—'

'Because there's no doubt in my mind that I'd be happier doing detective work. In almost every way, it's a move I'd love to make. Problem is . . . I can't accept a promotion from someone who's about to fire my husband. And since I know you'll have noticed that he's currently doing his best to get himself kicked out of the job . . .' Charlie shrugged. 'Frankly, I won't blame you if you're considering him for the chop, but I'm here to say: please, please don't do it. If you can promise me you won't fire him or . . . go after him in any disciplinary way – if you can just, like, leave him to come round in his own time and not make a fuss if he's a bit strange in the interim—'

'Then what?' Fran Whittingham asked. 'What are you offering me, Sergeant, if I agree to ignore the basic standards of professional behaviour and the responsibilities of my position?'

That didn't sound promising, though the super's delivery, as always, was as bland as that of a saleswoman showing prospective buyers around a show home.

'I'm offering: me taking the job and sorting Simon out,' said Charlie. 'That'll give you everything you want: Simon back on form and working well, me in charge, keeping everything under control. That must be what you want, or you wouldn't have offered me the job.'

'Do you know where DC Waterhouse is at the moment?' the super asked.

'No.'

'Neither does anyone on his team. He isn't responding to anyone's attempts to contact him.'

'Oh – yes, he has.' Charlie was pleased to be able to share good news. 'For a while he didn't, that's true, but I spoke to Sam just now. He saw Simon this morning, brought him up to speed.'

'After a day of his being inexplicably missing, and after he encouraged a young woman to kill her stepmother the previous evening – a stepmother who, as it turned out, had recently been stabbed to death in her garden.'

How the fuck did she know Simon had told Jemma to do it? Sam would never have told her that.

'I'll be honest, Sergeant. I'm disappointed by your request. You must know that you don't get to come in here and offer me a deal. That isn't how this organisation works.'

'Yeah, I know,' said Charlie wearily.

'I'm sure you also know that your husband has been uncontrollable and unaccountable since the day he first set foot in this building.'

How do you know? You weren't here then. You've only just gerbilled your way in.

'For some reason, no one before me has felt inclined to tackle the problem,' Whittingham said. 'I'm not sure why. Nobody seems able to explain it to me.'

'So you are planning to fire Simon.' Charlie felt something as heavy as a rock inside her, slowly sinking.

'I'm not discussing my plans with you, Sergeant Zailer. And, though I'm sorry to have to say this, please consider the offer of the DS position withdrawn. I've been scrupulously fair with you – I didn't want to tar you with any brushes just because you're his wife—'

'Who the fuck do you think you are?' The words were out of Charlie's mouth before she could stop them. 'To be clear,' she went on smoothly, 'I know you're the new super, but you don't get to talk about Simon as if everyone agrees he's a piece of shit. I don't agree, because he isn't. Lots of people here know he's irreplaceable, even if you don't.'

'Nobody is irreplaceable.' The pouchy cheeks just couldn't wait to squeeze out that time-worn platitude.

'Yes, they are,' said Charlie. 'You're not, but lots of other people are – people like Simon who think for themselves. Don't all the cases he's closed pretty much singlehandedly count for anything? His one hundred per cent success rate?'

'He's undoubtedly talented, yes,' said the super. 'The problem I have is that other things matter too.'

'If you fire Simon, or he goes, I'm going too,' Charlie told her.

'Of course.' Whittingham smiled. 'I completely understand. You must do what's best for you.'

'Maybe I'll go and be the new CEO of Dickhead Quotes on Wedding Pictures. How about that?' Charlie pointed to the framed photograph.

That got a reaction. Pink blotches appeared at the top of the super's neck.

' "A princess from a dream", really?' Charlie couldn't stop herself. 'That a typo? Was it meant to say, "Fran looked like an abscess from a nightmare"?' *Juvenile.* She needed something sharper, that would go in deeper. 'I'll tell you one thing,' she said. 'There's no way he still loves you as much as he did then. He's known you too long, and you're awful, aren't you? He must have noticed by now.'

The expression on the super's face wasn't one Charlie could stand to look at for more than a fraction of a second. No need to ask herself if she'd gone too far.

She left the room as quickly as she could, slamming the door behind her.

'I don't know what you're talking about,' Olly says. 'I don't know any man with grey hair and a ginger beard . . . I don't know the person you're describing.'

'You're lying.' I lean forward in my chair. 'Thought you weren't going to do that any more. It's okay. I keep lying to you too: you're fair game, aren't you?'

'What have you lied about?' He doesn't like the sound of this at all. Good. Serves him right.

'This isn't the first time I've booked to see you under a false name,' I tell him. 'Do you remember a missed appointment two weeks ago – new client? Cindy Riley?'

'That was you?'

'I was going to be Cindy Reller.' I smile. 'As in Cinderella, she of the Wicked Stepmother. Then I decided that sounded too made-up. I did turn up for the appointment, by the way. Got as far as walking up to the building, but then something happened that threw me and made me think I wasn't ready to talk to you after all. I had to go home and think it through.'

Olly's eyes flit around the room; he's trying to piece it together.

'Ask me what happened to throw me off course,' I say. 'I know you're wondering. Shall I tell you? That man happened. Same one I've just described: I saw him here, two weeks ago. I was about to open the front door and walk in when he came striding out. He didn't recognise me, I don't think, but I knew him instantly. I'd only seen him once before, but it was a memorable once because of the circumstances. It was definitely the same man, though he was quite a bit older.'

'Where had you seen him before?' asks Olly. 'And when? "More than ten years ago", you said.'

'Who is he, Olly? You recognised him instantly from my description. I saw it in your face.'

'Where did you see him, the first time?'

If I tell him, will he then answer my questions? Probably not, but if I don't try . . . 'Walking through the grounds at Dad and Marianne's,' I say. 'Looked as if he was coming from the house, heading for the road. It was late afternoon and pretty dark already, and it certainly wasn't more than a year after you and I broke up. Funny thing is . . .'

I can hear Olly's breathing from across the room. He's impatient to know what's coming next.

'I got back two hours earlier than I'd told Marianne I'd be back. Dad was out. She does like her secret meetings when she thinks she's got the house to herself, doesn't she? First you, now this mysterious man. Mysterious to me, that is – you're not mystified, because you know his name and you know what he was doing there that day. Don't you? And now you're going to tell me.'

I adjust my position, hoping to make it clear that I'm settling in, staying right here in this chair until I get the answers I came for. 'Marianne lied when I asked her. Said he was a landscape gardener, there to give a quote for some work that never happened – what a surprise. I believed her, though, until I saw the same man walk out of this building two weeks ago.'

Olly is staring down at his desk.

'Who is he, Olly? Whatever the secret is that you and Marianne are keeping, he's involved, isn't he?' I wait a few more silent seconds, then say, 'I think his first name is Oliver. I think he might be the person who cut Marianne's throat in 2012 and left her for dead.'

'He isn't.' Olly sounds angry. 'Jemma, I'm begging you to drop this. Do you think I don't want to tell you?' His voice cracks. 'I'd love nothing more, but I can't. Look, Marianne's alive, isn't she? The person who tried to kill her failed. They won't try again: that I can promise you.'

'You promised not to lie to me any more,' I remind him.

'And I'm not. Keeping a secret is different from telling a lie. The man you saw . . . his name isn't Oliver. His name is Mark.'

This sounds so familiar. *Mark. Mark* . . .

'His middle name's more unusual,' says Olly. 'Rowan.'

Mark Rowan . . .

A shiver passes through me. Oh, my God . . .

'I can see you don't need me to provide a surname,' Olly says. 'You remember.'

I do. And I understand even less than I did before.

20

SIMON

'So you're saying me and Jemma could be done for conspiracy to commit murder and . . . whatever the other thing was you said?'

'Soliciting to murder. Yes,' said Simon.

'Even though we never did anything?'

Tom Tulloch looked as alarmed as he deserved to be, Simon thought. The two of them were at Tulloch's brother's house in Little Holling, in a grim sitting room with a gas fire turned up too high and windows that looked as if no one had opened them for years.

The brother, Lucas, had gone out and left them to it.

'That's right.' Simon wished he'd brought a handkerchief to mop up the beads of sweat forming on his brow. 'You made a plan together, to kill someone. Legally, I'm afraid that counts as doing something.'

'But Jemma changed her mind, right? You said she came clean. So what's the problem?'

'One problem is that Marianne Upton ended up dead, murdered in the very particular way that your and Jemma's plan specified, so . . . Put yourself in the shoes of a jury – all twenty-four of them.'

'Only twelve on a jury, mate. Dunno what films you've been watching.'

'Twelve people. Twenty-four shoes,' Simon said.

'Oh, right. Fair.' Tulloch put down the beer he'd been holding and grabbed his long, wiry beard with both hands as if it were an instrument he was about to play. 'You said the Domino's driver told your sergeant I was here when I said I was, yeah? On Monday?'

'He did. That doesn't change the fact that you were involved in making a murder plan that came to fruition.' How much, Simon wondered, would that driver have wanted in exchange for lying? Probably not a lot. And if Tulloch hadn't done it, then who? According to Sam, they were all on the couldn't-have-done-it list: Jemma and her husband and daughter, Marianne's husband, Oliver Mayo, Jemma's best friend Suzanne Lacy . . .

Tulloch said, 'Look, I'll be honest with you: I'd already decided I wasn't going to do it – for other reasons, nothing to do with it being a crime.'

'Yeah. Wouldn't want to let a trivial detail like that stop you,' said Simon.

'I'd started to think it wasn't worth it. I don't mean financially – the money was generous, but I stopped believing it'd get our friendship back to where it had been. I'm not sure Jemma's a very forgiving person, and Paddy's neither here nor there. She makes all the decisions. And I mean, I'd passed the test, hadn't I?' Tulloch sounded almost offended. 'Said I'd do it, ready to put my neck on the line. But there was still nothing said about whether I ought to move in with them for a bit, just while I got myself sorted. No one told me I wouldn't have to live in this dive any more.'

'So if Jemma had given you the green light, you'd have told

her you'd changed your mind?' Simon asked. 'Even though she'd already paid you part of the money? That's what you told DS Kombothekra, right?'

'Dunno. I don't think she'd have made me give it back,' Tulloch mused. 'She's loaded, Jemma. The kind of loaded that means you don't really keep track of money – where it's gone, if it's coming back.'

'Must be nice to live like that,' said Simon.

Tulloch snorted. 'Why'd you think I was so keen to move back in with them? It's nice having rich friends, that's for sure. All kinds of perks. Don't know why Paddy bothers with the crappy bar jobs. He could live off Jemma for ever if he wanted to.'

'Any idea who might have killed Marianne?' Simon asked. Disappointingly, his instincts were telling him the amoral gnome in front of him wasn't the stabber he was looking for.

'Jemma's the only person I know who wanted her dead,' said Tulloch. 'Look, if I help you out, can you make this conspiracy to murder thing go away?'

Simon couldn't, but didn't say so. 'How can you help me out?'

'Wait there.'

Tulloch left the room, not shutting the door behind him. Immediately, the heat was less intense as cooler air from the hall entered the room. Simon took the opportunity to reach over and turn off the gas fire. A whirring whine came from above his head. A printer? Was the gnome printing something out upstairs?

After a few minutes, Tulloch returned with some papers he'd rolled into a tube shape. Simon nearly retched when Tulloch tossed them into his lap and he saw they were being held in place by a black elastic hair bobble that still had quite a lot of hair attached to it: dyed red, dark brown at the root.

'Take them out of that . . . thing,' he said, pushing them off his knees and onto the carpet. 'What are they, anyway?'

'Lots of diary entries, written by Jemma – though I've got my theories about the typed ones, as you'll see if you read the emails I've printed out for you.' Tulloch's stubby fingers pulled at the hairband. 'The handwritten ones with the messy edges are from Jemma's 2006 diary, and the rest, the typed ones, are from between July just gone and about two weeks ago. Meant to be from a diary file on Jemma's laptop. Marianne sent me them as attachments. They're all dated.'

'*Marianne* emailed them to you?' Simon straightened in his chair. 'How did she get your contact details?'

'She'd been in Jemma's laptop, hadn't she? Snooping around.'

'When did this happen? When did she first contact you?'

'Can't remember,' said Tulloch. 'Everything's dated though. You just need to read it all yourself.'

'Oh, I will,' Simon assured him. 'I want to hear it from you too, though. In your own words.'

Tulloch sighed at the imposition. 'Marianne got in touch, asked if we could meet. I was shitting it: thought she must have found out what Jemma had asked me to do, you know? Well, I knew she had, 'cause she told me. Said if I told Jemma she'd contacted me, I'd regret it for the rest of my very short life.'

'Death threat?' said Simon.

Tulloch nodded. 'Sounded like she meant it too. So I kept my mouth shut, went to meet her, and afterwards she sent me those.' He nodded down at the papers. 'All the diary bits are on the same theme: how much Jemma hates Marianne. They're really bitter and horrible. Reading them did make me wonder . . .'

'If you'd picked the wrong side?'

'Kind of, yeah,' said Tulloch. 'I mean, obviously Marianne only sent me the worst bits, given what she wanted me to do.'

'Which was?'

'Kill Jemma.' This was said matter-of-factly. 'She knew about Jemma's plan – found the diary file on her laptop and read the whole thing. Told me she'd suspected for ages that something wasn't right, so she'd got into Jemma's computer and had a bit of a shufti. Didn't like what she found, so offered to pay me twice as much.'

'To kill Jemma?' Simon thought it was worth checking.

Tulloch nodded.

'When and where was this meeting?'

'Early September, in London. She invited me to lunch. Restaurant called Gymkhana in Mayfair. She paid, obviously. Way beyond my means. Paid for my train and taxis too. Crazy woman made me eat goat brains.' Tulloch chuckled. 'Side dish: goat brains, I kid you not – haha, pun intended. She promised me I'd love it if I could get past my squeamishness, and she was right. Delicious.' He patted his belly.

Simon felt nauseous.

'You know, I think that's how I knew Jemma wasn't really serious about going through with it.' Tulloch tilted his head to one side and his beard moved with it like a solid piece of wire sculpture. 'I sat there listening to Marianne, thinking, "This is someone who *really* wants her enemy taken out." She wouldn't take no for an answer at first. I had to get a bit firm with her or she'd never have left me alone. I'll be honest with you: I've not slept nearly as well since, but I will now. Now I know she's dead,' Tulloch clarified, apparently unaware of what he'd revealed.

'And you still didn't tell Jemma,' Simon said pointedly. 'You didn't warn her or go to the police?'

'No way.' Tulloch reached over and turned the gas fire back on. 'Like I said, I wasn't keen on the prospect of killing anyone.

223

I didn't want Jemma deciding we'd better strike first, before Marianne had a chance – which I was pretty sure Marianne wouldn't do, by the way.'

Spoken like a seasoned analyst of criminogenic risk factors, thought Simon.

'She'd have known if anything happened to Jemma, I'd be in a position to tell the police everything. No way she'd take the chance.'

'She could have paid a third party to remove the problem of both you and Jemma,' Simon suggested.

'Could have, I guess.' Tulloch scratched the side of his face. 'I never thought of that possibility.' Helpfully, he reminded Simon once again that what he'd lacked in opportunity, he made up for in motive. 'Luckily, I don't have to worry about it now, do I?' he said. 'Now Marianne's dead, I mean.'

Simon pulled over as soon as he'd turned a corner and was sure he couldn't be seen from the too-hot lounge he'd just escaped from. He picked up the papers from the passenger seat next to him and started to leaf through them. As promised by Tulloch, there were handwritten diary entries and typed ones. His eye landed on an email from Marianne, which seemed as good a place as any to start.

From: Marianne.Upton1955@gmail.com
To: TomJBTulloch@yahoo.co.uk
12 September 2023

Dear Tom,

In the hope that it might persuade you, I'd like you to read the attached extract, dated 7 July this year, from the diary I found on Jemma's laptop computer, which I only went searching for once I'd decided that she and her privacy deserved as little respect as she has shown for me and mine. I told you when we met about her approaches to Norman Pelphrey and others. In this diary entry, she refers to that unsavoury episode as if she were the victim of it and I the evil, entrapping monster. I hope you'll be able to see that, given what she has done already and her grotesque plan to eliminate me, this mealy-mouthed offering is the writing of a manipulative, narcissistic snake. You cannot imagine how painful it is for me to write those words about my own daughter.

I beg you, Tom – think about everything I've told you. Read again, more than once if you have to, the diary pages I've posted to you from 2006. Also read the entries I emailed you yesterday (they're not dull, I promise. They include Jemma's plan to murder me, using you as a weapon). Read it all, and try to imagine even a fraction of the misery I've experienced. I think you'll change your mind. I profoundly hope that you will.

Warmest best wishes,

Marianne

Simon turned to the piece of paper beneath: another email from Marianne to Tom, sent after he'd failed to reply to her first.

From: Marianne.Upton1955@gmail.com
To: TomJBTulloch@yahoo.co.uk
13 September 2023

Well? If £10,000 isn't enough to tempt you, I'm willing to double it. £20,000. That's my final offer.

M x

Tulloch had taken eight days to reply to this one. Simon wondered if that was because he'd been too tempted by the money to shut down the possibility with a swift 'No'. He'd said no eventually, however, and deprived himself of twenty thousand pounds by doing so:

From: TomJBTulloch@yahoo.co.uk
To: Marianne.Upton1955@gmail.com
21 September 2023

Dear Marianne,

Jemma's not your daughter, she's your stepdaughter. Please don't write to me again. I've said no already and I won't change my mind. You must think I'm stupid. Jemma obviously didn't write this diary entry you say you found on her laptop. The dates are written differently for a start. In all of them, the month comes first, in capitals, then we have the day – just the number – then a comma and then the year. In the handwritten diary pages from 2006, the dates are in a different format: first the number of the day with 'st' or 'nd' after it (as in 1st, 2nd, etc.), then the month and year with no commas anywhere.

Also, in the handwritten ones from 2006, the first line of each entry is indented, but in the typed 2023 ones, everything is left-justified. Then there's the fact that no one writes a diary on their computer. It just doesn't happen. And Ollie's name is spelled wrong in the laptop diary. Remember, I've known Jemma since school. I dug out a couple of emails from her from 2005 where's she's raving about her amazing new boyfriend: Ollie with an 'ie'. Did she forget how to spell his name between then and this year? Unlikely. We both know how important he was to her. It's pathetic, frankly, that you'd stoop so low as to impersonate her and write all this weird shit just to try and make her seem scarier than she is and manipulate me into doing your bidding.

She hasn't been in touch with me for weeks, anyway, and I predict she won't be. Even if she did get in touch, I'd steer clear. This whole thing's too messy and complicated for me, so I'm out, and I won't be replying to any more emails from you.

Cheers.

Tom

Simon moved the email to the back of the pile. He needed to see this famous diary on Jemma Stelling's laptop with his own eyes. She'd been keeping one – that wasn't in doubt. Since July, wasn't it? So Tulloch was wrong to say that no one writes a diary on their computer, but were these printed pages Simon was looking at now genuine extracts from that diary, or fakes created by Marianne?

There was only one way to find out.

10th July 2006

Had a bit of a revelation this morning. Instead of pretending Paddy is a hundred per cent the one I want, as I've been doing so far, what if I decide instead to start believing that's the actual truth? Less than ten seconds after putting this hypothetical proposition to myself, I had a massive 'eureka' moment. Two important things occurred to me, one after the other. The first was to do with driving and speed cameras, and the second was going to the doctor.

Someone once told me (I've no idea if it's true) that there's a machine you can buy and put in your car that tells you when speed cameras are coming up. This enables you to slow down to whatever the speed limit is before you get snapped going too fast by the camera. The fact that such machines exist tells us something: that there are lots of people out there who want to avoid getting fines and points for speeding, but who haven't considered the obvious, brilliant solution of . . . just not speeding! The customers of the company that makes those machines are asking themselves, 'How can I carry on speeding but not get in trouble for it?' And maybe this clever machine can make that work pretty well for you most of the time, but would anything work quite as well as deciding never to drive above the speed limit again, and then sticking to that decision? I doubt it.

It's the same as going to the doctor for a health check-up. How often have you heard people say, 'I'm not eating chocolate/cakes/ smoking cigarettes at the moment – I've got a doctor's appointment next week for a health check-up and I want my weight/blood sugar/ blood pressure/cholesterol to be down, not up, so that I get praised instead of ticked off by the doctor'? And what do those who say that, or think that, secretly plan to do, immediately after the doctor praises them for their efforts and great results? They're obviously going to be straight back on the burgers, booze and fags, aren't they? Feeling all smug about the pat on the back they've just earned, they trot off to carry on with their usual hedonistic, health-disregarding habits until they're summoned for their next health check-up – but they'll worry about that then.

Instead, they could give up fried, fatty foods and alcohol for ever. They could change their habits permanently, and know that from that point forward, they could get their check-up summons on any day and not worry about it. There would be no need for panicked, last-minute crash diets. They could live longer and feel the glow of true, meaningful achievement rather than a sense of 'Phew! I got away with it, and the doctor will never know I'm plan-ning to clog up my arteries again as soon as I get out of her office.'

I've just read back what I've written, and I sound like a pompous prig. I promise you, I'm not speaking from a position of superiority – I'm describing my own tendency to come up with brilliant plans that don't actually solve the problem. That's what I do – it's what we all do - when there's a massive advantage to be gained by letting the problem linger in our lives. (Eating sugary carbs is fun! Driving fast is fun! Resenting Paddy isn't fun, but continuing, secretly, to prefer Ollie definitely is, and I can't pretend I don't enjoy, on some level, having a big secret in my life. It makes everything so much more interesting.)

But what if both are possible? What if I can prefer Ollie and at the same time genuinely believe Paddy wasn't the wrong choice?

What if Paddy is still, despite my preference against him, the perfect boyfriend?

This was the question I asked myself, and immediately afterwards I had this rush of 'Oh my God, it's true. It's really true.' I didn't even have to convince myself. Of course Paddy is perfect – because Ollie would have been TOO GOOD.

I need to think about this more and make sure I understand the implications, but I know I'm on to something. I can feel it.

Here's what I've realised: you can have everything you want in life, as long as you're willing, when necessary, to want the thing that's been forced on you and is beyond your control. If you can make that work, no one will ever be able to win against you.

This is everything. This is going to be my salvation.

21

Wednesday 1 November 2023, 12.30 p.m.

JEMMA

I open the front door and find DC Simon Waterhouse on the other side of it. He looks so odd, so very urban amid the greenery that surrounds him on all sides – like something that's landed in the wrong place after being blown in from a nearby, down-at heel city.

Paddy and I did the opposite of what Dad and Marianne did when they bought Devey House. Marianne fell in love with the house and grounds, and didn't much care where it was. If the location happened to be a featureless Fenland village, so be it. I love my house because it's home, and I love it even more because it's Lottie's home, and the home I share with her, but I'd be the first to admit there's nothing pretty or special about it as a building. It's a low, red-brick cheat of a bungalow with just one tiny staircase and a triangular white-painted wooden 'dormer' section sticking out at the top, boasting three horrible PVC windows that we haven't yet got round to replacing with wooden ones.

It was this location I knew I had to have as soon as I saw it, not the house. You can't see a single other building, though there are plenty in Little Holling down the road, and the view

233

of trees, fields and hills from the front door and from every window, even the ugly plastic ones, would make anyone want to drop everything and take up landscape painting. On a day like today, with bright, clear skies, it's exceptionally beautiful.

DC Waterhouse doesn't seem to have noticed. I'm not surprised. There's something intrinsically idyll-repellent about him.

'Can I come in?' he says, and I wonder why he sounds furious.

Do I have a choice? I don't think I do, so I might as well sound welcoming – as much as I can fake, anyway. 'Sure.' I stand back to let him pass.

'Are your husband and daughter in?' He stays where he is, as if he's had second thoughts about entering my home.

'No. Work and school respectively,' I say. *Thank God.* I don't want this strange man anywhere near Lottie. 'I'd normally be at work too, on a Wednesday, but they've given me compassionate leave. Ironic, some might say.'

'Where's your laptop?' he barks at me.

Shit.

'It's here, isn't it? I need it, and any passwords?'

'I—'

'DS Kombothekra says he's got all the devices belonging to your family, and they've got your phone, but no computer for you.'

'You seem agitated,' I tell him. 'Remember, you don't care if people murder their stepmothers.' I flash him my most annoying fake smile. 'You made that clear on Monday. Not that I did – kill Marianne, I mean.'

'Where's your laptop, Jemma?'

'At my work,' I lie.

'So I can collect it from there?'

'Yup. The Vanadiss School in Lower Heckencote. And also

the only school in Lower Heckencote.' I laugh nervously at my own feeble joke. 'Is that all? Because I should probably—'

'No, it's not all. Not by a long way,' says Waterhouse.

Damn. 'You'd better come in, then.' My bag, with my laptop inside it, is hanging from the newel post at the bottom of the stairs, just a few inches from where I'm standing. 'Come through,' I tell Waterhouse.

Why did he have to turn up now, when I'm finally feeling human again and breathing normally for the first time since Monday evening? I've only just managed to convince myself, with a lot of help from Suzanne, that I'm not going to end up in prison, despite the many rash, stupid things I've done. 'Send the mother of a thirteen-year-old girl to jail – a nice, upper-middle-class mum with no criminal record? No way. You're a crime *preventer*, Jemma. No, I mean it. You effectively handed yourself in *to save Marianne's life*, remember? That shows good character.'

From the expression on Waterhouse's face, I don't think he'd agree. Maybe I should ask Suzanne to speak to him on my behalf, or to DS Kombothekra.

I have to destroy my laptop before he gets his hands on it. If no detective ever reads my diary entries about the plan to kill Marianne, then they won't be able to prove any such thing ever existed. I never sent anything to Tom – we only ever discussed it in person – so I can pretend I was just desperate for attention and talking nonsense when I went to Spilling Police Station on Monday, as long as there's nothing in black and white, nothing that can be read out to a jury.

I'll be fine. We'll be fine, me and Lottie. Wasting police time is a far less serious offence than conspiracy to commit murder.

I offer Waterhouse a cup of tea and he says yes, then doesn't respond to any of the pleasantries I throw out as I make it –

just sits at the kitchen table, waiting to have my full attention.

'What do you know about the terms of Marianne's will?' he asks as I hand him his drink.

The question takes me by surprise. 'I've never thought about it. I assume everything she owns goes to Dad.'

'That wasn't always the case. Not according to DS Kombothekra. I just spoke to him before coming here.'

Well, bully for you.

'He's talked to Marianne's lawyers. Her most recent will was signed and witnessed on 13 December 2012, not much more than a month after she was attacked and left for dead on her kitchen floor. Before that, there was another will – one that left you a million and Paddy five hundred grand.'

'*What?*' My stomach lurches. 'I . . . I didn't know that. That's a lot.' I take a gulp of my tea. It's too hot and burns my mouth: a welcome distraction from the confusion.

13 December 2012 . . .

'I don't want her money,' I tell Waterhouse. 'Not a penny of it.'

'Good, because you haven't got it,' he says. 'She's left both you and Paddy nothing in her new will.'

'Suits me.'

'The timing's interesting, though, isn't it? Can't help thinking you or your husband might have known she was about to cut you both out and decided to deprive her of the chance. I'm talking about in 2012.'

'Are you asking if it was Paddy and me who tried to kill her? No, it wasn't. We were—'

'I know where you were meant to be. I also know you're a liar.'

I smile at him coldly. 'And I know you're a weirdo who helps would-be criminals commit murder and get away with it. So I guess we're even-stevens. I'd love to know, though, since we're hanging out: what changed? You didn't give a shit on Monday. Now you do. Why?'

'I want to know the truth, that's all. What happened to Marianne, in 2012 and . . . this time. For my own satisfaction, no other reason.'

Is he being serious? 'What about the reason of locking up criminals to keep them off the streets, keep society safe?'

He shrugs. Suddenly, he looks sad. He puts down his mug of tea and says quietly, 'Thing is, you don't care about telling me the truth, do you? And I can't make you care if you don't. That's the trouble.'

Something not one single real detective would ever say. What the hell is going on with this man?

'Well . . .' I begin tentatively. 'I suppose that might be the "me" part of the trouble, yeah. But what about the "you" part? I'm sensing it's substantial.'

I brace myself for his anger, but instead he nods. 'You lied to both me and Sam Kombothekra about Tulloch.'

'What? No, I didn't,' I say.

'You did. You've already paid him part of the fee for killing Marianne. After he house-sat for you this year.'

'Right. That's what I told you the plan was, remember? I told DS Kombothekra too. The money for Marianne was going to be hidden in overly generous house-sitting wages.'

'*Going to be.* Right.' Waterhouse glares at me. 'You presented it as something that would happen in the future, never said a word about having paid Tulloch two-fifths of the total already.'

'No I didn't. Didn't mean to, anyway. Really. I'd happily have told you I'd already paid Tom two grand if you'd asked me. If I gave the impression the payments were all yet to be made, then I gave an incorrect impression—'

'You're telling me.'

'I didn't lie when I spoke to you on Monday or when I spoke to DS Kombothekra,' I tell him.

'If you'd made a down payment on the hit on Marianne, then you wanted it to happen,' he says in a hard voice. 'You intended it to happen and – lo and behold – it did.'

'No. No! It's not as simple as that. I've always, from the start, both wanted and not wanted it to happen. I've told you all this. Yes, I wanted to . . . secure Tom's commitment, I suppose. It's pretty normal to pay a chunk in advance and then the rest once the job's done.'

'And it'd suit Tulloch to do it at his earliest convenience, wouldn't it? To claim the rest of his money.'

'No, it can't have been him,' I say shakily. 'It wasn't. I made it very clear: nothing was to happen unless I said so.'

Waterhouse nods. 'Here's a straightforward question for you: what would it take to make you tell me the whole truth – everything you've lied about so far, everything you're withholding? What if I did the same? 'Cause there's plenty I haven't told you, that I'm not allowed to tell you. But I'm willing to, if you're willing to level with me. What if I promised anything you told me would go no further than these four walls?'

I run what he's said through my mind a couple of times. 'You're actually insane,' I say.

'Maybe.'

Bad idea, Jemma. Terrible. Definitely inadvisable. You have no reason to believe he'll keep his word.

Somehow, the more like an unhinged zealot he seems, the more I want to trust him. In a way, he reminds me of myself: a reflection of my own desperation to know everything that's been kept from me for so long.

'My laptop's in my bag, in the hall,' I tell him.

Idiot. Biggest idiot in the entire world.

'The password's "Lottie". Help yourself.'

'Thank you.' He smiles. 'I'll have a look. I won't take it anywhere, or tell anyone I've seen it.'

'But I thought you said the police—'

'Fuck the police,' says Waterhouse.

I laugh. 'Wow.'

'So we've got a deal? Full disclosure both ways?' His stare is terrifying. What was I thinking? 'You give me everything you've got.' He makes it sound like an order. 'You hold nothing back. In return, I'll do the same. And nothing you tell me will go any further. Agreed?'

'Full disclosure both ways,' I mumble, feeling as if my heart might jump out of my mouth and fly across the kitchen table at him. I can only hope and pray that this won't turn out to be the biggest mistake of my life.

He nods, and holds out his hand for me to shake.

12th July 2006

I've been giving my 'Too Good' idea some proper thought. It works. I've stress-tested it from all directions. No one can put a dent in it, I don't think — least of all me, and, let's face it, I'm the only one likely to try. Perverse as it seems in so many ways, I think the Too Good Ollie theory is the magic ingredient I need: the conceptual foundation (listen to me!) that cannot be argued against, that's going to make me believe, forever, that of course Paddy has to be, and was always going to be, the one. Of course Paddy's perfect and Ollie isn't.

Why? Because Ollie IS perfect!!

It's taken me two days to fully understand it, and I'm the one who invented the proof. Yes, I'm calling it a proof because isn't that what mathematicians and scientists call it when they formulate watertight theories?

Here's how it goes, in full (allow me to 'show my workings'!):

a. Ollie is perfect.
b. Anyone who would even consider choosing, let alone actually choose, someone inferior in every way (Paddy) over Ollie must be very inferior themselves (harsh, yes, but how can this not be true?).
c. Anyone very inferior to Ollie doesn't deserve to be with Ollie; he deserves to find someone as high quality and impressive as he is.

d. Therefore, who is the perfect choice of love object and romantic partner for an inferior person who would choose Paddy over Ollie? Why, Paddy, of course!

I can't say this makes me at all happy (I'm crying writing it) but I don't need to be happy in order to go along with what the Tyrant has decreed. I just need to be able to believe that it's somehow right and, most importantly, a blessing for Ollie rather than a tragedy.

22

SIMON

'Soon as I'd said it, I thought, "What horrendous thing have I just done?"' Simon told Jemma. He hadn't been able to admit it to himself until now, let alone to anyone else: exactly how much he'd regretted those terrible words.

He and Jemma were sitting in her lounge with new mugs of tea: her second, his third. 'I could hardly take it back, though, or say, "Actually, forget you heard that. I don't really want you to kill anyone. I'm just in the worst mood I've been in since records began." Didn't want to come across as weak or mad, so I had to try and convince myself I'd only said it because I was absolutely sure you were a time-waster who'd never harm anyone. That's what I told Charlie, myself, everyone. I mean, I thought you were probably an attention-seeking weirdo, talking shite—'

'Gee, thanks.' Jemma smiled.

'—but I couldn't know for sure, could I? And then when I went back to the nick and Doug Brodigan told me Marianne Upton was *dead*.' Simon shook his head. 'You can't imagine my relief when it turned out she'd been killed while you and I were together. Thank Christ! It wasn't my . . . encouragement that moved the needle and got a woman killed. I was off the hook.'

'And I wasn't,' said Jemma.

'I believe you, for what it's worth,' Simon told her. 'I just don't see how you can know Tulloch didn't go rogue. I've met the man, and I can easily imagine him turning round and going, "Oh, sorry, misunderstanding! Still, you'd better pay me the full five grand now." '

Jemma was shaking her head. 'Totally get why you'd think that, but no. Doing that would alienate me for ever and he knows it. What Tom wants most is to get back under my . . . wing, I guess. He'd never risk it. Plus, Tom's the only one, out of everybody, who had no way of finding out what was in the diary file on my laptop. How would he have known I'd picked Monday 30 October at quarter past five? I don't believe the timing of the murder can be a coincidence.'

Simon didn't either. 'Who do you mean by "everybody" and when could they all have got into your diary?'

'Last Sunday, and so many times before then as well,' said Jemma. 'For all I know, there were regular . . . invasions, dating all the way back to when I started writing it earlier this year.'

'By last Sunday, you mean—'

'The day before the murder,' said Jemma. 'God, it seems like years ago. We were at Dad and Marianne's for a family lunch: me, Paddy, Lottie, Dad and Marianne. I had my laptop in my bag, which was hanging up in the boot room under my coat all afternoon. Anyone on their way to or from the downstairs loo could have got it out and had a good nosey. And if it was Marianne, she could have told Ollie.' Jemma's face twists in apparent pain. 'What if it's not true that they've done nothing but send Wordle scores to each other since last year, with no other contact or communications? That could easily be a lie.'

'It could,' said Simon.

'And then there's Suzanne, who knows absolutely everything thanks to me always opening my big gob and telling her everything. But . . .' Jemma stood up, started to pace around the room. 'I can't see why anyone would do it, apart from Marianne. I think it must have been her. Who else would get a kick out of taunting me by changing the spelling of Ollie's name? That's got Marianne written all over it.'

'Does that mean you think Ollie Mayo's the most likely murderer?' Simon asked. 'She told him the plan she'd read about in your diary, and he decided to put it into action?'

Jemma came to an abrupt stop in front of him. 'What? No. Ollie's not a killer. He's . . . Ollie is lovely. I just . . . no, he wouldn't kill anybody.'

'I suppose Marianne could have read your diary and told any of them, couldn't she?' Simon speculated aloud. 'Your dad, your husband, your daughter, Oliver Mayo—'

'If Marianne was the one who broke into the diary, then yes, she must have told someone,' Jemma agreed. 'Didn't stab herself to death, did she?'

'What about Oliver Mayo's dad?' said Simon. 'Mark Rowan Mayo?'

Annoyance flashed across Jemma's face. She'd told Simon while making his latest cup of tea how disappointed she had been when the mysterious man she'd seen, both in the grounds of Devey House and outside Oliver Mayo's therapy practice, had turned out to be nothing but a giant red herring. This had struck Simon as an odd conclusion for her to draw; how could she be as sure as she seemed that Mayo Senior wasn't the person who had twice tried to kill Marianne?

'What about him?' she said. 'I told you: I've seen him twice – once outside Dad and Marianne's house in 2006, quite a while after Ollie and I split up. He didn't see me. Then I saw him again in late June in Cambridge, coming out of the Cedarwood Centre where Ollie works.'

'And you never met him when you were seeing Ollie in 2006?'

'No. He was desperate to introduce me to his dad and tried to arrange it twice, but the selfish shit-bag cancelled both at the last minute – found something better to do.'

'And Mayo wouldn't tell you why his dad had visited Marianne in 2006?' said Simon.

'No.' Jemma looked angry. 'Are you saying Mark Mayo might have killed Marianne?'

'Well . . .' Simon thought about it. 'He's worth adding to the list of who might have known what was in your diary file. If Marianne could have told Mayo, then Mayo might have told his dad. Can't rule it out.'

Jemma shook her head. 'It's not only the who that I'm worried about. There's a more important question to answer first.'

Simon waited.

She sat down again, further away from him, in the chair nearest the window. She didn't look at him as she spoke, but stared out at the patchwork of fields in front of her house. 'Whoever killed her . . . did they do it for themselves, for their own reasons – or did they do it to help me? Or . . .'

'What?' Simon had thought of another 'or' but didn't want to be the one to say it.

'Or do they want me to get the blame?' said Jemma. 'It's like Sergeant Zailer told me: the murder happened just before half past five on Monday, and where was I, the only person who seems to want Marianne dead? At the police station, spilling the beans about a plan I'd made to have her killed at that exact same time. That could look pretty incriminating to anyone who wanted to see it that way: like I'm some sort of criminal mastermind who thinks she's been oh-so-clever and committed the perfect crime.'

'Possible,' Simon conceded. 'I'd say the opposite's equally likely: someone thought, "I'll do Jemma a favour, do what I know she wants done while she's at the police station, so she can't be suspected for it. She'll have a rock-solid alibi." '

Jemma nodded. She was still facing towards the window, her shoulders shaking slightly. Simon was glad he'd decided not to tell her about Marianne's attempted bribing of Tom Tulloch. The last thing Jemma needed was to have her emotions stirred up any more than they were already.

'I'd just like to know,' she said quietly. 'Whoever did it, are they my enemy or my friend?'

23

JEMMA

Even if I couldn't hear her talking, I would know it was Suzanne at my front door from the chaotic sound of metal hitting wood, then metal, then wood again as she repeatedly misses the lock. She never stops talking, and rarely looks at a door while trying to insert a key into it.

Eventually I hear the door open, followed by her voice and Lottie's quieter one, and then a scuffle of coat and bag divestment in the hall: rucksack scraping against wall, shoes hitting the floor.

'I'm in here making supper,' I yell, squeezing the juice of half a lemon over the mixture in the bowl in front of me: turkey mince, feta, parsley, garlic, red onion and mint. I decided to cook a proper meal – one of my regulars, homemade healthy hamburgers – because after Simon left, cooking was the last thing I felt like doing. I decided that choosing the opposite of what felt tempting and easiest in the moment was probably the right call, since all I wanted to do was curl up in a ball and cry forever, in preparation for perhaps spending the next twenty years in prison.

The bowl I'm using for the hamburger mixture is too small,

but it's my favourite of the kitchen things I inherited from Mum, who bought it from a jumble sale at my playgroup. It's full of cracks now, and very likely a health hazard, with an uneven navy-blue rim and a pattern of bright yellow lemons that look as if they're dancing. My favourite thing about the bowl is that Dad lied in order to be allowed to keep it. He told Marianne he'd been the one who'd bought it and was the only one who'd ever used it – that he'd picked it out especially because it 'looked fun'.

'So she said it was disrespectful based *only* on the shirt not being tucked in?' Suzanne is saying to Lottie as they appear in the kitchen. 'Like, there was nothing else to go on? No insubordination?'

'I don't know what that is, but no,' says Lotts. 'Nothing at all.'

'Wow. That's wild.' Suzanne shakes her head. 'Like, there's no way a shirt might escape from a teenager's belt without that teenager noticing, of course – it *has* to be a planned act of rebellion.'

Normally I'd be feeling myself tense up at any hint of trouble at school, but I already don't care about whatever this is, even before I've heard the story. A teacher being unfair to Lottie might soon be the least of her problems. *Try: mother charged with conspiracy to commit murder . . .*

Stop it. That hasn't happened. It won't happen.

Ollie once said that the worst problems we ever have are the ones we don't have yet. 'Eh?' I said to him, getting ready to take the piss. 'It's true,' he replied. 'Because we can't solve them. There's no action we can take to make anything any better. How can you solve a problem that doesn't exist?'

'Something smells delicious.' Suzanne leans towards Mum's bowl and inhales.

'Please stay and have some,' I say.

'Can't. Got a dinner date and I need to shower, wash my hair, do all the things. I should head home, start getting ready.'

I look at my watch. Nearly five. 'You really should,' I agree, feeling guilty for making her drive out here to the middle of rural nowhere. Her flat and job are both in Rawndesley, not exactly close to our house or Lottie's school. She's done the school run for two days now. Paddy hasn't felt up to all the driving, what with having to go to work as well. He seems a bit more thrown by Marianne's death than I'd have thought he'd be.

'I've got a strong suspicion my hot date will turn out to be tepid,' Suzanne says. 'I'd much rather stay here with you and Lotts. Still, I'd better give the latest applicant a chance.'

Lottie laughs. She adores Suzanne, and seems as relaxed in her company as she always has. *Thank God.* She's very different today from the hunched, haunted-looking Lottie I found at Devey House on Monday when I got back from the police station.

'Tell me about this one,' I say. 'Is he also from the internet?'

'Yup. Bumble,' says Suzanne. To Lotts she says, 'Will you listen to your mother? "From the internet"! Not all of us met our husbands when we were, like, three and before typewriters had been invented.'

'His name is Bumble?' I try to look open-minded.

'Oh, my God.' Suzanne puts her head in her hands. 'No, Jemm, the app's called Bumble. The dude is called . . .' She breaks off suddenly, looking furtive.

'You have to tell us,' says Lottie.

'Okay, look, it's not great, but remember it's not his fault. His parents chose the name, so he can't be held responsible.'

'What's he called?' I can't help laughing.

'He's known as Diz, but his actual name is Digory.' Suzanne

sighs and holds up her hands. 'I know, I know. It's from the Narnia books. So . . . if by some remote chance it works out between him and me, my parents-in-law will be lunatics, apparently.'

'Deal-breaker.' I shake my head. 'What's the latest school drama, Lotts?' I tip the turkey patties into a frying pan. 'Did you get told off for an untucked shirt?'

'Not me. A boy in my class did.'

'Right. Well, you can untuck yours without reprisals, now you're home,' I tell her. 'Why don't you run up and get changed before supper?'

She nods. A few seconds later, I hear her footsteps on the landing above me, and questions and anxieties start to pour out of me: 'How do you think she seems? Did she say anything about Marianne or what's happened? Does she seem her usual self? What did you notice?'

'Woah, slow down.' Suzanne walks over to me and gives me a squeeze around the shoulders. 'I'm much more worried about you than Lottie. She's doing pretty well, I'd say, for a kid whose step-grandmother's just been murdered. How are *you* doing? Bearing up okay?'

'I'll be fine if Lottie is.'

'If she isn't already then she will be,' Suzanne says with certainty. 'When I turned up, she was chatting away to her little gang of girly mates. But . . . there is one thing I need to tell you about. Lotts said something in the car this morning—'

'Oh, my God.' Fear floods my body. 'What?'

'Don't panic, Jemm. It's bullshit.'

'Why didn't you ring me straight away, if it happened this morning?'

'Will you please calm down? I didn't ring because my goddaughter begged me not to tell you she knows, and I wanted to have a good, long think before rushing into anything.'

'Knows what?' I say, and my voice sounds like it's coming from somewhere remote.

'Thing is, she *doesn't* know it,' Suzanne says. 'She can't, because it's not true. To be honest, I don't even think she really believes it.'

'Just tell me.' Nausea curls around the back of my throat. 'What did she say?'

Suzanne takes Mum's bowl out of my hands, puts it down on the counter top.

'That Paddy's not her real father. Not her biological dad.'

'What?' Someone must have whipped my brain out of my skull and stamped on it before shoving it back in.

'Oh, God, don't cry, Jemm.'

If I could speak, I'd explain that it's not sadness, it's relief. *Thank God. Lottie hasn't confessed to killing Marianne. Of course she hasn't, because she didn't. Couldn't have. Simon Waterhouse said so.*

I didn't know until just now that I've been carrying that subliminal fear around with me. Once I've recovered a little, I try to make a joke of it. 'So who's her real dad, then? Let me guess – who would she most like it to be? Andy Murray, the tennis player? She likes him.'

Suzanne doesn't laugh or smile and, suddenly, I know what's coming. I want to shout all my objections at once – *That's impossible. Did you tell her it's impossible?* – but I can't make any words come out, and Lottie's feet are moving again, upstairs.

Any second now, she'll be back and I'll have to . . . I don't know what I'll do. I can't imagine surviving the next five seconds, let alone anything beyond that.

'She told me her biological dad's name is Oliver Mayo,' says Suzanne.

24

SIMON

'There's good news and bad,' Sam Kombothekra said. 'Who wants which first?' He, Simon, Proust, Sellers and Gibbs were in the recently renamed, newly done-out Joyce Magrane Meeting Room, with a computer and monitor sitting side by side on the shiny fake wood table in front of them. They were about to watch the last recorded footage of Marianne Upton before she was murdered, captured in the video of her husband's Zoom meeting on Monday 30 October.

Simon would have preferred to watch it on a laptop at The Brown Cow. He'd disliked this room since the day of its pathetic, ribbon-cutting launch, and hated it even more now that he saw Spilling Police Station as enemy territory. Who was Joyce Magrane anyway? And what was the point of having pelmeted curtains and a cushioned window seat when no one who ever came in here gave a toss?

Simon wanted to tell the others everything he knew, but how could he without risking a solve, or two? He wasn't prepared to contribute to any result that would make Dooper look good, and do nothing to persuade her to let Proust and Sam stay put.

'Let's have the bad news first,' said the Snowman. 'My brain is older and wearier than any of yours. The less work it has to do on the context-switching front, the better.'

'Context-switching?' Gibbs sneered. 'Does that mean thinking about one thing and then thinking about a different thing a bit later on? Is that also supposed to be harmful now?'

'Did I say anything about harm, DC Gibbs? Am I not allowed to say my brain feels somewhat fatigued?'

This might be the last ever pointless squabble between Proust and Gibbs, Simon realised, and the idea squeezed something already sore inside him.

'I agree,' said Sellers. 'Bad news first.'

'Fair enough,' said Sam. 'There's still nothing from the lab on the physical evidence, so we don't know if we've got anything useful there.'

'It's not even been forty-eight hours,' Sellers pointed out.

'I know, but they did say we'd have it yesterday. Oh, and some more bad news: I can't get this recording to play any more. Can you have a go?' He handed the remote control to Sellers. 'I don't know if it's out of battery from the number of times I've watched it already today. Marianne Upton is very much alive in it, guest-starring at 5.10 p.m. when she appears on the screen behind her husband. Then at 5.20 his mobile rings and you see him answer it. That was Marianne – both their phones' call logs corroborate. His call to emergency services, after he found her dead, was at 5.27. This gives us a very narrow time window for the murder: seven minutes. Narrowest we've ever had, I think.'

'I'm ready for the good news,' said Proust.

'That also involves Marianne's phone,' Sam said. 'Oliver Mayo's all over it, proving true what Suzanne Lacy suspected: Marianne and Mayo exchanged Wordle scores – every day, first thing. Even on the day she died, and going back more than a year.'

Simon did his best to look as if he hadn't already been told this by both Oliver Mayo and Jemma.

'Apart from that, there was no other communication between them that we've found so far,' said Sam. 'Someone needs to go to Cambridge and talk to Mayo as a priority. I know he can't be our man, now or then, but he could well know something that'll help us.'

Simon gave a convincing impression of someone who hadn't been to see Mayo in Cambridge yesterday.

'There you go, Sarge. It's playing now.' Sellers handed back the remote control to Sam.

Gareth Upton's Zoom meeting from Monday afternoon filled the large screen: a grid of faces staring out from their separate boxes. 'This is Upton here.' Sam pointed at the man for Simon's and Proust's benefit, since they hadn't met him. The meeting was quiet and full of pauses. All the faces on display were men and none seemed eager to speak. When they did, the technical language made no sense to Simon: nodes, algorithm implementations, microcontrollers. A thin man with a white goatee beard was the main contributor, while everyone else either listened or pretended to. Simon shuffled his chair closer to the table to get a better view of Marianne Upton's husband – Jemma's dad – who had a round, lumpy face that brought to mind a potato, and sandy-coloured hair that stuck out awkwardly on either side of it.

The team watched in silence until Marianne Upton appeared behind her husband, at which point Sellers made an exclamatory noise, as if a superstar had just walked onto the main stage.

'Calm down,' Gibbs muttered.

Gareth and Marianne didn't communicate at first. She was

wearing something lilac-coloured and floppy that could have been sportswear or nightwear, and holding a black bag. Yoga attire, Simon guessed, knowing she'd been on her way to a yoga class when she was killed. Big white trainers – bright and shiny new-out-of-the-box white. Did people wear trainers to do yoga? He hadn't thought so; he'd imagined it was a bare-footed activity. Still, she had to get there, he supposed.

Marianne bent down, disappearing from view. When she popped up again in the distance, behind her husband's right shoulder, there was something in her hand. Pale blue: a cloth of some sort. She was dusting things and putting them back on a shelf – photos probably, or certificates; all Simon could see for sure was that they were a variety of sizes.

If Gareth Upton was disturbed by his wife fussing behind him, he showed no sign of it. Then he turned and it looked as if he and Marianne exchanged a few words. Then she left the picture.

'Nothing happens now till twenty past so let me fast-forward . . .' said Sam '. . . to when Gareth gets a call. As I said, we know this was Marianne. Here he is picking up his phone, talking . . . He's muted himself, like most of them, and we can't read his lips because the quality suddenly deteriorates. It's gone all blurry, see? But then watch.'

Simon stared at the screen. Despite the fuzziness, which made it difficult to see Upton's expression, it was clear that after a few seconds his body language changed. He seemed more agitated, and moved his phone away from his ear a couple of times to look at it.

'I think this is when Marianne's getting attacked,' said Sam. 'See, Upton's looking at his phone as if to say, *Where's she gone?* And now he's putting the phone down, and watch how he's sitting from now on – not nice and relaxed like before.

He's worried about her now, keeps shifting and shuffling, no doubt telling himself Marianne's probably fine. But he can't convince himself, so . . . here he is getting up and leaving the room. He's decided to go and check on her.'

'And he couldn't have stabbed her by her car when he got there?' Proust asked.

Sam shook his head. 'No blood on his clothes, no weapon in sight. He wouldn't have time to wash, get changed, hide the knife. No way. Uniforms were there too fast.'

'The house and grounds and the woods adjoining the garden have been searched,' Sellers told the Snowman. 'No bloody clothes have been found, nor the murder weapon.'

'So if it wasn't Upton, then who?' Simon asked. 'There are no viable suspects, unless the brother and the Domino's pizza guy are lying to protect Tom Tulloch. Press play again.' He nodded at the screen. When the video restarted, he said, 'Look at the guy in the green tie. Bottom row, third from the right. Watch him.'

'His eyes are moving up and down,' said Gibbs. 'Probably watching porn.'

'He's totally on his phone,' said Sellers.

'Interesting blue and white vase he's got on the cabinet behind him,' said Simon. 'Notice anything about it?'

'Who is he?' Sam asked.

'No idea.' *Stop showing off. More importantly, stop taking them closer to a solve.* The know-it-all inside him couldn't resist, though. Surely they could see it? It couldn't have been more glaring.

'Why are we interested in this man?' the Snowman asked.

'I'm not,' Simon told him. 'He's no one. Notice anything about the vase?'

'What are you on about?' said Gibbs. 'It's just a vase.'

'What's that at the bottom of it?'

'It's a white square with initials on it: TKC,' said Sam. 'Probably the potter's initials.'

'Definitely watching porn.' Gibbs chuckled. 'He's gone red now. Looks guilty as fuck, too.'

'Nah, no one watching porn's that bored. He just tried to stop himself yawning.'

'What's your point, Waterhouse?' asked Proust.

Simon knew he had to come up with a presentable lie, and quickly. 'I was just thinking: his wife's obviously put that vase there, hasn't she? No way a bloke arranges a Zoom backdrop like that if he's got any say in the matter. He looks like he's been abandoned in an art gallery.'

Sellers frowned. 'It's just a big vase. Nothing wrong with it.'

'What are we supposed to notice about it?' Sam asked.

'Just how stupid and weird it is, that's all,' said Simon, hoping he'd get away with leaving it at that. There was no way he was going to tell them – not with his brain buzzing like a bomb about to go off and when he still didn't quite believe it himself.

25

JEMMA

I knock on Lottie's bedroom door, loud enough to make sure she hears it over her music, then walk in and close the door behind me. I don't have time to wait for permission. Paddy could be back any second. This conversation needs to happen before he gets home.

'Hey, Mum.' Lotts doesn't seem to mind me barging in. She's sitting with her back against the wall, legs up on her bed, phone in her hands. Her room's still tidy – has been for the last month. Ever since she and her friends painted the walls a colour called 'Sardine' and we swapped her old faded curtains for white-painted wooden shutters, she's been keeping it spotless. I try not to think about the clothes strewn all over the floor in Paddy's and my bedroom, which has become a junkyard in recent months – since July, when my obsession with Marianne and secrets and murder first took hold.

'How are you doing?' I ask. 'Are you okay?'

'I'm fine,' Lottie says in a measured voice, as if she's antici-pated the question and prepared her answer in advance.

'You sure?'

She nods.

'Suzanne says you told her something today.'

'Oh, great. Thanks, Suzanne.'

I walk over to her bed, sit down on the end of it. 'She says—'

'Look, Mum—'

We both stop talking at the same time. Then Lottie says, 'I was talking rubbish, okay. I know Dad's my dad. I was just being an attention-seeking brat, I guess.'

'You've never been a brat, Lotts. You're perfection on a stick.' I smile. I've said this to her regularly since she was little. 'And there's no question about it: Dad's definitely your dad. I wouldn't lie to you about something so important.'

'Guess I'm the only liar, then,' she mutters. 'Suzanne must think I'm a total dick. I'm going to have to apologise to her, aren't I?'

'Of course she doesn't think you're a dick. Suzanne adores you. You know that. Lotts, how did you know Ollie Mayo's name?'

'Heard the police talking about him on Monday, at Grandad's. But, I mean . . . that wasn't the first time I've heard his name mentioned, was it?'

'I don't know,' I say. 'Wasn't it?'

She sighs. 'No, Mum. You and Suzanne whisper about him all the time.'

Great. No parenting awards coming my way any time soon. I don't know what to say. I feel not at all like the parent in this moment. Desperately in need of one, more like.

'I'm going to apologise to Suzanne for lying to her,' says Lottie. 'I just wanted to see how she'd react.'

'She'll understand. After what you've been through—'

'No.' Her voice is quiet but hard. 'I haven't been through anything. You don't understand.'

'Tell me.' I have to know, though I'm not sure I want to hear it, whatever it is.

It can't be Lottie. Lottie can't have done it. You know this.

'Losing your grandmother's different when you know she must be evil,' she says eventually. 'Like, not as sad. Don't you think? And she wasn't even my proper grandmother.' Then a flood of words bursts out of her: 'She was the one who lied. Granny. She told me Ollie Mayo was my real father, not Dad. I didn't believe her. Whenever she said it, she sounded like she really, really needed me to believe it, which made me think it had to be a lie. And she said I could never tell anyone, especially not you. I know I should have anyway, but . . . I didn't want her to do bad things to me like I'd seen her do to Dad.'

It feels impossible that I'll ever be able to understand what I've just heard, but I have to try. 'You . . . you'd *seen* her . . .?'

'And when it first started, I was still little,' Lottie blurts out. 'I was scared of what would happen if I didn't just agree with everything she wanted me to do.'

'Do?' My heart thuds.

'She kept taking me up to her study – her locked room. Never when you were at the house. Only when you were out or at work. Sometimes Dad was there, but he'd be chatting to Grandad and didn't notice if Granny took me off somewhere. And whenever we were up there, the same thing would happen: she'd talk about how Ollie was my real dad and how one day I'd be able to have my proper family all together again, and . . .'

How could I have been stupid enough to leave Lottie in her care, ever, even once, when I wasn't there to keep an eye on things? I sensed what Marianne was capable of on the first day I met her, then spent a little over thirty years trying to talk myself out of what, deep down, I knew. Why did it take me until July this year to trust my gut instinct?

I realise Lottie's come to a stop. 'And what?' I manage to say.

'I don't remember everything,' she says. 'Granny stopped taking me up to her study when I was about three or four, I think. Maybe a bit older, I can't remember exactly when. Sometimes I've wondered if I can trust any of my memories of it. Like, what if they're just stories I've made up in my head? But . . .' Lottie curls her body away from me, so that I can't see her face. 'I do have a memory of her saying you've always loved Ollie way more than you love Dad.'

The pain of hearing those words come out of her mouth is almost unbearable. I have no idea what I'm supposed to do or say. I shouldn't have let Suzanne leave; she'd know what to do. All I know is, I'm glad Marianne's dead. Glad she got murdered, violently. I've never been gladder about anything. No one could deserve it more.

Why? Because she told your daughter the truth, and ruined your happy family lie?

But it wasn't the truth. Not all of it, anyway. Paddy is Lottie's biological father, not Ollie.

And what about the part that's true, about loving Ollie more?

'I used to have dreams about him,' says Lotts. 'For quite a while after Granny stopped taking me up to her room. In the dreams, Ollie was always my dad.' Lottie turns back to face me. 'You know the hexagon duck pond, where you and Dad used to take me to feed the ducks – by the old bandstand?'

I nod.

'In the dream I had most often, we were there, except with Ollie Mayo, not Dad. You, me, Granny and Grandad. And every time I'd wake up so sad because I wanted Dad to still be my dad. I loved Dad, not Ollie Mayo.'

I reach for her hand and squeeze it. 'Dad loves you more than he loves anyone or anything else in the world,' I tell her. 'He's your real dad and he'll always be your dad. Nothing can ever change that.'

She half smiles. 'Another dream I used to have was just me, Ollie Mayo and Granny. We were having a tea party with my old tea set, just the three of us – you know, the one with the pattern of fairies with different-coloured wings? There was a round window, like the one in Granny's study, so I think we were in there in the dream – but we were also on a station platform, because there was a thick yellow line on the platform. And we were also on a beach.'

'Can you remember anything else Marianne said to you?' I ask her. 'Anything she told you not to tell me?'

Lottie nods. 'She said she knew Ollie was my real dad because she'd had a special test done that proved I was his daughter. Which must have been an outright lie, right?'

'That wouldn't have fazed her,' I say. 'Marianne didn't recognise any difference between what she wanted to be true and what was. That's why she was an effective liar. She always knew what she thought ought to be true, and tried to impose it with sheer force of will.'

'She lied to you about Dad,' Lottie says. 'More than once. And you believed her.'

'What do you mean?'

'She used to put drugs in Dad's coat and trouser pockets. So you'd find them and think he was still a weed-head.'

Oh, my God. This can't be real. 'Lottie, even Granny wouldn't—'

'She did, Mum. I saw her do it, more than once.'

'But . . . did Dad know—' A loud creaking sound cuts me off. Slowly, Lottie's bedroom door starts to open.

Paddy is standing there. I didn't hear the front door. I don't know how long he's been listening.

'Many times, more than once,' he says. 'It's true, Jemm. Maybe you'll believe it now Lotts has told you. You'd never have believed it if you'd heard it from me.'

26

Thursday 2 November 2023, 4.50 p.m.

SIMON

Nobody had any idea that Simon Waterhouse was in Cornwall, apart from Simon himself – a fact he couldn't help finding amusing. He'd chuckled to himself at least three times during the eight-and-a-half hour drive. That was before the dulling, greying effect of being on car-and-truck-jammed motorways robbed him of his ability to find anything funny.

Now, almost fully recovered, he was sitting at a table in the Orangery restaurant of the Lannanta Blue Hotel, watching people walk their dogs on the sandy beach below. A few minutes ago, he'd seen four fools in wetsuits walk into the sea. He'd expected them to run out screaming a few seconds later, but they were still in. In November. *Madness.*

The hotel was an imposing Victorian mansion, sitting squarely on a plateau that formed part of a steeply ascending wooded bay. Simon had thanked and said goodbye to Belynda Simmonds, Oliver Mayo's former client and alibi-provider, and was now waiting for the person he'd next arranged to meet: ex-Cambridge college chaplain Jason Moorhouse. After that conversation, if it went the way he assumed it would, he'd drive home – through the night if he had to, though he'd need to find a way of guaranteeing he'd stay awake. Maybe it would only be seven hours on the way back, if he left it late enough.

His phone buzzed on the table in front of him, knocking against the side of the pint glass full of Coke that he'd insisted on being served. *Charlie.*

She launched straight in: 'That gerbil-faced bitch is still avoiding me.'

'Dooper?'

'I've sent her three messages asking for a meeting, so I can apologise for my . . . vicious outburst. She knows that's why I want to see her, and she's ignoring me. Clearly thinks I deserve to feel awful forever. I mean, just fire me and put me out of my misery! Where are you, anyway? No one knows.'

'Cornwall. Near St Ives.'

'For God's sake . . .' A loud sigh travelled much more efficiently from the Culver Valley than Simon himself had. 'Simon—'

'What's wrong with Cornwall?' he asked.

'Nothing, apart from you've got absolutely no reason to be there.'

'It's where Belynda Simmonds lives: the therapy client Oliver Mayo saw on the evening of 8 November 2012, when he couldn't have been cutting throats at Devey House.'

'She confirmed the Ollibi?'

'The what?' said Simon.

'That's what Sellers and Gibbs are calling it. As you might know if you were, you know, hanging out with your team instead of taking yourself off for little jaunts to the seaside. Why the hell didn't you ring the Simmonds woman, or get her on Zoom?'

'It's not the same,' said Simon. 'You miss out on the subtle gestures, the body language. If I'd suspected Mayo any less, maybe I'd have been happy with a phone call.' He took a sip of his Coke. 'No point suspecting him now, though. I'd wondered if maybe Simmonds and Mayo had been more than client and therapist, but she told me she'd engaged him as a therapist because she was having an affair with someone else – one she described as "all-consuming".' Simon winced as he said it. 'It's still going on, too. Crazy story she told me: she couldn't take the pressure any more, so she persuaded her husband to move down here, forcing a separation from the other guy – but he followed her. Left his wife and kids and moved in down the road from her here. As if that's not mad enough, guess what he was before he did that, when he lived in Cambridge?'

'A lowlife?' said Charlie.

'Yeah, and also the chaplain of St Saviour's College.'

Charlie made a noise. 'Well, it's lucky he gave that up. Obviously Goddish behaviour was a struggle for him.'

'Must have been. I wonder if he'll confide in me.'

'What?'

'I'm meeting him in an hour,' Simon told her. 'Looked him up soon as Simmonds left. He's got his own cleaning company now, so he was easy to find.'

'I don't get it,' said Charlie. 'He's nobody's alibi for anything, is he?'

'No. I just want him to look me in the eyes and say, "Yes, Belynda Simmonds and I were seeing each other in November 2012 and yes, that's why she needed therapy every Thursday evening." '

'You don't entirely believe her, then?'

'I just want to make as sure as I can . . . make,' Simon said. 'I keep thinking, it *had* to be Mayo who did it in 2012. Everyone else was vouched for by at least one stranger who owed them nothing. Whereas . . . ask me how hard I find it to believe that a devoted and grateful therapy client would lie for her shrink . . . Oh – have you tracked down Mark Mayo yet, Ollie Mayo's dad?'

'Yes, I've done all the little chores you assigned me,' Charlie said in an acerbic tone. 'Mayo Senior's not an option for 8 November 2012. He's a roadie now, for bands. Been doing that for over a decade. Have you heard of Audio Entry? Of course you haven't. Why am I bothering to ask?' She muttered something Simon couldn't catch. 'Mark Mayo was with them at the Toros Stadium in Birmingham on 8 November 2012.'

'And on Monday?' Simon asked.

'Leeds, with Discocode, another group you won't have heard of. I've told Sam. And I couldn't persuade Mayo to tell me why he went to see Marianne Upton in 2006, though he did admit he was there – and saw Jemma seeing him walking through the garden. It wasn't an enjoyable conversation; he got all excited about telling me as little as possible. Kept saying, "This is my son's mess to sort out, not mine. Ask him." I've passed that on to Sam too. And I've spoken to Farida Suleyman.'

'Who?'

'Mayo's client from five o'clock on Monday,' said Charlie. 'Ollibi number two. She was having her therapy session with Mayo when Marianne Upton was killed, and she's already emailed Sellers her Cedarwood Centre car parking receipt to prove it. The receptionist saw her . . . Rock solid. And she had only good things to say about Mayo: best therapist ever, already changed her life in just a few weeks, blah blah.'

Simon managed to stop himself from asking, *But did anyone see Mayo himself at around 5 or 5.30?* It wasn't impossible that he and Farida Suleyman had—

Stop. Give up. It's not Mayo, however much you want it to be. Which meant it had to be somebody else.

'So what should I do about Dooper?' Charlie's voice in his ear sounded uncharacteristically whiny.

'Apologise by email,' said Simon. 'Or leave her a voicemail, message, whatever.'

'Tempting. I did the damage face to face, though, so the apology needs to be face to face too, or I'll feel like a coward.'

'So when it suits you, being in the room with someone counts for something?' Simon said.

'Er . . . when it means I don't have to drive all the way to Cornwall, mainly.' Some exasperated mumblings followed. 'Maybe I'll just stand outside her office until she agrees to have a conversation.'

'I wouldn't,' said Simon. 'Easiest thing's to stop feeling sorry about what you said. No further action required.'

'Do you think I haven't tried that, as my first resort? I failed to convince myself. I said at least one thing that was inexcusably cruel. Simon? Are you there?'

He was, but he could no longer hear her because he'd moved his phone away from his ear and was now staring at it, trying to take in the words. And the numbers. Never had a gigantic motive for murder had quite so many zeros at the end of it.

Sam had sent a text that read:

'From Marianne's lawyer: money Jemma and Paddy aren't getting isn't going to Gareth, Lottie or charity. Going to Oliver Mayo instead. The whole £1,500,000.'

27

Thursday 2 November 2023, 5.15 p.m.

JEMMA

'I knew what Marianne had been doing, yeah,' says Paddy. 'Never saw her, but who else could it have been?' He's taken the day off work and might or might not be going in tomorrow, or ever again, for reasons I couldn't be bothered to pay attention to when he reeled them off. *There goes another bar job.*

We're at Lazy Cave in Little Holling, the only café-bar that's walkable from our house. It's tiny: two small square rooms with low, beamed ceilings, sea-green-painted walls and lots of small, uncomfortable wooden chairs like the ones Van Gogh liked to paint. The mug of tea in front of me is cold, and was tepid when it arrived at the table.

This place is incapable of delivering a hot drink that's actually hot.

'I didn't know Lottie had seen it, though,' Paddy says. 'If I'd known . . .'

You'd have done nothing.

'Where would Marianne have got weed from?' I say. 'It makes no sense. A woman of her age who never took an illegal drug in her life? How many teetotallers do you know who have drug dealers in their contacts lists?'

'Anyone can get hold of weed. It's not hard. Jemm, I never smoked any of it. I chucked it away every time. Unless you got there first, which you sometimes did. And I told you, I don't know how many times, that I hadn't bought it and wasn't smoking it again. You never believed me.'

'Because you were lying, Paddy.' He shouldn't need me to explain. It's so glaringly obvious. 'I think I'd remember if you'd ever said, "These bags of weed keep appearing in my clothing and I'm not putting them there, so I think Marianne must be." That's not what you said, though, is it? Instead it was always, "Oh, that's funny, I don't know how it got there, it must be from ages ago." And that I knew wasn't true, because I do all your laundry and ironing.'

'I was telling the truth when I said I wasn't smoking it,' he says. 'Look, maybe I should have told you the whole—'

'Maybe?' I can hardly stand to look at him.

'All right, then, I should have,' he snaps. 'But you wouldn't have believed me. You never do.'

'I don't believe you when you *lie to me.*'

I hear him take a series of deep breaths. 'How could I prove it was Marianne when I hadn't seen her do it? I knew what you'd say – you've just said it: there's no way Marianne'd buy drugs when she doesn't even drink alcohol. And God knows what she'd have done to me if I'd tried to turn you against her.'

'I can't believe I'm hearing this,' I say, staring down at the oily surface of my cold tea. 'I was already against her. You knew that. I understand that you were scared of her, but – I mean, what about your lies to me?'

He grabs me suddenly, twists me round so that I have to look at him. 'Is Lottie really mine?' he asks.

'Yes. But I had a one-night stand with Ollie.' I ought to be nervous – scared, even – to tell him this, but I'm not. I don't want to be needlessly cruel, but I also don't mind if finding out upsets him. I can't afford to care any more if I hurt him. I just can't.

'It happened when I was already pregnant but didn't know I was,' I say. And then a strange feeling takes hold of me. For a few seconds I can't work out what it is. Then I recognise it: peace. It feels so good to be telling the complete truth. I should have done it years ago.

'I figured something like that had happened,' Paddy says, and he doesn't sound angry. 'I've spent most of our marriage wondering when you were going to leave me for him. I'm glad about Lottie, though.'

'I wouldn't allow you to believe you had a child if you didn't.'

'We can make it work, can't we?' says Paddy. 'The whole separation, co-parenting thing. I mean . . . sorry if this sounds crass, but we've both kind of lied to each other, haven't we, so there are no good guys or bad guys invol—' He frowns. 'What?'

I don't know whether to laugh, cry or pour the rest of my tea over him. 'Wait, did I miss something?' I say. 'Have you just broken us up, without consulting me?'

'I assumed you were breaking us up,' he says. 'Aren't you? Or aren't you about to?'

'Paddy, I can't think further than the next breath at the moment.'

'Right, but you must know if there's any hope.' He's using his most reasonable voice, the one he only wheels out for very special occasions. It would be unacceptable for me to scream at him: *Why does all the hope always have to come from me? Why is everything down to me?*

'Is there anything else you've been lying about or with-holding?' I say. 'Because there's zero chance for our marriage if you don't tell me everything now. This is your chance.'

One. Only. Last.

Paddy's eyes move uneasily away from me. 'No,' he says, starting to run his finger around the rim of his glass of water. 'There's nothing else.'

He's lying.

28

SIMON

Jason Moorhouse, when he turned up twenty minutes late to the Lannanta Blue Hotel, looked less like a former Cambridge college chaplain than Simon had imagined he would, though maybe it was the 'former' that should have given the clue. Moorhouse was tanned, with a forehead that was all wrinkles but smooth skin on the rest of his face, which made it hard to guess his age. He was wearing faded jeans, gleaming white trainers that looked fresh out of the box and a grey T-shirt bearing, in black, the slogan 'ANGLICAN FUNDAMENTALIST – BASED AF'. Both his arms were tattooed: a series of what looked like small bird and animal skulls on the left and 'Belynda' in curly letters on the right. That would be awkward if he ever bumped into Belynda Simmonds' husband on his way to St Ives, Simon thought. *As I was going to St Ives, I met a man who had one wife – with a very unusually spelled name that I'd stupidly had inked into my arm, so I got my head kicked in.*

Simon could happily have started an argument about the T-shirt, too. He didn't consider himself a Catholic any more – hadn't been near a church in years, much to his mother's disgust – but he could still join in with the part of being religious that he'd always enjoyed most: disapproving of others. What kind of Anglican fundamentalist betrays his wife and his God at the same time by committing adultery?

Luckily, Moorhouse turned out to have no illusions about his own moral character. 'What can I say?' He spread open his extensively vandalised arms with a chuckle, then pointed up at the ceiling. 'I was tested by Him Up There, and I failed about as badly as it's possible to fail. Still, you've met Belynda, haven't you? Then you'll know what I'm up against. Temptation doesn't come much stronger. But here's the thing about Jesus: who did he focus on? Who did he used to consort with? Sinners! That's one of the things I always loved about him as a kid.'

'So when you and Belynda lived in Cambridge—'

'He's still the centre of my life, is Jesus, even though I've left the church.' Moorhouse pressed the flat of his hand against his chest. 'Still my daily companion, still my best friend.'

Lucky you. Some of us have to make do with Colin Sellers and Chris Gibbs. Simon tried again. 'When you and Belynda were still in Cambridge, did she ever talk to you about her psychotherapist, Oliver Mayo?'

Moorhouse nodded. 'She certainly did. I got quite jealous, the way she talked about him: "Oliver thinks this, Oliver says I should do that." And she'd never miss a session with him, not for anything. I said to her, "I don't want to see you on Thursdays from now on, not after you've been with him – all you do is witter on about how brilliant he is."'

So that was that, Simon thought: 8 November 2012, the night someone had tried to kill Marianne Upton, had been a Thursday. They were all telling the truth: Moorhouse, Belynda Simmonds, Oliver Mayo.

It made sense, because – yes, this was it, this was what had been prodding at the edges of Simon's awareness for a while now – if it had been Mayo who'd attacked Marianne in 2012, then it was all too convenient to be plausible. Simon went over it again in his head, the Guilty Mayo version: he wants to kill Marianne and, lo and behold, he's got Belynda Simmonds, a loyal client, willing to lie for him. Conveniently, Thursday nights are when she sees him for therapy – and this has been going on for fourteen months by the time the attack on Marianne happens. No one sets up an alibi that far in advance, surely. And Thursday also just happens to be the one night Marianne can be guaranteed to be the only adult at home at Devey House; her husband is always away for work on Thursdays, and Paddy and Jemma Stelling are at a hotel for their weekly date night, trying to save their marriage – that's been going on for nearly a year too.

In other words, if Mayo was guilty, then all the surrounding circumstances were conspiring like crazy, well in advance, to help exonerate him. It would be an every-murderer's-dream scenario, especially when you factored in Marianne insisting he hadn't done it, even though she'd initially claimed he had.

Whereas if someone else, not Oliver Mayo, had tried to kill Marianne in 2012, there was no implausible coincidence to grapple with, only several different people doing their various activities on Thursday evenings.

Maybe Simon needed to think less about the living and more about Marianne herself. Why had she said 'Oliver' when asked in 2012, if he hadn't done it? He thought back to what Jemma had told him at her house, while they'd been busy confiding in each other in a way Simon never had with anyone before: Marianne had almost insisted Jemma stay with Paddy, after the one-night stand with Mayo in 2010. Why? Why try and persuade anyone you cared about to stay with a weed-addicted loser who went from one dead-end bar job to another? Oliver Mayo, meanwhile, was charming, professionally successful . . . True, there had been a baby on the way – Paddy's baby – but still, what kind of stepmother would do everything she could to make her stepdaughter stay with an obvious loser she didn't love any more?

Moorhouse was talking about his great relationship with Jesus again. The laces of one of his trainers was undone. The newness and shine of them made Simon wonder where he'd last seen . . . That was it: Marianne had been wearing gleaming white trainers too, in the background of her husband's Zoom meeting, before she left the house and walked over to her car and to her death.

'How long have I been here, and no one's offered me so much as a bread roll?' Moorhouse said suddenly.

'Sorry, I should have thought,' said Simon, hoping he wouldn't be required to watch him eat, or eat in front of him.

'I hate hotels,' said Moorhouse. 'Horrible, impersonal places, most of them are. No one cares about good service any more. I'm glad Belynda and I aren't reliant on hotels now we're down here. I live alone now, so . . . I tell you, the amount of money the Gresham Hotel in Cambridge made out of us.' He whistled. 'We never spent a single night there either, that was the saddest part. All those nights we could have had together that were ours by right, all bought and paid for . . . but we both had to sleep at home, keep both sham marriages intact with no one wondering where we were overnight.'

Simon wasn't fully paying attention. Something was wrong. It was the trainers, the untied laces . . . No, not the laces . . .

Then everything rearranged itself in his head and he knew what he'd missed. Not just him, either – they'd all missed it. *Unbelievable.*

Not wanting Moorhouse to think his attention had wandered, he said, 'You and Belynda saw each other in the day, then?'

'Yep. Still do. Midday on the dot. That's always been our time.'

'Before, you said . . .' Simon shook his head. 'Forget it.' He was clutching at straws.

'No, go on,' said Moorhouse. 'Ask me. Open book, me.'

It couldn't do any harm, could it? Just to make sure. 'You said you didn't like seeing Belynda on Thursdays after she'd had a therapy session with Mayo. I was just thinking: those sessions were 7.30 at night – so if you'd ever seen her after one, that would have been 8.30 or later – evening, not daytime.'

Moorhouse looked surprised, and was shaking his head. 'No, she always saw him first thing in the morning on Thursdays, before the receptionists were in, even. "I'm his early bird", she used to say.'

Simon leaned forward, his heart hammering. Unless there was something he was missing, Ollibi number one had just fallen apart.

He needed to move, quickly. 'Excuse me a sec,' he told Moorhouse. 'Got to make an urgent call.' Less than a minute later he was standing in the hotel's main car park in the dark, wishing he had more than two bars of phone reception.

Sam Kombothekra picked up on the second ring.

'Oliver Mayo wasn't with a client on the evening of 8 November,' Simon told him.

He raced through a summary of his day so far.

'Incredible,' said Sam. 'We'll need to look more closely at this other client, then, the one he was allegedly with on Monday between five and six.'

'Don't bother,' said Simon. 'That one's legit. Mayo's not the killer.'

'How do you know?'

Shit. In his excitement, Simon had forgotten he'd vowed not to help any crimes get solved.

'Don't ask me that yet,' he said.

'Can I tell you something instead?' Sam sounded hopeful.

'Go on.'

'The whole of Devey House and its grounds have been searched, top to bottom. Among other things, we've found lots of photos, quite a few with Jemma Stelling in – but she's smiling in none of them.'

'So?' said Simon.

'Gareth Upton told Sellers that Marianne had kept all the photos of Jemma smiling and looking happy in her locked study. He also said that when she stripped everything out of her study, the photos were moved somewhere else, put with the rest of the photos. But they're not. No happy, smiley photos of Jemma anywhere.'

'In that case . . .' Simon thought as he spoke. 'They might be in the same place as the killer's bloody clothes and the murder weapon. Bet you haven't found those yet either, have you?'

'No,' said Sam. 'Where are they, then?'

'Look closer to home,' Simon told him. *Shit.* He had to stop giving the game away. How, exactly, was he going to resist the urge to tell Sam everything the moment they were face to face?

'I told you, we've searched Devey—'

'No, look closer to *our* home. The nick,' said Simon. 'Spilling Police Station. That's where you'll find everything the murderer wanted to hide.'

29

Thursday 2 November 2023, 10.04 p.m.

JEMMA

A few minutes after ten o'clock, I decide I've sorted my head out as much as I can for the time being, and pick up my phone to ring Simon Waterhouse. Lottie is staying overnight with Suzanne, who kindly offered to do some 'marriage-saving babysitting – or divorce-hastening babysitting; whichever you want it to be, Jemm'.

Upstairs, Paddy is snoring. I wonder if I should go outside and call Simon from the farthest end of the garden, but in the end I decide not to bother. It's cold tonight, and it isn't as if being that little bit further away when you tell a virtual stranger you no longer love your husband makes anything any better, morally.

Funny thing is, I've known Paddy since I was a child, yet he feels more like a stranger to me than Simon does – Simon whom I met on Monday for the first time in my life.

He picks up immediately, and I'm about to say I'm sorry if I woke him when I hear voices and a clattering noise in the background. 'You sound like you're somewhere busy,' I say.

'Motorway services,' he says. 'What's up? Has something happened?'

'Kind of. I hope you're sitting down and not in a hurry.'

'Tell me,' he says.

I give him an update: everything I've found out since we last spoke. He listens without interrupting. There's a short silence after I've finished. Then he asks, 'When did Marianne give up drinking?'

I make a frustrated face at my phone. How can that be his first question, after everything I've just told him? 'What's that got to do with anything? She didn't give up, as far as I know. She just didn't drink. Never did. Not that I can remember, anyway. I mean, she'd have the odd sip of champagne at a special occasion – she did at Lottie's christening, I remember.'

'Tell me about Christmas in the Cotswolds,' says Simon.

'*What?*' I'm tempted to ask if he's the one who's been hitting the bottle. He seems to be trying to have a different conversation from the one I started.

'There was a Christmas before 2006 that you spent with Oliver Mayo in a rented house in the Cotswolds. True?'

'That's right, 2005. Probably the only great Christmas I've ever had since Mum died.' Something twists inside me. That whole period – the week away, the weeks before, the months after when Ollie was the main focus of my days – was one of the happiest of my life, except I didn't realise it at the time. If you'd asked me then, I'd probably have said I expected to maintain that same level of happiness for the rest of my life.

'Who went?' Simon asks.

'To the Cotswolds? Me, Ollie, Dad and Marianne.'

'Just the four of you?'

'Yes. Simon, what have Marianne's drinking habits and a trip to the Cotswolds from nearly twenty years ago got to do with anything?'

'Unbelievable,' he says, as if he's just received shocking news. 'Okay.'

'You're not making sense,' I tell him. 'Why's it unbelievable? Who else would you expect to have spent Christmas with us, the Archbishop of Canterbury? Plenty of photos got taken, if you need proof it was just us four.'

'No, I didn't mean I don't believe you—'

'Dad got Marianne a posh camera as a Christmas present and, boy, did she use it. Dad joked all week that she was secretly planning to sell an exposé of our holiday to *Hello* magazine.'

'And you had a great time even though Marianne was there?' Simon asks.

'Yes. Ollie was my main focus, not her. Actually . . .' Is it strange that this hasn't occurred to me before? 'I hated her significantly less that week. Probably because she and Ollie kind of . . . bonded. Or seemed to get on really well, anyway. It was kind of like . . . I saw her liking him. So I liked her more – or at least, I could cope with her company more easily.'

Even though she was running a regime in which it was pretty much illegal to mention your mother, or your grief at losing her.

True – but that week in the Cotswolds was the height of the 'Nothing Matters But Ollie' season of my life.

'So Marianne wasn't trying to persuade you to dump Mayo and throw in your lot with Paddy Stelling at that point?'

'Paddy hadn't yet declared himself willing. He was still believing he was too young for a committed relationship, so there was no Ollie/Paddy choice to make until late May 2006. Christmas 2005 we were still in the Golden Age of Marianne letting me choose who I wanted to be with. God knows what changed between then and her weeping hysterically a few years later, as if the world would end if Paddy and I got divorced, but something definitely did.'

'Were you surprised when that happened? The hysterics?' Simon asked.

'That's an understatement. I literally wouldn't have believed it if it hadn't been happening in front of my eyes.'

'Why not?'

'Disapproval because I'd had a one-night stand? Sure,' I say. 'A smug lecture – that's what I'd have expected, and maybe a "Look, you really need to tell Paddy the truth." Instead, what I saw was . . . proper anguish and heartbreak. That's what it looked like, anyway. Made no sense to me – still doesn't. Why would Marianne care so much? It was my marriage, not hers. But she cared all right – enough to fund nearly a year of date nights for me and Paddy in a posh London hotel, while she babysat Lottie.'

'Right. Right.' Simon sounds as if everything I'm saying is confirmation of what he's worked out. I'm about to demand to know what that is when he says, 'Back to alcohol. Do you drink?'

I make a rude face at my phone. 'I wish you'd tell me what booze has got to do with any of this. Yes, I like getting tipsy now and again, and I like a glass of wine or two with dinner. I definitely put away more units than my GP would recommend. In fact . . . I lied to her recently when she asked me what my weekly alcohol intake was.'

'Ha!'

'What the hell are you sounding so excited about?' I ask irritably.

'When was the first time you did that, do you remember? Or . . . Sorry, scratch that. This recent time, when your doctor was asking you about your drinking – did she ask you any other questions as well? How did alcohol come up?'

'It was just a routine questionnaire, and no, she didn't. Simon, what's going on?'

'Never mind. I can't talk now – have to get home, unless I want to spend the night on the M4. Just one more thing: do you like cocktails—'

'*What?*'

'—and if so, do you have a favourite one?'

30

CHARLIE

Charlie looked up from her book as Simon walked into the lounge. There was a green folder tucked under his arm. He dropped it on the sofa next to her, then snatched the novel she'd been reading from her hand. Noticing her offended expression, he said, 'You wouldn't have been up reading in the first place if you hadn't been waiting for me.'

'This had better be worth it.' Charlie opened the file and tipped out its contents into her lap.

'Read what's in there. Carefully. I'll be back in about half an hour.'

'You're going out again? Where?'

'I need some fresh air, get my head straight.'

'It's 2 a.m.!'

'You want me to restrict my actions based on the position of the sun in the sky?' he said. 'I'll walk to the corner of Offin Street, sit on that bench under the tree for a bit.'

'Didn't that kind of thing lead to the invention of Buddhism once?' Charlie muttered as Simon headed back out, and she began to go through the bundle of papers. Mainly, they were diary entries: Jemma Stelling's. Handwritten ones from 2006 and typed, printed ones from between July 7 this year and two weeks ago. *Blimey*. Here was the murder plan in all its cold, meticulous detail. It made Charlie shiver. And here, a few weeks later, was the new plan to go to the police and lay it all out: the full confession of intent, in a desperate bid to avoid becoming a murderer 'on my CV as well as in my heart' was how Jemma had put it.

It wasn't long before Charlie saw something she knew was wrong. The last in a series of emails between Marianne Upton and Tom Tulloch contained an accusation that Marianne had written the diary file on Jemma Stelling's laptop. Charlie knew that wasn't true; Jemma had told her all about the diary she kept on her computer. *Unless Marianne had deleted it and written a new one . . .*

She had a question ready for Simon when he returned an hour later: 'Why would Tulloch leap to the conclusion that Marianne wrote the laptop diary? I mean, yes, the style's a bit different, but the 2006 one was written seventeen years ago. I hope my writing style's improved in the past nearly two decades.'

'Different spelling of Ollie, dates written differently,' said Simon. 'Different tense, too. The one from the laptop's written in that pretentious present tense I can't stand. Everyone does it these days. It annoys me.'

'What's wrong with the present tense?' said Charlie. 'It's where and how we live our lives, so why not write that way?'

'Reads like you're trapped in a jar with a buzzing fly.'

'The style's neither here nor there, is it? Anyone can decide to change their writing style – and the different spellings of Ollie aren't enough to prove Jemma didn't write the laptop diary. She's explained that: Marianne went through the file and changed all the "ie"s to "y"s, either to wind her up or threaten her or . . . just generally mess with her mind.'

'Oh, Jemma wrote the laptop diary.' Simon smiled enigmatically as he sat down on the sofa next to Charlie.

'So Tulloch's wrong?' she said.

'He is and he isn't.' The infuriating smile widened.

'What do you mean? Simon, it's the middle of the bloody night – just tell me. You mean he's not wrong because Marianne did change something?'

'Nope. I mean—'

'I know!' Charlie was determined to get it right. 'Marianne forged Jemma's 2006 diary – the handwritten one – in order to make Tulloch believe Jemma was nastier and more deranged about her than she ever really was?'

'You think the writer of the 2006 diary is nasty and deranged?' asked Simon.

'Aha! I'm right, aren't I?' Charlie clapped her hands together in triumph. 'And yes, obviously: the writer of the 2006 pages is a stone-cold bitch, I'd say. Whereas Real Jemma, in the laptop diary, is more measured, more sensitive . . . I mean, she's also someone who plans murders in a very step-by-step way, like a conscientious teacher planning a school trip . . . but wait, Tom Tulloch was at school with Jemma, right? Wouldn't he have spotted if this wasn't her handwriting?'

'No,' said Simon. 'Think about it. Who were you close to at school? Would you recognise their handwriting now, or spot it if someone had forged their handwriting? Did you exchange lots of letters with your school friends and keep them into adulthood?'

It was an excellent point. 'No,' Charlie said. 'So . . . Wow, so Marianne *forged* these handwritten diary entries and sent them to Tulloch, claiming they were Jemma's?'

'Nope.' Simon's face was expressionless.

'Clumps of hair are about to be torn out in front of you,'

Charlie warned him. 'If it wasn't Marianne and it wasn't Jemma, then who the hell wrote these 2006 diary pages? Oliver Mayo? Paddy Stelling? Lottie? Can't be Lottie – this isn't a thirteen-year-old's handiwork.'

'Did you read the bit in the 2006 diary about the "Tyrant's" favourite cocktail?'

Charlie nodded. 'Mai Tai, wasn't it?'

'I asked Jemma Stelling what her favourite cocktail was,' said Simon. 'Guess what she said?'

'If you think I can guess, then it must also be Mai Tai.'

'It is. But there's no "also".'

'Simon, I'm going to throw myself out of a window.' Charlie groaned. 'And we're on the ground floor, so hopefully that shows you how desperate I am.'

'This diary isn't a forgery by Marianne,' he said. 'She's not writing it pretending to be Jemma, hoping to fool Tom Tulloch or anyone else. She's writing it as herself.'

Charlie felt her mouth drop open.

'These handwritten pages from 2006 *come from Marianne Upton's 2006 diary*,' said Simon. 'And, what's more, she never said, wrote or pretended any different – not to anyone. Read them again. It's obvious, once you know.'

31

Friday 3 November 2023, 12.55 p.m.

JEMMA

'Do you have an appointment?' today's receptionist at the Cedarwood Centre asks me. It's a different woman from last time. For my second visit to Ollie's workplace, I have come as myself, not as Jenny Judge or under another false name.

You mean you've come as the walking definition of crazy and deluded: believing Ollie will tell the truth this time even though he didn't in July.

Don't they say that expecting a different result from the same action is the definition of madness? I prefer to think of it as dedication mixed with optimism, the only two things keeping me going.

The effort of hoping for the best – proceeding as if the best might be true – is exhausting. My marriage is falling apart, and looks likely to take Lottie's safe and stable home life with it. Most of my dreams are of being in prison. Still, somehow I'm still functioning. Somehow I managed to get myself to the station and onto two trains today.

Possibly the most kidding of myself that I'm doing is in relation to Simon Waterhouse. I don't know why I can't shake the belief that he'll fix it all. Desperation, probably. *He has to.*

If I'm to get through the next hour, the next day, the next week, I have to believe he'll be able to prove someone else killed Marianne, someone who's nobody I care about. Then that person can be locked up instead of me.

'Jemma?' Ollie's voice comes from behind me.

I turn, and the strangest thing happens: we hurl ourselves at each other, even though there are people watching: someone waiting to see one of Ollie's Cedarwood Centre colleagues, the receptionist behind the desk. It's as if Ollie and I decided at the exact same moment that we'd only survive if we clung to each other and never let go – either that or we didn't decide at all, it just happened.

It's been waiting to happen for years.

I don't care that we're kissing like shameless exhibitionists in the middle of the reception area. I don't want it to stop. The Cedarwood Centre is my favourite place in the world and I want to marry Ollie right here, on this spot where we're standing now.

And none of that means I'm going to let him get away with anything.

A few minutes later we're upstairs in his therapy room. The heavy stone of dread that I've been carrying around inside me is back; it reappeared as soon as the kissing stopped. Ollie has made us a mug of tea each – I've got the 'As I Suspected, I Was Right About Everything' one that I saw when I came here in July. *Talk about inappropriate.* I've been wrong about so much.

'You could get reported for snogging a client,' I tell him.

'I told Gayle you were a friend, not a client,' he says.

'We're hardly friends. I'm sure you lied convincingly, though. Ollie—'

He raises a hand to stop me. 'You don't have to say it, Jemm. I don't want you to have to say it.'

'But I want to and need to.' I take a deep breath. 'You have to tell me everything: the locked room, the secret between you and Marianne, why your dad went to see her at Devey House. Anything you've ever kept from me—'

'I know, Jemm.' There's a tremor in his voice. 'I'd already decided before you got here. You'll hate me once I've told you, and it'll destroy me, but I still have to try. Just in case there's a chance—'

'If you tell me the complete truth, and if you love me as much as I love you, there's more than a chance for us,' I tell him. 'And . . . if you can bear the fact that I may one day be convicted of Marianne's murder.'

'Did you kill her?' Ollie asks.

'No. I tried to do the opposite.'

'What do you mean?'

'I'll tell you, but I'm not going first,' I say. 'I've waited long enough to hear the truth from you.'

He nods. 'You've no idea how much I wanted to tell you at first. But then . . . November 2012 happened. After that, I decided I couldn't. The chance had gone. Except it hadn't.' A look of disgust twists his face. 'Even then, I could and should have told you the truth and trusted you not to . . . I don't even want to say it.'

Not to tell the police I'd tried to kill Marianne – is that what he's about to say? I steel myself to hear the worst, and know, at the same time, that it wouldn't be, even if he's about to tell me he was the one who picked up a knife and used it to slash my stepmother's throat. None of that would be as painful as hearing him say he doesn't love me any more.

'I should have trusted you not to stop loving me,' says Ollie.

'I think . . .' I begin slowly '. . . if there was any chance of that happening, it would have happened already.'

'I know I have no right to ask for anything, but . . . will you promise to carry on?' Ollie asks me.

'Loving you?'

'Even if you want nothing more to do with me once you know everything. It's not an either/or, you know. You can love someone and not be willing to see or speak to them, or have them in your life.' He sounds like he's talking to one of his therapy clients.

It would be so easy to reassure him; it would only be telling the unedited truth. I won't ever stop loving him. He could tell me it was him in 2012 and him now, a failed murderer and a successful one, and it wouldn't kill my love for him. But I don't want to say it. Not yet.

'I'm not doing it,' I tell him.

'Doing what?' he asks. 'Jemma, I've loved you so much, for so long—'

'I'm not reassuring you about anything or promising you anything until I've heard what you've got to tell me.'

Ollie nods. 'Put down your tea. The truth is quite a bit worse than whatever you think it is.'

It's as if my muscles are attached to his words. My hands feel weak and wobbly.

Carefully, I place my mug down on the floor next to my chair.

'You have to understand one thing first,' Ollie says quietly. 'I get you at the end of this story. Paddy Stelling doesn't. And . . . I really believe this: the future in which you and I are happily married already exists. We can't make it *not* happen, however hard we try. Believe me, I know how crazy that sounds. And it might be some bullshit fantasy. But it's what I know to be true.'

Or want to be true.

Then he starts to tell me: all the things I wish weren't true, but are. I sit, still and quiet, and listen to it all: everything he's done, nearly done, refused to do; everything he's thought and felt and feared, everything he knows.

All of it.

Apart from who killed Marianne – because, Ollie tells me, and I believe him, that's the one thing he doesn't know anything about.

32

SIMON

'I don't get it,' said Sellers. He and the rest of the team had met Simon and Charlie at The Brown Cow after an urgent summons from Simon. 'You're saying the handwritten diary bits from 2006 were written by Marianne Upton, but she lied to Tulloch and said Jemma Stelling had written them? 'Cause if it's not that, I'm clueless.'

'Bless him,' said Charlie, who was on to her second gin and tonic.

Simon decided to be gallant and not mention that it had taken her a while to get it too. 'Sorry, mate,' he said, appreciating Sellers's eternal willingness to admit to being stumped. 'Marianne didn't lie or mislead Tulloch in any way. He misled himself – completely.'

'Meaning?' said Gibbs.

'Waterhouse is suggesting that the misleading of Tulloch was done by none other than Tulloch himself,' said the Snowman in a monotone.

Simon said, 'Marianne posted the handwritten diary pages, snail mail, to Tulloch with a note saying "Read these." That's all it said, apart from her initial, M. It's in that lot somewhere.' Simon pointed to the papers on the extra table they'd pulled up. 'She never pretended Jemma had written the 2006 diary. Tulloch *assumed* that what he'd been sent were extracts from Jemma's diary. Why? For the same reason I assumed it when I first read them. "The Tyrant", all of that. Until you know different, it reads like a daughter, or stepdaughter, who hates her tyrannical mother – which is what Tulloch knows Jemma is. Of course he thought it was her.'

Sellers looked unconvinced. 'How can you be sure, if the Tyrant's not referred to as Jemma even once?'

'She's never referred to as Marianne either,' said Simon. 'Unlike the villain in the laptop diary, which Jemma *did* write, in which the villain's name is Marianne throughout. Now, is that alone enough for us to be certain? No. So here's the rest, and when you've heard it, you'll be as sure as I am. First of all, the easy one: cocktails.'

'Mine's a Negroni,' said Gibbs. 'Porn Star Martini for him.' He nodded in Sellers' direction. Both had empty pint glasses in front of them; neither had ever been seen drinking anything but beer.

'Marianne didn't drink alcohol,' said Simon. 'Jemma does. Jemma has a favourite cocktail: Mai Tai. First diary entry in the batch sent to Tulloch, or maybe second, I can't remember – mentions that the Tyrant's favourite cocktail is a Mai Tai.'

'But whoever wrote the handwritten pages is evidently madly in love with Oliver Mayo,' Sam Kombothekra said. 'Are you thinking—'

'That Marianne was in love with Mayo?' said Simon. 'No. She wasn't. Go back over all of it, carefully, and you'll see that absolutely nowhere in those 2006 diary pages is there anything that specifies this is *romantic* love we're reading about. You assumed it was on your first reading, like I did and like Charlie did, because you assumed Jemma was the writer.'

'What about the part where she talks about Mayo's great beauty, and how stunning his kids would be?' Sellers asked.

'Recognising beauty doesn't necessarily imply romantic attraction,' said Simon.

'We all want beautiful things in our lives, don't we?'

'You might want to tell that to your shirt and trousers,' Proust said. Gibbs laughed.

'I'm not sure about this, mate,' Sellers told Simon. 'I still think Jemma could have written it.'

'How about the part about speed cameras, and going for health checks?' said Simon. 'The gist of all that was: do things properly, don't just pretend or do half measures. So rather than look out for speed cameras, stop speeding altogether. Instead of getting a good blood sugar result from the doctor and then celebrating by scoffing a load of doughnuts, just change your diet forever and eat only healthy foods.'

'How does any of that prove—' Gibbs started to ask.

'That Marianne wrote the 2006 diary pages? Jemma Stelling's never learned to drive.' Simon tried not to sound too triumphant. 'She came to the nick by cab on Monday, and Charlie had to arrange a uniform to drive her to Devey House afterwards. Which means speeding and speed cameras aren't part of her life, never have been.'

'People sometimes use metaphors that don't come from their own personal experience, Waterhouse,' said the Snowman. 'That's not illegal yet in this once-great nation, though I'm sure it soon will be.'

'Would avoiding speeding fines be the first comparison that sprang to mind for a non-driver?' Simon looked at each of them in turn. 'I don't think so. And what about the health check stuff? Jemma Stelling was twenty-one years old in 2006. What twenty-one-year-old has GP health checks, blood pressure and high cholesterol in their head as a point of reference? Whoever wrote the diary is drawing from the metaphor bank of a much older person, and one who's been driving cars for years.'

Sellers and Gibbs exchanged a look. Were they each trying to work out how convinced the other was?

'Need more, still?' said Simon. 'I can keep going. How about the story of the time Ollie Mayo went with the Upton family to a cottage in the Cotswolds for Christmas? He was worried they were going to be late and said to the diary writer, "Didn't you tell them we'd be there at four?", to which our narrator replied with something along the lines of "Yeah, I said four, but they won't mind if we turn up an hour late." Crucial part there is the "I" in "I said four". I asked Jemma who went to the Cotswolds that Christmas. It was her and Mayo, and Gareth and Marianne Upton. Remember, Jemma's twenty-one in 2006, and younger than that before 2006. And this was the family Christmas trip.'

'And no twenty-one-or-younger person would be the one handling the communications around the booking if their rich, control-freak stepmum was also going on the trip.' Sam sounded excited.

'Exactly,' said Charlie. 'Marianne would for sure have been the one telling the property caretaker or whoever, "We'll be there around four."'

'I think I'm starting to be convinced,' Sellers told Gibbs.

'Good,' said Simon, 'because I rang Jemma this morning and asked her. These pages don't come from her 2006 diary, she told me. Categorically not.'

'What about the friend, Rosie, the Royal Family fan?' asked Proust. 'That was about the pain of being stopped from marrying the person you love – written by someone it had happened to.'

'Nope,' said Simon. 'Jemma's never had a friend called Rosie, she told me. That was Marianne, saying she'd rather be part of the Royal Family, where duty and the wishes of your elders count for something – much easier to stop junior family members following their hearts if you're a Royal. Whereas she, Marianne, came from a family where *in theory* everyone can choose to be with the people they love most. In fact, Marianne loved Oliver Mayo best – her perfect son, son-in-law, confidante, person to talk to for hours – and she'd been deprived of him forever by Jemma's choice of Paddy. And, unlike a Royal matriarch, there was nothing she could do about it.'

Gibbs gave a small whistle. 'It's insane how much all of that writing could totally be either of them. Like, the part where she says, "I should never have let Paddy and Ollie meet each other and be in the house at the same time" – that's not Jemma saying, "I shouldn't have acted like a slapper with no class whatsoever", it's Marianne saying, "I shouldn't have let Jemma flaunt her cheating and behave badly under my roof."'

'I'm convinced now too,' said Sam. He'd picked up one of the 2006 diary pages and read aloud from it: ' "There would be no sympathy for me, even if I were honest about how I feel. No one would understand. I could well be the first person this particular awfulness has ever happened to. No one on this planet has felt what I'm feeling now – at least nowhere near as strongly – for someone who is forbidden to them for the particular cruel, senseless reason that Ollie is to me." ' Sam looked at Simon. 'If that was Jemma talking about being separated from the man she loved by a disapproving parent, or parental figure, she wouldn't think she was the first, or that no one would sympathise.'

'"Senseless".' Charlie shook her head. 'That's how Marianne described Jemma having the temerity to . . . choose her own boyfriend, basically. Woman must have been a nightmare.'

'Well!' The Snowman clapped his hands together. 'I'm delighted that you know who wrote a particular diary in 2006, Waterhouse. If your job were "Diary Authorship Identifier"—'

'I know who killed Marianne too,' Simon spoke over him. 'And who tried and failed to do it in 2012.'

'Same person?' said Gibbs.

'Different people.'

'Are you going to tell us?' Sellers asked hopefully.

'If you want me to, yeah. But you might not.'

'Why wouldn't we want to know?' Sam looked anxious.

'Because . . . to put it crudely, the only proper villain in this story, the only person both capable and guilty of true evil, is the one who's already dead,' Simon told him. 'I don't want anyone locked up for years for anything Marianne Upton-related. You won't either, soon as I tell you what I know. Both crimes were self-defence at heart, if not legally. Most people would vehemently disagree with that, and they'd be wrong. Both were psychological self-defence if not physical. So, yeah, I'll tell you the full story if you want to know – and then I'll beg you all to pretend you're still in the dark as far as anything official's concerned. Want to hear the other option?'

'Can't wait,' Gibbs muttered.

'I can tell you nothing,' said Simon. 'That's the easy route for you. I keep it to myself. No agonising choice between doing your professional duty and being loyal to me.'

'There's a much more appealing third option,' said the Snowman. And then, for the first time in his police career, he made a suggestion that all present liked the sound of.

33

Friday 3 November 2023, 10 p.m.

JEMMA

Paddy's still up when I get home at ten, sitting facing the TV in the lounge as if he's watching it, but the screen's a square of black. He's in his pyjamas, a half-drunk mug of tea balanced on the sofa arm next to him.

'Is Lottie still at Suzanne's?' I say.

He nods. 'Where've you been?'

There's no point lying any more, and I don't even want to. 'Cambridge.'

'I thought that's where you'd be. Did you . . . Did it go well?'

'I got a lot of answers that I've wanted for a long time, so . . . yeah, it did,' I say, lowering myself into the armchair in the corner of the room. This is where I've got the best view of Paddy's face. I don't think I've looked at him properly for years. 'I owe you an apology,' I say. 'A big one.'

'No, you don't,' he says. 'I had a one-night stand too – also after we were married. Just the one . . . episode. Wasn't even a night.' He picks up the remote control, points it at the TV, but doesn't press any of the buttons. A few seconds later he puts it down again on the sofa. 'Are you going to hate me now?'

'No. Of course not.' It's a surprise – and it probably shouldn't be – but I'm not hurt or angry. The person I was a week ago would have been, or would have pretended to be, to justify demoting Paddy to even lower in her estimation. 'Who was she?' I ask, feeling nothing but emptiness for this man I've been married to for so many years.

'First name was Chloe. Never found out any more than that. She was out drinking with friends at the bar where I worked – can't remember which one. She was the one who did all the running.' Paddy smiles sadly. 'That probably won't surprise you to hear.'

'Paddy, when I said I wanted to apologise, it wasn't for sleeping with Ollie thirteen years ago,' I tell him. 'That's obviously something I shouldn't have done, but—'

'Is it? What if Ollie's the right man for you? Jemm, don't take this badly, but . . . you've kind of been leaving me, very slowly, while pretending not to, since . . . I don't know when. But years. I think we're probably talking double digits.'

He's right. For the first time in our marriage, I'm not at all sure I'm the better person out of the two of us, and I'm relieved not to have to pretend to be. 'That's what I'm sorry for.' I start to cry. 'For the hundreds of mean, blamey, judgey thoughts I've had about you. I can see how I've made it impossible for you to feel secure, and be yourself – certainly to be your best self – and . . . I've been judging you too harshly and thinking the worst of you since before Lotts was born. If I hadn't done that, everything might be very different now.'

'Or it might not,' says Paddy. He doesn't sound as unhappy as I feel. 'Anyway, we can make it work now, for the future,' he says. Seeing my confusion, he adds quickly, 'I don't mean as a couple. I know that's over. But together or apart, we're Lottie's parents. We're family and always will be.'

'Yes, we are. And I want to think the very best of you from now on.'

'Or you could be less perfectionist about everything,' says Paddy. 'Including me. Maybe nothing has to be "the very best".' He makes quotes with his fingers. 'Not me, not your opinion of me. Like, what you just said about stopping me from being my *best self* . . .'

I appreciate the effort he's putting into not sounding scornful. It's difficult to hold up for scrutiny words you'd never dream of using without allowing scorn to creep in, but he pulled it off.

'If you're into that way of thinking about things, that's great,' he says. 'But I'm not. I don't have a best self. I'm just me. But . . . maybe you can just stop hating and resenting me, and then everything could be . . . okay-ish?'

I wipe my eyes. 'Deal,' I say. 'Let's have a properly okay-ish co-parenting relationship.'

'When will we tell Lottie?' asks Paddy.

'Soon.'

I know what's coming next before he says it. I only have to wait about three seconds.

'Are you going to be with Ollie now, then? Are you and he . . .?'

I wish I didn't have to answer. Our lounge fills with the howl of a long silence.

Then I nod. 'I'm so sorry, Paddy.'

The shattering is silent, invisible, unmistakable. I've just thrown my whole life at the wall, deliberately smashed it to pieces. It had to happen; that doesn't mean it's not terrifying.

'Don't be.' He says it emphatically, and I wonder if his vehemence means that me leaving him is the best thing that could ever happen to him, or that he blames himself, or something else altogether.

34

CHARLIE

No matter how many times she ordered herself to direct her gaze elsewhere, Charlie's eyes kept coming back to Superintendent Fran Whittingham's framed wedding photo. She couldn't stop reading and rereading the stupid caption:

Hands down the most magical day of my life. Fran looked like a princess from a dream. —Lloyd Whittingham.

Charlie remained convinced that it couldn't be real, yet here it still was.

This morning the super's resemblance to a princess from a dream was at an all-time low. Persuading her to agree to see the six of them together had taken all of Sam Kombothekra's charm, and she looked ready to pulverise the first person who opened their mouth.

'Well?' She scowled around the room.

'I'll start,' Charlie said. Dooper hadn't looked at her since she'd entered the room, and, to ram the point home, there had been generous amounts of eye contact doled out to all the men – even Proust, whom she was rumoured to hate most of all.

Whittingham wanted Charlie to know she'd been selected for special persecution.

It was hardly surprising. Just as Charlie would never forget what she'd said that day, neither would the super. One didn't often speak, or get spoken to, quite so viciously.

In spite of the discouraging signals, Charlie was determined to do her best to atone. 'I was unforgivably rude to you the other day, Superintendent. I'm sorry. I've felt awful about it ever since, and I've been trying to apologise, but—'

'It doesn't take six people to apologise for one person's rudeness,' Whittingham said, staring at Sam. 'What do the rest of you want? I'm busy.'

'We'll be as quick as we can,' Simon told her. Charlie felt awful for hoping that the stunt he was about to pull might put her transgression into perspective for the super. There was throwaway viciousness, and then there was what Simon was about to attempt.

'Our team has the option of closing two cases today if we want to,' he said. 'Not only Marianne Upton's murder but also the attempt on her life in 2012. We know who's responsible for both.'

'What do you mean you "have the option"?' the super snapped. 'If you can close both cases, excellent. Do it.'

'There's another option, though,' said Simon.

Charlie couldn't help being impressed by his performance. Nothing about his tone or demeanour was giving any hints that this was the start of anything but a routine conversation. He sounded every inch the uninspired plod who needed reminding of the basics of his job.

'Instead of closing them, we might choose to let them sit on the record as unsolved,' Simon told Dooper.

Charlie took a quick survey of the others' expressions: all flat and emotionless apart from the Snowman, who was beaming.

Charlie did a double-take; yes, he definitely was. He'd never looked jollier. To be fair, he had never looked jolly at all until now.

Fran Whittingham's gerbil-like cheeks hadn't moved for a while. How long since someone had spoken? Charlie wasn't sure, and hoped someone in the room was in the process of deciding that the onus was on them to talk next. An awful, worse-than-you-could-imagine outcome still felt very possible. Likely, even.

'Why would you leave cases unsolved when you can solve them?' Dooper snapped at Simon. 'I don't understand.'

'Because any good work we do is going to reflect well on you, as our line manager,' Simon said. 'Which is why, if only we could think well of you, we'd want others to do the same.'

'I beg your pardon?' Whittingham sounded exactly halfway between angry and puzzled. She couldn't work it out, Charlie suspected: was this two people with very little in common talking at cross purposes? Or was it something much more alarming?

'But there's only one way I'm going to be able to think well of you, and the rest of the team feels the same,' Simon went on. 'I'm sure you can guess what that one way is. And the—'

'DC Waterhouse, if this is your idea of a joke—'

'Deadly serious,' Simon bulldozed Dooper's interruption out of the way. 'Let our team stay together and you'll get two cases, nicely closed. Two killers – one successful, one failed – behind bars. We're also asking for one more thing in return for the two solves. Let Charlie come back to CID and work with us. We'll be a team of six instead of five from now on. Effectively we have been for years.'

'Are you trying to blackmail me, DC Waterhouse?' The super stood up behind her desk and folded her hands together, as if for an official portrait.

Charlie imagined the scene captured in a framed photograph with a caption:

Hands down the most terrifying moment of my life. Dooper looked like a vengeful rodent who was about to end my career. — Sergeant Charlotte Zailer.

'I mean . . . if you want your glass to be half empty, it can be,' said Simon. 'What I'm trying to do is offer you, and all of us, a brilliant opportunity. If we do it my way, we all get to win.'

Whittingham turned to Sam. 'DS Kombothekra, am I correct in thinking that you want to be part of this career suicide mission?'

Shit. Also: no surprise. Anyone who was shocked by the words 'career suicide mission' had to be a naive idiot, right? Of course that was where this was always heading. What had Charlie expected? Not everyone wanted to run to Simon, hug him to within an inch of his life, tell him he was the best thing ever to grace the earth.

'I want to be part of whatever this is, yes,' Sam replied with a smile. 'I don't see it as career suicide. Simon's right: there's an opportunity here for excellent outcomes across the board.'

'I assure you that's not the case,' Whittingham told him.

'Ma'am, if I may?' Sam cleared his throat. 'I know that as a team we can be . . . inconvenient to have as people to manage in your downline, I can completely see that. And . . . well, of course, I'm sorry if we've been a challenge for you in that way. But please don't miss the most important part of the overall picture: there's been case after case that no team but ours could or would have closed. I believe you know that's true. No team but ours would have caught Billy Dead Mates, the Culver Valley's only serial killer. And countless murder victims would have been denied the justice they deserved: Jane Brinkwood. Helen Yardley. Judith Duffy. The Gilpatrick family. Damon Blundy—'

'Stop reciting their names!' Dooper snapped.

'Of course,' said Sam. 'My only point is: we're exceptionally good at what we do. And none of us would be anywhere near as effective if we weren't all doing this work together.'

'Enough.' Fran Whittingham sat down at her desk again. Was that a smile? Charlie was impressed. She'd taken a nasty blow, but she was rallying. 'I'm sure nothing I'm about to say will come as a surprise to you, but you're all off the case. Both cases. You're to take no further action on anything relating to Marianne Upton. Is that clear? Now, all of you get out of my office without uttering one more word. Return to your desks and await further communications.'

'Acting against us now is going to make life much easier for every would-be murderer, all over the region you're supposed to care about keeping safe,' Simon told Dooper. 'You know that as well as I do. Your decision, though.'

Charlie thought about the silly self-help catchphrases her sister Liv was always inflicting on her, picked up from a range of internet-based gurus with bouffant hair. Normally Charlie waved them away with a snort and a raised eyebrow, but one came back to her now: *It was always meant to happen this way. Everything unfolds exactly as it's supposed to – and that's as true of the painful things as it is of the ones we welcome and celebrate.* Total bollocks, probably, but perhaps helpful when it came to feeling better about the end of a career you'd loved.

It took an uncomfortably long time for the six of them to exit the super's office. Charlie was last but one in line, with Proust behind her. She wanted to turn round on her way out, look at the 'princess from a dream' photograph one last time to check she hadn't imagined it. None of this seemed particularly real at the moment, not even Fran Whittingham being the person whose office this was; Superintendent Barrow had been its occupant for so long.

'Don't weaken, Sergeant,' Proust muttered from behind.

Charlie stepped out into the corridor and exhaled with relief. Simon squeezed her arm. 'Don't worry, Char,' he said. 'We're winning this one.'

35

SIMON

'Marianne never wanted to save Jemma and Paddy's marriage,' said Oliver Mayo. He and Jemma were sitting across from Simon in one of the wooden booths at The Brown Cow. It was where they'd been sitting when Simon had arrived, and he hadn't felt he could reasonably ask them to move to the table he thought of as his, even though it was available.

'All she wanted was to have Devey House to herself every Thursday, the night Gareth was regularly in London overnight for work,' Mayo went on. 'That was what prompted her to come up with her "Date Nights in London" plan for Jemma and Paddy. How could they refuse? Overnight in a fancy spa hotel with a gorgeous pool once a week, all paid for, dinner and breakfast paid for, free childcare thrown in, a guaranteed good night's sleep, uninterrupted by—'

'Lottie was a terrible sleeper until she was about three,' Jemma cut in, and Mayo stopped talking instantly, as if afraid to miss a precious utterance from her, even though she was speaking in a matter-of-fact way about an unromantic subject. The two of them had been holding hands since Simon got there.

'As soon as Marianne suggested the London arrangement,

all I could think about was the miracle of being able to guarantee one whole night a week of proper sleep,' Jemma said. 'It's funny thinking about it now that Lottie's thirteen and it's nearly impossible to drag her out of bed in the morning, but I can remember fantasising about it: turning out the light at nine or ten and sleeping right through until eight the next morning.'

'And meanwhile, Marianne would babysit Lottie at Devey House – but not alone,' said Mayo. 'The point of the whole scheme was to invite me round too, every Thursday, so that the three of us could play happy families: me, Marianne and Lottie.'

'Not the only point,' Jemma said quietly. 'Don't forget the me-and-Paddy bit.' She looked at Simon. 'The London hotel nights were supposed to reveal to me, slowly but surely, that even in luxurious conditions, I really didn't want to be with him. Marianne was banking on me not being able to get my love for Ollie out of my system. And I'd finally give myself permission to leave Paddy, because I'd be able to tell myself I'd done right by Lottie and given the marriage my best shot, but it just wasn't going to work. Does that make sense to you?' Jemma asked Simon.

He nodded.

'It didn't to me when Ollie first told me,' she said. 'A few months after Ollie and I briefly . . . reconnected in 2010, Marianne found me trying to have a secret cry one day. I ended up telling her I was convinced I'd made a terrible mistake by marrying Paddy, that Ollie was the one I wanted to be with . . . That was when she out-hystericalled me and started weeping as if me having a one-night stand had ruined her life.'

Simon noticed that Mayo had winced at 'one-night stand'.

'She came as close as she could to forbidding me to leave Paddy,' Jemma said. 'Said things like "How can you think about divorcing him when you're pregnant with his child? That would be a tragedy – for all three of you, the baby too." But if all she'd wanted, since 2006, was for me and Ollie to get back together—'

'We've worked it out, though, right?' Mayo said. 'You wouldn't have left Paddy then, however much you'd wanted to. Because of the baby.'

'I once had a good mother.' Jemma's eyes filled with tears. 'Not for long, but I did. I had the best mother. And I was, I still am, determined to be the best mother.' She looked at Simon. 'I've racked my brains to try and remember exactly what I told Marianne that day. Like, the specific words I used. And . . . I think I probably said something about how unbearable it was to realise with so much clarity that Ollie was the one I wanted when it was finally too late, when I had no choice but to stay with Paddy because of the pregnancy. Marianne tried to persuade me – not that I should leave someone whose baby I was expecting, but that the baby might be Ollie's. It lasted ages, that argument. It felt . . . very bewildering at the time. Marianne wasn't normally quite so irrational. I kept telling her: I knew for a fact Ollie wasn't the father. It had to be Paddy. The dates put it beyond doubt. But it was like she didn't hear me. She kept insisting strange things can happen and "Doctors don't know everything you know, Jemma", and could I really be *that* sure?'

Mayo was nodding. 'And that's why she didn't say, "Leave Paddy and be with Ollie if that's what you want." You'd made it clear you weren't prepared to leave Paddy, having just found out you were carrying his child. So Marianne decided to play a longer game.'

'Much longer,' said Simon. 'Lottie's thirteen now. When did the nights in the London hotel start?'

'Beginning of 2012,' said Mayo. 'Lottie was fifteen months old, the first Thursday night I went round.'

'So Marianne was prepared to wait out the pregnancy and the whole first year of Lottie's life before getting going on her plan?'

Mayo was shaking his head. 'That's not how she saw it. By that point she and I were meeting regularly, in secret, in her study at Devey House, right up until November 2012 when—'

'Doing what, exactly?' Simon asked. 'Sorry to interrupt.

'We just talked,' said Mayo. 'Mainly about how sad we both were. I was devastated for obvious reasons, and at first I felt utterly alone and cast out, but then . . . I saw that Marianne was too. In the seven months Jemm and I had been together, Marianne had become very fond of me and started to hope that I'd one day . . . well, be part of her family. Be her son-in-law. Knowing she wanted that as much as I did was comforting. I'd just lost everything I cared about, and then suddenly I felt as if I was part of something again – and not just any old thing. The thing I yearned to be part of: Jemma's family. Marianne kept saying, "The story isn't over, Ollie. Who knows what might happen soon, or at some point?" Kept telling me I was infinitely, and obviously, superior to Paddy and that Jemma would see that one day, when the time was right. I . . . I believed her because I desperately wanted to.'

Jemma leaned in closer to him.

'Marianne could have that effect on you,' Mayo said. 'She'd bring this whole . . . vision, this imaginary world, to life for you and you just couldn't help believing it. I was soon so convinced that I told my dad: not to worry, I was miserable now, but I'd be getting Jemma back sooner or later. How did I know? Because Marianne had said so, and Marianne had a plan. Dad thought the whole thing sounded sinister as hell and couldn't be talked out of going round to Devey House to give her a bollocking—'

'That was the day Jemma saw him in the garden at Devey House?' Simon cut in.

'Yes,' said Mayo. 'It's the only time in my entire life that he ever went into protective father mode. He stormed round there, ordered Marianne to leave me alone and let me get on with the rest of my life. She just smiled sweetly at him and kept her cool, knowing I'd side with her over him any day. That was partly what made me want to train to be a psychotherapist: Marianne saying one day, "The ability to remain calm when others are losing their minds is one of the biggest psychological advantages a person can have." '

'Probably true,' said Simon.

'It was Marianne, not Dad, who cared enough to spend actual time with me on a regular basis,' Mayo said. 'She asked me more questions about myself and what mattered to me in the first two weeks of our . . . new, secret relationship than Dad has in my entire life. She really seemed to care for me in . . . I suppose I thought of it as a properly motherly way, even though I didn't have any experience of that. She gave me firm instructions, right from the start: I was to think of her as my mother-in-law, because one day she would be, officially.' Mayo smiled sadly. 'She was such a strange mixture of . . . attributes. As much as she was comforting, which I needed, there was also a hard, warrior side to her.'

'Understatement,' Jemma muttered. 'She could have defeated an army of thousands.'

'I was convinced that if she said we could win, if she really believed it . . .' Mayo shrugged to indicate that he'd finished for now.

'When what?' Simon asked him.

Mayo and Jemma exchanged a puzzled look. Then he said, 'I'm not sure what you mean.'

'Before, you were saying: you and she met regularly, in secret,' said Simon. 'In her study at Devey House between 2006 and November 2012 *when* . . . You didn't finish the sentence. When what?'

There was a short silence. Jemma looked down at her cup of tea. Then Mayo said, 'When I slashed her throat with a knife. And left her for dead on her kitchen floor. Although . . . No. I'm not going to make excuses. I did it. I'm . . . I'm sorry I wasn't honest with you about that straight away.'

He exhaled several times, staring at the air in front of him as if expecting to see something appear there. Jemma clutched his hand more tightly.

'Understandable,' Simon told him. 'I'm the police. No one's honest with me. But you're going to be now, aren't you?'

'I just have been,' said Mayo.

'Mainly. But you described yourself as Marianne's confidante, and that's not all you were. More of a collaborator, surely?'

'Yes.' Mayo squeezed Jemma's hand. 'That's true. I wanted Jemma back – whenever, however that could happen. It all came from Marianne, not me – certainly all the ingenious aspects – but I was an active part of it. That's how I know you're wrong about her waiting it out for years. That's not how she saw it, not at all.'

'Enlighten me,' said Simon.

Mayo took a sip of his pint of lime cordial and soda. 'She'd orchestrated her response – every stage of it – within a few days of the argument Jemma's described. Marianne wouldn't have liked that one bit, losing it and weeping hysterically in front of another person – especially Jemma, given the tensions between them. She was driven by a strong need for control and power, always. Which is why it took her less than a week to come up with something to make herself feel properly superior and all-powerful again. She'd have been in a hurry to . . .' He seemed to be searching for the right phrase.

'Regain ascendancy?' Simon suggested.

'Precisely.' Mayo nodded his approval. 'And the waiting for years, while on the surface doing all she could to seem supportive of Jemma's marriage and pregnancy and the "happy family" charade – that was all part of the . . . not fun exactly, I don't think she saw it as fun, but part of the drama for sure. From Marianne's point of view, she didn't wait years. She got started straight away, calculating that the more supportive she seemed, the more Jemma would feel trapped and unhappy in the marriage. Plus there was a new baby to contend with – always challenging and exhausting, always a bit of a marriage-tester.'

'I did all the things she hoped I'd do, right on cue.' Jemma sighed. 'Grew more and more unhappy, saw every day how enthusiastic Marianne apparently was about me and Paddy and Lotts as a trio – what she called our "perfect little family" – and I just kept thinking, "Why can't I feel as good about it as she does?" Because I was in love with Ollie, obviously, and that wasn't going away. And Paddy . . . it was probably horrible of me, but I started to notice every insensitive thing he did or said, each time he sat on his arse and watched me, yet again, haul myself upright to go and deal with whatever Lottie wanted this time. I was constantly on the lookout for evidence to justify my quickly deteriorating opinion of him. I started to feel really, really desperate – and that's exactly when that bitch suggested the Posh Hotel Rescue Plan. All me and Paddy needed was regular quality time alone together and proper rest, she said – that would sort us out, and she was happy to make it happen for us.'

'It must have seemed like an unbelievably kind and generous offer,' said Simon.

Jemma looked unsure. 'Yes and no. There was such a strong vibe of "I want this, so it must happen." There usually was, from Marianne. I wasn't going to say no – I wasn't an idiot, and it did sound blissful and too good to be true in many ways – but the message I was receiving in no uncertain terms was, "You will put all thoughts of Ollie out of your mind right now and throw yourself into this attempt to make your 'perfect little family' work – the one you've been ungratefully trying to wreck for so long." '

'Marianne told me she'd put money on it,' said Mayo. 'Jemma and Paddy would break up within a year of the Thursday nights in London starting. And once that had happened, I'd be able to slot neatly into Marianne's *real* perfect family. Lottie would already be helpfully familiar with me, from all the Thursday nights of me playing Daddy, and—'

'Playing Daddy how exactly?' Simon asked. 'Or do you just mean being there, and Lottie seeing you there?'

'No.' A look of guilt, or perhaps shame, passed across Mayo's face. 'She was only little then – too young to understand – but Marianne would say to her, "This is Daddy, Lottie – your real Daddy." And . . . she'd expect me to do the same – play the role of Lottie's father.'

'And you agreed to pretend? To lie to the kid?' Simon probably hadn't done a great job of concealing his disapproval. He didn't care.

Mayo was shaking his head. 'I didn't think it was a lie. You have to bear in mind . . . Marianne had become my only family, effectively. Week after week, she filled my head with . . .'

'Propaganda,' Jemma said, supplying the missing word.

'Kept saying it was down to the two of us to keep the faith, keep the fire burning, that she loved me and always would – I'd always be her perfect son-in-law, she was so proud of me.' Mayo sighed. 'She never ran out of powerful, inspiring metaphors to describe what we were doing. And no one had ever . . . spoken to me like that, believed so hard on my behalf that I could get what I wanted, that I could be a winner and not a reject. She also managed to persuade me that Paddy would lose interest in Lottie and fatherhood the second Jemma dumped him. That's not true.'

'No, it isn't,' Jemma confirmed.

'That was either a big lie on Marianne's part or else she just underestimated Paddy,' said Mayo. 'We're all flawed, him included, but . . .' He stopped.

'He loves Lottie,' said Jemma. 'She's never felt unloved by him.'

Simon was still at a bit of a loss. 'So you're saying you felt as if it was true that you were Lottie's dad to all intents and purposes, or soon would be?'

'No. Marianne lied to me. That's why I did what I did, because I found out about the lie. That and . . . the other reason. She told me I was Lottie's biological dad. Said she'd sent off some of both of our DNA and proved it beyond any doubt.'

'When did she say that?' asked Simon.

'A few weeks after the Thursday nights had started.'

'Did you ask to see the DNA results?'

'Of course,' said Mayo. 'She was well prepared for that question. Said she'd torn them up and binned them – that it wasn't safe to keep them anywhere in the house in case someone found them. I said, "But you've got this study, that you keep locked." That didn't go down well at all. She looked angry and snapped at me: "I told you, I've torn them up." Maybe that was true, I don't know — but the part about me being Lottie's dad was a lie, as I found out in 2012, on 8 November. I read all about it in one of Marianne's diaries: she'd had private DNA tests done, yes, but the results were the opposite of what she'd told me. No match at all between me and Lottie, but a clear result for Paddy and Lottie. He was her father, no question. And she'd told me the opposite. The diary entry I read made it clear she was proud of her ingenious idea: to get me even more on board and invested than I already was, by adding that one lie to the mix.'

'Unbelievable,' Simon murmured.

'Yeah, I was pretty shocked when I read that,' said Mayo. 'And I only saw it sort of by accident. For the first time ever, on 8 November 2012, Marianne had left the study first, without me, and gone downstairs, leaving me sitting in a chair, too stunned to move. Why was I paralysed? Because she'd just told me that there was now no other way for our plan to work – I was going to have to kill Paddy.'

'What?' Simon hadn't been expecting that.

A tear had escaped from the corner of Mayo's left eye. He wiped it away. ' "Important developments!" That's what she said when I arrived that night – as if something exciting had happened. And it had, but it wasn't exciting. It was terrifying. She'd realised, she said, that Jemma had more grit and determination than Marianne had expected from her. She really did seem determined to stick it out with Paddy, for Lottie's sake, and it was already November – the Thursday nights had been going on for eleven months by then, and Marianne was sick of waiting. So, her workaround was to tell me I had to kill Paddy. As a fireman, she said, I must know a way to do it, something involving fire, that would look like an accident. She said . . .' He stopped. Shuddered. ' "Burn down the whole of Devey House if you have to. You have my blessing." Those words actually came out of her mouth. Then she said, "Let's go downstairs and open a bottle of wine – we need to drink to this new arrangement." And she . . . she just walked out of the room. I hadn't agreed – I'd been too gobsmacked to say anything – but she behaved as if I'd said, "Sure, no problem" and it was all in the bag, a done deal.'

Jemma had covered her face with her hands.

'I heard her calling me from downstairs and eventually I managed to stagger to my feet – and in doing so, clumsily, I knocked against Marianne's desk. Her diary, which was on it, slid off and landed on the floor. I picked it up, not planning to read it, and I was about to put it back when I realised she might have written something about what she'd just done – what she'd asked me to do, I mean. Maybe she'd decided the day before that she was going to ask me to kill Paddy, and written about it. Or maybe I'd find something reassuring like, "I've thought of a brilliant trick to play on Ollie . . ." So I looked. And kept looking. And saw that it wasn't a prank – she was deadly serious. And I found the page where she'd written about the DNA test lie.'

'You must have been angry,' Simon stated the obvious.

'I didn't feel it, weirdly,' said Mayo. 'Utter shock – that was all I felt. Like the world wasn't real any more. Or I wasn't real. So I went downstairs and sat across from Marianne at her kitchen table, feeling numb, with this horrible buzzing in my head. She was chatting away cheerfully about me murdering Paddy, as if it was the most normal thing in the world, and I couldn't listen any more. That's when I attacked her.' He wiped his forehead with the palm of his right hand. 'I should have come clean about all this a long, long time ago, but I thought Jemma would hate me, and I still . . . even after I'd nearly murdered someone, I still hadn't given up hope of getting my happy ending.'

'I'm glad you hadn't,' Jemma said quietly.

'The woman I love is an extraordinary person,' Mayo told Simon.

So's the woman I love. Simon didn't say it. It would have sounded weird, and it wasn't a competition.

'My best mate Suzanne would use a different adjective,' said Jemma. 'Many different ones, in fact. All of them rude.'

'At what point did you involve Belynda Simmonds?' Simon asked.

'I rang her soon as I got out of Sleatham St Andrew,' said Mayo. 'Pulled over, called her. I knew she'd cover for me – she was very loyal. But also . . . I mean, to put it crudely, I had something on her. I knew about her adulterous affair, and I also knew something else about her home life, which is probably why I thought of her straight away: every Thursday evening, her husband was out with his mates for five-a-side football followed by a curry. I only knew that because it was a point of contention between Belynda and her lover. She couldn't understand why he would never agree to spend those Thursday evenings with her, when she was home alone and it would have been so convenient. Apparently, it was down to me.' Mayo sounded surprised, and looked exasperated as he said it. 'The lover said he didn't like seeing her on days when she'd seen me already. Some weird sort of misplaced jealousy, I think. Anyway, that's how I knew that she spent Thursday evenings home alone.'

'Which prompted you to think of her as a possible alibi-provider,' said Simon.

Mayo nodded. 'She agreed to tell the police she'd been with me on the evening of Thursday 8 November 2012, and that we'd been seeing each other on Thursday evenings at 7.30 going back fourteen months. It was true she'd been my client for that long. I faked some retrospective records at the Cedarwood Centre, got the fake history put into the system – really easy to do. No one's generally in of an evening, so no one could have said, "Wait, I remember that night and Ollie wasn't in with any client then." '

'And the Ollibi was born,' said Jemma.

'The police descended on me very quickly,' Mayo told Simon. 'I had no idea Marianne had survived, or that she'd named me as her attacker. She very quickly took back her accusation, though. That and the . . . er, Ollibi saved me. A month or so later, Marianne wrote to me – a proper letter that she sent through the post.'

'Saying?' asked Simon.

'It was an apology. For naming me, for driving me to it. She blamed herself for all of it, and . . . I forgave her. I wouldn't have thought she'd be capable of . . . But she was. I wrote back, saying I accepted her apology and I wished her well. Neither of us said so, but there was an unspoken agreement that our meetings would stop. All communications would stop – that seemed clear somehow. And then, years later . . .'

'Wordle,' said Simon.

Mayo nodded. 'For the last year or so, until she died, we swapped Wordle scores most days. It felt . . . I don't know. Nice, somehow. In spite of the monstrous things both of us had done. Perhaps that was it: we were two monsters who had been through a lot together. And sometimes she used to . . . goad me, using whatever happened to be the Wordle word of the day.'

'What do you mean?' Simon asked.

'When there was a word she felt was especially relevant, she would sometimes add a comment or . . . punctuation mark when she sent her score, no doubt designed to make me think or do something. Like when the word was "Flirt", she sent me two exclamation marks. When it was "Dream" she sent the question "Do you still?". Once I got an angry red-face emoji — that was when the word was "Rival". She was trying to make me jealous, to remind me that Paddy had Jemma and I didn't — as if that were something I might forget.'

'I'd like to see the photos now,' said Jemma. 'From Marianne's locked room. Full disclosure, remember? Have you got them?'

Simon shook his head. 'They're at your dad's: our next port of call. He's expecting us. Asked me to tell you he's made lunch. And I did disclose: I told you about the photos this morning, and you said you'd already heard about them from . . .' Simon nodded to indicate Mayo.

'I'm not going to believe they're real until I've seen them with my own eyes,' said Jemma.

'I assume you're also going to tell us who killed Marianne?' Mayo said.

'If I have to,' said Simon, thinking there was a good chance they would both misunderstand him.

36

JEMMA

I watch as Dad lays out the photographs – twenty-seven of them – in a grid-like formation on his desk. Simon and Ollie are standing on either side of me.

'Is this all of them?' I ask.

'Yes,' says Dad.

'And they're all from her study?' As I say it, I notice what's different about Dad's home office. The two large portraits of Marianne aren't here any more. I wonder where he's moved them to, and why.

'When she decided to . . . empty out the room, she took all the photos out of their frames and gave them to me,' says Dad. ' "Put them somewhere safe", she told me. "Somewhere unfindable." So I did.'

I barely hear him. Ollie did his best to describe these pictures to me last Friday, but it's different now they're in front of me. It's so hard not to run away, scream, grab them and tear them to shreds.

Because they're it. They're the big reason Marianne's study had to be locked for all those years – well, them and the piles of notebooks Ollie's told me about, the ones she wrote her

331

diaries in: always with flowers on the cover, always wide, faint lines inside. She loathed notebook pages with lines that were too narrow or too bold, apparently.

I force myself to stand still and keep looking at the pictures, not trusting myself to touch them. I don't want to go to pieces in a room with three other people. 'I thought you said you found them?' I ask Simon eventually.

'I did,' he says. 'I found them in the safe place where your dad put them.'

'Did you . . . make them for her, Dad?' I ask.

'No, and I don't know who did,' he says gently. 'She and I always kept our financial affairs separate, and she never told me any more than she wanted to, about anything. I assumed she'd paid someone to do it – maybe a graphic design type person.'

'These pictures always creeped me out,' Ollie says in a whisper. 'I couldn't understand how Marianne was able to . . . believe in them. For me, all they did was remind me that what I wanted so much was no more than a fantasy. I wanted it *for real*. Her insisting we had to pretend made it so much worse.'

I reach out and almost touch the photograph closest to me. 'They're the scenes from Lottie's dreams,' I say.

Family photos, all of them. *Sort of.*

They are and, at the same time, they are absolutely not photographs of our family: on holiday, in front of crashing waves at Porthgwidden; on a railway station platform nearby – Lelant Station – about to catch a train. It was high tide and the sea was right there, next to the platform edge. I remember saying to Lottie, 'It's just like being on a beach, isn't it? Except the platform's where the sand should be.'

And she dreamed about all those places, blending the scenes together to form a surreal landscape that was none of them as much as it was all of them . . .

332

I take a deep breath and pick up a photo of the five of us outside a tea shop in North Yorkshire, with a bandstand to our right. Except it isn't the five of us – or rather, not the five who were actually there. It's a lie, just as all these photographs are lies; Paddy isn't in any of them. Everywhere he ought to be – everywhere he was, when we went to those spots and had our picture taken, pictures Paddy was in – Ollie is there in his place. I'm in most of them too: smiling, looking like the perfect, happy daughter.

Marianne replaced Paddy. With Ollie. Over and over again.

In some of the photos, it's only the head that's been replaced, not the body. There are several in which a man of Paddy's height, wearing Paddy's clothes and shoes, has Ollie's head. In others, the whole person is Ollie, tall and wearing Ollie's clothes.

It takes me around half a minute to realise that I recognise all these faces of Ollie in front of me; I've seen them all before. Marianne used the photos she took that week in the Cotswolds in 2005, using the camera Dad bought her as a Christmas present, for her great picture-faking initiative.

How many times did she take Lottie up to her study, show her these photographs, tell her that Ollie was her dad and not Paddy?

'She used to say, "In this room, everything we want to make happen has already happened. It's already true." ' Ollie's voice pierces my numb shock. 'There were so many of the Photoshopped pictures, covering every shelf. Why did there need to be so many? I'd have been able to believe so much more in the future happy family we talked so much about if those awful pictures hadn't been distributed all over the room, looking so obviously like hideous fakes. Everything else we did and said was real – I didn't get why there had to be this . . . creepy fake stuff too. But Marianne obviously loved the photos, and I didn't want to . . . I don't know, upset her or spoil anything for her, I suppose.'

'Sweetheart?' says Dad. 'While we're on the subject of photo-graphs . . .' I feel something against the skin of my hand, and turn. He's trying to pass me something.

Please, not more twisted, fabricated pictures. I half expect the ones I'm holding to turn out to be all of us replaced – five happy Ollie-faces, each one at the top of a different body, standing underneath a tree in Devey House's garden.

I gasp when I see what Dad's given me: the three pictures of Mum I used to keep tucked into my mirror when I was much younger: the ones that disappeared from my bedroom soon after Dad and Marianne got together. I've been convinced, all these years, that she stole them.

'Did you find them in her things somewhere?' I ask Dad, unable to stop the tears that are rolling down my face. Ollie puts his arm round me, and I allow him to half hold me up. I press the photos against my chest. No one is ever separating me from these again.

'No,' says Dad. 'They were in the same place where I stored all the other photos when Marianne asked me to hide them.'

'But . . . are you saying . . .?' It's too much. I can't trust what I think I'm hearing, in case it turns out to be wrong.

'Yes, sweetheart. I took your photos of Mum,' Dad tells me. 'I know you thought it was Marianne, but it was me. I was worried she might . . . I don't know. React badly if she saw them. Destroy them, maybe. So I stashed them away to keep them safe for you.'

'What do you mean, "for me"? I haven't had them, Dad. If Marianne hadn't died, I still wouldn't have them now.'

'I know. I've handled everything terribly.' Dad looks down

at his feet. 'I know that. Believe me, I know. I'm trying to make up for it now by telling you everything, if you'll let me.'

'There's more?' I'm not sure I can take in anything else. I know there are questions I ought to be asking, but I can't think clearly.

'There's a letter,' says Dad. 'Marianne wrote you a letter.'

'I never got it,' I tell him.

'No, she didn't send it. It's . . . well, I put it in the same hiding place. She gave it to me.'

'She wrote Jemma a letter and sent it to you?' Ollie says, to check Dad hasn't got mixed up.

'Yes.' Dad sounds uncertain now. 'DC Waterhouse, perhaps you could . . .?'

'This hiding place,' says Simon, looking at me. 'Where your dad put these . . . doctored family photos, the photos of your mum that he'd taken from your bedroom, the letter Marianne wrote you. Other things were hidden there too.'

'What do you mean?' asks Ollie.

'It's where the person who killed Marianne hid the bloody clothes, the murder weapon, their blood-spattered shoes.'

'They used the same . . . So they saw what Dad had hidden there?' I ask.

Simon looks very serious, all of a sudden. 'Not quite. I mean—' He's looking at Dad as if waiting for him to say something.

And he does. 'I think we all need a little break,' he says, sounding as nervous as he used to when Marianne was grilling him about something he hadn't done to her satisfaction, or strictly according to her orders. 'Who fancies some lunch?'

No one is in the mood for eating, but we sit in the kitchen with our plates and bowls of hard-boiled eggs, salad, sliced ham and cucumber between us for nearly half an hour, drinking from our water glasses and talking about anything we can think of that isn't Marianne or who killed her. None of us wants this break to end, except perhaps Simon – but he doesn't rush us.

Dad apologises for the inadequacies of the meal. Ollie says, 'Actually this is a very good lunch,' and I shoot him a puzzled look. 'I keep hearing people say it,' he explains. 'The healthiest kind of meal is when everything on your plate has only one ingredient. An orange, for instance, or a boiled egg.'

Dad looks so much thinner and older than he did before Marianne died, but Ollie's praise brings a smile to his face. *Another reason I'll never stop loving Ollie: his kindness.*

I've decided to stop questioning my love for him – to stop forever. And I'm aware of it growing bigger and more powerful inside me every day, whether he's just done something silly or something brilliant. I love how thoughtful he is, and that he's quite weird too. I've found out a lot I didn't know about him since last Friday. He really does believe that the future is already decided – completely pre-determined – and that nobody has free will. He's twice mentioned a book I ought to read that proves it and explains why it's great news for humanity. I asked him to summarise the book's main theory, which he did straight away and at great length, because – and this is a huge difference between him and Paddy – Ollie is someone who loves, wherever possible, to say yes and make people happy. Paddy feels more comfortable if he's saying no to something, or he's not sure, or he doesn't really think so. His yeses take a long time to coax out of him, after initial refusals.

The theory in the book Ollie wants me to read sounds completely insane – as insane as some of his more neurotic messages (*'I'm probably going to be three minutes late'*, *'No, sorry, I'm likely to be a bit early, in fact – maybe two or three minutes'*, *'Me again, sorry – turns out I'll be exactly on time'*) and his take on religion. 'I'm agnostic, I guess,' he told me as he drove us to Dad's today. 'Though I seriously considered joining the Church of Jesus Christ of Latter-day Saints last year. I wanted to be part of something bigger than myself, and Mormonism's my favourite of all the faiths I know of. Or is it Mormonhood?'

I told him I had no idea and asked why it was his favourite.

Deadly serious, he said, 'When *The Book of Mormon* the musical came out, the Latter-day Saints bought advertising space in the theatre programmes: "You've seen the musical – now come and discover the real *Book of Mormon*, which is even better." So clever. Also, I love the origin story, with the gold plates.'

'I can't tell if you're serious or joking,' I told him.

'I can't either,' he said. 'Anyway, I didn't join in the end. I looked up where the Church of Latter-day Saints headquarters in Cambridge was, and it's one of my least favourite roads, so . . . that was that.'

'Mormon-y God must have been so impressed by your dedication,' I told him, thinking that I could stay married to Paddy for the rest of my life and he would never say anything so bizarre or entertaining.

Yes, there are moments when anger blazes through me and I fear nothing will be left of my love for Ollie by the time it's done – because he kept all those secrets for so long, lied to me for so long – but I'm starting to realise that none of the pain takes away any of the love. None of it stops my heart from soaring with joy when he says the things only he would ever say. On Saturday, after I saw him in Cambridge on Friday, he messaged me saying: *'You're wrong. Us starting again is not Back to Square One. It's Forward to Square Two.'* You know you've got it bad when you're dizzy with desire from the way someone uses capitalisation.

I force my attention back to the conversation I'm supposed to be part of. 'So the superintendent still doesn't know who killed Marianne?' Dad is saying, as if he and Simon are old friends, or work colleagues catching up. What else did the two of them discuss this morning that Ollie and I weren't privy to, apart from Dad wanting us all to come for lunch?'

'And she never will,' said Simon. 'She rejected the terms we offered, so we kept the information to ourselves. And will continue to do so.'

'But will you lose your job?' Dad asks.

'No idea, but . . . I don't think so,' says Simon. 'I'm quietly hopeful – and that's not my natural tendency, believe me. But we were all told to sit by our inboxes and await career-ending news . . . and no such news has arrived. Not yet, anyway. And yesterday, at the end of the day, the chief constable turned up at The Brown Cow – that's the pub we go to, me and my team – and asked us if we knew where the super was, if anyone had heard anything from her. We hadn't, and we told him. Seems like she's gone AWOL. No idea what that means for the plan to move my DI and our skipper to Lincolnshire. My wife keeps trying to make deals with deities she doesn't believe in: if by some miracle we survive this, we'll do everything by the book from now on, that kind of thing. She tries to rope me in, too: no more the-rules-don't-apply-to-us, no insubordination.' Simon looks unimpressed by that prospect.

'Anyway, we're not here to talk about my dog's breakfast of a career,' he says, evidently embarrassed to be the centre of attention. 'I'm here to say: whatever happens to me and my team, the truth about who killed Marianne, and who tried to in 2012, won't be going any further, ever, than me, my team, and the three of you. I've made sure it can't.'

'What does that mean?' I ask him.

'You don't want to know, and I'd rather not tell you,' Simon says bluntly.

I wonder if he's destroyed evidence. He must have, if he feels able to promise that.

'The way I see it, both incidents were self-defence,' he says. 'Prison time, for either . . .' He shakes his head. 'Doesn't feel right. And I want to keep my word to you, Jemma.' To Dad and Ollie he says, 'Jemma's told me things she wouldn't have told me if I hadn't promised her it would stay off the record.'

'Thank you,' says Ollie.

Simon gives Dad a pointed look.

Dad clears his throat. 'Sweetheart . . .' He looks at me. 'There's something I need to tell you.'

'I know what you're going to say, Dad.' The truth is, I didn't – not before he said that. I had a funny feeling, though, and tried to persuade myself it was nothing.

My hands feel shaky and alien . . . as if they might detach from my body and float away. I want to grip the table, but I can't. I can't move . . .

'It was me, Jemma,' says Dad. 'I killed Marianne.'

Breathe. Breathe.

Seeing I'm unable to speak, Ollie comes to my rescue. 'Gareth, Jemma understands better than anyone what hell you must have had to live—'

'Oh, no. No, no.' Dad looks troubled. 'No, it wasn't that at all. She was going to kill Jemma. That's why I did it.'

'Marianne was?' Ollie sounds as shocked as I feel.

Has someone thrown me across the room? No, I still haven't moved.

Shock on top of shock on top of shock . . .

'Marianne was going to kill Jemma?' I can hear from his voice that Ollie doesn't believe it, and won't – not without a repeat and a lot more detail. I half expect him to ask Dad to name the prime minister, just to check he hasn't lost it completely.

I believe it. A large part of my wanting to kill Marianne was a fear that something like this was going on in her mind.

'Or have her killed,' says Dad. 'If she could find the right person to do it. But if not, she told me she'd . . . she'd do it herself if she had to.' His face crumples and he starts to cry. 'It was never part of my life plan to become a murderer, Jemm.'

'You aren't a murderer, Dad,' I tell him. 'Not in your heart.' *And you don't have to plead with me as if I'm some kind of judge. Remember what I was planning to do to Marianne? I'm in no position to judge anyone. Neither is Ollie, and neither is Simon, who encouraged me to commit murder and advised me on how to get away with it.*

I wonder if he's told Dad about that: what he said to me on Monday; our non-disclosure pact and all it entailed.

'It really did feel like . . . not self-defence exactly, but defence of you.' Dad sends another pleading look my way. 'The thing is, she'd never have given up. She'd decided she wanted and needed it done, and she'd have made it happen. She spoke about it like a military general planning a world-saving campaign. She said it was the only way she'd ever have true peace of mind, and of course in her eyes it was fully justified because she'd read your diary, the one on your computer.'

I nod to let Dad know I'm listening carefully.

'She knew about your . . . plan,' he says. 'Didn't seem to care that you'd thought better of it. "Don't be naive", she said when I tried to reason with her. "Jemma could revive the plan at any moment, find a different method, set herself up with a nice alibi—" '

'I'd never have done it once I'd been to the police,' I say.

Ollie – whose arm around my shoulders has been holding

me upright all this time, or at least that's how it feels – gives me an encouraging squeeze.

'Everything was my fault, sweetheart,' Dad says. 'That you needed to make a plan like that in the first place . . . In all the years since Marianne joined our family, I'd never once disagreed with her or stood up to her. That's the only reason she told me what she intended to do. Why would she imagine I'd suddenly start objecting to her behaviour now?'

'She thought she had you fully under control,' I say.

'Well, she did. She was right about that.' Dad sounds angry. 'I'd have lived happily under her . . . regime for ever, if she hadn't threatened you. When she did, I knew I had to do something. I . . . I started to have dreams about your mum. My late first wife, Nancy,' Dad tells Simon. 'The same dream over and over: her begging me to save Jemma's life. And . . . well, you know the rest.'

'I only know some of the rest,' said Simon. 'Do you mind if I ask you a few questions? So that I can understand everything properly?'

'I'm hardly in a position to mind anything,' Dad says. 'I have some questions for you as well. The main one is: how did you know I was the guilty party? You said this morning you've known for some time.'

'It was the white trainers that first started me off down the right track,' says Simon. 'I was in Cornwall, talking to an ex-Cambridge college chaplain. Yes, that one,' he tells Ollie. 'Belynda Simmonds' bit on the side. He was wearing bright white trainers, and I realised I'd seen some that looked brand spanking new like that somewhere else recently. Then I got it: Marianne was wearing trainers like that, in the background of your Zoom work meeting, the one I'd watched with my team that supposedly proved beyond doubt you couldn't have killed her. Her trainers were clearly visible, which means she can't have been in the room with you – she had to have been much further away if we could see her feet, when we could only see your top half, sitting at your desk. Plus, she was dusting things in the video and putting them back on shelves, and there aren't any shelves in your home office, are there? There's very little in there – just computers of every possible size. Some huge.'

'Some huge,' Dad repeats.

'So Marianne must have been in her study, across the landing,' says Simon. 'Now, you might think, so what? So what if she wasn't in your office with you? So what if she was in her study? She was still there, wasn't she? In the video, demonstrably alive at 5.10 p.m.? Here's the thing: Marianne had stripped that room of all of its contents long before Monday 30 October. On 7 July, she showed Jemma the completely bare, empty room.'

'What a fool I am,' Dad says, and it sounds as if he's reminiscing fondly about a complete failure whom he loves in spite of everything.

I hope he does. I hope he can go through the rest of his life liking himself, feeling okay about himself. If I need to spend the next however many years convincing him of all the reasons why he should love himself, I'm ready to do it.

He saved your life. You only succeeded in saving the life of Marianne – the woman who'd have killed you. He saved yours. Don't be too hard on him, Jemm.

Tears fill my eyes as I realise that wasn't my inner voice talking to me: it was Mum.

'To plan what you really believe is the perfect murder and neglect such a fundamental detail . . .' Dad shakes his head.

'You're not the first,' Simon told him.

'I didn't think of her study and whether it was full or empty, or whether it would be visible, or noticed – not for a second.

I was too busy counting myself lucky that she wore the same outfit every Monday to go to her yoga class.'

'You had a lot on your mind,' says Simon. 'Planning a killing is stressful. And if it's any consolation, I'd begun to suspect you even before I saw those white trainers in Cornwall and made the connection. You were the only one on the list whose alibi was a Zoom, not an in-person encounter. Everyone else had been seen in the flesh by another person at the relevant time, in a place that meant they couldn't have been here killing Marianne: Jemma, Paddy, Lottie, Suzanne Lacy, Oliver Mayo – much as I wanted it to be you for a while,' Simon tells Ollie with an apologetic half smile.

The mention of Suzanne's name gives me a heavy feeling in my stomach. Will she ever speak to me again? She promised she would. 'Hey,' she said, 'if our friendship can survive you marrying one man I disapprove of, then why not two? You're off into the sunset with a guy who claims to love you, having withheld the truth from you for seventeen years? Great! If you're happy, if he makes you happy, I promise not to keep saying inconvenient things like this.'

Still, I'm worried about me and Suzanne. I don't want to have to feel ashamed whenever I think about her, and don't know how to forget that I've lied to her for the first time in our decades-long friendship. I told her it wasn't Ollie who attacked Marianne in November 2012. The rest of the truth I was happy to share with her, but not that. And I won't tell her about Dad either. For the same reason Ollie didn't tell me all the secrets for so many years: fear. I can't be sure Suzanne wouldn't go straight to the police.

'Even Tom Tulloch had an alibi provided by real people, albeit biased and unreliable-seeming ones,' Simon tells Dad. 'And the other day Charlie and I – that's my wife – we were arguing about whether I could have saved myself a drive to Cornwall by just Zooming with the people I went there to see. I said to her: "Talking to someone on Zoom isn't *really* talking to someone", or words to that effect. Which is true – seeing someone on a Zoom isn't actually seeing that person. It's seeing an image of them. When I watched your Zoom meeting with my team . . .' Simon shakes his head.

'Image quality?' Dad grimaces. 'It was inconsistent, wasn't it? The trouble is, the recordings sent out after those meetings are made by different people, with different Wi-Fi connections, on different machines—'

'That was one clue among many,' says Simon. 'Your face was all fuzz and stripes, but no one else's was. One guy had a vase behind him. You could see every movement that man's face made, as well as the initials of the pottery maker at the bottom of the vase: TKC. I thought: why would Gareth Upton have so much worse video quality than everyone else? I mean, it could have been your Wi-Fi signal, but again . . .'

'Someone in my line of work would make sure he always has a fully functional internet connection,' Dad says.

'That's exactly what I thought,' said Simon. 'Which led to me wondering how hard it would be for someone with your tech expertise to . . . I don't know, get a massive screen, much bigger than the one that's doing the recording of the Zoom, and set it up so that it's positioned in the one and only spot that'd make it look like he's sitting there in his room. The screen playing the video would need to be quite a bit bigger than the one recording it, I reckon. I know I couldn't make it work myself, but I didn't doubt that you could. And you could arrange it so that it looked like Marianne came in and spoke to you at the moment you wanted, and rang you at the moment you wanted – because that all happened, didn't it? Just not on

Monday 30 October. But you remembered a previous Zoom work meeting, same people, in which all of that happened.'

'It was a Zoom call from several months ago,' says Dad. 'The physical set up was easy enough to do. I've got several computers in the house with larger screens. Well, I did have, until your team and their helpers carted them off.' He smiles at Simon to show he's not trying to be critical. 'And I've never once said a word, or been called upon to do so, in any of those pointless, interminable meetings, so I reckoned I was safe enough from that point of view.'

'You must have killed Marianne long before 5.25, right?' Simon asks him.

'4.25,' says Dad. 'Pretended I'd found a problem with the car and asked her to come outside so I could show it to her. Earlier that day I'd hidden my change of clothes – same ones I'd worn for the Zoom I was planning to pass off as me in real time – in the woods near where we park our cars. I . . . did the unthinkable, then got changed and carried the plastic bag full of bloodstained clothes and shoes and the knife I'd bought back to the house.'

'And hid them where you'd previously hidden the pictures Marianne gave you from her study,' says Simon. 'The doctored family photos with Paddy taken out and Oliver added in.'

Dad nods. 'And the three pictures I stole from Jemm's bedroom many years ago, so that Marianne couldn't destroy them. Yes.'

'Where did you hide so many things, Dad?' I ask. 'Must have been somewhere pretty spacious, for clothes and shoes and everything. In the house? How come DS Kombothekra and the others didn't find them? I thought you said they searched the entire house and grounds.'

'They did,' says Dad.

345

'I thought exactly the way you're thinking,' Simon tells me. 'Yeah, everywhere had been searched, so if your Dad was the one who'd done it, which by then I knew he was, where had he put all the evidence? I felt pretty pleased with myself when I worked it out.'

'What did you work out?' Ollie asks, as desperate as I am to know.

'It seemed obvious once I thought of it,' says Simon. 'The massive computers our SOCOs had removed from this house – from your home office, Gareth – and taken to the nick in Spilling.'

'You can hide a lot in a full tower case if you take out all the other components,' Dad says. His face twists, as if at a sudden spasm of pain. 'Isn't it funny how you can think you're being so clever while being a fool of the first order? I thought it was perfect. Foolproof! No one would ever convict me of a crime someone else was confessing to wanting to commit at the very moment I was supposedly doing it. I knew about the diary file on your computer, Jemm. Marianne had read it and told me all about it, so I knew that on Monday between five and six you'd be at the police station. "Perfect", I thought. "Jemma can't be blamed. She'll have the most solid alibi imaginable: vouched for by the police." And I thought my clever Zoom recording plan would work just as well for me.'

'And you didn't think about the conspiracy to murder charge that would almost definitely have been coming Jemma's way,' Simon says, with a small shake of his head at Dad's reckless stupidity.

'How can we be sure that won't still happen?' Ollie asks him. 'The conspiracy charges.'

'We can be sure because . . .' Simon reaches for a slice of cucumber from the bowl in the middle of the table. Instead of

346

eating it, he starts to pull it apart with his fingers. 'What murder plan?' he says. 'What laptop diary? Is anyone going to step forward and say they've seen such a thing, or read it, or even heard of it? No. They're not.'

'I see,' says Ollie. 'Thank you so much.'

Thank you.

I'm too overwhelmed to speak. I don't care if Simon's doing all this for me and my family or for his own strange reasons, but I don't care. I'll be grateful to him for the rest of my life.

'I want to make it very clear . . .' Dad starts to say, and for a second I nearly laugh, imagining he might be about to complain about Simon's bad table manners and the shredding of the cucumber, but of course he doesn't. Instead he says, 'After today and . . . everything we've all done, after all of this . . .' He gestures around the table. 'You're not the only one who's going to be doing everything by the book from now on, Simon.'

'No. You are,' Simon tells him. 'The only one out of you and me, anyway.'

'What do you mean?' Ollie asks.

'I don't know,' our strange police detective friend says. 'I just . . . I don't have it in me to live by anyone else's rules, even if it means keeping a job I need. Never have and never will. That won't change.'

'I thought you said your wife wanted the two of you to make a deal with . . . gods you don't believe in,' Dad says.

'True, and well remembered,' Simon smiles. 'But she's about to find out, along with everyone else who knows me, that unfortunately for them, I'm still Simon Waterhouse.' He reaches for another piece of cucumber. 'To be honest, I can't see myself stopping being Simon Waterhouse any time soon.'

23rd October 2023

Dear Jemma

You won't ever read this letter. Very soon, I hope, I'm going to do to you what you planned to do to me, but chickened out of doing.

I won't be chickening out. I'll be going through with it — or someone acting on my behalf will — and you will deserve it. In due course, you'll be a body, not a person any more, and your father and I will bury you in the grounds of Devey House with a great fanfare. Your wake will, of course, be the party to end all parties. And this letter will be buried alongside you, because that's the closest I can get to what I want.

What I'd ideally like is for you to be able to read this before you die, but that can't happen. No, that's wrong. What I'd like even more, but know is impossible, is for you to see the light in time to save yourself. (A woman can dream, can't she?) If only you could promise to change and start loving me . . . God, you've no idea how often that passionate wish has passed through my mind over the years.

I'm not perfect, Jemma, but I did want to be your mum. I was the only mum you had, and you rejected me over and over again. I loved you and was ready to carry on loving you forever. You were the one who ruined that with your endless, ongoing, year-after-year refusal to show me any affection or loyalty whatsoever. You did one good thing, though: you found Ollie and brought him to our home, our family. Then you stupidly ditched him in favour of Useless Paddy, but I forgave you for that — because I saw a different way forward. Ollie and I would sort it all out, I thought, and you'd love it once you had what I knew you truly wanted deep down. And once we were all together and everything was as it was supposed to be, you'd start to love me then — I was sure of it. Why? Because Ollie did. That's right, Jemm — Ollie really loved me, like the best possible son loves his mother. He'd have persuaded you round to his point of view about me, given the chance.

Remember the brilliant time we had in the Cotswolds, Christmas 2005? It really crushed me when you spoke so harshly about Ollie afterwards — him ringing to say we might be late when there was no need - because we were all so happy that week, you as much as anyone. Later, I realised why you were so determined to trash Ollie in the immediate aftermath of you dumping him: you were trying to brainwash yourself, weren't you? You were already starting to worry you'd made the wrong choice, and it was you that needed propagandising as much as me.

Because you loved Ollie, and I did too, and that's what would have made you love me too, eventually. Except I messed it all up. I lied to Ollie about the DNA test, told him Lottie was his when I knew she was Paddy's. I shouldn't have done any of that. I should have been completely honest with him and trusted him. Most of all, I should never have assumed he'd be willing to kill Paddy. It's to his credit that he wasn't, and I saw with blinding clarity, as I lay bleeding on my kitchen floor, that I should never have been willing to take it that far either.

I did everything I could to put right the catastrophic mistakes I'd made: wrote Ollie a long letter of apology, told the police I'd made a mistake when I'd named him, assured them it wasn't him. They would have charged him with attempted murder, which would have been too stupid for me to bear. The whole awful mess had only happened because Ollie was so against the plan I'd made for him to kill Paddy. What he did to me was a protest against murder — as I said to DC Brodigan, it was the opposite of murder. (I had some fun, winding the police up with my cryptic comments.)

I cannot tell you how much I missed Ollie, once he stopped coming to the house. I felt exactly like a mother who had lost her beloved son. You can't get over a loss like that. Many years later, when I became a Wordle fan, I risked making contact with him again, hoping enough time had passed. I was delighted when he sent me his Wordle result in response to me sending him mine. That became our new relationship. It wasn't everything I wanted, but it felt like enough — for the time being at least. I'm a patient woman, Jemma. And I never, ever stop believing I can get what I want. (Oh — once I sent my Wordle score to you by mistake — you might remember. As I said, I'm not perfect.)

As compensation for the anguish I'd caused him, I changed my will to leave Ollie (who knew nothing about it — I decided it could be a nice surprise for him after my death) a lot of money — money I'd previously allocated to you and Paddy. But you didn't deserve it, Jemm, which meant that you certainly didn't deserve Ollie.

In fact, that was the rather brilliant way I reconciled myself, quite genuinely, to the catastrophic boyfriend choice you made in 2006. Here's what I told myself: if Jemma was worthy of Ollie, she wouldn't have rejected him. Therefore she isn't — so maybe she and Paddy actually deserve each other. Maybe everything is exactly as it should be. And Jemma will need to work on herself and improve her character and suffer rather a lot, probably, in order to learn her lesson. Then, once she's deserving, that's when she and Ollie will be reunited. I had it all worked out neatly, to my own satisfaction.

I wasn't prepared for how devastated I'd feel when you told me about your one-night encounter with Ollie in 2010. Remember how you cried on my shoulder, telling me you'd made a terrible mistake and that Ollie had been 'the One' all along? But you couldn't leave him because you were pregnant with Paddy's child? The injustice, the waste of it, combined with the shock — it just tore me apart. The lost years! And now everything was just so utterly, tragically ruined! That was how I felt at first, and it was unbearable.

Very soon afterwards, I rallied, of course, and made a much better plan. Here is some invaluable life advice, Jemm (not that you'll need it, as you'll soon be dead): there is always a much better plan than sitting around feeling tragic and moping. You just have to find it. If it doesn't exist already, you have to make it. That's what I did, though, as I say, I got a few elements disastrously wrong. I like to think I was, nevertheless, much less wrong and foolish than you were. You stubbornly made yourself immune to learning any lessons at all, didn't you? You knew you'd made a mistake picking Paddy over Ollie, but you could see he and Lottie loved each other — playing happily together for hours, silly games of the sort that only entertain children and fools, people with no sense of adult responsibility. You decided — a grave error on your part — that you owed it to Lottie to stay and suffer in your marriage to Paddy. That was stupid, Jemma. Moronic. No child is ever better off with a parent who is visibly unhappy.

I'll tell you something I've never told another living soul or even admitted to myself until now: your stubborn resistance, year after year, to accepting the inevitable, leaving Paddy, choosing Ollie, finally . . . It all suited me rather well. As time went on, I started to wonder if I almost preferred having Ollie all to myself, as he and I planned and schemed and even as we exchanged Wordle results in secret. I didn't have to share his attention with you. It was me and him, and no ungrateful Jemma around to spoil anything or take up his time and energy. Just me and Ollie: bliss. And, of course, we also had the fantasy of our future happy family life, in which you were very much involved . . . I discovered that I preferred my imagining of it to the reality. The make-believe version allowed me to spend so much more time with Ollie than you ever would have, if you and he had got back together.

I'm sorrier than you'll ever know, Jemma, for what I now know I have to do. Murder should never leap out of the list of available options as being the best way forward. Quite the opposite.

I love you. You should have let me.

Marianne xxx

2 January, 2025

Dear Marianne,

Well, it's only taken me fourteen months to start and finish this letter. When I read yours to me, I thought, 'I'm not letting that stand. I'm writing a reply.' I thought I meant soon, or soonish, but it's taken me this long to work out what I want to say, and then change it and change it again to get it right. Luckily, I've had time to do that.

Having more time – time left – is a great thing. You'll have to take my word for it.

I made it clear right from the start: this is my story and no one else's. That's the only reason I'm writing to a dead woman: because you tried to turn me and my life, all my romantic relationships, even my planned death . . . You tried to turn all of it into part of *your* story.

You failed. It's still my story and only mine. In it, I'm no longer a murderer. You still are and always will be, even though you didn't kill anyone. You've run out of time to change for the better and make adjustments to how you will be remembered by everyone you cared about (I won't say 'loved', since your version of love wasn't anything deserving of the name).

The bald fact is: you died wanting, and fully intending, to have me killed. That can never change, so redemption is beyond your reach.

It's funny to think that even Tom Tulloch (I know you'd see him as your inferior) has fallen accidentally into a happier ending than you've had. Simon Waterhouse visited him again and put the fear of God into him in a way that made sweat ooze from his pores, apparently, after which Tom vowed, repeatedly, to be a fully law-abiding citizen for the rest of his life. Will he stick to that? Who knows – but at least there's some hope for him.

Here's how I like to look at it: the only person in this story who got a true and significant punishment was you, Marianne. That's as it should be. Most people I've written about in this . . . whatever it is did plenty of things wrong, of course, but there's only one of us who doesn't deserve another chance, and, by happy coincidence, it's the only person who isn't getting one.

Simon Waterhouse believes this outcome was created by the internal politics at Spilling police station; he sneers at me when I tell him it's what the universe wanted to happen, but I'm going to believe my preferred narrative. And, though he'll never admit it, he loves it when I disagree with him and has occasionally phoned me so that we can argue about it. I think he finds it reassuring to hear the strength of my certainty. He's admitted that, even in the unlikely event of his superintendent having agreed to his demands, he and his team would never have divulged what they knew about what Dad did, what Ollie did, what Tom Tulloch and I planned to do . . . Clearly it would make him feel better if he could convince himself, or if I could convince him, that keeping the truth to himself would have been – no, *is* – acting in accordance with the universe's idea of justice.

The last time I spoke to him was about a month ago. He rang me at eleven at night and mumbled something about loose ends and peace of mind before asking me if Ollie knew what he was doing when he attacked you in 2012, or if he lost control and wasn't responsible. 'I can imagine it happening either way,' he said. 'The thing is, by Mayo's own account, the two of them did have a glass of wine together in the kitchen *after* he read the diary entry about the DNA test—'

'So what?' I said. 'Why does it matter, after all this time?' I knew why he was asking, though: he wants to think of Ollie as someone who would never do something so violent while in his right mind. At first I didn't want to answer (I mean, for God's sake, Waterhouse, you're a murder detective who's decided to let people who are technically criminals walk free, so why not own it?) but then I took pity on him and told him exactly what Ollie had told me: 'All he knows is that there's a gap in his memory,' I said. 'One minute Marianne was fine, and talking, and the next she was on the floor bleeding from her throat. He says it doesn't matter if he chose to do it or lost control and did it, because he remembers *not* ringing an ambulance, *not* doing anything to save her life. That was a deliberate choice he remembers making, and that's bad enough, he says.'

I don't know if I agree with him. Obviously it's not ideal 'in the best of all possible worlds' (as Ollie would say), but I think it's totally understandable that he behaved the way he did, and that I did, and that Dad did. It's funny how quickly healing happens once the poison is removed. Ollie and I are blissfully happy together, and Dad and

Paddy look as if they're both heading towards happiness too, each with their new partner. It's early days for both relationships, but Dad's girlfriend Janet has the patience of a saint and is trying to train Dad to work out what his own wants and preferences are, instead of just saying what he thinks will please her most. Paddy's new partner seems to think he's wonderful for just existing, which I freely admit has brought out the best in him. He and I were totally ill-matched and brought out the worst in each other; I can see that now. Our relationship is so much stronger and more relaxed now that we're not together. The main thing is that Lottie is massively happier. She doesn't know the truth about what happened to you, Marianne, and she never will – she and Spilling Police have that in common. For them, and for most of the world, your removal will remain a mystery, with no responsible party ever identified.

Unless Lottie reads this one day, which . . .

I could take steps to make sure that doesn't happen. Suzanne says the only way to be as certain as I want and need to be is to delete and destroy.

I might. One day. Not yet.

Acknowledgements

As always, huge thanks to my publishers, Hodder and Stoughton, my wonderful agent, Peter Straus and my brilliant editorial first ports of call, Emily Winslow and Kate Jones. I particularly want to thank Phoebe Morgan, who slaved over the earliest and messiest versions of the text, hour after hour and month after month, and copy editor Gabrielle Chant, whose long paragraph of enthusiasm for the novel came at exactly the right time – after I'd spent more than a year seriously wondering if I had accidentally produced something that made no sense – and proved to me in an instant, as if by magic, that I wasn't going mad and had indeed written exactly the book I had wanted to write. Special thanks also to Jo Dickinson who read the penultimate draft and responded to it with such care and passion that I was able to fall in love with this novel properly, and all over again.

Thanks to Gillian McAllister, who is incredibly clever, got everything straight away, and repeatedly gave sound advice; to the brilliant Sarah Phelps for being such a fervent supporter of the phrase 'monarch amnesia'; to the Curry Club Board Members for helping me to distinguish between the acceptable and the unacceptable; to Nina Pottell and Mark Nattrass for their help with firefighter-related queries; to Luke Hares for helping me 'hide the evidence' and get away with fictional crimes; and to my sister Jenny for the 'Thursday night date night' part of the plot.

Thanks to my husband, children, mum and dog for putting up with all the melodrama as I rewrote this book five times. It won't happen again, I promise.

DON'T MISS SOPHIE HANNAH'S OTHER UNGUESSABLE THRILLERS

'Hannah [always] comes back with her trademark
flair, creativity and stylish prose'
GILLIAN MCALLISTER

OUT NOW
PAPERBACK, EBOOK AND AUDIO

.